Blood & Water:

Yorgos the Damned
Part One

J Michael Braiden

DEDICATION

This book is dedicated to my family, in particular my mother, Jo Anne Sallia, who has always encouraged me to be myself–no matter how weird–and to be creative. Thank you, mom!

I would also like to dedicate this book to my adopted dads, Gary Matson and Merv Chaplin. Without their support this book may not have ever been published. Thank you, dads!

This book is also for Scott Nespor. His home is sometimes my home too, and it is always my home-away-from-home. Thank you, Scott, for giving me a place to work when I had no where else to go, because I couldn't afford a cup of coffee for the free internet.

CONTENTS

CONTENTS

CONTENTS

ACKNOWLEDGMENTS

There are a number of people I'd like to thank for supporting me while I wrote Blood and Water parts One and Two.

Sharon Peterson should be sainted for the ways in which she supported me during our bimonthly get-to-gethers. She patiently listened to me read the work-in-progress not once, not twice, but countless times while I wrote, revised and revised again, until it was finished.

I am also greatful for Lisa Kelly who edited; Kim Myron who loaned me her eyes; and Jules London who created the cover. Without Lisa's work this book would be in sorry condition. Without Kim's last minute readthrough, numerous mistakes would have made it to the the printed page. Without Jules' artwork I would have had to create the cover myself. No one wants to see *that*.

Two former coworkers, Beth Smith and Kristy McNamee, have supported this work from its very inception. Beth suggested a number of ideas that helped shape the story in the early stages of development.

Speaking of coworkers, I would also like to thank Barbara McCloud, Kerry Barajas, Denise Johnson, Georgia Fouseki, Claire Manely, Bobbe Abts, Vicky Held, Lyn Metzner, Danny Martinez, Lance Burcham, Allison Brown, Bree Holmes, Lisa Newman and Arlene Spaniol. Like Beth and Kristy, they've supported me from the beginning, each one in their own way. Every time they asked me "How's the book" or "When's it coming out" I was encouraged to press on, especially during times of dreaded writer's block.

I would be remiss if I failed to thank my Greek hosts, Mel Aligizakis, Yota Theod and Sophia Theodorakopoulou. They welcomed me into their homes and treated me like a part of their families while I was there. Their hospitality enabled me to see and experience Greece first hand, which helped me to write more authentically.

Last, but by no means least, are the friends and family (and two or three strangers) who contributed to my fundraising campaign on indiegogo.com: Heather Ross, Lori Sandoval, Kathy Wharton, Adel Epley, Sharon Peterson, Shari Hammond, Kamala Parris, Devon White, Kathy Wilson, Michael Airhart, Anthony Caruso, Melissa Chamberlain, Gayle Ruddell, Autumn Decesare, Scott Nespor, Shin Evans, Teddie Tomaselli, Brian Hickey, Eduart Marishta, Megan Floto, Gary Matson, Merv Chaplin, my sisters Cari Ramirez and Tracy Derwey and our mother, Jo Anne Sallia. Without their financial contributions "Blood and Water: Yorgos the Damned" would not have made it to print so easily.

Thank you. I am indebted.

Blessed are those who hunger and thirst for righteousness. For they shall be filled.

Matthew 5:6 New King James Version.

Prologue

Greetings.

Because today is my Name Day I will begin my introduction by writing about my name. Over the centuries I have gone by many names, but none of them have strayed far from the truth. They have all been my own name in its various international forms. My sister, always the crafty one, is an ever-creative inventor of aliases and persona. I am not.

My name is Georgios, pronounced in the Greek of my youth, *Ghe-or-ghe-os*.

Yorgos, with a subtle roll to the 'r', is the nickname I most commonly went by. When I left my homeland, I left behind the native pronunciations of my name as well.

I became George, in London; Jorge, in my brief stint in Latin America; and Georgie—which I loathed—in the earliest of my years spent in the United States. Now I am Georgeo, which is the more Italianate way of saying it.

I think, other than Yorgos, which is the name my ancient soul most responds to, Georgeo is my favorite.

Though it is my true name, and any other name is foreign—no matter how close to the original—I despise being addressed as Yorgos. It grieves me to respond to it because that name represents my more innocent, and mortal self before I became this . . . this creature that I now am.

In telling my story, I am aiming for truth, not perfection. So I won't even try to capture the cadence, rhythm, or idioms of the old Greek we used in the 1600's. Besides, I am in the New World now, and an even newer century.

If there is a modern English idiom that will nicely convey the meaning I am going for, I will use it with out hesitation. Please don't let that get in the way of your enjoyment of the story. I would quite hope that it will make following my story that much easier for you.

Besides, you didn't pick up this book because you wanted lessons in old Greek. No. You wanted a good story. Well, I have got a story for you. I will let you be the judge as to whether or not it is any good.

Georgeo Godevenos
April 23, 2010, the Feast of Saint George

Post script,

Where my memory fails, I have asked Mister Dumitru to fill in the gaps. I think that you will agree that, though his perspective differs greatly from mine, his contributions round the story out.

PART ONE:
GIFTED & CALLED

1 An Odd Little Boy

1626, The Pindus Mountains, Greece

"You are an odd little boy, Yorgos."

From where I knelt, I looked at my oldest brother, Theophilos. I didn't understand why he'd say a thing like that. My chest tightened.

He had caught me in the act of prayer, with three ikons I sneaked from the family altar. I had arranged them on a flat rock under the interlacing branches of several trees, at the bottom of a wooded ravine behind the inn my family owned. At the base of each ikon, a burning candle stuck out of the dirt.

"Don't you talk to God and the saints?" I asked.

He chuckled. "Yes, during Divine Liturgy and other services like everyone else."

"I always talk to God. He's everywhere, not only in the sanctuary." Theophilos broke a twig from a tree and plucked the leaves off one at a time, tossing them into the air.

"I know." Once he stripped it bare, he discarded the stick and crouched, reaching for one of the ikons. He lifted it, looked at it without *seeing* it, and set it back down in front of one of the burning candles.

It was a temperate afternoon in Zagoria, the remote region of the Pindus Mountains where I had been born and raised. Indolent clouds grazed an expansive cerulean

3

sky. Zagoria boasted imposing peaks, abysmal ravines, and extensive forests. Though rugged and forbidding, the area consisted of 46 villages and countless smaller hamlets.

Without warning, Theophilos stood, walked several paces, and began to urinate. I didn't mean to look at first, but curiosity seized me. His penis was larger than mine, with a shock of coarse hair that it seemed to grow out of, like a tree springing from the grass and shrubs surrounding it. The clear liquid streamed out, pooled on the ground, and ran away in muddy rivulets. Seized with wonder, and awash in a heady mixture of shame and excitement, I wanted to reach out and touch it but feared that doing so would have been wrong. When he noticed that I watched, I averted my eyes. I plucked one of the prayer candles out of the ground and snuffed the flame.

"It's okay, Yorgos. It's normal to be curious." He turned to face me full on. His penis, still exposed and hanging flaccidly over his trousers, dripped on them. The liquid spread out, making a dark spot on the fabric.

"It's so big." I whispered. He laughed while tucking it in his pants.

"No, not really. It only looks that way to you. Don't worry, you're a kid still. Yours will grow in time."

The desire to look at his penis and touch it did not disappear when he tucked it away. Both horrified and aroused, what I felt was stronger than curiosity. Watching my brother urinate gave me an intense feeling of pleasure which mounted giving way to an equally intense feeling of shame.

In a flurry of movements, I gathered my ikons and prayer candles. I pressed them against my chest and scrambled through the back door of the inn to the kitchen, the breeze extinguishing the remaining flames. On the way, I dropped one of the ikons. I didn't stop or look back. I pressed on, wishing I could move my legs fast enough to lose the feelings that were surfacing in me, to leave them far behind. I didn't know it at the time, but it was impossible to outrun them. I and my new feelings were inextricably one.

Panting, I ran through the kitchen, past my mother, aunt, and Grandmother Yaya, who were preparing supper. I ran straight into the adjoining storage closet and shut the door. Spreading the remaining two ikons out on the floor in front of me, I made the sign of the cross several times and asked the saints depicted on the small wooden panels to pray for me.

"Yorgos, is something wrong?" Mother called through the door.

"No, Momma, I'm praying." I knew she would be satisfied with my half-truth; praying with the old ikons was not unusual for me. I began to recite the Jesus Prayer, my eyes misting with tears that caught in my thick lashes. "Lord Jesus Christ, Son of God, have mercy on me, a sinner." With each repetition I made the sign of the cross until peace gentled my turbulent soul. I remained on my knees, reciting my favorite prayer, letting the peace take root in me. Mother didn't disturb me again until just before mealtime.

As was common in those days, our household was a large one. It consisted of my immediate family; my mother's sister, Aunt Petra, and my father's brother, Uncle Petros. They moved in at separate times when they lost their spouses. With my aunt and uncle came several cousins of various ages. My three living grandparents lived with us too. Add to that the number of guests at the adjoining inn that my family operated—which could range in number from one to eight—and you'll understand why I often sought solitude but rarely found it.

Mother called me to supper early, as usual. I collected myself, brushing dirt off my limbs and drying my eyes. If they were puffy from crying, I couldn't do anything about it. However, I wanted to avoid having to answer any uncomfortable questions.

I pulled the latch string and pushed the door open. When I saw Mother waiting for me, concern filling her brooding eyes, all my efforts to make myself presentable and brave crumbled. She dropped to her knees and I ran to her. Before I reached her the scent of her perfume enveloped me. It smelled like jasmine, and it comforted me.

"What's gotten into you?" she asked, supporting me with an arm around my waist and a hand behind my head. Her familiar scent grounded me.

"Nothing, Momma. I'm okay."

Still kneeling she pushed me back with both hands on my shoulders, but only far enough to get a good look at me.

"Are you sure?"

"Of course. I just lost one of my ikons outside." She regarded me closely for a moment.

"Alright," she said, biting her lip. She shrugged, "I don't know why you insist on taking them outside to play. It's not proper."

"I don't play with them Momma. I *pray*. I feel closer to God out there, that's why." She mussed my hair, accepting my explanation.

"Are you ready?" I nodded.

Every night, before she called the rest of the family to the table, Mother and I carried food-laden trays down the hall to the room that my father's parents shared. They were old and had been bedridden for years. Grandma Nona only left the comfort of their quarters on Sundays when she braved the dangers of the world to attend Divine Liturgy. Every Sunday, while Theophilos and I guided her down the street to the neighborhood church, she said, "I have never missed a service and I am not about to start."

I loved it when Nona said that. It made me smile and aspire to be like her. Papus, my grandfather, would have gone to the service too, but he couldn't even walk with a cane anymore. Nona was some twenty years younger than him and could still walk. While Nona attended the liturgy, Papus recited the entire service from memory. Afterward, Father Elias would come home with us to bring Papus the Holy Communion.

"You ought to let me bring the Holy Communion to you too," he would say to Nona, while helping her to the front door and across the threshold. Grandma scoffed whenever he said that and repeated her favorite refrain: "I have never missed a service and I am not about to start."

Together, my father's parents were my greatest inspiration. They taught me how to love and revere God and how to pray with ikons. If I could be half as devoted as they were, I would have a rich spiritual life.

Before joining the others at the table, Mother and I propped my grandparents up in bed with plenty of pillows and made sure they were comfortable. Together, the four of us made the sign of the cross and Grandfather said the same blessing over the food that he always said. After that, we helped them eat, cutting their food for them and holding the glasses to their lips when they wanted a drink.

In contrast to the raucous mealtime conversations in the crowded dining room, mealtime conversations with Nona and Papus were quiet and reflective. They both told anecdotal stories from their lives. Papus usually forgot what story he was telling half way through and Nona would have to finish it for him. I heard the stories so many times that I memorized them. Toward the end, before both of them died, I was the one who would finish the stories when Papus got stuck. Nona always nodded along with me, smiling because I had gotten it right.

After they were done eating, we prayed with them and tucked them into bed for the night. Careful not to wake them, we gathered the dirty dishes and carried them to the kitchen.

Finally, Mother and I joined the rest of the family in the large dining room. Mother stood behind her seat at the opposite end of the table from Father.

They each balanced one of the three-year-old twins on their hip. Father held Zoe-Sophia and Mother held Zosimos. As always my sister carried the rag-doll Mother made for her in the crook of her arm. She and 'rag-doll-sister,' as she called the thing, were inseparable.

Yaya joined us and gathered my little brother into her arms so that Mother and Aunt Petra could begin to serve us once we had prayed. Theophilos entered behind my uncle and cousins, and placed a small bouquet of wild flowers in the middle of the table while kissing Mother on the forehead. In front of me, he placed the ikon I dropped.

"You left this outside, little brother." He winked at me while standing behind his seat.

"Who will say the prayer?" Father asked. My cousins giggled until Aunt Petra quieted them with a glance. I looked at the image of the Good Shepherd, staring into the eyes of Christ.

"Well?" Father prodded.

"Yorgos can do it." Theophilos suggested. In light of my experience in the ravine, I didn't feel worthy. How would I explain that to my hungry family?

We held hands while the twins and other young children fussed, and I proceeded to bless the meal saying one of our customary prayers, "The poor shall eat and be satisfied, and they who seek the Lord shall praise him; their hearts shall live to the ages of ages." I also prayed for Zosimos, that God would make him well, because he had been sick and weak for as long as I could remember. Silently each of us made the sign of the cross and added our own private prayer. I asked God to make me good and keep me.

"That was beautiful, son." Mother reached for me and twisted a lock of my curly brown hair around her finger. Father, too, seemed proud, and the other grownups smiled at me. We each filled our bowls with soup and ate all the hot, oven-fresh bread we wanted, with olive oil for dipping.

While Theophilos told the grown-ups about my prayers in the ravine, I scrutinized the ikon, wanting to crawl into it and lose myself in its painted landscape. I wished I could run to Jesus. It seemed he welcomed me, even though he bore the weight of the lamb on his shoulders.

"I think we may have a young monk or priest in our midst," Theophilos said, his cheeks plump with bread. I lightly touched the ikon by my steaming bowl, continuing to study it.

"I have wondered the same thing," Mother mused. "Your grandparents would be so pleased if you grew up to be a priest."

I tried to remain aloof until I felt Mother's hand touch my shoulder. "Hmmm? Nothing would make me more proud than to have a monk or a priest in the family, Yorgos." I looked up at her, knowing that she wanted me to, "I've always known that when God put you here He gave you an extra special purpose."

"How did you know that Momma? Did God tell you?" Mother shook her head gently.

"No. Not with words at least. It's hard to explain, but I'll try. On the night you were born I sensed a disturbance. I know it sounds ridiculous, but I had the distinct feeling that you were in danger. And then," she snapped her fingers, "just that fast, the feeling was gone. I've always believed that an angel saved you from some terrible, unseen peril."

"Really?" Dumbfounded, I said nothing more, but my heart welled with a cacophony of discordant feelings. Excitement! It had never occurred to me to think about what I wanted to be when I grew up. I believed that my childhood was eternal and that it would never end. Until that moment, the future seemed too distant to think about. But there it was, taking root in my understanding. It was full of endings and beginnings and brimming with possibility.

In addition to being excited about having a spiritual call, I felt ashamed of the strange new feelings I discovered earlier that afternoon. I couldn't keep from wondering if someone like me could be a worthy candidate for serving God as a monk or in the priesthood.

My excitement won. My mouth stretched into a radiant smile. I felt encouraged when I looked into the faces of my extended family and saw that everyone agreed. Everyone, that is, except for Father.

"Yorgos will find a master and apprentice in a trade. Letting him serve God as a priest is an extravagance our family cannot afford. We will find a paying apprenticeship for him." My joy shattered like a clay chalice colliding with the ground. I tried not to show it.

For the rest of the meal we ate in relative silence. The twins chattered and babbled and my cousins whispered. Mother looked at me with concern misting her eyes. I imagined myself escaping into the ikon. The painted world was as solid and real to me as my village in Zagoria. I wished I could lose myself and become a part of the great cloud of witnesses, if they would have me.

2 Learning To Write

While the weeks and months passed, the discussion about my future continued. Of course, officially speaking, my parents left me out of it. In private, Mother asked me what I wanted to do and she tried to convince Father to let me do it. "God has clearly given him a spiritual vocation," she'd reason. "I've known it all along. It would be wrong of us to keep him from fulfilling it." My aunt, all three grandparents, and Theophilos tried to prevail upon him too, but that only made him more resolute. When her attempts to convince Father failed, Mother turned her full attention on me, consoling me in ways that only a mother could.

Time passed. She found other ways to encourage my interest in spirituality. When I was eight, she learned that one of the guests at the inn was a painter, of no small renown, from Venice. She implored him to teach me to use the egg paints. He dismissed her request, yet gave her a few scraps of unused pigment before departing. He also included a single frayed paint brush and a couple small squares of wood that were prepared to receive to the paint.

"What shall I paint, Momma?" I asked when she gave me the brush, wood, pigments and an egg.

"Paint whatever is in your heart to paint," she answered. "I only know beautiful things will flow out of it."

Of course she knew that I would paint ikons. I experimented, figuring out that the results were better if I

11

separated the yolk from the white first. It was a messy task that I was sloppy at. My first ikons weren't masterpieces, but they possessed a crude beauty. I had spent enough time holding, touching, and simply being with ikons in my devotional life that it was natural for me to express myself by creating them. By Mother's estimation, I was gifted.

Several weeks later, the artist traveled through our area again. When mother showed him my work, it astonished him. She implored him to take me on as an apprentice, believing that Father would be appeased. He said he neither had the time nor patience to take on another, especially a child as young as I was. However, upon reflection he admitted to being intrigued by my lone efforts and decided to spend an afternoon with me.

Only a few days before he was supposed to depart for Venice, he set up a work space behind the inn where Father had discarded an old table. There he arranged several items, most of which were familiar to me because they came from Mamma's kitchen–things like earthenware plates and cups, one of them full of water to the rim. There were other items too, unfamiliar to me because they belonged to him–dull knives, brushes and square pieces of wood that were made ready for paint.

"The first step," he explained, "the egg must be separated from the yolk." Between his forefinger and thumb he displayed a brown egg that came from one of our chickens. With an artist's flair he raised it above his eyes, and then lowered it level with mine. "They must be completely separated. If any white remains in the yolk, the paint will dry too quickly and it will drag on application." He pointed to one of my little masterpieces where this had happened. "If you are careful and patient, these mistakes are easily avoided." His voice was both stern and tender.

"When you crack an egg open, allow as much of the white to drain off as you can without dropping the yolk." He did with the egg exactly as he described, carefully halving the shell and passing the yolk back and forth several times. He allowed the slimy clear substance to drip to the ground, while instructing me. "Continue the separation by transferring the yolk from the palm of one hand to the other until yolk is all that remains. Place the yolk on a towel and gently roll it to the edge." While he spoke his demonstration continued.

He reached for one of the cups. "Pierce the yolk sac like this," he said, using a sharp stick he whittled for the occasion, "and allow the yolk to drain into a clean container." He smiled while showing me how to do it. "I suggest that you use a fresh egg each day, because they dry out."

When he finished showing me how to separate the yolk from the white, he produced an egg from the pocket of his jacket with the theatrics of a magician. "Your turn," he said. When I followed the instructions, obtaining similar results, he patted me on the head.

In the clay cups from Momma's kitchen, he showed me how to mix the dry pigment with water to create a paste. Using an old plate, calling it a palette, he demonstrated how to mix the colored paste with equal amounts of yolk saying, "Mix it well or there will be lumps. You don't want there to be any lumps." He also taught that some pigments require more egg and others require less. He was confident that my skills would improve with practice.

In fact, he encouraged me to practice daily if I wanted to be any good. For the rest of the afternoon, and the two that followed, he and I painted. He discovered that he was willing to spend more time with me than he anticipated; telling Mother that teaching me had been a pleasure. In three days, I produced an image of Theotokos that astounded him.

While he demonstrated his technique, he painted a portrait of me. The morning after the third day, when we said our goodbyes, he gave me a couple more of his old brushes, several dry pigments, and a dull knife that he used for mixing the paste. He told Mother that he was certain I had a gift. He regretted that he couldn't apprentice me, but he urged me to practice. I gave him the ikon of The Mother of God that I painted under his tutelage and he gave me, or Mother rather, the portrait of me that he had done.

I never saw him again. Over the next several years, at regular intervals, he sent me letters, including pigments for me to use. Occasionally, he included things like brushes too. These things always came with the admonishment that I continue painting. Which, of course, I did.

I practiced my skills. In the excitement that comes with inspired creativity, I tended to rush, always wanting to move on to the next. The earlier examples of my work were proof of this. Over time, I learned to slow down and be patient with the process. I was learning in practice what I knew in theory, painting ikons was as much an act of prayer as venerating them. In time I had painted so many, that I gave everyone in my family at least one or two. Several of the ikons on the family altar in the eastern corner of the common room were replaced with ones painted by me as well.

When Grandfather's seventy-fourth birthday drew near, I decided to paint him a copy of his favorite ikon, called Christ Emmanuel which means 'God is with us.' Several times I had seen him hold his old fading ikon of Christ Emmanuel with tears streaming down his cheeks.

Once, when I asked him why he cried, he said, "Because God left paradise and became one of us. *That* is love." Christ

Emmanuel is the first ikon I remember painting slowly and prayerfully with an eye for the smallest detail. This was for Papus. It had to be perfect. I completed it several days before his birthday and couldn't wait to give it to him.

I was the one who heard Nona weeping the morning Papus died. I woke at dawn, as was my custom. After dressing, I headed, with Zosimos lagging behind, to the ikon corner, ready to welcome the day with my family in the traditional Orthodox fashion. Hearing my grandmother crying, I knocked on their door, opened it, and peered in.

"Nona, what's the matter?" I asked. She didn't look at me, or even answer. At first I thought Grandfather was asleep on his back with Nona curled up beside him. One of her knees was bent over his thigh and her hand was on his chest. Her lips, against his ear, were moving. When I opened the door wider and spoke, she tried to rouse him by shaking him.

"The boy is here. Wake up. Wake up." She shook him with more vigor.

"He won't wake up, Yorgos." She wailed even louder than before. I tried to help her out of the bed and into the chair next to it so I could see what was wrong with Papus, but she threw herself on top of him and clung to him.

Before long, other family members came to the room, spilling out into the hallway. The women gathered around Grandfather's bed and gave voice to their unutterable grief by groaning, wailing, and beating their chests.

When the priest, Father Elias, arrived, my family parted for him as if for a herald bearing urgent news. After confirming that Grandfather had died, he began the First Parastas, a short memorial service, which is celebrated soon after the time of death and several times thereafter until the burial. For more than a day, the women continued to perform the constant funeral dirge over Papus' body.

I had been thrust into a surreal existence. In my ten years of life, no one close to me had died. I kept expecting Grandfather to wake up, but of course, he didn't. When the First Parastas was completed, all of the women of the family, including my six year old sister, handled Grandfather's body with reverence. They began to wash it and prepare it for burial. I watched while the older women showed Zoe-Sophia how to do this.

They explained to her that there was nothing to be afraid of and that by handling his body with care and respect, and by sharing their unfathomable grief as best as they could, they were expressing their love for him. Throughout all of it, Father and Uncle Petros stayed with them and assisted.

Mother found Zosimos and me in the corner, trying to understand what the commotion was all about. She explained that Grandfather died in his sleep, which meant he would never wake up. He was with Jesus now and a part of the great cloud of witnesses that I so longed to one day be part of. She led me and my brother from the room and explained that Nona must be allowed to stay and grieve.

Zosimos and I were allowed to watch from the hall. After the ceremonial washing, the women clothed Papus for burial and placed a crown of myrtle leaves upon his head. Woven into it was a strip of paper with the Trisagion written on it, "Holy God, Holy Mighty, Holy Immortal, have mercy on us."

From the hall, I saw Father lift the ikon of Christ Emmanuel from the shelf in their bedroom and approach Grandfather's body with it. Nona shook her head. She pointed to a small silver cross that hung from the shelf. Father returned the ikon to its place, took the cross in hand and went to his father's body. Lifting Grandfather's right hand, he placed the cross in it. Nona then placed a prayer rope on Grandfather's left wrist.

16

When the preparations for burial were complete, the men of the family carried Papus' body to the common room where Father Elias waited with an empty casket. Father and Uncle Petros lifted the heavy unhinged lid, which was decorated with an Eastern Cross, the only flourish on the otherwise plain burial box. They placed the lid outside next to the open door, a sign that our household was in mourning.

Father Elias sprinkled holy water on all four sides of the casket before the body of my beloved Grandfather was placed inside it. After that they double checked everything. Did his hands need to be adjusted? Was the silver cross in place? Did the crown need to be adjusted?

When everything was set right, the wake commenced. It consisted of a continuous reading of the Psalms which was only interrupted by an occasional Parastas. Anyone present was allowed to read, and it was customary for everyone, including family and friends, to take turns. When I screwed up my courage, I read Grandfather's favorite passage from scripture, and mine too, a portion from the Book of Lamentations. It was my favorite because it was the first portion of scripture I memorized, and Papus helped me learn it.

"A reading from the Book of Lamentations.

My soul is deprived of peace,
    I have forgotten what happiness is;
I tell myself my future is lost,
    all that I hoped for from the Lord.
The thought of my homeless poverty
    is wormwood and gall;
Remembering it over and over
    leaves my soul downcast within me.

But I will call this to mind,
  as my reason to have hope:
The favors of the Lord are not exhausted,
  his mercies are not spent;
They are renewed each morning,
  so great is his faithfulness.
My portion is the Lord, says my soul;
  therefore will I hope in him.
Good is the Lord to one who waits for him,
  to the soul that seeks him;
It is good to hope in silence
  for the saving help of the Lord.

This is the word of the Lord."

3 Death In Residence

Temporarily, life as I knew it stopped. The women didn't take a break from their guttural expression of grief, even to prepare meals. Meals were provided by our neighbors. They came and went at all hours through the front door of our home which we left open until the end of the wake.

Early in the afternoon of the second day, Theophilos guided me and Zosimos to our bedroom to get us out from underfoot. To pass the time, he started a game of knuckle-bones, before leaving to join the grownups.

Not long after that, Niko, a boy my age who lived in the village, came with his mother and infant brother. They brought a plate heaped with spanakopita. I recognized him because he regularly attended the Divine Liturgy with his family. Though I wanted to, I'd always been too shy to introduce myself to him after the service. I was happy when Theophilos escorted Niko to our bedroom and encouraged him to play the game with us. We welcomed him and started a new game. Theophilos leaned against the doorjamb for a few minutes and watched us.

"May you have an abundant life," Niko said when Theophilos introduced us. It was a traditional thing to say to the bereaved during a time of loss.

"Thank you," I answered my palms moist with sweat.

When I saw Niko up close, I knew that I liked him. I was unable, at first, to look at him after that. When our hands connected, when his skin touched mine, I felt the undeniable shock of attraction. My heart fluttered, skipping circles in my chest.

We played several rounds of knuckle-bones, laughing and joking the whole time until Aunt Petra shushed us. We stopped playing the game for a few moments and a deep silence flooded the bedroom.

Finally, Niko spoke. "Tell me about your Grandfather. I don't remember ever seeing him at Divine Liturgy." A mournful grimace contorted my face.

"Papus hadn't been to the liturgy in a long time. Father Elias used to bring him the Eucharist and serve him here, in his bedroom." Pain pierced me through when I heard myself speaking of my grandfather in the past tense.

"I'm going to miss his stories," Zosimos said.

"Yes," I agreed, and Theophilos nodded.

"Tell me one of his stories," Niko said. "Please?"

"He used to tell me all the stories about the saints. My favorite one was–"

"That sounds boring," Niko interrupted. "Didn't he know any other stories?"

I stammered. "Oh . . . uh . . . ?" Theophilos chuckled.

"He did love the stories about the saints," he said. "You're just like Papus, Yorgos." I felt proud to be compared to my grandfather, and embarrassed that Niko thought my interest in the lives of the saints was boring. I wanted him to like me, to find me interesting.

Zosimos had a coughing fit, taking the attention off me. He held a handkerchief up to his mouth and we all waited in silence for the fit to end.

"He knew all the stories about the heroes," Theophilos said.

"And the gods and goddesses," Zosimos added, when he could speak without coughing.

"You mean he told you the myths?" Niko asked. Zosimos nodded, still holding the cloth to his mouth.

"Yes," he finally said.

"Tell me your favorite one." I slumped back against the edge of my bed.

"All of his stories were good. It's hard to choose . . . ." Zosimos scratched his head. With Niko's attention on my brother, I felt like Zeus bereft of thunder.

While we waited for Zosimos to decide, I rattled the knuckle-bones in my cupped hands.

"I know the one. Theophilos, tell the story about the haunted cave at the lake."

"Well, yes," Theophilos started. "Grandfather used to say that all over Greece there are sacred places; groves, springs, and mountain passes, that have been considered holy since before Christianity was ever preached here. There's such a place in the hills above the lake. It's a cave where nereids have lived for thousands of years. Did you know that?"

"I didn't know about the cave, but I've heard that people often see nereids up there," Niko answered.

"It's true," Zosimos said. "Yorgos, do you remember the story?"

"Yes, of course. Water drips from the roof of the cave. People believe that the stalactites are the breasts of the nereids and the water is their milk."

"That's right," Zosimos said, satisfied. He started to cough again and indicated that I should wait to continue.

"It is believed that the water dripping from the stalactites will cure any illness," I said when he was finished coughing. "However, if anyone wishes to take some of the water to a sick friend or relative they must be careful to do it the right way, or they will have to face the wrath of the nereids." I glanced up at Theophilos. He nodded and

21

turned to rejoin the other adults to help with the funeral preparations.

"What happens if they don't do it right?" Niko asked. Zosimos lowered the handkerchief from his mouth and leaned toward him.

"First, while he is on his way to the cave he can't speak to anyone. Speaking will nullify the effect of the water."

"Oh!" Niko gasped.

"And he must bring a green lamp to light once he is inside, and a green pot to collect the water in." Zosimos paused for a moment to catch his breath.

"That's not how to tell the story," I said. Niko and Zosimos looked at me.

"Well . . . ?" Niko prodded while I gathered my thoughts.

"Let me start all over. The nereids aren't gods at all, but they're not people like us either. When someone sees a nereid they almost always see a female. People who see them say that they are unnaturally beautiful. They dress in flowing white gowns and have veils that cover their faces. If you look real close, you can see through the veils. If you're lucky, you might glimpse a nereid without her veil on. That means a blessing is sure to come your way. It doesn't happen often, though. Nereids are rumored to be extremely private creatures. Occasionally someone will see a male nereid, but that's even more rare than seeing a female without her veil. Seeing a male can signify either a blessing *or* a curse. There's no way of knowing . . . until it's too late."

Zosimos interrupted me, "Yorgos, that's boring. Just tell the story."

"Okay." I shrugged. "I'm sorry."

"I didn't think it was boring," Niko countered. I bit my cheek to hide my smile and turned to my brother, feeling more confident.

"You'll like this part, Zosimos. Nereids live a long time, a lot longer than people do."

"I wish I could live a long time," he said, drawing in his breath and holding it.

"They still die."

Zosimos exhaled, "Just tell the story."

"Please," Niko agreed. "Tell us about the cave. You said there was a cave nearby?"

"There is. In the hills above the lake." I leaned back into the hard edge of the bed, thinking for a moment. "Suppose there is a young boy who is always sick." In unison Niko and Zosimos nodded. "He has a brother who would do anything to help him get well."

"Would he go to the cave?" Zosimos asked.

"He would go to the cave," I answered. Zosimos smiled. "He would do anything to help his brother get well," I said, adding under my breath: "Anything for you, Zosimos." His smiled widened.

"He needs a green pot for the water," he said.

"He takes one."

"He also needs a lamp, a green lamp."

"He takes one of those, too."

"What does he do with the pot and the lamp?" Niko asked.

"He uses the lamp to see, and the pot to collect the water, of course," I answered. "On his way out of the cave he isn't supposed to look behind himself no matter what. The lamp is for lighting the way ahead, not for looking behind."

"What will happen if he does?" Niko asked.

"If he looks back—"

"The water will lose its power and he will lose his mind," Zosimos answered with maniacal glee. He laughed until he started to cough again.

"Don't forget the clothing," I said, speaking over the sound of his hacking. "He is supposed to leave behind a favorite piece of clothing as a kind of offering. If he doesn't, it won't work."

"That's right," Zosimos agreed with a hoarse voice. "What does he bring to leave for an offering?" he asked me.

"I . . . I don't know."

"It sounds like it won't work unless everything is done perfectly," Niko said.

"It's true," I agreed. "At least that's what Papus told us. The nereids are sticklers. If you make one mistake, or you bother them on a bad day, they'll make sure you have a bad day too."

"A *really* bad day," Zosimos added. He paused, coughed once more, and then wiped his mouth. "On his way home, just like on his way there, he must not speak to anyone." Zosimos leaned back for a moment to catch his breath again.

"That's what Papus said," I agreed. "Grandfather told us several stories about people who went for the healing water that drips from the nereid's breasts."

"Did it ever work? Did anyone ever do it right?" Zosimos asked. I threw an expression at him.

"You know the stories as well as I do."

"Yes," he agreed. "But I want to hear you say it. Did it ever work? Were their loved ones healed?"

Understanding illumined my mind.

"Zosimos, have faith in God."

"What if that's not enough?" he asked, his muscles tensing. I swallowed my piety and gave him the consolation that I knew he sought.

"I remember at least one story in which, yes, someone perfectly accomplished everything the nereids required of him, and when he gave the water to his loved one, his loved one got better."

Zosimos relaxed. "Yorgos, would his brother really do that for him, go up there to the cave alone and risk angering the nereids?"

"If he asked, yes, I am sure his brother would." Zosimos lay back against his bed, satisfied.

"Thank you," he said simply.

"Do you have any other favorite stories from your Grandfather?" Niko asked.

Zosimos and I had enough favorite stories that we could have entertained Niko with them for hours. Halfway through the next one, it was time for Niko to go home. I enjoyed his company so much that I almost forgot that it was Grandfather's death that brought him into our home in the first place. When his mother finished giving her condolences and was ready to go, I didn't want him to leave.

Between the time of Grandfather's death and the funeral, there were innumerable special prayers said and services held on his behalf. Finally, three days after he died, on the eve of his burial, and after the Final Parastas had been said again, I went to Nona. I found her secluded in their bedroom, a rare thing since Papus had passed. I climbed onto the bed and she sat down next to me.

"I want to show you something, Nona." Grandmother smiled at me and put out her hand. I set the ikon of Christ Emmanuel on her upturned palm. "I wanted to give this to Papus on his birthday," I fought to suppress my tears. The next day would have been his birthday. Instead of celebrating his birth, we were going to put him in the ground. It was incomprehensible that my life would continue without him. He had been a part of my every day since I was born.

She held the ikon before her failing eyes and peered at
it. When she recognized the image, she kissed it, crossed
herself, and gave it back to me.

"It's beautiful, Yorgos. You have a gift. God has blessed
your eyes and your hands. Most importantly, he has blessed
your heart. To paint such beautiful ikons, one must have
a beautiful heart." I pressed my lips together in a grateful
and self-conscious smile.

"Thank you, Nona."

"Your Grandfather would love it. I know it. And he
would be so proud of you." I clasped Nona's hand and patted it.

"Nona, do you think Papus would mind if I kept one of
his ikons?"

"No, son. I don't think he would mind at all. I think
he would like that." I went to their ikon collection, in the
eastern corner of their room, and selected the one I wanted:
Christ Emmanuel, because I knew it was his favorite. I
showed it to her for her approval. She nodded.

"I think that is the right one, Yorgos. What will you do
with the one you painted for Papus?" I lifted it from where
I laid it on the bed and placed it in her hands again.

"Do you want it? I can put it on the shelf where this one
was." She patted my hand.

"No. I think you will come up with a better idea than
that."

After the Final Parastas, the slow procession to the
church commenced. We were a throng of mournful black
that wound its way from the inn to the church like a ser-
pent. The only things that broke the black monotony were
the flowers people clutched in their hands.

While we walked, I made my decision regarding the
ikon I painted for Grandfather. I knew exactly what I
wanted to do with it.

When the procession arrived at the church, the casket was placed in the center of the nave with Grandfather's feet facing the altar. Four candle stands were arranged around it in the shape of a cross while Father Elias swung the censer over it. With Mother standing behind me, her hands on my shoulders, and Nona to my right, I watched Father and Uncle Petros remove the heavy lid and place it outside the door of the church like they had done at home. There it stood, an invitation to all who might pass by to come and join us in our mourning.

Before the Divine Liturgy began, I broke free of mother's grip. I ran to the casket. Curiosity and dread twisted my stomach. I feared I approached a bottomless hole. Grandfather lay still and breathless. I stared at him. His face, sagging toward the earth, was the most subtle shade of blue. It looked like wax, having the same pale sheen as candles. His hands were crossed over his chest. Emotion swelled, but I couldn't cry. My tears were stuck, piling up behind my eyes. Finally, I lifted one of his cold hands and placed Christ Emmanuel under it and set the hand on top of the ikon. I looked at Nona. She nodded once, a reserved smile touching her lips.

"I painted this for you, Grandfather," I said. "I hope you like it. Maybe from the great cloud of witnesses you can see it. I don't know. I hope so . . . . Grandmother said you'd like it." I half-expected him to respond, to pick it up and hold it to his weak eyes. I wanted to hear him tell me himself, in his creaky voice which had been weathered by more than seven decades of living, that he loved it. But he just lay there, dead.

I understood something that I hadn't grasped before. Every time I wished to escape sin and the pain of life by becoming a part of the great cloud of witnesses, I wished to die. I wasn't ready to die. Life was too precious. Papus taught me that by living nearly seventy-four years and loving God, life, and family until the end. I wanted to follow his example.

When I returned to Nona, she squeezed my hand. Pressing her lips into my ear, she whispered, "That was the right thing to do with your gift, Yorgos. I am so proud of you."

During the Divine Liturgy I was usually captivated by the myriads of ikons that surrounded me like little portals into heaven. On this particular occasion, however, I couldn't take my eyes off Papus lying in his casket.

Once Divine Liturgy ended, the funeral service commenced. Everyone held lighted candles, and Father Elias swung the censer until the air inside the sanctuary was thick with incense.

Toward the end of the service the people chanted these words, "We mortals are formed from the dust of the Earth and to dust we shall return. To whatever place we mortals wend our way we make into a funeral dirge the song: Alleluia! Alleluia! Alleluia!"

I couldn't say it. Grandfather was dead. To me that didn't seem to be much of a cause for celebration. I didn't think I would ever want to celebrate anything again.

After the service, while everyone gathered around Grandfather's casket for the last kiss, I ducked outside. I said my last goodbye when I placed Christ Emmanuel in his hand. I didn't want to see the empty shell of his body ever again. He was gone, that was clear to me now. Gone.

Mother followed me. When I submitted to her embrace, the scent of her perfume filled my nostrils, and though it comforted me, I knew something now that I hadn't known before, something that tempered the solace. People die. Someday it would be her time to go. And someday, after that, it would be mine. I didn't want her to ever stop hugging me.

I found that I wanted the whole affair to be over. I was tired of prayers, Parastas, and reading Psalms. It all felt empty to me. During the funeral, I examined the faces of the people who knew and loved Papus. Yes they wept, they were clearly sad but I saw *joy* when they sang Alleluia. It wasn't empty for them. I didn't understand it.

"Momma, why are we celebrating? I don't feel like singing Alleluia. I don't know if I ever will." She stepped back, lifted my chin and looked me in the eye.

"If you don't feel like singing Alleluia, then don't. It's okay. But the *reason* we sing it is because we know that death has not defeated your grandfather. When Christ rose from His grave He defeated death for us. Papus is alive with Christ now. What he has hoped for he has attained: eternal life with Christ. That is the same hope we all have. Do you understand?"

I nodded yes. I so wanted to understand, but I expected that this was something I would not fully grasp until I was older. To me, dead was dead. Perhaps in some inexplicable way Papus really was alive and with Jesus in some other place. What difference did that make to me here on earth? Here, on earth, he was dead. That his cold, stiff, unbreathing body was lying in that horrid wooden box was proof enough of this to me.

A procession formed again. This one was much shorter than the one that went from our home to the church building. It led behind the church to the cemetery.

Upon arriving at the spot where Grandfather would be laid to rest, and covered with dirt, the Parastas was chanted yet again. Nona, Aunt Petra and Mother served koliva in clay cups from a table set up beside the grave. Traditionally served at funeral and subsequent memorial services, koliva is a sweetened mixture of boiled kernels of wheat, dried fruit and nuts, made in the shape of a mound to resemble a grave.

Father Elias sealed the coffin with three nails which were meant to remind us of the three nails with which Christ had been crucified. As the nails were beat into the box I felt they were being driven into my heart. With each resounding strike my body shuddered and for a moment, with my heart pierced, I felt I had been paralyzed.

While the casket containing my beloved Grandfather's body was lowered into the earth all the people gathered around and chanted, "Open wide, O Earth, and receive him that was fashioned from thee by the hand of God before time, and who returns again unto thee that gave him birth."

Father Elias poured a shovelful of dirt on the casket in the form of a cross saying, "The earth is the Lord's and the fullness thereof."

Everyone who brought flowers threw them down on top of the casket, along with a handful of koliva, and then Father Elias finished burying it–casket, flowers, koliva, and all–under a thick blanket of earth.

At that moment, while Father Elias threw shovelful after shovelful of dirt on Papus's casket, I couldn't breathe. It was as if I were being blanketed with a thick heavy covering of earth. A covering so thick and heavy that I couldn't overcome it. I shook the thought from my mind and turned my back on the sight of it. I had never imagined anything more horrifying. *What could be worse,* I wondered, *than being buried under so much dirt?* The idea itself was suffocating.

4 Driving Death Away

My family grieved an epic length of time. The traditional period of mourning for Orthodox Christians was forty days. For the Godevenos household, the number was nearly doubled because Nona passed away sixty days after Papus. I suppose they spent so many years together that their souls were fused into one, so the one couldn't live without the other.

Though Death seemed to have taken up permanent residence in the Godevenos home, once the official period of mourning had been observed for both Papus and Nona, life in and around the inn returned to its regular daily rhythms. During this time, however, Death waited patiently to claim one more member of our family. It sneaked up on us, though really we should have seen it coming.

One morning, a full hour earlier than I normally woke up, I was raised by the sound of Zosimos coughing. Far away, in her own bedroom, Zoe-Sophia cried.

"What's wrong with Zosimos?" Slapping sounds from her feet grew louder as they repeatedly struck the floor. Soon she blocked the doorway and peered in with wild, tear-filmed eyes.

Mother was already in our bedroom with Yaya, bending over Zosimos' bed. Father came rushing in. My sister hid behind his legs and peeked around them at her twin, trembling. Mother turned to Father with the grimmest face.

"Titus, he's coughing up blood." She held up a towel with a deep red stain on it. "He's never coughed up blood before." Zosimos had another coughing fit. When red droplets splattered Mother's cheek and her white nightgown, she started to cry. Theophilos came up behind Father and pulled Zoe-Sophia into his arms.

"Will he be okay?" she whimpered. When Mother reached for my sister's cheek her fingers glistened with spittle and blood.

"Honestly, sweetheart, I don't know this time." Mother looked at me and then Theophilos while wiping the blood on her nightgown.

"Theophilos, please get her out of here." My brother turned to leave, Mother called out to him. "Please, son, go get Father Elias. Take Zoe-Sophia with you."

From my bed I watched Yaya and Mother tend to Zosimos. Father paced in the hallway saying nothing. Aunt Petra and Uncle Petros went with their children to the common room to pray.

I was reminded of the fuss we made over Papus in the predawn hours on the day that he died. I feared that Zosimos wouldn't make it until morning light either.

When Nona was dying, I learned that if Father Elias was summoned, it meant death was near. Zosimos wasn't dead *yet*. I could pray. I pulled the blankets up to my chin and made the sign of the cross several times searching my memory for the right prayer, or the right saint to address. I was at a loss and started to pray from my heart. Silently, I begged God to keep him from dying and make him well.

Theophilos returned with Zoe-Sophia asleep in his arms. Mother looked up, searching with her eyes for Father Elias. She exhaled when she saw him following close behind my brother.

Watching from the hall, Theophilos let the priest pass and stood in the doorway. Father Elias made the sign of the cross.

"May Theotokos comfort you in your loss," he said, addressing Mother. "She knows what it feels like to lose a young son." Mother held both hands over her heart and nodded her acknowledgment.

"Zosimos, I am so proud of you for your courage," she said, leaning over him. "No one has fought Charon more valiantly than you." Her tears fell on his forehead. She brushed them off, in the sign of the cross, and then she brushed his hair from his eyes while pressing hers closed. The copious flow of tears wasn't staunched.

Father Elias waited. He murmured a prayer with his prayer rope in hand. A black knot pinched between his forefinger and thumb. Clearing his throat, he began to recite the Office of the Parting of the Soul from the Body.

"O Holy God, Holy Mighty, Holy Immortal One, have mercy on us," he said three times. My heart dropped into the earth.

"No!" I shouted. Theophilos passed Zoe-Sophia to Yaya and came to collect me. While he carried me out, Mother caressed the back of my head.

"Yorgos, please! This is hard enough." Zosimos coughed again. I covered my ears to block out the sound. Mother continued speaking. Her lips formed these words,

"We knew this day would come."

"Why?" I yelled. "Why now? Too much! There has been too much death!" When I said that, Zosimos fought to rise up in his bed.

"I don't want to die," he said. "This isn't fair." He paused to catch his breath and continued, "Papus lived to be old. I want to, too." He slumped into the mattress and pillows and tried not to cough.

"Please!" Mother begged. Father embraced her.

"I can't handle another death in the family. Not our son. He hasn't lived." Father's chest muffled her voice.

"Theophilos, take Yorgos to your aunt and uncle," Father instructed. While Theophilos carried me down the stairs, Zosimos called out to me, "Yorgos go to the cave. Bring me back the water."

Theophilos carried me to the common room and returned to our bedroom. I found my tattered scarf, passed down to me from Papus, on the divan where I left it. I wrapped it around my neck and tied the ends into a knot. My cousins, aunt, and uncle were praying for Zosimos. I joined hands with them, closed my eyes and tried to focus. I couldn't. My heart kept thumping in my chest, and it hurt to breathe.

I slipped away from the prayer circle and retreated to the kitchen. Before sneaking out of the house through the back door, I selected a suitable oil lamp and a pot with a lid. Neither were green. I rummaged through the place where I stored my painting supplies and found the ingredients for green tempura paint. I threw them together, not at all meticulous about separating the yolk from the white. I was in a hurry.

While I rummaged, I also found a piece of flint and a rock to strike it on. I dropped them into the pot. In haste, I coated the pot, its lid, and the lamp with a single, thick layer of green and struck out on my errand of mercy. By the time my feet hit the dirt road, the sun was beginning to brighten the morning sky and warm my skin.

At a regular pace, a walk to the lake was forty minutes and the caves in the hills beyond were another fifteen. On my way, I passed by two neighbors. It was easy to be silent in response to their casual conversation because I was running. When I slowed to a walk and passed another two, it was harder for me to ignore them. Though I feared being rude, I kept my gaze fixed to the road.

When I passed her house, Mother's friend Dorcas, who was working in her garden, came into the road to greet me.

"Good morning, Yorgos!" she said. I glanced at her but didn't stop. I didn't greet her. I feared that if I did anything more than walk to the cave I'd nullify the effects of the water.

"Is anything the matter?" she called after me. I didn't respond. Instead, I started to run again.

By the time I reached the lake, it felt like my lungs were on fire. I stopped for a drink and to catch my breath. I splashed water on my warm and blood-flushed face, and brought cupped handful after handful of it to my mouth. While I drank, I feared that by the time I got home it would be too late and Zosimos would be dead. I hoped that God would delay the seemingly inevitable.

"Please give me enough time," I prayed.

Feeling as refreshed as I could under the circumstances, I bolted for the cave where the nereids lived, heading in the direction I expected to find it.

I remembered Papus mentioning that a stream passed by the cave. When I came across one, I followed it up the hill. The higher I climbed, the thicker the trees, until I couldn't avoid being scratched by their growth. I ignored the irritation.

In the distance, the mouth of the cave rose above the treetops. I followed a curve in the stream until I heard singing. I stopped. My chest expanded and my heart beat behind my eyes. The cave was still a considerable distance away, but through gaps between the trees, I could swear I saw a man with his arms raised. He was unusually tall and wore radiant white robes. Four equally tall women who also wore white, held hands and danced circles around him.

A fierce wind upset the trees and saplings making it difficult for me to see the people–the nereids–that I had been spying on. I pressed through the swaying foliage hoping I could get another glimpse of them and beg them for help. When I stumbled into a clearing, the cave was only a few meters ahead. I expected to see the nereids. Instead, I saw the tail ends of three white deer while they escaped into the concealing ground cover and low hanging trees. A fourth deer and an immense stag looked up at me. The stag nodded before sprinting away, followed by his companion.

My feet had fused with the ground. I swallowed, breathed through my nose and forced the air out of my mouth. I couldn't take a step, not without anyone to push me. I was alone. I mustered the courage to push myself, approaching the cave with trepidation.

When I reached it, I crossed myself and asked God to go with me. I took several swift steps before fumbling with the flint and the rock to light the lamp. While I knelt, I heard a chorus singing. It came from the deep recesses of the cave. It was beautiful and moving, inexplicably scaring me.

I stood up to my full height and held the lamp above my head. I peered into the darkness, took a deep breath, and resumed walking. A thousand shadows danced around me; on the floor, walls, and ceiling of the cave. They even passed before my face. While I edged in, the light from the lamp scattered them. The singing faded until it was so indistinguishable from the wind that I doubted I had heard any singing at all.

I walked several more meters. Water dripped on my arms and the top of my head. It saturated my hair, running down my forehead into my eyes. I looked up to see thousands of stalactites pointing down at me. They reminded me more of swords than breasts. Yes, some demi-god or ancient hero had driven thousands of swords through the roof of the cave and the tips of them continually dripped. It struck me that blood would be a better metaphor for what dripped from the stalactites, not milk. Of course, in truth, it was nothing but water.

I decided that I had gone far enough. I set down the empty pot and hoped it would fill up quickly. Holding the oil lamp with one hand, I cupped the other over the flame. I didn't think I could be courageous enough to stay if the lamp went out.

I sat on the ground next to the pot and listened to the soft spattering of the water strike the wet floor. While the water level slowly rose, the sound of the dripping inside the pot grew louder, echoing in the silence.

After a while, I was able to relax. I crossed myself and concentrated my thoughts on God and Theotokos, asking her to pray for my brother. I figured if she knew what it was like to lose a young son, she would also know what it was like to hope that his life would be spared. I hoped that she would listen to my prayer. I made it on my mother's behalf and on the behalf of my entire family. Surely Theotokos and God would be moved.

I interceded for my brother for perhaps an hour. By that time, I was drenched but I was no longer afraid. My prayers had centered me. Thankfully, however, the flame was still strong and burning bright. I peered into the pot. It was three-quarters full.

That should be enough, I thought. *I hope it's enough.* I made the sign of the cross over the pot saying: "In the name of the Father, and the Son and the Holy Spirit." I covered it, gathered it in my arms, and stood up. A green puddle was where the pot had been. The required color had been washed off! I bit my lip. *What if I've upset the nereids, and ruined the whole thing?* I had already done my best to meet the traditional requirements. What more could I do?

When I rose, the light on the cave walls rose too. The shadows that scattered before came rushing back. They threatened to extinguish the light. I held the pot against my stomach with my right elbow. With my right hand, I held the lamp and covered the sputtering flame with my left. When I started for the mouth of the cave, a warm wind blew past me. In its wake, the lamp went out.

I heard a sound like the rushing of many feet. It brought with it shadows that enveloped me. I twirled, screamed, and flapped my one free elbow trying to lose them, determined not to drop the lamp or the pot of potentially life-saving water.

Though the shadows lacked substance, they did not lack the power to scare me. Breathless and terrified, I pressed on to the mouth of the cave and ran out of it. I expected the shadows to stop following me once I made it outside, dispelled, one would expect, by the daylight. However, the diaphanous black wisps were not put to flight by the direct light of the sun. Like leaves lifted by wind, they swirled around me. I ran, yelling, down the hillside along the creek.

Though petrified, I managed to recall that I was supposed to leave behind an article of clothing. I mustered my courage and returned to the cave, defying every instinct which told me to go home. I also recalled that I wasn't supposed to look back. So, while I ran I was careful to look at nothing but than my feet.

On my way I shielded my eyes with my left hand, holding the lamp and the pot with my right. When I could tell I was near the cave's mouth I closed my eyes and tore off Papus' scarf. I fumbled blindly, reaching for a tree that was beside the cave. When a branch scratched me, I draped the scarf over it, turned, and bolted for home. I didn't dare glance behind myself, though it sounded like a multitude persued me. I didn't want to see whatever terrible phantom throng it was that followed.

When I had run three-quarters of the way home, the sound of my pursuers stopped as if they had been called into retreat. I paused, feeling it was safe to do so, but I didn't look up the road the way I had come. I didn't want to risk nullifying the effect of the water.

Sitting on one of the many boulders that were along the side of the road, I rested, but not long enough to catch my breath. I needed to get the water to my brother before he died, if I wasn't already too late. I prayed it wasn't too late.

The moment I rose to my feet, a hand touched my shoulder. I turned. A woman, unusually tall and thin, stood behind me. Her face was veiled. When she lifted the sheer cloth to speak I saw that her features were similar to those of a human, but they were subtly too perfect and slightly like a deer. Her brown eyes were too big, her nose was too long, and her ears were just a little too pointy, yet her features were elegant. She was something more, or at least different, than I, or any other Greek I had ever known. She wore a white gown that went from her chin past her toes. It pooled on the ground around her feet and shone in the sunlight. Her wheat-colored hair reached past her shoulders and had tiny flowers braided into it. She was beautiful. When I looked into her hazel eyes, my insides quivered.

"You have great faith and courage, young Master Godevenos." Her lips moved imperceptibly, yet I heard her clearly. While she communicated, her steady gaze was unblinking. I closed my eyes and bent, fumbling for the lamp and the pot that were beside the boulder. She grabbed me by the shoulder and pulled me back up. With my eyebrows knit and mouth shut, I shook my head no.

"Do not fear. You may speak. My father, the king, has sent me to you." I slapped my hand over my mouth and shook my head again. I didn't want to be deceived by her flattery or her charm.

"You have followed our ways perfectly. It is clear that fear does not sway you or stop you from doing what must be done. We perceive that your heart is pure." The sunlight caught in her hair. It seemed to catch on fire. "The God you believe in and love has heard your secret prayers." I nodded, affirmatively this time, and stepped away from her. She reached for my hand and pulled me to a stop. Her expression was grave and utterly sincere. "Your prayers are being answered, young Yorgos, but the day will come when you wish they hadn't been. Such is the burden of being pure of heart."

She held together her middle finger, forefinger and thumb, kissed them on the tips and touched them to my forehead, my chest, and my right and left shoulders, making the sign of the cross. Then she reached both of her hands into the sky. They stretched out and disappeared into it. The rest of her body turned into a tornado that shone white in the sunlight. It twisted around me, picking up leaves and twigs that lay at my feet. While it lifted off the ground, I remained in its center. It rose up and over me, taking flight into the sky, moving toward the cave from which the woman came. Bewildered from the brief encounter, I rubbed my eyes, watching the tornado disappear.

"May milk and honey be in your path," I whispered, while picking leaves and twigs from my hair.

I climbed the four steps to the inn, a burden in each hand. I paused at the door. I was afraid to enter and I was afraid not to. If Zosimos was dead, my journey would have been for nothing. Worse than that, however, I would have missed my last opportunity to say goodbye. Nevertheless, the nereid, if that is truly what the woman was, said that my prayers would be answered. The only way to know for sure was to seize the moment, no matter how dreadful.

I filled my lungs with air and pulled the latch, while giving the door a push. It swung open for me in a creaky arc. I found Uncle Petros, Aunt Petra, and my cousins still downstairs. Aunt Petra and Theophilos rushed to me and embraced me. They both had bleary red eyes and puffy cheeks.

"No," I cried. "He hasn't–?"

"No, he is still with us," Theophilos answered. "I don't know how, but he has found the strength to hold on." Aunt Petra picked a leaf from my hair. Upstairs Zosimos groaned. I thrust the lamp into Theophilos' hands and clutched the pot of water in mine.

"He keeps asking where you are with the water." Theophilos pointed to the pot. Without further word I ran up the stairs to the bedroom I shared with my brothers.

I couldn't enter because Yaya blocked my way. Mother sat on the bed holding my brother's hand. Father and Father Elias stood beside it. I said nothing. Peering between the doorjamb and Yaya's body, I caught a glimpse of my brother convulsing.

"No!" he shouted. "I won't come!" His voice was both weak from his fight with death and shrill with intensity. His body stopped shaking and he settled.

"Zoe-Sophia, what are you doing here?" he asked, shouting at the wall. My sister, asleep at the foot of his bed, lifted her head from her pillow and blinked before speaking.

"I'm here, Zosimos. I fell asleep, I'm sorry." Zosimos didn't look at her or even acknowledge that she had spoken. Instead he stared dimly at the wall opposite his bed.

41

"No. Don't leave me, Zoe. If you must go, take Charon with you." He lifted his hand and pointed at the wall and then dropped it into his lap. "I don't like him staring at me like that, Zoe, take him with you." Zoe-Sophia's brown eyes were big and round as pomegranates.

"What is he talking about?" she asked. She peered at the same wall he had talked to and pointed at. Fear clouded her eyes. Mother touched her cheek without answering.

"He is hallucinating," Father Elias said. "He is close to death, but his will to live is the strongest I have ever seen in someone so sick." Zosimos glared at Father Elias. His eyes were now lucid.

"I won't die. Where is Yorgos with the water?"

"I'm here, Zosimos," I answered. "I have it."

When the adults heard my voice, they made room for me to pass through. Zosimos, though terminally weak, was breathing. His skin was pale like a dead man's. Mother came to me and dropped to her knees.

"Yorgos, where have you been? I haven't the strength to worry about two of my boys in the same day. You broke my heart, sneaking out like that." Zosimos struggled to sit up.

"Easy son," Father said. He pressed him back down with his hand on his shoulder.

"Help me up," Zosimos demanded. Determination steadied his voice. "Father, help me up."

When I got to him, Zosimos was sitting up and leaning against the wall, surrounded by pillows. I extended my arms until my elbows locked and offered my brother the pot of water. Without hesitation, he grabbed it from me and downed it in five gulps. He was so small and frail that in his hands the little pot looked like a large pail.

"Tell me about it, Yorgos. What happened? How did you get there?"

"I was afraid that if I didn't hurry, you'd die before I came home," I answered. "So I ran."

"The whole way?"

"No. I had to walk part of it. I lost my breath. That's a long way to run without stopping to rest."

"Someday, when I'm better, when I'm not so tired, I'll race you to the lake," he said. "You can't have all the fun." He collapsed back onto his pillow and let the pot fall to the floor where it shattered. I bent to pick up the pieces and nicked my finger. Though it was only a small flesh wound it bled profusely. I tensed and squeezed the wound closed. A little bit of blood landed on Zosimos' lip and on his bedclothes. He wiped it off his lip with the back of his hand.

"Yorgos, do you bring me blood *and* water?"

"Ewww!" Zoe-Sophia shrieked. She covered her eyes.

"No. Only water," I answered. "My blood won't heal you, Zosimos, but the water might." I reflected on my journey to the haunted cave and my encounter with the nereid princess. Yes. I was certain of it. He would not yet die.

"The water will keep you alive, Zosimos. I believe that God has blessed it." With trembling arms he reached for Mother. I could already see the color returning to his cheeks and hands. Indeed, all of his skin was being restored to a natural hue. I bent and kissed him on the forehead.

"I love you, Zosimos," I said. Though I had been squeezing the wound on my finger closed, a trickle of blood oozed out of the tiny nick. When I bent to kiss my brother a large dot splattered his white pillow.

"Oh, dear!" Mother exclaimed. "Let's go get you bandaged up."

I followed her to the kitchen where she cleaned and dressed the insignificant cut.

"I am proud of you, Yorgos," she said. "That was a brave thing you did, going up to the caves alone like that."

"Thank you, Momma."

"I am not finished," she added. "I never want you to do it again. Do you understand me? It was dangerous. You could have been hurt or even killed. I could have lost both of my precious boys today."

"You didn't," I said, lifting my shoulders.

"No. God is generous. He protected you, and it seems he spared your brother."

"Mother, something confuses me."

"What is it, son?"

"I went to the nereid cave for water to heal Zosimos."

"Yes. What confuses you about that?"

"We've prayed for Zosimos and he has never been healed. The nereids aren't Christian. If the water I brought from their cave works . . . I don't understand why. Why would the pagan water work when our prayers haven't?" Mother considered my question while she bandaged my finger.

"Is that all you did, Yorgos? Collect the water and bring it home?"

"No, Mother. First, the hike was strenuous. Once I found the cave, I had to wait for enough water to collect in the pot. I almost couldn't stay put, I was so scared."

"What else? Go on son, what else did you do?"

"I followed all of the rules that Papus said the nereids expected someone to follow. If it worked, however, I wanted God to get the praise. I also wanted to make sure I had God's blessing. So, once I had collected enough water, I prayed and made the sign of the cross over the pot." My mother secured the bandage to my finger and then she ran her fingers through my hair, picking out more twigs and leaves, taming its wild condition.

"You did well, son. If your brother has indeed been healed, or even if he is with us just a little bit longer, it is

God who has done it. Do you want to know why I believe that?" I nodded, listening intently.

"Because you loved your brother enough to take the risk and because you loved God enough to make sure that He got the credit, not some pagan creature."

"I think they respect God," I said. "And they helped me."

"They helped you? Who, dearheart? Who are you talking about?"

"The nereids," I said, adding, "The princess blessed me with the sign of the cross, before she disappeared into the wind."

"A nereid appeared to you?"

"Yes, Mother."

My mother regarded me silently. She stepped back and took in my full youthful stature, and then she smiled, her entire face bright with joy.

"That doesn't surprise me, son. I believe that you have the kind of faith and love that could move even the pagan gods to come to your aid and bless you." She sighed. "Now go." She bent and kissed me on the cheek before sending me off.

Yes, Death had taken up residence at the inn, but Death's stay was only temporary. With God's help, and the unlikely assistance of the nereids, I managed to drive death away before a third member of my family was taken from us.

Though Zosimos did not die that day, neither was he thoroughly healed. He clung to life with tenacity, determined to stay alive long enough to find the ultimate cure. I prayed daily that God would reveal it to him.

5 Challenging Father

The contention between my parents increased. I was eleven years old and they still hadn't agreed what to do with me. "Yes, he has an unusual interest in the religious life," Father agreed. "But a life of prayer cannot help support our family. Everyone must do their part." The open discussions were mostly calm, even dispassionate. However in private, Father and Mother argued like devils. Father was adamant that I find a trade. If she could find a paying apprenticeship with a painter he would be satisfied. Mother had no such luck.

Mother was equally adamant that directing me toward a trade, away from a life of devotion, was equal to squandering a precious gift. Back and forth they went, never reaching an agreement. It seemed that Father's will would prevail. Once he found a suitable Master, I would be sent away to learn a trade.

When I recall Theophilos' words, spoken so long ago, I find I must agree. I was an odd little boy. I couldn't see that spirituality and sexuality were two sides of the same fabric. I thought, in the way that an eleven year old boy would, that I must choose one aspect over the other. The way I saw it, my sexuality had to be repressed. From then on, and for all my mortal years that followed, a war raged in my heart.

As my heart grew, the war intensified. I could reach ecstatic heights in my worship of God, but one stray thought about my neighbor Niko could bring me crashing down into the bedrock of shame that lay in the bottom of my soul.

Increasingly, prayer with ikons became my retreat, as did painting them. I tried to excite my friend about them, offering to teach him how to paint them, but he wasn't interested. I feared that he agreed with my brother's assessment that, when it came to religion, I was odd. Niko didn't like to pray when it wasn't required of him. He liked to go on hikes through the hills and ravines that our houses were nestled in. He liked to climb trees and throw rocks into the creek bed or skip them across the water.

While I did agree that these activities were fun, they didn't excite me the way that praying with the ikons or painting them did. Being with my friend, however, did excite me in much the same way. Watching him undress down to his undergarments and leap into the cool waters of the nearby lake, eyeing the smoothness of his bare skin, and imagining him kissing me—these were the things that took me to ecstatic heights almost rivaling that of worship. This both delighted and terrified me, so back to prayer I would run, ikon in hand.

Though we were a poor family, my mother collected ikons. She always had. When my interest in them became evident, she collected them more liberally. One Sunday afternoon, after the Divine Liturgy, she called me into the kitchen. When I answered her she pulled from the folds of her simple dress an exquisite ikon of the crucifixion saying, "This is for you, for your collection. Paint one like it for me, will you?" Gingerly I reached out to take it. It was master-fully painted. I mouthed my thank you and slipped out of our home to the ravine behind it.

I examined the ikon in the sunlight. The gilding glittered and shined. It dazzled me. Though I was confident I could replicate its simple composition, some of the colors would be different. I didn't have any gold leaf. After examining it aesthetically, I placed it on my usual flat rock and started to pray. My focus intensified. I was drawn into the scene which unfolded like paper, surrounding me. It became real to me in a palpable way.

The ethereal sky above was golden. Jesus, hanging on the Roman cross, prayed for the souls that put him there. "Father, forgive them . . . ." His Mother and two of his disciples wailed. When they moved, I heard the sand grind under their feet and their garments rustle. I smelled their sweat. The sun baked my skin and grit lifted by the wind stung my cheeks. I ignored it, entranced by the naked body of Jesus hanging above me. Even pierced and bloodied, He was indescribably beautiful.

Something dripped on my forehead. I wiped it off with the back of my hand. Blood. This only deepened my devotion. I fell to my knees allowing it to cover me until I was drenched, imagining myself washed clean. All my sins and faults carried away by the blood of Christ.

The need to minister to my Savior overcame me. Climbing the cross, I pulled the spikes from His hands and feet and carefully carried Him down, bearing His weight on my young shoulders. I cleaned His wounds with my own shirt and lifted the crown of thorns from His head. I yearned to run my fingers through His hair and untangle it, so I did. I panted with desire. Oh, to cover Him with kisses. I kissed the wound in His side. I kissed His pierced hands and feet. I kissed His forehead. I kissed His lips. He smiled. Again I did it, I kissed His lips. Astonished by what I had done, I looked up.

The scene changed. Jesus was back on the cross hanging above me, weeping. His tears dripped on my forehead. The world came rushing, as if I were being dragged out of a room backwards. The ikon folded in on itself, reminding me again of paper. It lay before me on the flat rock, motionless, small and confined to the size and shape of the tiny piece of wood it had been painted on.

Sweating, and panting, I knelt on the dirt in my usual spot under the canopy of branches. What happened? What started as religious devotion turned to . . . what? Had I sinned? Was it wrong of me to feel attracted to the naked body of Jesus? I am not being irreverent. I did not want to molest His body when I ministered to His wounds. However the love, passion and desire I felt had been sensual beyond a child's understanding without being carnal.

Confused, I ran with the ikon into the back of the house, like I had many years before. Mother, Aunt Petra and Yaya were working in the kitchen. "Momma," I said. "Please keep this one for me. I'm not ready for it." When she looked down at me her dark eyes conveyed confusion.

"Not ready? You don't have to copy it perfectly Yorgos." I thrust it at her. "Okay, dearheart." She wiped her hands and took it from me, placing it on a shelf where it would be safe. "I'll put this on the family altar. Just ask me for it when you want it. It's yours."

I sought Niko's company more frequently. I was twelve years old now and well into puberty. My penis was starting to grow, like Theophilos said it would, and peach-fuzz pubic hair was coming in. I wondered, was my friend's body going through the same changes?

It was quite innocent, until the time that, just like my brother had done; my friend exposed himself and started to urinate. His acrid pee streamed onto the ground and splashed my bare legs.

Aroused, my heart danced in my chest like an ecstatic mystic beating on his drum. This time, without thinking, I reached out and grabbed hold of his penis, feeling the weight of it and the fine stubble of pubic hair that was just beginning to grow. Shocked, he slapped my hand away. Before fleeing, he gave me the most humiliating look one boy could give to another. He said nothing.

I ran to the inn. Taking the ikon of Jesus from its place on the family altar, I retreated to the storage closet. Kneeling, I held it close to my eyes. I hoped that it would open up for me again, that I would be drawn into the story of the crucifixion. This time it did not become a real and active scene unfolding for me in three-dimensional splendor. I did not feel the rays of the sun, hear the crunch of the sand, or the rustling of fabric. This time I did not physically minister to my Savior or cover him with kisses.

I hoped to feel the same love, passion and desire that I felt before. I longed for Jesus to smile at me. I wanted to compare my feelings for Niko with the feelings I had for Christ on the day I beheld his naked beauty upon the cross. Nothing out of the ordinary happened. From the square piece of wood, Jesus peered up at me. I was drawn to His eyes, but not transported. His eyes communicated love and acceptance, nothing more. Surely it wasn't that simple. Surely there must be something I must *do*. Not to earn His love, but to put to death the sin that claimed my heart with its roots and tendrils. I feared that the desire growing in me would be next to impossible to root out.

Momma called me to supper. The rest of the family had already assembled around the table. I came out of the storage closet, ikon in hand, and took my place across from Theophilos. I lay the wooden hand-painted image on the table in front of myself, holding it in a steady gaze, drawing strength from it through my eyes. Zoe-Sophia and Zosimos were seated across the table from each other. Father motioned for us to take each other's hands and proceeded to pray his usual blessing. After he said "Amen" I hastily jumped in adding my own prayer.

"Lord, please open Papa's eyes. Let him see that unless I am serving you I will never be happy. Amen." I fixed my gaze on my Father without flinching. Any words he might have said caught in his throat. Everyone else was speechless too.

"It's true," I said with a level of self-possession that was uncommon for a child of twelve. "I'm not hungry." Before leaving I snatched up my ikon, brandishing it like a shield. Without asking to be excused I turned my back on my family. All of them were stunned. Even the twins, as garrulous as they could be, knew better than to speak. I slowly ascended the stairs to the bedroom, listening. For several warm heartbeats, no one made a single sound. Dishes didn't clash. Eating utensils didn't scrape on plates and no one sipped from their glasses. As improbable as it was, even the children were quiet. No one spoke until Zoe-Sophia shattered the unnatural mealtime silence with a question,

"Is Yorgos in trouble?"

"No, dear," Momma said.

While I continued my slow ascent, they murmured. Mostly, my parents spoke. I stopped at the top landing. In the shadows, I leaned against the wall straining to hear the conversation. My efforts availed nothing. Back and forth my parents debated. I couldn't make out individual words, but I could hear the distinct sounds of their voices and even their tones. Mother was tender and imploring, Father was stern yet softening. Occasionally, I could make out Theophilos' voice, but not what he said. I quit trying, went into the bedroom, and lay down facing the wall.

Hours passed before the bedroom door creaked open. When it did, the room was brightened by dancing golden light. Soft footsteps approached me. A large, solid hand touched the top of my head.

"Son?" I turned to face Father, saying nothing. I knew he was about to deliver the final verdict. This was the first time I pressed the issue myself. I had forced him to make a decision.

"I didn't know that you feel so strongly." He moved his hand to my shoulder and gave it a squeeze.

"I do."

"You've never spoken of it so directly—"

"I was afraid, but Papa, why must I say something that is so obvious to everyone else? Don't you know me?" Father's grip on my shoulder tightened. He released it and brushed my hair from my eyes. Tears were collecting in his.

"I think I'm beginning to. You may do as your heart is directing you. I won't force you into an apprenticeship that would only make you miserable and quite possibly make you hate me."

"I don't hate you, Father."

He smiled.

"I am glad to hear that, son."

Mother came to the doorway and leaned against the jamb.

"The details will be figured out later. I wanted you to know." Before turning to leave, he bent over to kiss my forehead. On his way out he passed the oil lamp to Mother. She rushed to me from across the room and collected me in her arms. After holding me for a moment, she composed herself, urging me to come eat while Theophilos tucked Zosimos into bed.

6 When Strangers Are Strange

More than two years had passed since I confronted father. I was fourteen years old now, almost fifteen. Father had been working to secure my permission to go to Mount Athos, like he promised he would. One morning before dawn, while I helped Momma clean and prepare the guest dining room for breakfast, a stranger came to the open door and called out to us.

"Excuse me . . . ." His voice shattered the companionable silence we shared. Mother jumped. I froze in place, unable to complete my task of sweeping.

"Oh!" Momma gasped. "I didn't know anyone was there. Please, come in." He crossed the threshold swiftly and moved so stealthily over the creaky floorboards that his feet didn't make a sound when they touched down. I watched him and Momma in the mirror on the wall nearest me.

Mother set down her dust cloth. Stepping from the light of the candles on the table into the shadows, she approached him. He backed away. For several heartbeats I stared into the mirror, silent and still as I could be, with my back to them. I held the broom handle so tight with both hands that my knuckles turned white. While they spoke, an invisible hand wrapped its fingers around my heart and squeezed. My heartbeat slowed. The invisible fingers tightened their grip, making it hard for me to breathe. Sweat glazed my forehead and dripped down the sides of my face.

They talked in conversational tones while he paid for one night's stay. I listened. Mother told him about the surrounding area, beautiful places in nature that he might want to visit during the day when the sun was bright and warm, and when to expect breakfast.

"Oh, I won't be leaving my room until the cool of evening," he interrupted. "I am not to be disturbed." His lilting accent was unfamiliar to me. I thought it was lovely, though it stirred in me conflicting feelings I didn't understand.

At once the invisible fingers released my heart. It began beating faster and faster until my chest hurt.

When it occurred to me that I was standing unnaturally still, I made the motions of sweeping, without paying much attention to the results. I sensed that this was a momentous occasion; that this man had come to our inn for only one night, but everything would be different because of it.

"Yorgos, please help Mister Dumitru in with his things."

"Yes, Momma." I leaned the broom in the corner of the room and turned to face them. The twins banged around upstairs.

Staring into Mother's eyes, the man muttered under his breath. His face lacked expression. His eyes were distant and intense. He blinked.

At once Mother gathered her things saying, "I must check on the twins and finish preparing breakfast." Alone with Mister Dumitru, I inched toward him. He bridged the gap, stepping out of the shadows into the light of the candles.

Mister Dumitru had wavy auburn hair. It contrasted with his bone-pale skin, making it look like the painted hair of a statue. His skin, with a network of blue and violet lines pulsing underneath, appeared to have been polished. His most striking feature, however, was his eyes. They were a vivid green and a light shone in them that didn't belong to a normal person. They were perfectly unnatural. I gasped.

"You may call me Lucian," he said, leaning toward me and offering his hand. I was enthralled.

"My name is Yorgos," I said, shaking the hand he offered. It felt like a slab of cold marble. I let go and rubbed my palms together to warm them. "Don't you have any gloves? You're gonna catch cold." I both hated and loved the man, which confused me. It wasn't like me to hate, but he wasn't like most people. There was something about him that both thrilled and chilled me. I wanted to flee to the safety of my parents embrace, and I wanted to climb up inside of him, to be one with him. He laughed. I had no idea why. Without reason I found myself laughing too.

He led me out to where his team of four horses was lashed to a tree. Behind them was the simple wagon that contained his belongings. It was rectangular with an arched roof and varnished for protection from the elements.

He went to the front two horses and scratched under their chins before producing an apple and a knife from his pocket. I hovered several paces back, watching him from a safe distance. After slicing the fruit into wedges, he motioned for me to come closer. I denied him with an emphatic shake of my head. Commanding my attention with his penetrating gaze, he muttered something under his breath with the same expression I saw before when he spoke to Mother. I found myself complying, in spite of my apprehension. He smiled amiably and motioned for me to put out my hand. When I did, he held his closed fist over it and uncurled his fingers. Several pieces of apple fell onto my palm.

"They'll love you forever if you feed that to them." He indicated the rear team. One of them, the horse closest to me, stamped his hoof several times and whinnied. I offered the horse a couple pieces of fruit, which he nibbled from my palm, leaving it slathered with thick slobber. I grimaced and wiped it on my thigh. All the horses followed suit. I scratched their chins and ears and patted their noses, while giving each of them a treat.

"You'll care for them during the day for me, won't you? See to it that they are brushed and fed." My brows furrowed. "I would feed and care for them myself, but I never venture out during the daytime. I have a condition that forces me to avoid the sun."

"I've never heard of that. You really can't come out during the day?"

"Oh . . . If I really wanted to come out, or needed to, I could, but sunlight weakens me. It's best for me to avoid it." I scrunched my face trying to think of what to say next.

"Can't a doctor help you?"

"So many questions! No. I am afraid that nothing can be done. I like being nocturnal. Do you know what that means?"

"No, tell me."

"When a being is said to be nocturnal it means it is a creature of the night. It means it thrives in darkness, that darkness becomes it. That is me! I am nocturnal. And I love it." He smiled triumphantly.

"What do you do when everyone else is sleeping?" I asked. "Isn't it creepy? Don't you get scared?"

"No, I don't get scared in the middle of the night." He scoffed. "I am a potter. When I am at home, nighttime is when I get my work done—making ceramic dishes and such. It's also when I read or study. It's when I do any number of things that interest me. Because everyone else is sleeping no one disturbs me. That's the best part." I regarded him silently. He continued, "I love to travel through the night with only the stars to light my way. It invigorates me."

"I don't understand how you can see well enough to travel in the middle of the night. I can barely see out here and the sun is starting to come up." He stiffened, as if I had reminded him of an immanent danger.

"Ah, yes, the sun," he whispered, looking at the faint splash of light on the horizon. Dawn was breaking, though darkness still surrounded us. Turning to me he continued, "I see extremely well in the night; better, actually, than I can see during the day, in some respects. It's a part of being nocturnal."

He winked before hurrying to the back of the wagon, and then motioned for me to follow. When I stood beside him he opened the double doors revealing a treasure trove of various goods and wares. Lanterns hung from the roof beams. Shelves built into the side walls contained candelabra, vases, plates, pitchers and cups. All were formed from clay and nestled in a protective cloth. Netting made from thick rope was stretched over the shelves and nailed in place, to keep the wares from shaking loose when he traveled. The ceramic pieces ranged from the simple and functional to the ornate, painted with intricate and colorful designs.

In the center of the wagon was an oversized trunk made of wood, with a lock hanging from the lip of the lid. The trunk was rectangular, only a few feet wide, four feet high, and six feet long. Leaning against it, all the way around, were cloth sacks of different sizes filled to their capacity. He selected the smallest four and thrust two of them at me.

"Take these to my room. I will follow behind in a moment." I grunted when I felt the impact, wondering what was in them. They were the same weight and substance as the sacks of flour that Momma kept in her pantry. Faltering under their weight, I struggled to steady myself.

"What's in the trunk?" I asked. He ignored my question. When I lingered, swaying unsteadily, he repeated his request that I carry the sacks to his room. I complied, and he followed me. Holding one end of it, the trunk stuck out in front of him, lengthwise. Though it looked like it should be unwieldy, he managed it with ease.

"How did you do that?" I asked when he set it on the floor without making a sound. "I thought you'd need to get Theophilos to help."

"Nonsense. When you grow up to be like me you'll be able to carry heavy things too, without needing to be helped. You're still young."

"My brother and father can't carry things like that. Why should I be able to, even when I'm grown?"

"I said when you grow up to be like *me.*" For a moment we held each other's gaze. He looked away. "Will you please retrieve the other two sacks?"

When I returned, the door had been left open, but he was gone. I leaned the sacks against the trunk and saw that the lock had been removed. My heart quickened. Looking over both shoulders, I confirmed that I was alone. I nudged the door with my foot, leaving it open only a crack, before giving the trunk my full attention. My hands trembled. I touched the lid, jumped back, and then in one decisive moment rushed forward. I pushed up on the lid until my elbows locked. It was heavy. My arms quaked under its weight. Bracing it open with both hands I cocked my head to one side, listening for footsteps. I heard nothing. I turned back to the trunk intent on inspecting its interior when a dark presence rushed in from above and behind me. I felt an incredible downward pressure. It was too strong for my tired arms to resist.

"You should respect the privacy of your guests!" Startled, I gasped. Under Mister Dumitru's palms, the lid came down with a bang. I trembled. Backing out of the room, I apologized and ran to my parents. It was time for breakfast anyway.

1633, The Pindus Mountains, Greece, Mister Dumitru

I suppose that I am the villain of this sordid tale. Out of my own self-deprecating sense of humor, I will acquiesce to that. However, I can't help wondering, why does there always have to be a villain? It has been said that we're all the heroes of our own stories. From my point of view does that make me the hero and young Yorgos my foe? Preposterous. I'll gladly be the bad guy. This is his story, after all.

During that time, I lived as an itinerant artisan traveling from Eastern Europe through the Balkans. I earned an honest living by selling ceramic wares I formed with my own hands.

Though my intended destination was the city of Salonika, when I neared it, my intuition compelled me to continue west into the Pindus Mountains. I didn't know where I was going or what I would find when I got there, but the feeling that I should continue past Salonika was strong. The farther into the mountains I went, the deeper my sense of urgency became. I was rushing into the future. I could feel it. Not just the future defined as any number of vague possibilities. No. I was rushing toward something specific, something that would change my world—amend that—*the* world, totally, and forever.

It is not necessary for me to breathe, but you would not have known that by seeing me. I panted and gasped, pulling the air into my lungs in large drafts through my uncharacteristically wide and smiling mouth. I drove my horses as hard as I could until I feared for their lives. Necessity forced me to slow down, for their sakes.

Whenever I quiet my mind and listen to my gut, it takes me places and gets things done. My intuition never misleads me.

So, at the end of a dark and starry night, while I rushed through a winding pass in the high hills, I was glad when my intuition compelled me to slow down. I had been traveling over the Pindus Mountains and through Zagoria for many days and was eager to discover where I was being led to.

While I guided my team of horses around a bend in the road, I saw a small inn nestled in the hills and ravines not fifty meters away. Normally I would have passed it, but my intuition told me to stop. "I guess I'll be staying," I mused aloud, while lashing my horses and wagon to a tall pine tree growing to the left of the building. The timing couldn't have been better. The sky was beginning to brighten. I do hate to be exposed to the light of the sun.

Approaching the open door, I was hushed by the soft candlelight that spilled out of it. *Why have I been led to this place? What is my purpose here?* Pausing, I watched, touched by the simplicity of what I witnessed. A woman prepared the family business for the coming day. She hummed softly and contentedly, only interrupting her tune to say a random prayer for her husband, one of their four children or one of the other adults she lived and worked with.

Though I loathed disturbing her solitude, my intuition compelled me to speak. Before I composed myself the words, "Excuse me" tumbled out of my mouth. Good enough words for getting someone's attention, I suppose. But I wished, as I always do, to be in full command of myself with every action considered and well thought out. It was too late for that. With a start, the woman invited me in. Little did she know how that simple gesture tempted fate, or who she invited into her family's lives.

That was just too easy. Now, mind you, nosferatu—as we call ourselves where I come from—must only be invited into *private dwellings.* Public establishments, including hotels and inns, are ours for the taking. Be warned! However, a family lived and operated a business here. Out of respect, I waited to be invited in. I always do, even before entering a public space for the first time, because I am giving any person with half a wit of discernment the chance to consult their gut before entertaining me. If they're foolish enough to extend an invitation after that, whatever happens next is their own damned fault.

I crossed the threshold and tarried in the shadows near the door. The woman made her approach with swift strides, evincing no fear. I sensed in her simple gratitude over having a guest. While we discussed the price for a room, I noticed the reflection of a boy in a mirror. He watched us. If I had a living heart it would have skipped a beat before galloping off without me. It wasn't only his fragile frame or the youthful beauty he possessed. Something else about him gave me that jolt. Could it be true? I didn't believe it. The boy was much too young. I couldn't know for sure until I looked him in the eye.

He stood frozen in place for several moments before attempting to act normally. When he started to sweep again he merely spread around the dust and debris he had already swept into neat little piles to be collected. Reaching out with my senses, I detected that he was in physical pain and trying to comprehend what was happening. Yes, the boy sensed it too. His heart was beating so fast that if it wasn't a strong young heart, it would have burst. His mother and I talked in conversational tones while he suffered quietly in confusion. Wishing to be alone with him, I directed his mother's attention elsewhere.

The boy took a couple of hesitant steps toward me while I strode from the shadows into the light. Our eyes met. And with that, with just one look, the slow but steady twining of our lives commenced. Nothing could stop it unless natural death took him from me before I fulfilled the demands of the imprinting.

A nosferatu may only experience such a thing once, no matter how long he exists. There is no way for me to know for sure, but it is said that the experience is stronger for the mortal partner. If he desires such a thing, he will perceive it as falling in love. If he does not, if he is closed and afraid, it is pure agony.

When I sensed that poor Yorgos experienced the latter, my dead unbeating heart went out to him. *What can I do?* I wondered. *This can not be stopped.* Something had been set in motion that was bigger and stronger than a legion of us, with all of our preternatural strengths combined. This was a function of our evolution. Evidently, Yorgos would make a strong nosferatu. That would have to wait. He may have imprinted on me, but he was much too young to be turned. We have laws against turning one who could not survive alone in mortal society. If turned now, he would always be dependent on those of us with more mature bodies than his—no matter how mature his mind might become. If *I* turned him now, it would only be a matter of time before the Ancients found and destroyed him. I would not have *that* on my conscience.

I introduced myself and offered the boy my hand.

"You may call me Lucian," I said, capturing him in my thrall. I wished to alleviate the pain and confusion that imprinting caused him.

"My name is Yorgos." I found his thoughts to be delightfully capricious. He asked me if I had any gloves—my hand reminded him of a slab of cold marble. Yes! That's precisely what my hands are made of, marble. Delightful! He both loved and hated me. He wanted to be inside of me *and* as far away from me as possible, in the safe company of his parents. As if, in the end, they could save him. It was so deliciously innocent and heart rending. I loved it. I hated myself for loving it. And he made me laugh, for which I found that I loved him even more.

1633, The Pindus Mountains, Greece, Yorgos

When I joined my family for breakfast, Father, Uncle Petros, Theophilos, and my cousins were already traveling between our various fields, tending to the crops and feeding the livestock. Only the women and young children were left at the table. Zosimos was breathing heavily, as if he ran laps before joining us. Mother, brows furrowed, brushed his cheek and forehead with the backs of her fingers.

"Zosimos, how are you feeling?" she asked.

"I'm tired and I feel dizzy."

"Didn't you sleep well, honey?"

"No. I kept waking up."

She pressed her lips together. "Hmmm. I thought you were beginning to feel better."

"I did feel better, but it came back. It *always* comes back."

"Momma is Zosimos gonna die?" Zoe-Sophia asked, her voice pitched high.

"No, sweetheart, not anytime soon. He isn't nearly as sick as he was that one time." Mother forced a weak smile, patting Zoe on the head before returning her attention to Zosimos. "Isn't that true, son?"

"Yes, but I still feel pretty bad."

"Then I want you to stay in bed today and rest. I'll bring in the village healer to take a look at you." His shoulders slumped, but he nodded his understanding.

"You'll feel better again in no time." Then she directed her attention at me.

"Yorgos, did you help Mister Dumitru with his things like I asked you to?"

"Yes, Momma. He scares me. I hope he doesn't stay here for long."

"Why does he scare you?" I bit my lip trying to puzzle out just what it was about the man that I didn't like.

"He's so . . . strange, there's something different about him." Mother cupped my chin in her hand.

"Honey, he comes from another country. They have different customs and beliefs where he comes from, and they speak a different language. Why, even the way they talk when they speak Greek sounds strange to our ears. But being different doesn't make someone bad. And it shouldn't make them scary. They're just not the same as us. There's nothing wrong with that. Do you understand?"

I nodded saying, "I think so," because I genuinely wanted to understand what she meant. However, her explanation didn't change the way I felt. There was something about Mister Dumitru that enticed me while at the same time scaring me to the core.

"This reminds me, Mister Dumitru has asked that a bath be set up in his room by sundown. He's instructed me to unlock the door to his room and set it up for him. I would like you to do that for me, Yorgos. Later this afternoon, I'll give you the key and help you boil the water, and you can set it up for him, okay?"

"Okay, Momma. Just before sundown."

The rest of breakfast was filled with chatter and laughter. The twins, now ten years old, asked many new questions, like they always did. Their world expanded daily as they began to comprehend the breadth and width of it, and the wonders it contained. What child's mind could comprehend something as complex and vast as the world? I've spent my entire existence contemplating it and have only just begun.

Mother answered what questions she could and laughed with the twins. I could tell that she worried for Zosimos. Ever since he nearly died four years earlier, she took every sniffle and sneeze as a possible sign of imminent death.

Perhaps she even worried for me. I said little, only entering the conversation when Zoe-Sophia or Zosimos said something especially funny.

From time to time, Mother looked at me with her big brown eyes. I saw sorrow mixed with the mirth. Yes, she worried about me too.

After breakfast, I led the horses to the stable and fed them, like I promised I would, before catching up with Father and Theophilos. They were at the olive grove where they were pruning and fertilizing the trees. I helped carry the compost and mix it in the soil, turning the soil over with a shovel. Father said I was too small, too underfoot to be of much help for the load of strenuous work that needed to be done that day. He needed to stay focused on what they were doing, not worry about me. So, he sent me to the pasture to help Uncle Petros care for the sheep.

When I arrived, Uncle was feeding them. I grabbed a couple handfuls of feed and four of the youngest lambs stampeded me. I stumbled backwards, landed on my rear and found myself at the bottom of a pile of voraciously hungry animals. They nuzzled me with more force than I would have expected young lambs to muster while rooting for food. When I fell, my hands flew open and feed went everywhere, but mostly on my clothes. The lambs jabbed me with their cold, wet noses and licked me with their warm wet tongues until I laughed.

When I stood, they scattered and rejoined the flock. As soon as I turned my back, one of them came to me and stayed at my side. She bleated and repeatedly pressed her head against my thigh, my bottom, and my stomach. She was white, like all the others, but in the plane of her forehead, spreading down to the space between her eyes, was a brown spot roughly shaped like a diamond. I turned circles where I stood, trying to lose her. She only became more playful. I clasped my my hands together and held them against my chest to stop her from pressing her cold wet nose against my palms and licking my fingers.

Uncle Petros and I guided the flock down to the nearby stream, walking companionably. The same lamb followed close behind. I patted her forehead and wished that she'd stop begging.

"I don't have anymore food for you."

"I don't think she wants food. I think she likes you," said Uncle Petros. I stopped for a moment and knelt. She butted her head against mine and then covered me with little wet kisses.

"I like her too. I think she's my favorite."

"Well then, she needs a name. What will you call her?" I pursed my lips while considering the options.

"I don't know . . . I'll have to think about it. Maybe I will have a name for her by tomorrow."

When I returned home after helping Uncle Petros, I remembered that I was supposed to set up the bathtub for our strange guest.

I located the portable tub in the storage closet behind the kitchen and pocketed a couple of small wooden blocks from the fire box. I then pulled it into the kitchen by the rope that was attached to it. The tub had wheels, so it was easy to move. Mother helped me heat up enough water to fill it a third full. I added some soap to the water and mixed it until it was really sudsy. Then she handed me the key to Mister Dumitru's room and gave me an encouraging push. I pulled the tub by the rope down the hall of the guest wing, straining against its weight. The hot soapy water sloshed out and soaked my feet, drenching the floor.

I was surprised to find the door ajar. I pushed it open and stepped back. The room was uncommonly dark. Mister Dumitru had stretched thick wool blankets over the two windows and tacked them in place. They blocked out the sun so completely I couldn't tell if the man was asleep in his bed or not. I tugged the bathtub into the room and crammed the wood blocks against the back wheels, so it wouldn't roll around when our guest bathed. Once it was secure, I went to the kitchen for a lit candle so that he could see.

When I reentered the room with the light, it was clear that the bed had not been slept in. The trunk was still unlocked and Mister Dumitru was not there. I placed the candle next to the lock where it lay on the nightstand. The golden flame sputtered on its wick, causing the light to flicker and shift.

Where is Mister Dumitru? I wondered. *More importantly, what's in the trunk?* I had to know. I looked left and right before stepping up and touching the hinged lid. I knelt in front of the trunk. Pressing my palms up to the lip, with my fingers curling around it, I pushed with all my strength–bracing for the weight. Nothing happened. It didn't budge. It must have been stuck. Or was it locked from the inside? *Locked from the inside?*

I froze, afraid to move, my arms held ridged as boards against my sides. I scanned the details of Mister Dumitru's room, only moving my eyes. I scrutinized the trunk, the candle, the lock on the table, and the brown wool blankets that blocked out the light. What a dreary place this room had become. I didn't like it at all. Something thumped inside the trunk. I forgot my curiosity. I didn't want to know what it was. I stumbled over the bathtub while scrambling out of the room, thanking God I hadn't knocked the bathtub over.

Hours later, with an oil lamp in hand, I went to the guest wing for the bathtub. It was in the hallway beside Mister Dumitru's door. I leaned over it with the light to get a better look. The water was brown and murky: all the suds had gone flat. The bottom was covered with so much thick sediment and mud, Mister Dumitru must have been covered from head to toe with dirt when he bathed in it. I dragged it through the kitchen and out the back door. Once outside I turned it over, spilling the water out. It took me several minutes to thoroughly clean it.

Though it was my Name Day, the next day started like most. I woke before sunrise and compelled Zosimos to get out of bed and come with me downstairs. After morning prayer, I dashed outdoors intent on feeding and brushing Mister Dumitru's horses before breakfast, like I promised him I would. I wasn't especially partial to the man, but his horses were something else.

Horses were uncommon in our parts and illegal for non-Turks to own or ride. Mister Dumitru's were magnificent animals. I wondered how he got away with owning and riding them without incurring the wrath of the Ottomans. Whatever his secret, I felt lucky to be charged with their care.

Theophilos arrived before I did and was brushing one of them. I was glad to have his help. I learned the day before that brushing four horses is a time consuming task. Uncle Petros arrived soon after, to admire the beasts on his way to check on the sheep.

"What strong beauties!" he said, passing by. He tossed Theophilos a sack containing four apples saying, "Those are for the horses, boys," while ambling down the trail to the corral.

"Yorgos, are you certain about wanting to go to Mount Athos?" Theophilos asked while brushing out an especially ratted knot in the horse's mane.

"Yes. I want to go more than I've ever wanted to do anything. Why do you ask?" He said nothing for a minute and shook his head as if coming to a decision.

"I will miss you if you go is all." Silently, I considered his words while focusing on the task at hand.

"I'll miss you too. I don't think I'll be leaving anytime soon though. We're still waiting to hear if they will let me come."

I finished brushing out the first horse's mane and started brushing its neck and flank.

"This is hard," I said. "It takes so long. I'm glad you're here to help," Theophilos chuckled.

"Get used to it, little brother."

"What?"

"Hard work. Did you think that on Athos you'd pray all day and do nothing else? There's cooking, cleaning, laundry, chopping wood for fires, tending to the animals . . . . I am sure the list of chores is nearly endless. Remember, women aren't allowed there. The men have to do all the work themselves, even woman's work. I laughed hard for a moment. For some reason the mental image of monks sewing clothes and baking bread, washing dishes, and weaving cloth, struck me as funny. It didn't bother me though. All my life I had been the one to help Mother with woman's work around the house and inn.

"I hadn't thought of that before—all the work I'll have to do," I said. "Of course it makes sense. It's all a part of worship, isn't it?"

"I suppose it is, little brother. You really were made to for this, weren't you?"

"I think I was . . . . I hope I was . . . ." I stopped mid-stroke, to ponder Theophilos' question. Yes. The answer resounded within me. "Yes. I was."

I repeated it quietly, not with outward gusto, but with inward certainty. It gave me a feeling of great satisfaction. I let that feeling sink in, taking possession of it before continuing my brushstroke where I left off.

When we were finished, Theophilos and I gave each of the horses an apple before heading home.

When we were about to leave, Uncle Petros came dashing up the trail, carrying my favorite lamb on his shoulders. I recognized her by the diamond spot on her forehead. I rushed to him to take the animal into my arms when I saw blood smeared on his shirt and hands.

"When I was counting the sheep, I discovered this." He lay the animal on the ground, panting heavily. The animal's neck was ripped open. I turned to Theophilos and hid my face in his chest.

"Uncle Petros! What were you thinking?" Theophilos put his hands on my back and patted me while I sobbed.

"Yorgos is nearly a man. Death is part of life. He cannot bury his head and hide from it forever. Look at this, Yorgos." I pressed my head even deeper into my brother's chest, shutting out the horrors of the world. "A wolf did this, I am sure of it. There's probably a pack. At least two or three others are missing."

"The dogs?" Theophilos asked.

"They're fine. Two of them were sleeping when I got there, but none of them were hurt. Just how the wolves got past them is the real question."

"Yes," Theophilos agreed.

Slowly I turned, out of curiosity, and looked. My lamb lay lifeless on the hard ground. I dried my tears with my palms and determined to face the situation like a man. At first I deliberately focused on the animal's rear end and stomach, trying to avoid looking at the wound.

While Uncle Petros and Theophilos talked about what must be done to protect the livestock from predators, I examined the contours of the animal's body. I started at the tail and continued past the hind legs. The belly was still pink and covered with soft downy fur. I stopped at the neck, skipping over the wound and looked my lamb in the eye. I regretted that I never gave her a proper name. Every creature deserves to be loved and remembered by name when its time for passing comes.

The eyes were empty and lifeless. No personality emanated from them, no presence. I wished that someone would close them. Theophilos and Uncle Petros continued to discuss the problem, but I didn't pay any attention. I went to my knees beside the lamb and closed her eyes before laying my head against her stomach for one last time. Her fur was soft and her skin was cold. I ran my hand up to scratch her chin, forgetting the horror I would find. Her torn-open flesh was sticky with half-coagulated blood. I withdrew my hand and sat up, deciding to look at the wound and acknowledge the manner in which death had claimed my pet. The wound reached from her collar bone to her chin.

"I have never seen a wolf attack like this," Uncle Petros said. "The neck was ripped open, but none of the flesh appears to have been consumed, it's as if the wolf killed the animal for sport, not sustenance."

"That is strange," Theophilos said. "Yorgos, go home and eat breakfast. Uncle Petros and I will deal with this problem." I took one last look at my poor dead lamb and ran home.

I scrambled through the back door and kitchen. In the dining room, I found the usual assortment of relatives coming and going from breakfast in shifts. I took my seat and blessed my meal when Mother placed it in front of me.

"Yorgos, have you been crying?"

"Yes, Mother. It's my lamb. A wolf killed her last night. Uncle Petros says that several of them are missing. I never even gave her a name." Mother stopped what she was doing and embraced me from behind. I started to cry again.

"Why does everything have to die, Momma? It's cruel that life must end. Why are some left behind? That's cruel too. I'm not sure which is worse. I wish I didn't have to die, or you, or Papa. I wish Nona and Papus were still here. Why can't we all just live forever?"

All of my jumbled thoughts came tumbling out. Ever since my grandparents died I contemplated these questions, without voicing them.

"I think living forever in this present life would be the most cruel, Yorgos. More cruel than you could possibly imagine." Aunt Petra quietly agreed while gathering up dirty tableware.

"Why, Momma, why do you say that? Life is wonderful. Don't you think it is? Why do you say living forever would be cruel?" Mother walked around the table and sat next to me.

"Yorgos," she pinched my exposed forearm. "This flesh was not made to last forever. Our bodies grow old and get weak. Parts even stop working. Remember your Grandparents?" I nodded that I did. "Your grandfather's eyes had grown weak and he couldn't hear well. He couldn't even walk anymore. Do you think he was always like that?"

"He was like that my whole life."

"Yes," she said. "But he was once a boy, just like you. He could run, he could see and hear."

"I understand, Momma."

"Both your grandparents were getting very wrinkly." I smiled, remembering them, what they looked like.

"They were wrinkly," I agreed. "Grandfather's face looked like a walnut." Mother laughed.

"Yes, it did, that's exactly it."

"Momma, isn't it the sin of vanity to worry about such things? Everyone gets old and wrinkly."

"Exactly son. And everyone dies. *All* of God's creatures die. Like your lamb." She opened her arms to me. The scent of her perfume was strong. It comforted me. "I am sorry for your loss. I know how it hurts to lose something you love. Whether a family member or an animal, it hurts just the same." Rising to her feet she placed her hands on my shoulders and peered into my eyes.

"Don't be so quick to judge the vanity of the old. When people age and their bodies change, there is a tremendous sense of loss and sadness. Watching your youth slip away, only to be replaced by wrinkles and aches, it's dreadful."

"Maybe it would be better for us if we weren't even born, if life is so dreadful." Mother shook her head at me. Even as I said it, I knew I didn't believe it.

"Son, living is wonderful, as you say. The awareness of the passage of time, and the inevitable changes time brings, sometimes these feel like dreadful things. I don't expect you to understand now. Wait until you've lived to be fifty . . . then you'll *know*."

"I wish that God made things differently." Mother lifted my chin.

"So do I, son. So do I. I wish I could tell you why we must die before we can live forever, but I don't understand it myself. I do believe God will give us life again, and new bodies. Our new bodies won't age or get wrinkly or stop working. That is the promise of the Resurrection."

7 The Feast and Midnight Escape

Mother excused me from work and told me to grieve for my lamb however I needed to. I stole away into the ravine behind the inn with the ikon of the crucifixion that she gave me. I laid it on the flat rock, pushed the fat end of a prayer candle into the dirt above it and set flame to the wick. Sitting cross-legged with the ikon in front of me, I made the sign of the cross several times and tried to concentrate on my prayers. I couldn't. I repeated the Jesus Prayer, which usually helped me to focus. That didn't work either.

Mister Dumitru's lilting voice began softly droning in my mind. Though the words were indistinct, his accent was unmistakable. I ignored it, trying to focus on the image of Jesus hanging on the Roman cross. I hoped the scene would come alive again. Nothing unusual happened. I didn't have any visions. With my own imagination I tried to picture Jesus smiling at me and beckoning me to come to him. Nothing. My mind was filled with Mister Dumitru's voice, and his voice was getting louder. I couldn't understand a word of it. Either he spoke in a foreign language or his Greek was too slurred together with his thick accent, I couldn't tell which. Never mind.

On and on he chattered–until one, unmistakable word demanded my attention: *nosferatu*.

"What is nosferatu?" I wondered aloud. The word caught in my throat, compelling me to make the sign of the

77

cross again. I made a mental note to ask what nosferatu meant at the dinner table. I was sure that the twins would have many new questions of their own. What's one more? I couldn't clear my head of Mister Dumitru's incessant talk. I gave up, blew out the candle, and went inside.

It was early afternoon and I had nothing to do. Out of boredom I told Mother that I felt better and offered to help her. She mussed my hair and asked me to sweep the hallway of the guest wing.

When I passed Mister Dumitru's door I couldn't shake the urge to test it. It was unlocked. I cracked it open and peered in. The room was too eerily dark for daytime hours. Thick wool blankets still blocked out most of the daylight. I opened the door all the way to see by the light that filled the rest of the house. The bed was empty; it appeared he had not slept in it. The lock was on the nightstand, just like the night before.

Creeping farther into the room, I pulled the corner of the blanket away from one of the windows, and closed the door behind myself–making sure that the latch didn't catch.

I dropped to my knees in front of the trunk as one would kneel before an altar, only I wasn't entering into prayer, I was snooping. *Father better not find out or I'll be in big trouble.* I steadied myself with three deep breaths, before pressing the heels of my hands against the edge of the trunk with my fingers curled over the lip of the lid. I took one more deep breath, the deepest yet, and released it while pushing the lid open. I leaned forward to get as good a look at the contents as I could in the dim light.

I couldn't believe what I saw. I would sooner have believed that my ikon of the crucifixion was truly a portal into another realm than I would believe what lay before me. With one tired hand, I held the lid up and with the other I rubbed my unbelieving eyes. I looked again. No, I hadn't imagined it. Mister Dumitru lay with his hands crossing his chest, and he was covered with dirt. In fact, he was laying in at least five centimeters of it. Crumpled at his feet and under his head were the sacks I carried in for him when he arrived, now empty.

I reached in to touch him. My hand hovering over his body, I flashed back to my grandfather's funeral. I recalled how his complexion was a pale blue shade of white, and his skin sagged. It was clear when I saw my grandfather's face that he was no longer alive. That is exactly how Mister Dumitru appeared. I lowered my shaking hand until the tips of my fingers touched his skin. It was cold and clammy, just like Grandfather's had been when he lay in his casket. *CASKET!?!*

I gasped, dropped the lid and turned to flee. A cold hand gripped my wrist. Mister Dumitru sat up, caught the falling lid, and drew me close.

I made the sign of the cross. It availed nothing. His grip was tight, his eyes were closed, yet he appeared to be dead. I resisted him, but couldn't break free. Without opening his eyes he leaned closer to me and his lips curled, revealing a pair of sharp teeth. He pressed them into my neck.

He sniffed my skin and let me go. I ran to the door to make my escape and turned to see his body descend into the box. His eyes flashed open revealing the same unnatural light I saw when I met him. The door closed behind me and I brushed my neck with my fingertips to see if I was bleeding. Nothing. He hadn't broken skin.

Screaming, I ran to the kitchen where I knew Mother would be. I tried to tell her what happened but I was in hysterics. She knew this was no sibling spat gone too far. She dropped to her knees and opened her arms to me, asking Theotokos to protect and calm me. When I could finally breathe evenly enough to speak, she asked me why I was crying. I opened my mouth to tell her and found I couldn't remember.

1633, The Pindus Mountains, Greece, Mister Dumitru

Please don't hate me. Yorgos was never in any mortal danger. Like he discovered, sleep, for a creature like me, resembles death. I am not dead, at least not in the conventional sense of the word.

It was instinctual to grab hold of him and attempt to bite, in self-defense and completely autonomic. In this case, because he imprinted on me, it would have been impossible for me to harm the boy. I am his guardian angel, if you will allow the twisting of the metaphor.

1633, The Pindus Mountains, Greece, Yorgos

Once I calmed down and it was clear that I was alright, Mother reminded me that it was time to prepare Mister Dumitru's bath. She helped me fill the basin with hot water, just like the day before, and sent me on my way, telling me that when I was done I should come to dinner.

When I arrived at his door, I hesitated. I felt a new uneasiness and entered with caution, trying not to make a sound. I placed the wooden blocks against the wheels and hurried to the dining room where I found my family assembled around the table. Everyone stood behind their chairs, waiting for me. Embarrassed for the attention I knew I was going to have to endure, I narrowed my eyes.

"Happy Name Day, Yorgos!" they chorused. I was so preoccupied with the death of my lamb that I wasn't in the mood to celebrate.

"A letter came from Mount Athos," Zosimos blurted. Father shushed him, and Zosimos slumped back into his chair in a fit of coughing.

"It's true, son," Father said. "Word came yesterday." He produced a letter from the breast pocket of his coat, waved it, and set it on the table.

"What does it say?" I asked with a grin, my voice cracking with excitement.

"Let us pray." Father raised an eyebrow. "We'll discuss the contents of the letter in a bit." He clasped Mother's hand and she clasped Theophilos'; we formed a chain of hands around the table.

"Christ, our Lord, please bless the food and drink of your servants, for you are holy always, now, and forever, to the ages of ages." He prayed and we all echoed, "Amen."

Everyone seated themselves except for Mother. She tended to Zosimos before taking her seat.

"I cooked all of your favorite foods to celebrate your special day." Mother pointed to the center of the table at a steaming pot of Avgolemono, or egg-lemon soup. Enough bowls for all of us were stacked in the center of the table. Mother reached for the bowls, and began to ladle soup into them and pass them around the table.

"We have agreed not to discuss the situation with the wolves tonight," Father said. "This is your night, son. I don't want it to be spoiled."

Theophilos spoke next, "I have something for you, little brother." From his lap he produced something small and square. It was wrapped in plain paper, which was held in place with a ribbon. He set it on the table in front of me. I stared at it.

"Aren't you going to open it?" Theophilos asked.

"Yes, open it!" the twins demanded. I tore the ribbon off, and the paper fell to the floor. It was an ikon of Saint George the Dragon Slayer, the saint I was named after.

"Thank you, Theophilos."

"Let me see," Zoe-Sophia asked.

"Yes, what is it?" Zosimos interrupted her. I held it up so that everyone could see it.

"It's Saint George. He's my favorite saint. Well, one of my favorites . . . there are so many." When she saw the picture of the saint and the dragon, Zoe-Sophia gasped.

"That's scary," she said. Her eyes were as big and plump as over-ripe olives. Mother shushed her, chuckling, and reached for the ikon.

"May I see?" she asked. "This is lovely. He slew the dragon. See?" She pointed to the black, evil-looking beast that Saint George had pierced with his sword. The blade went right into the dragon's mouth, and blood poured out of it onto the ground. "Whenever you're scared, or feel something bad is near, ask Saint George to pray for you and protect you. He'll do it. He's part of the great cloud of witnesses that watch from heaven and pray for us." Mother handed me the ikon.

"Thank you, Theophilos," I said again. "It's beautiful. I love it." He mussed my hair.

"I knew you'd like that one." I smiled.

"Son, do you know the story?" Father asked. Emotion caught in my throat when I recalled my dead lamb. I nodded.

"Please share it with us." I closed my eyes, steadied myself with a breath, and the lump in my throat dissolved. It was replaced with gratitude and joy. I nodded at Father again and then I began.

"There are many stories about Saint George," I said. I paused and glanced at the ikon on the table at my elbow. It was painted in the usual Eastern Orthodox way. The colors, bright and deep; the composition, stylized. It was meant to be a thing of beauty, to tell a story, to teach theology and to draw the observer into deep meditative prayer—all at the same time.

"The story that most people know is the one about how he killed a dragon that terrorized a little village far from here."

Both of the twins looked up. Zosimos stopped fidgeting and Zoe-Sophia hugged her rag-doll—their gazes fixed on me. I paused again and glanced down.

"Go on, son, you're doing just fine. Tell us the story," Mother encouraged.

I imagined that the ikon at my elbow was a window. All I had to do was look into it and describe what I saw.

"This story takes place a long time ago, and far from here. Saint George had been traveling many months by both land and sea when he came to a place called Libya. There he met a poor Christian hermit who devoted his life to prayer.

"Thank God," said the hermit. "I have been asking God for help, and here you are, a knight from the Crusades."

"What has God sent me here to do for you?" asked the saint.

"Not far from here is a village named Silene," the hermit began. "The people of Silene are pagans; they don't believe in the one true God, they believe in many gods."

When I remembered what came next, I hesitated. The legend came too close to recent events. I lowered my head and looked at the hand-painted image of the saint. I decided, just like my patron, to face the things that scared me, and caused me pain. I started the story again.

"The hermit continued to explain to George that there was a lake near Silene where the villagers got their water. Every day the people offered a sacrificial lamb to a dragon that made his lair in a cave beside the lake."

I paused again to steady myself. Mother placed her hand on my shoulder. I glanced at Uncle Petros, and he nodded. I think he was remembering my lamb too. I pressed my lips together and gathered my thoughts.

"Take courage," I whispered. "Just like Saint George."

I continued, "If they didn't give him a lamb to eat, the dragon would kill anyone who came too close to the water. So, they did what the dragon demanded of them. Every day they brought him a lamb and he ate it in one big gulp."

I peered up from the ikon and into each person's eyes. They all listened attentively. Encouraged, I pressed on, in spite of my sadness. In fact, in that moment it dissolved into something less clutching.

"The dragon didn't care that they weren't cooked. In fact, if he wanted them cooked he could have breathed fire on them and cooked them himself, but he didn't bother. He ate them raw."

"The dragon ate the little lambs?" Zoe-Sophia whimpered.

"Yes," I answered. "And he swallowed them whole. He spit out the parts he didn't like, the bones, the fur, and the hooves."

"Yuck!" Zoe-Sophia yelled. Everyone laughed, including me.

"Where was I?" I asked. "Ah yes . . . the dragon would eat the lambs whole. Once the villagers appeased him they collected the water they needed as quickly as they could. They had to hurry in case the dragon was still hungry and decided to eat one of them too."

When I glanced up from the ikon, I saw Zoe-Sophia hiding behind her rag-doll.

"Poor little lamb," she said, her voice muffled.

"That's not the worst of it," I taunted. At that, Zosimos leaned in closer, and my sister lowered her doll to her lap and peered up at me with eyes and mouth wide open.

"When they ran out of lambs, the dragon demanded that young girls be offered in their place." Zosimos laughed out loud, and Zoe-Sophia shrieked. He patted her on the head.

"Don't worry; I won't let any dragon eat you." He knew he was playing to the crowd; he looked up at the faces of the laughing grown-ups and laughed right back at them.

"Continue, please," Father said.

"Well, the fairest way to choose a girl the villagers could think of was to have them draw lots. The girl with the shortest piece of straw would be the dragon's next meal."

"I don't like this story," Zoe-Sophia complained.

"I do," countered Zosimos. "I love it! Go on!"

"Well," I continued, "it didn't matter if they were rich or poor, noble or common. Every girl was expected to draw a straw. When the monk told this to Saint George, it made him especially angry. He asked the hermit how to get to Silene and departed at once.

"On that very same day, the king's daughter drew the shortest straw. The king looked high and low for a lamb to offer in her place and urged the villagers to help. They found nothing. He was so overcome with grief that he offered the people all of his riches and half of his kingdom if they would spare his daughter the fate chosen for her by lot. The people refused because that meant one of their own daughters would have to be sacrificed.

"On his orders, the king's guards brought the princess out. While she was guided through the streets, villagers followed. Though she wore her most expensive finery, the princess was solemn faced and sad. She took each step with slow precision. When they reached the water's edge, the king relieved his guards and led the princess to the opening of the lair, where they wept. Father and daughter held onto each other like they would never let go. Finally, the king's guards pried them apart."

At this point, I glanced at the ikon again. I lifted it and inspected it closely. In my imagination I could still see the scene like I watched it through a window. The villagers were becoming restless. Some prayed out loud for the pagan gods to intervene. Others cursed and chanted, wanting to rouse the dragon. They were drawn to the excitement, the spectacle of it all.

"While they waited, a knight of the Crusades approached on strong white horse. It was none other than Saint George. He rode up to the princess. Being brave, she begged him to leave, warning him that a terrible beast was on its way and would eat him and his horse too if he didn't go. Saint George was grieved by her plight and moved by her courage. He vowed to remain until it was over.

"A monstrous wail came from the center of the lake. Everyone—man, woman, and child—turned to see what could make such a horrid sound. When they saw the dragon lifting his head out of the water, they gasped and scrambled out of its way. The beast lumbered toward its chosen victim.

"The princess tried to be brave, but her chest heaved and tears streamed down her face. She winced and closed her eyes when the dragon reached her.

"Do not fear this dumb beast or put your trust in your many pagan gods," Saint George called out, shouting over the din of the crowd. Everyone heard him and every head turned, including the dragon's. Saint George invoked the name of God, while making the sign of the cross. Having protected himself by making the sacred sign, he charged.

The beast laughed. He thought that Saint George was too small a man to harm him, but the saint had faith.

While his horse ran past the dragon, he threw his sword with all his strength and it plunged into the dragon's heart. The beast lumbered forward, stumbled, and plummeted to the ground, sending up a large cloud of dust. Saint George climbed onto the monster's stomach and withdrew his sword. He hacked off the dragon's head with it. The head was larger than he was. He lifted it for everyone to see, his knees buckling under its weight.

"The people cheered and praised Saint George. He waved his hands in front of himself to quiet them. 'Do not thank me. Thank the Father of the Lord Jesus Christ, for it is by his grace that I was able to accomplish this.'"

"The whole village lifted their eyes heavenward and believed in God. On that day, all of the people of Silene, including the princess and the king, converted to Christianity."

I paused and looked at my family. Every eye was on me. When the praises started, I lowered my eyes and cleared my throat. Feeling self-conscious I didn't look up, I peered at the ikon in my hands and continued, "That is the legend of Saint George, but I don't believe it's true. I don't . . . I don't believe in dragons."

"*I* believe in dragons," Zosimos interjected. The adults around the table murmured.

"What do you believe?" my aunt asked. When I looked at her I saw something I hadn't seen before. She was sitting next to Uncle Petros, and they were holding hands.

"Well," I started, "I do believe that Saint George was a real person, but that story is a legend. It's meant to teach us that with faith in God we can overcome any evil, and that God will save anyone from their dragons if they ask Him."

"What about the dragons?" Zosimos asked. "Doesn't anyone care about them?" Smiling, I looked at my brother and wagged my head.

"Thank you for the story, son," Father said, while mother rose from her seat.

"Eat up everyone–supper is getting cold," she urged.

"Here's to Yorgos!" Uncle Petros lifted his wine glass. All of the grown-ups followed suit, and Mother poured me a spot of wine so I could participate in the toast. "He is our own little saint," Uncle Petros continued. "May God bless his heart and accept the offering of his life." I eyed the letter lying on the table at my father's elbow.

"Father, what does the letter say?" I asked. In anticipation, I balled my hands into fists, and opened and closed them.

"Did Yorgos tell you I helped him feed and brush our guest's horses?" Theophilos asked, looking at Father. "They're beautiful."

"And strong," I added. "Father, the letter!"

"Yes, they are strong," Theophilos said. "I wonder what the breed is."

"You did this for our guest?" Father asked.

"Yes!" I slumped back into my chair, folding my arms across my chest. "Mister Dumitru won't come out during the day–he says he has sensitivity to the sun." I sulked, wondering why they avoided my question.

"That's odd," Father said, slurping up his soup. "I am pleased that you agreed to be helpful."

Mother and Yaya excused themselves and, with Zoe-Sophia's help, began to bring the rest of the food in from the kitchen and place it on the table.

"Yes, Father." I looked at him, begging him with my eyes to answer the one simple question I had posed.

"Alright. I hate to give you disappointing news on your special day." He lifted the letter. "You have been denied.

You are too young. The Protos said that you may inquire again when you are eighteen years old. Because the letter Father Elias sent was such a radiant recommendation, you are assured admittance once you reach the appropriate age." I pressed my lips together, trying not to let them quiver like a little child's. I wanted to be grown up so that I could move through the world without restrictions imposed by others, by adults.

When the table was laden with my favorite foods, Mother, Yaya, and my sister returned to their seats.

"Son," Mother said, "You're looking at this the wrong way. You will be allowed to go. In less than four years. I know that that seems like a long time to you, but really it isn't." I nodded and Mother continued, "Yesterday you didn't know if you would ever be permitted to live your dream. Now you know it is in sight. That is worth celebrating, don't you think?" I mulled it over for a moment. Yes, I decided she was right. I sighed.

Mother prepared two main courses: oven-baked lamb with mixed vegetables, and moussaka. She served Spanakopita (my favorite), dolmas, and artichokes with olive oil, too. For dessert, she made baklava. I filled my plate until a mountain of food was balanced on it. Theophilos chuckled.

"Looks like Mount Olympus."

"I'm hungry enough to eat Mount Olympus," I teased with my mouth full.

Father laughed along with us saying, "It seems you have the appetite of a god."

"Yes," Mother agreed before changing the subject. "Yorgos, after supper would you get the bathtub and clean it out for me?"

"Sure, Momma. Have you been in Mister Dumitru's room?"

"No, I haven't disturbed him, like he asked. Why?"

"I found the door open a crack. Yesterday, and again today, I didn't need to use the key."

"He must have forgotten to lock it." I considered that for a moment and shrugged. Then I remembered something that seemed important earlier.

"Papa, what is . . ." I wracked my brain, trying to remember the word. "What is nos . . . fer . . . nos . . . feratu?" I said finally. His cheerful face went blank and he thoughtfully put down his spoon. Looking up from his soup he made the sign of the cross.

"What is it?" Mother asked. "What's wrong?" Father scrubbed his forehead with his hand.

"Son, don't ever say that word. It is evil."

"What is it? What is nosfer–"

"Hush! Where did you hear that word?"

"I don't know. Earlier when I was trying to pray I couldn't focus and that word popped into my head. I like the sound of it. Nosferatu." Father slammed his fist on the table causing soup to splash and dishes to rattle. Everyone jumped and looked at him. He lifted his napkin and wiped his mouth clean, his cheeks flushed.

"Nosferatu . . ." he whispered so low I could barely hear him. "Nosferatu . . . . That is the Romanian word for vrykolakas." He glowered at Mister Dumitru's door down the hall from the dining room. "Did our guest teach you that word?"

"No, not really. It just . . . popped into my head. I don't even know what it means or what vrykolakas means. Don't be angry, Father. I am just curious."

"Vrykolakas," Theophilos said. "A vrykolakas can be one of two things." Instinctively, I grabbed my ikon of Saint George the dragon slayer and hugged it against my chest.

"What, Theophilos? What does it mean?" I pleaded. Father cleared his throat, trying to silence my brother, but Theophilos ignored him and continued.

"Don't be so superstitious. That's what will scare the children more than the truth. A vrykolakas is a person who turns into a wolf during the full moon. When they are wolves, vrykolakes hurt people." When Mother heard this she ignored the rest and gathered the twins in her arms. My aunt and uncle followed her lead and corralled their children too.

"I want to stay and listen to the story," Zosimos protested, resisting her. Mother pulled him along, but left him when Zoe-Sophia's lips began to quiver. Mother took her by the hand and led her to her bedroom.

"You mean they kill people," I said. It wasn't a question. I wanted him to know that I could tell when he held something back.

"Yes, son. That's what your brother means. Vrykolakes don't just hurt people; they kill them and feed on their meat. I don't like this conversation."

Theophilos looked at Father. "It's not as if we're inviting them into our home by speaking of them."

"Are you sure about that?" Father mopped his forehead again.

"What else does it mean, Theophilos? You said that vrykolakas could mean one of two things." Father growled. At last, Theophilos deferred to him.

When Mother rejoined us, Father cleared his throat and leaned forward saying, "I don't want to speak of these things in my home again after tonight. Is that understood?" I nodded without speaking. "Good."

"All this talk of dragons and monsters scared your sister," Mother said.

"I'm surprised she fell asleep so quickly." Father gave Mother's hand a gentle squeeze before he continued. "A person who becomes a wolf during the full moon when they are alive becomes something else entirely after they have died."

"What do they become?" I intoned, giving little breath to the words.

"A revenant; one who returns from the grave. But what I speak of is something much worse than that. Revenants do not always kill, or do harm, but those I speak of do. They thirst for the blood of the living. They kill their families, and after that their neighbors. They keep killing until they are stopped. Unless they are properly destroyed, they are a menace that lives forever. They are truly frightening."

"I want to live forever," Zosimos said, covering his mouth while he coughed. Father threw him a discouraged look. "You don't know what you are saying, son. Have faith. Eternal life with God should be enough." Father directed his attention at me. "There isn't an exact word for this in Greek. Vrykolakas comes closest. The Romanian word describes more precisely what I am trying to explain. Not all vrykolakes are nosferatu but all nosferatu are vrykolakes."

"Do all vrykolakes become nosferatu?" I asked. I couldn't wrap my mind around it. My head was filled with Greek words I didn't know, foreign words I had never heard, and concepts that threatened my belief that the world was mostly a safe and predictable place. For a long time Father was silent.

"It has become too confusing," he whispered. "Nosferatu . . . . Never speak of it in this house again."

"How do you stop a vrykolakas, Father?" I held the ikon to my chest, as if it were a breastplate that could protect my throbbing heart.

"Enough of this conversation. Say your prayers, love God, and you will never have to find out." One last time Father mopped his head with his napkin. "Never speak of this again." A short silence followed, interrupted by a quiet knock on the doorjamb. Everyone around the table jumped.

"Good evening," said Mister Dumitru. "Am I intruding on a celebration?"

"We are celebrating, yes, but you aren't intruding at all," Mother wiped her hands on her towel and stood to greet him. "I haven't prepared a proper meal for our guests because everyone else checked out today, and I wasn't sure when you'd come out of your room. You're welcome to have some of our food and join our celebration. It is my son's Name Day."

"No, thank you. I am not hungry. I want to check on my horses. I thought you should know that I would like to extend my stay by at least day or two." Father, brooding with his brows knit and his arms crossing his chest, harrumphed.

Mother smiled saying, "Thank you for letting me know. You may pay when you leave." Mister Dumitru bowed his head.

"You are most kind," he said, adding, with a look at me, "Happy Name Day, young Yorgos." With that, the meal ended. Zosimos, Theophilos, and I each grabbed a second helping of baklava before vacating the dining room, and scattering in different directions.

1633, The Pindus Mountains, Greece, Mister Dumitru

I relished my stroll under the canopy of stars. Save for the white hot flecks of light, the sky was a fathomless well of India ink, total in its darkness. This was my hour. All

of the hours of darkness were mine. They were my possession, my solace, and my refuge.

Heading back to the inn, I pulled my handkerchief from
my jacket pocket and wiped my mouth clean. I stopped to
pat my horse's flanks and scratch their ears while I thought
of Yorgos. I regretted scaring him. Already the boy was
dear to me. I knew I couldn't leave him behind. Surely, he
was mine, just as the hours of darkness were mine. With
time, he would become my solace and refuge too.

For four hundred years, I have traveled through the
mortal world alone, hoping to be one of the rare and lucky
ones to be imprinted on. I wanted an end to be put to my
solitary existence. I wanted someone to share immortality
with. Until now my pottery and my private studies had
been my only salvation. Of course, once I'd given up hope
it happens! A shock, to be sure, that one so young could
imprint on me. I would have to wait for him to grow up. I
wouldn't touch him, and certainly wouldn't turn him until
he reached the appropriate age. However, I was relieved
to know that the end of my interminable loneliness was at
last in sight. What's a few more years after several hundred had already been endured? Though the thought made
me giddy I became pensive.

Under the stars, I found myself sighing in relief. Such
a mortal gesture. Imprinting made the idea of being separated from Yorgos unbearable. It caused me great anxiety.
What an invincible nosferatu I've turned out to be! I can't
bear to be separated from a mere boy. I laughed at myself
thinking, *I can not leave him behind.* I reached out with my
preternatural senses and probed his mind, continuing on
to the minds of his parents, and their youngest, Zosimos.
When I brushed his mind, Zosimos stirred, and yielded to
my touch. His thoughts opening to receive me, he became
half aware of my presence. I quickly moved on to the oldest

child, Theophilos. I didn't have to dig too deeply into any of their minds. Something I could easily exploit unfurled like a moonflower, clinging tenaciously to its vine. It was a minor family drama which had been satisfactorily resolved. I would stoke the flame and make that drama blaze again.

Ebullient, I basked in the glow of my new and forming scheme. I climbed into the back of my wagon, and scrounged for a wooden box before rummaging through my wares. Into the box went matching candelabra, a vase and several mis-matched bowls, plates, and cups. Because these were some of my most intricate and fragile pieces, I nestled them in a protective cloth before returning to the inn.

I was glad to find Yorgos' parents still conversing. For a moment I eavesdropped, standing at the door that separated their business from their home.

They were discussing their children while picking at the remains of the baklava. She was filled with a mother's concerns. Something was the matter with Zosimos. Her instincts told her that he was not recovering from his illness, though for a short time it seemed that he had been. She felt it was time for Theophilos to think of settling down and starting a family of his own. And Yorgos. More than anything she wanted him to be happy but secretly she feared for him. She was relieved to learn that he would have to wait to go to Mount Athos, and glad that he would remain within her protective sphere for four more years. She felt guilty for feeling glad. Zoe-Sophia was the only one of her children she did not worry about. Her husband held her and assured her that all of their children would be okay. They would be better than that. They would all thrive.

I cleared my throat, leaning from the inn toward their private quarters, unable to enter. They turned, looking over their shoulders at me.

"Hello, Mister Dumitru," the woman said warmly. Her husband frowned under dark brooding eyebrows. Would you like some baklava?" The plate she offered me was covered with broken pieces and crumbs.

"No, thank you." I took a step forward asking, "May I come in?" My foot encountered an invisible barrier. "I have a gift for you." Mr. Godevenos put his arm around his wife and drew her close.

"Yes, of course," she answered, breaking free of his embrace long enough to clear a spot on the cluttered table. Observing my hesitation she added, "Please, come in." She relaxed against her husband's body again. I held the box lower than eye level for their inspection before placing it on the table.

"I would like you to have these. I made them at my studio in Romania." She pushed the box away, shaking her head lightly.

"We can't accept this," her husband said before falling back into brittle silence.

"These are too beautiful, too costly. I would hate to rob you of any income," said the woman.

"Nonsense!" I countered. "You and your family have been especially hospitable to me. Young Yorgos in particular. He has been most helpful, feeding and brushing my horses and preparing my bath. I would like to show my gratitude with these gifts." I looked her in the eye, and held her gently in my thrall. She reached into the box and randomly withdrew the items, one at a time, inspecting them. Without speaking, she consulted her husband who gave a curt nod yes.

"Thank you," she said. "We would never be able to afford such fine things." Seeing my opportunity, I took another step and stopped when Mr. Godevenos threw me a warning frown.

"I would like to talk with you about that."

"About what?" The man barked, his arms wrapped tight around his chest.

"I mean you no disrespect. It appears that your family is experiencing difficult times."

"What is that to you?" he asked. "Under Ottoman rule, we are all experiencing difficult times."

"I would like to make you an offer. I am interested in having Yorgos come apprentice with me in Romania. I sense an artistic inclination in the boy that I feel should be nourished. Of course, you will be compensated. One day, only a few short years from now, your son will be able to make his own ceramic wares to sell, just like these." I pointed at the box on the table. "I have a friend and neighbor who is a skilled painter. I am sure he would also be glad to take Yorgos on. Your son is a talented painter. The evidence is all around this place–his ikons and portraits are everywhere. Talent like that mustn't be squandered. With guidance and practice, he will be producing beautiful works of art in no time. I mean in both mediums: ceramics and paint." Having been released from my hold on her, the woman turned away from me and began to clear the table. Her husband leaned closer in.

"I am sorry. We know best which inclinations should be encouraged in our son. We are already making plans for Yorgos to serve God at a monastery. He lives to serve God. I will not deprive my son of his dream." I paused for a minute before persisting, pretending to consider the man's words. When I opened my mouth to speak the woman cut me off.

"–Tell me, Mister Dumitru, if one had to choose between artistic talent and religious devotion, which would be the worst to squander? The love my son has for God is uncommon. It is what sets him apart." Abruptly, having spoken her mind, the woman returned to her cleaning. Mr. Godevenos regarded me with suspicion.

"Of course, we would continue with his general studies as well. He will have a well-rounded education."

I locked eyes with Yorgos' father. I soothed and wooed him. I stirred his doubts and fears about sending his son to Mount Athos. I inflamed his monetary concerns and nudged his thoughts in the direction I wished them to go. Yes, Yorgos is a talented painter. Yes, they would be compensated. Yes, he could go with me. *Yes.* When I knew the thoughts I planted had taken hold, I blinked and released him. However, my spell had not been broken, he sat deep in thought while his wife went in and out of the kitchen sweeping, clearing the table, and wiping it clean. I knew she was lingering—wanting to know what her husband would decide.

"Yes," he whispered, as if talking to himself, and then louder, "Yes." He looked up at me. All suspicion and distrust evaporated. "Perhaps I should reconsider. I have always hoped that my son would choose a trade. I do believe he would do well as an artist."

Mrs. Godevenos threw the cloth she was cleaning with on the table and turned her smoldering eyes on me.

"I wish you had never come here. Why do you disrupt us? Take your things. I don't want them. Truly, they are too costly for us." Mr. Godevenos went to his wife and tried to console her. She shrugged him off.

"Please forgive my wife. Leave the items. I will show them to my son in the morning and discuss this with him. I will strongly encourage him to reconsider." I nodded and retreated to my room without another word, certain that I would prevail.

1633, The Pindus Mountains, Greece, Yorgos

That night my dreams were filled with an odd mixture of joy and sorrow, loss and expectation. I dreamed of death. I dreamed that when my grandfather's casket was lowered into the ground I jumped on top of it and clung to it, ignoring the fists-full of dirt that pelted me. Sitting up, I rubbed the soil on my face and in my hair before stuffing handfuls of it in my mouth and swallowing it.

I dreamed of life. Zosimos stalked a dragon and healed himself by piercing the beast's heart and drinking from the wound.

I dreamed that Zoe-Sophia had her heart broken but managed to expand and grow in spite of it. Her heart was filled with more love than she could contain. Her love went out like concentric ripples in a pond until everything was included in their circumference.

Last of all, I dreamed again of Grandfather. He lay cold, dead and alone in his casket. The scope of my vision narrowed onto Grandfather's face. It turned into Mister Dumitru's dead-looking, soil-smudged countenance. His eyes opened, revealing the odd light that shone in them.

"Yorgos," he whispered in my dreams. "Yorgos . . . ." *Come to me!* I heard him now, not in my dreams, nor with my ears, but in my mind. My eyes fluttered open. Disoriented. *I am waiting.* I sat up, fully awake and rubbed the seeds of sleep from my eyes before throwing my feet over the edge of my bed. I hesitated and found that I couldn't refuse his command. I tiptoed out, careful not to wake my brothers, and headed to Mister Dumitru's room.

He waited for me, sitting on the top of his wooden box. I lingered in the doorway not wanting to enter. An oil lamp flickered and sputtered on the nightstand.

His voice in my mind said, *Come in,* and he patted a spot on the box next to himself. *I promise I won't bite.* I was reluctant, but found again that I couldn't refuse him.

"What is this box for?" I asked, aloud.

"It is what I sleep in." He answered, audibly. *One day, I will make one like it, just for you.*

"What if I don't want one?" I asked. The idea of sleeping in a wooden box repulsed me.

"You will." *One day, you will.* "Trust me."

We regarded each other. My heart began to beat more and more rapidly.

I don't understand. I wish he'd tell me what I'm doing here.

"I felt we needed to get to know each other," he whispered, like he could read my mind.

Mister Dumitru's eyes opened wide and our thoughts connected. He probed my mind and began to pull images from its depths. My thoughts came up and out of me like plants yanked out at the root. Only he wasn't exactly taking my thoughts from me. The images he drew out of me also remained. He was learning what he could of me, getting to know me in his peculiar fashion.

He started to weep and turned away from me, releasing my mind. His shoulders shuddered. I patted his back, not knowing what else to do to comfort him in his distress. He rubbed his eyes and cheeks clean before turning to face me. His usually pale white face was smudged red.

"I regret that I must break my promise to you," he whispered into my ear. I have no memory of what happened next.

1633, The Pindus Mountains, Greece, Mister Dumitru

I drew Yorgos into an embrace and, with my chin resting on his shoulder, wept into my handkerchief.

"I'm sorry," I whispered. He didn't flinch or pull away. He gently squeezed me, wanting to offer whatever consolation he could. That's when I knew I had come to the right decision. Placing my hand on the top of his head, I positioned it so that I could access his carotid artery.

When I first called the boy to myself, it was my intention to suggest to him that he would rather be my apprentice than devote the remainder of his mortal years–whatever their number might be–to asceticism and solitude. His father was already convinced that a lucrative apprenticeship would be better for him and the family. If Yorgos could be swayed next, his mother would certainly follow. With no one to object, he would be mine, and we could depart for Romania at once to begin his instruction.

I believed that like most mortals, he had a secret price I could uncover by digging into the depths of his soul, a price that perhaps even he himself had no conscious knowledge of setting. I would uncover it, expose it to the proverbial light of day, and offer to pay for it many times over. It was in my power to do it.

When I held him in thrall his soul opened for me. No matter how deep I searched, I found no such price. He wanted nothing more than to be a monk basking in the goodness of the God he loved. I recognized that he was one of the few mortals with a pure soul.

With that recognition came the belief that he needed time to discover himself; to develop his mind, and to learn how to love. His own heart had to be revealed to him. Only time, *mortal life,* would do it.

I had to allow him that. Our eternity together would have to wait.

Having peered into his soul, I arrived at my decision and began to weep. *The circuit of blood must be made.* Steadying myself, I dried my eyes before initiating the *little exchange* with a bite. I only needed enough of his blood (which would immediately be given back) to create an unbreakable connection between our minds; to seal the bond that imprinting started. With it, no distance would be far enough to keep me from knowing him. If he ever needed his guardian angel, I would be there. Yes, as fleet as the wind, I would come to him.

If his soul was pure, his blood was more so, a distillation of his soul's very essence. Steadying myself before it was too late, I withdrew my fang-teeth, and rubbed a mixture of blood and spittle into the puncture wounds. They healed without leaving a mark. The circuit was only half complete. I bit into my own wrist and compelled him to drink. I gave him only enough to bind us together. When the deed was done, I released him from my thrall.

He looked at me, dazed.

"What am I doing here?" he asked. I stood, went to the window, and peeled the wool blanket away. I gazed at the fingernail moon that glowed like a sliver of polished silver in the pre-dawn sky.

"You must have been sleep walking," I answered. "Go back to your bed." Previously, I buried his memories of the last two days and locked them in his subconscious. When he left me I released them. *You will only recall what you must,* I whispered in his mind.

1633, The Pindus Mountains, Greece, Yorgos

I dreamed of Grandfather again. He lay cold, dead and alone in his casket. The scope of my vision narrowed onto Grandfather's face. It turned into Mister Dumitru's dead-looking, soil-smudged countenance. When he opened his eyes, I fell headlong into the depths of his unflinching gaze, swallowed whole by the unearthly light that shone from it.

I bolted up, screaming, in my bed. Through the window, the sliver moon was the faintest white, and veiled by rolling gray clouds. Theophilos was by my bedside in an instant, and Zosimos sat up, lost in a fit of coughing.

Mother ran in to see what was wrong with me; Father was in tow. Uncle Petros and Aunt Petra followed behind. My entire family was roused by my hysterics.

"I had a bad dream," I said. My voice was muffled by Mother's bosom and I was swathed by the scent of her perfume.

"Tell us," she said. "It was only a dream, everything is alright. Everything is as it always has been, you'll see."

I knew that she was wrong, though I didn't comprehend why. Or how I knew it.

"What did you dream?" Father asked.

Only images came to me. I described them as I remembered them: images of myself covered in dirt, Papus lying in his casket and myself on top it, shoving dirt into my mouth. I described how Grandfather turned into Mister Dumitru, and that he was also lying in a casket. Then I remembered.

"He has one in his room, a casket I mean. I peeked into it. It's filled with dirt." Father groaned and rubbed his temples with his forefingers and thumbs.

"Why didn't you tell me this?"

"I was afraid you'd be angry with me for snooping." I confessed. Father flew down the stairs, heading for the guest wing.

When I reached Mister Dumitru's door, father stood in the way. I ran into him and Theophilos caught me when I reeled backwards. Father stumbled into the room and everyone crowded in. It was empty of all of Mister Dumitru's belongings. The ring of dirt scattered on the floor in the shape of a casket was the only evidence left that he had been there. Both wool blankets were removed from the windows and folded. He left them on the bed with a wad of money on top. Mother counted it.

"He left enough for half a year," she said, ruefully. Father reached for it, pulled out several bills and gave what remained back to her.

"Guilt money," he said. He palmed the cash saying, "The damn bastard has paid for our journey." Then Father turned to me.

"Get dressed quickly, son. We must leave at once. We have to go as far as we can while there is still daylight to protect us."

"From what?" Mother insisted. Father peered out the window. He turned from it to her.

"From that evil man."

"I don't understand."

"He wants Yorgos." Mother gasped when comprehension dawned. She crossed herself.

"Take Theophilos with you," Uncle Petros said. "My boys and I will stand watch here." Father nodded.

"Where are we going?" I asked, confused by father's sudden urgency.

"I'm taking you to Mount Athos."

"But I thought I was too young." Father bent so he could look me in the eye.

"I will convince them to make an exception." He stood and addressed Mother. "There has to be a way."

Everything was prepared within the hour. I was instructed to only pack what I absolutely needed. Yaya and Aunt Petra presented each of us a jug of water. We ate with haste and stuffed dried fruit and nuts into our pockets for the journey.

When it was time to leave, I ran down the stairs to catch up with Father and Theophilos. Halfway down, I realized I had forgotten my prized possessions. Returning to collect them from the ikon corner in my bedroom, I grabbed the image of the resurrection and the ikon of Saint George–the ones that were gifts, not the versions I painted myself. While I dashed through the house, and past my parent's room, I stopped. Mother's favorite perfume bottle was sitting on top of her dresser. I snatched it and shoved it in my pocket. I took one last sweeping gaze at the only home I had ever known and made haste to catch up.

When I descended the porch stairs, everyone I loved was waiting. Mother was closest. She and Yaya carried large knapsacks filled with food and other supplies–one for each of us–which they fitted on our shoulders. Zoe-Sophia, a step behind Mother, came out from hiding with her ragdoll pinned to her side by her elbow.

"Goodbye, Yorgos. I love you." She stood up on the tip of her toes and kissed my cheek. When everyone echoed her farewell I started to cry.

"I am going to miss all of you. Can't everyone come with me?" I knew I should be joyful, but I was scared. Father wasn't acting like himself. Mother wiped her tears with her apron.

"Zoe-Sophia and I can't," she said plainly. "Women aren't allowed on Mount Athos."

"Who would take care of the inn and the farm?" Father asked. "Theophilos and I will have to come home and continue with our lives, just as you will be continuing with yours."

"I want to know why women can't go there. That means that Momma can't ever come to visit me." I felt entirely insecure and unsure of myself. "Maybe I'm not ready," I said, looking at my toes. Even while I said the words, I was shocked by them. Mother ran her fingers through my hair saying, "Hush, dearheart. Relax. Sometimes it's scary to get the things we want. You will be happy. I promise." She cupped my chin with her fingers and lifted it so that we were looking into each other's eyes. "I love you. You will always be welcome at home. Do you understand? You can always come home. So it doesn't matter if I can visit you or not." I took a deep breath and nodded.

While Father, Theophilos, and I took to the road, headed to Mount Athos, it struck me that what should have been perhaps a bittersweet, yet joyous moment, was tainted too much by panic and haste.

8 The Road To Mount Athos

From daybreak to twilight, Father, Theophilos, and I descended the dirt road. Under the heat of the merciless sun, sweat adhered our clothes to our bodies like glue and our exposed skin burned. After several hours of traveling by foot, I was wearier than I'd ever been. My muscles were sore, my feet ached and my back hurt. The journey seemed impossible to endure.

We continued on.

While we went, I mulled over the events of the last few days. They had been strange days that were packed full of happenings that, upon reflection, were significant. Take, for example, Mister Dumitru's mysterious arrival and even more mysterious departure, the death of my nameless lamb and the disappointing news, in the middle of it all, that I was too young to become a monk. Add to that my nightmares and Father's insistence that we leave, at once, for Mount Athos, in spite of their decree that I wait. I found it all to be dizzying.

When I thought of Mister Dumitru, for an instant my mind was not my own. I saw—through someone else's eyes—that I lay horizontally in a dark, confining space. A plank of wood was above my face. In fact, wood surrounded me on all four sides. Unable to breathe, I began to panic. Mister Dumitru's unmistakable voice resounded in my mind, *Goodbye, my darkling*. And everything was again as it should be. Theophilos touched my shoulder.

"Are you okay, Yorgos?" he asked. I stopped and took a swig of water, while pondering the question. *Yes, everything is good.* I knew it in my soul. I felt released from some gripping menace.

"Yes." I said aloud. "I'm great."

Father, called out to us while walking backwards. "Hurry up, boys. Keep moving. Are you going to let your old man get down the mountain before you?"

He turned and sprinted ahead, urging us to catch up.

All day, Father drove us like a merciless shepherd goading his sheep with a stern rod to encourage them. He allowed us to stop at hourly intervals, but only long enough to catch our breath and drink a swig of water. By midday I was ready for a longer break. Father insisted that we continue.

"I think we have gone far enough," Theophilos challenged. "We need to stop for awhile." Grudgingly, Father relented. We settled on the ground by the side of the road. Under the shady canopy of a black pine, we unpacked our lunches and consumed them in an uncomfortable silence. We were so rushed we forgot to say the traditional blessing before we started to eat. Unthinkable, that, especially for me.

1633, The Pindus Mountains, Greece, Mister Dumitru

I cannot describe the pain I felt when I left Yorgos behind. If I were to say, in modern parlance, that I experienced separation anxiety, would that make me the fool? Would I sound childish and immature? Perhaps. As I am a being who is well acquainted with his own faults, I try to hide nothing–especially from myself.

Dawn was breaking, daylight was killing the night. I traveled only seven kilometers before necessity forced me off the road. I held myself together until I found a good secluded place in which to park my wagon and secure my horses to a tree.

Before I went into my casket and the dark grounding soil from Romania contained therein, I locked my wagon doors from the inside. After climbing into my casket, I locked it from the inside too, and settled into the soil. Taking it up by the handful I poured it over my body. I rubbed it in my hair and on my face. It was a small bit of home that always soothed me. Once secure, I had a good cry.

I know it's preposterous–all of this emotional fuss over a mere boy. To me, Yorgos was more than that. My maker abandoned me well over three hundred years before. I spent a good number of those years alone. Meeting Yorgos meant I would now have a companion.

Though I would have loved to bring him with me, I knew that I had to release Yorgos to his own mortal destiny. His *im*mortal fate would have to wait. When I peeked into his mind prior to making the *little exchange,* I learned two things about him. First, he was good. Everyone who knew him recognized it. Unfortunately, he did not. He needed mortal time away from the center of my dark circumference to learn this about himself. The second thing I knew was this: if I were to take him now, he would always hate me for it. For a creature like myself, always is *truly* a very long time.

I couldn't sleep. After pondering my lonely existence for hours, I reached out with my mind and lightly touched Yorgos'. I saw through his eyes. The bright light of the ascending sun hurt mine even from a remove. Making the connection however, took no effort at all.

109

"Yes," I whispered, "the *little exchange* worked!" I lingered in his mind, for a moment, before whispering *goodbye*. Extricating my thoughts from his, I continued to weep.

Though the few years I would have to wait seemed like an eternity, when Yorgos imprinted on me it meant that my loneliness would soon come to an end. How does one compare years with centuries? I could wait. I would *have* to wait. "Be patient," I whispered while falling asleep. *Patience be damned!*

1633, The Pindus Mountains, Greece, Yorgos

"What are you so afraid of, Father?" My brother asked.

"That man . . ." Father said under his breath, with his head turned away from me. He squared his shoulders, blocking my view of my brother. I strained my ears to listen.

" . . . That man wants Yorgos," he whispered.

"What do you mean he *wants* him?" Theophilos asked.

"He is vrykolakas. I know it. The moment I looked him in the eye I felt I was looking into the gaze of a dead man. His eyes were so odd, so . . . unnatural. I should have trusted my instincts and driven him out of our home right then and there." Theophilos laughed.

"Surely you're joking, Father. You don't actually believe the folktales, do you?"

"I am being most serious, and yes, I do believe the old tales." Father wagged his head and muttered, "He must have had me under some kind of spell."

"I think that Mister Dumitru is an eccentric artist from Romania," Theophilos suggested. "That, I am sure, is the extent of his oddness."

"You're wrong, son. That man is bad."

They continued to talk about our strange guest, Mister Dumitru, and how I had to be hidden away from him. In truth, the conversation was one-sided. The longer it went on the more it seemed that Father was talking to himself, convincing himself, and answering himself.

"Yorgos will be safe on Mount Athos," he said after much mumbled deliberation. "An infernal creature like that man cannot possibly set foot on holy ground. Yes, Yorgos will be safe there."

Theophilos raised an eyebrow, "So this is why you've been pushing so hard to put the inn behind us, to cover so much distance in so little time?" His incredulity was palpable.

"Yes. The man himself told your brother that he cannot come out during daylight hours. We have to take advantage of his weakness." They both turned toward me.

"Isn't that what he said?" Father asked.

"Not exactly," I corrected. I fidgeted under their piercing stares, trying to recall his exact words. "He said he prefers to avoid the sun. He can come out if he wants to. He told me so. But he has a condition–"

"A *condition* . . . ?" Father sneered. "Well yes, I suppose so. His condition is that he is *dead*. I fear he means to share that condition with you."

Theophilos laughed, and this time I did too, although I secretly feared that Father might be right. However, having been burnished by the relentless heat and light of the sun, my memory of recent events had lost its sharp clarity. The night terrors that seemed pressing before dawn seemed unreal in the bright light of day. Perhaps Theophilos was right and Mister Dumitru was nothing worse than an eccentric artist and just as harmless. Wouldn't Father feel foolish to find that that was so?

"Well then, we only have twelve hours to take advantage of his aversion to the sun," Father declared. "We have used nearly half of that already. We must cover more ground."

With that, we packed ourselves like unfortunate mules and set off again on the road to Mount Athos.

By nightfall, we set up camp not far from the side of the road. Without speaking, we ate the simple supper that Yaya and Mother prepared and packed for us.

Afterward, sitting on a log by the campfire, I meditated on the ikon of Saint George, holding it between my knees. I sought to emulate his courage.

"Father," I said, looking up from it, "I want you to know, I'm not afraid."

He regarded me for a long moment, before mussing my hair. He pushed his lips together in a failed approximation of a smile.

"I am glad that one of us is not."

"Why, Yorgos?" Theophilos asked. "Why are you not afraid?" I shrugged and looked from Theophilos, to the crackling flames and back to the ikon.

"God won't let anything bad happen to me." I said, glancing up. "I will be given the faith to repel evil if I must. Besides, I haven't fulfilled my purpose yet." Father's wide smile was genuine.

"You are your grandfather's grandson, aren't you? You have his faith."

"I always hoped I'd be just like him," I said.

"Well, rest assured, son, you are."

Father decided that I would sleep through the night, and he and Theophilos would keep watch in alternate shifts.

I spread out my bedroll and smoothed it on the ground. Kneeling on top of it I riffled through my knapsack, searching for the ikon of Christ Emmanuel I inherited from Papus. I wanted to pray with it before I went to sleep. I couldn't find it. The deeper I dug into my bag without uncovering it, the more afraid I was that I forgot to grab it in my haste to get on the road, even when I went back for the others.

Exasperated, I dumped the entire contents of the knapsack on the bedroll and tossed the items aside, one by one, into a not-so-neat pile. Once I moved everything from the original pile, where I dumped them, to the new pile, I knew that I had indeed left it behind. My chest ached. Nona entrusted me with Papus' very heart, when she gave me that ikon and I neglected it. At least Mother would add it to the collection in the ikon corner where everyone could appreciate it. I found some small consolation in that.

While I returned the contents of the pile to the knapsack, I lifted Mother's perfume bottle. It was an intricately cut and faceted glass orb that fit in the palm of my hand. The mechanism for spraying it was a black bulb, made out of leather or some kind of treated cloth, on the end of a shiny silver tube.

I spritzed the air with it and leaned into the floral scented mist, thinking of Mother. Though the sun hadn't yet set on my first day away from home, when I thought of her my heart was expanded and then rent by nostalgia.

My eyes closed, I clutched the bottle with both my hands cupped around it.

"What's that you've got there?" Father asked, walking up behind me. He came around and knelt, looking at me.

I presented it on my right palm for Fathers inspection.

"It's Mother's perfume. I took it," I said, with a sheepish smile and a shrug. Father crossed his arms and narrowed his eyes. "Don't be upset with me. I thought that when I really miss her . . . well . . . at least I could smell her perfume. It would almost be like she was with me." I held my breath, anticipating his wrath. His expression softened.

"I am not upset with you, Yorgos. Of course, I will have to replace it, but I understand why you took it. I might have done the same thing myself when I was a boy."

Father mussed my hair and turned to stoke the fire while I continued to repack my knapsack. I placed the ikons on the top and drew the string closed.

With my head on my pillow, I watched the campfire consume the wood. The crackling and popping relaxed me. I finally nodded off. A couple of hours later, I stirred and opened my eyes to slits. Theophilos was asleep beside me. Father, half awake in his bedroll, struggled to keep his eyes open and his head up. Sitting with his back against a log near the remnants of the fire he stared at it vacantly, his head bobbing. All that remained of the flames were red-hot embers scattered throughout blackened wood and ash. Feeling warm, safe and protected, I nodded off again.

While I slept, something tickled my cheek. I brushed it away and turned in my bedroll to face the other direction. As if in a dream I became strangely aware that a creature with four soft-padded feet circled me. The sound of purring assaulted my ears and something tickled my cheek again. I reached my hand to brush it away and struck a hard, furry body that vibrated. With a start I opened my eyes and looked directly into the reflective eyes of an impossibly large black cat. The shock rendered me mute. *I'm dreaming,* I reasoned, squeezing my eyes closed. The sound of the creature's purring became louder, and I felt its hot breath on my face. It butted my forehead with great physical force and then it licked me. *This is not a dream.*

I bolted up, screaming. Theophilos was on his knees beside me in seconds. Father, slumped over by the burned-out campfire, bolted up too.

"What is it?" they both asked. I pushed my brother aside and scrambled over the ground on my hands and knees.

"Where's the cat?" I stammered. Squinting to see in the nascent morning light, I looked in vain for the cat, or evidence that it had been there. I found nothing. Off in the distance, I heard the animal passing swiftly through shrubs and ground-cover.

"Son, what are you talking about?"

"Right there." I pointed to where my head lay when the cat butted its forehead against mine. "It was right there. A really big cat. It woke me up." Father's brows furrowed and he pushed his lips together.

"Another nightmare. This isn't like you, Yorgos, to have nightmares."

"No it isn't." Theophilos agreed.

"I wasn't dreaming. Well, at least not *after* the cat woke me up. It licked me." At that Theophilos laughed in spite of his effort not too. So did Father. I scrambled around on my hands and knees again, looking for paw prints, whiskers, anything that would prove I had not dreamed up the cat, and they laughed at me even harder.

"What are you doing now?" Theophilos asked, trying to stifle his errant laughter.

"I'm looking for proof. There *was* a cat."

"If there were any paw prints, I'm afraid you've just erased them," Father said. If I had learned by then how to swear, I would have employed a choice expletive or two to give expression to my frustration. Instead, I slumped, and threw my hands up before letting them fall limply to my thighs.

"It was here," I whispered, more to myself than either of them, because they were certain that I was delusional.

"Your brother is not himself, Theophilos," Father said, shaking himself free of the momentary lapse into frivolity. "I am afraid for him."

"I am too, Father." They both regarded me with sober intensity.

"They'll know what to do for him on Mount Athos," Father declared. Theophilos nodded in agreement. "Yes, yes they will," Father muttered, staring off into the trees. As if reaching an immutable decision he looked up. "Let us eat quickly and be on our way. We have another twelve hours in which to travel."

Over a rushed breakfast, I listened while they discussed what should be done for me. Not once, as was typical, did they seek my counsel. Only this time there was a difference. In the past, Father was adamant that I *not* go to Mount Athos. Now, he was equally adamant to get me there, and quickly.

The second day of our journey was much like the first; few breaks, little water, much sweat. The heat of the sun beat on us, burning painfully.

Early that evening, when the sky turned purple with twilight, Father and Theophilos selected a suitable clearing, a little ways of the road, to set up camp for the night. Waiting for the fire to be lit and supper to be unpacked, I stiffened when horses and a wagon approached from a distance. The blood vanished from my cheeks.

"It's Mister Dumitru!" I gasped.

"Theophilos, take your brother into the woods. Don't come out until I call for you." My brother grabbed my hand and dragged me behind himself while running into the denser growth farther off the road.

He found a large boulder to hide me behind and peeked around it to watch Father. When I came from behind it he shoved me back.

"I can't see, Theophilos. I want to see!"

"Shhh!" he hissed. "I'll tell you what happens." When a horse-drawn cart, piled high with wares and supplies, came around a bend in the road and stopped, I peeked and Theophilos shoved me behind the rock again.

"That's not Mister Dumitru's wagon," I said. "It's too small for a person and there is only one horse." Though the cart I caught a glimpse of came to a complete stop, I heard wheels and horses approaching.

"Yes," said my brother. "A horse with a rider, no less. More of them are coming, Yorgos. You're right. It's not Mister Dumitru after all." For the third time I stood beside him, and for the third time he shoved me back. This time he only pushed me behind himself.

"Watch carefully," he whispered. "We don't want to be seen until Father calls for us."

Three more well-packed horse drawn carts with riders came up behind the first. Their cargo jangled and clanged from hanging pots and pans striking each other. Two horses flanked each cart. An elderly man dismounted from one of them and a younger woman, accompanied by a girl roughly my age, dismounted from the other.

To my young, inexperienced eyes, the women's clothes seemed to be exotic. Their colorful dresses reached to the ground and their shoulders were draped with layers of shawls. Scarves on their heads secured their long brown hair away from their faces. While the three of them approached my father, bells sewn into the hems of the women's dresses tinkled. When they reached him, the man bowed and the women curtsied before standing to the right of the man and taking a step back.

While Father and the man talked, several other men and women arrived on horseback. Five more carts, also piled high and swaying with wares and supplies followed.

Behind these a small mass of people, perhaps thirty-two in all, traveled on foot.

"Who are these people, Theophilos? They don't look like Greeks. They don't look like Turks either. Who are they?"

"I think they're Gypsies. I've heard of them, but I've never seen any before."

"They have horses. They must be Turks." I surmised.

"Yes, probably. Who knows where they're from. Gypsies are nomads, wanderers."

While we watched from behind the boulder, Father reached into his pocket and retrieved the money that Mister Dumitru left when he vacated his room. The old man waved his hands in front of himself, refusing payment, but Father insisted. He peeled off three bills and pushed them at the man. "Theophilos, Yorgos, it's okay. Come out," Father called.

Theophilos went to them without hesitation. I jumped behind the rock and peeked out. The old man and the women squinted in the purple haze of twilight, to see me. Before dropping her gaze to her toes the girl peered from behind her chaperones, raised her hand and waved. I was struck shy.

"Yorgos!" Theophilos called. "It's okay." I assumed an awkward smile and joined them.

The old man bowed his head saying, "I am Fonso." He gestured toward the women. "This is my granddaughter Dika and my great-grand—" Dika stepped forward and interrupted him, "Excuse me, Grandfather," she said before addressing us directly. "Florica. This is my daughter Florica." Florica smiled and looked away.

"Yes. The lovely Florica." Fonso said through his teeth. The girl looked at me again. In her eyes I saw a deep sadness that was incongruous with her tender age. Her fear and shame were almost palpable. She looked away.

"You and your sons are free to join us in all that we do while you are with us." Fonso said. "We have found that it is far safer to travel in numbers. We are glad to have you."

The Gypsies repositioned the carts to create a barrier from the road. After that, they set up camp. With dizzying speed, a bonfire was made, and several benders were erected around it with enough space between for tables and chairs. Benders, I learned, were tents made from withies and tarps. Withies are long, flexible branches of hazel trees. Driven into the ground, they were bent and woven together to create a strong domed form. Tarps covering the dome were strapped into place.

Father and Theophilos helped set up the benders. I offered to help too, but the Gypsies moved with such practiced and competent swiftness that I soon felt underfoot and in the way. I found a place by the bonfire and watched in amazement, feeling that I had found the one calm spot in a storm of activity.

Camp was set up in a matter of minutes, complete with food being warmed over the fire. Soon dinner was served. With a steaming bowl of stew, I looked around in wonder of it all. Lanterns hung from the branches of trees, children ran, skipped and played, musicians created music, and the people danced and sang with joy. In a short time, this small plot of unused land by the side of the road was transformed into something more than a campsite. The Gypsies had made it a home. At that time and in that place, it was easy to forget the fears that accompanied me and my family on the road thus far. While I waited for them, I prayed that Father and Theophilos would find the same relief.

A few minutes later, they joined me at the table. Together we blessed the meal and crossed ourselves.

While we ate, a group of scantily dressed women came out of one of the tents and danced around the campfire.

Going up to various men, they lured them up onto their feet and into the dance. The women punctuated the beat of the music with tiny cymbals on their thumbs and index fingers. I tried to look away but it was not easy to ignore their lithesome and graceful, if not provocative, gyrations. To my astonishment, Dika and Florica were among them. Mother and daughter dancing together in such a shameful way! My cheeks flushed red and I looked at Father, aghast. He laughed at me heartily while tipping a flagon of strong alcohol to his lips.

"Perhaps I have allowed your mother to shelter you to a regrettable degree. Settle down, son. It is all for fun and relaxation. These people have known hardship and too many long days on the road. This is how they celebrate the fact that they are *alive!*"

He leaped to his feet, took Dika by the hand and spun her in circles, laughing. Theophilos downed his own frothy beverage and joined in. I was mortified. I had never seen Father behave like this. I especially had never seen him dance with a woman other than my mother.

Florica danced circles around me, shielding her face with a veil and peeking at me from behind it. She dropped the veil and laughed. Never once did she break eye contact. She tried to coax me from my seat, but I responded with an adamant shake of my head. She would not accept my refusal. She followed the circumference of my table and when she made her way back to where I sat, she reached for my hand. I smiled at her sheepishly and acquiesced, allowing her to pull me to my feet and drag me into the crowd.

The dancers spun, gyrated, and moved as a cohesive whole through the camp. We joined, becoming one with them. We reached for each other's hands. Our palms touched, our fingers twined. I recalled the many evenings that my family and all of our neighbors gathered to play music and dance all night. I danced with my aunt, Mother and Yaya. I danced with my friends' mothers and sisters and once, before I scared him away, I even danced with Niko. I knew how to dance, how to lead. So I decided it was time to take charge. With our fingers twined I lifted my hand and hers with it and tried to spin her. This time she denied me with an adamant shake of the head. She used all the strength in her arm and upper body to take control and then she spun me. Arm wrestling on our toes, we both fought playfully to take control, to lead the dance. I twirled her, she twirled me. I led right, she led left. I began to dip her. She stiffened, forced me back and dipped me instead. At last, and without warning, Florica danced me to the table and pushed me back into my seat. She laughed heartily, flashing all of her teeth, and then danced away, disappearing into the crowd of merrymakers.

After supper, the people repaired to wood basins, on opposite sides of the camp, that were set up for bathing. One side for the men, and the other for the women. Father and Theophilos went ahead of me, but I refused, initially, as I was not accustomed to bathing in public.

The music was now slower, less celebratory. I lingered by the fire to listen to it. It was sorrowfully beautiful music. Paradoxically, it consoled an inconsolable ache in my soul. I couldn't tear myself away.

When the crowds in and around the bath basins thinned, and at Father's urging, I made my way to them. There were four basins in all. Three of them were grouped together in the clearing. The forth was off to the side under the canopy of a leafy tree. A single lantern hung from a branch throwing light upon the water. It appeared to be unoccupied. I thanked God, because the others were still brimming over with boys, teens, and men who splashed in the water while rubbing soap into their hair and over their bodies. Alternately, I averted my eyes and glanced furtively at them until a fevered shame set flame to my cheeks. I felt a twinge of guilt and hurried by, rushing to the far basin, the one removed from all of the naked flesh. With my back squarely facing temptation, I was determined to avoid it.

While I made my way, the boys splashed me without mercy and invited me to join them. I crossed myself, said the Jesus Prayer, and kept walking.

With my head up and facing forward I saw—when it was too late to gracefully back away—that the basin was not empty after all. Florica rose out of the suds, spitting water from her mouth. I dropped my gaze to the ground. Though it was an accident, seeing a naked girl embarrassed me. I decided that I didn't care about being graceful. I turned on my heel, about to give up completely on the idea of bathing when I heard her call "Yorgos, it's okay." I stopped mid-step and looked back in her direction, refusing to look at her directly.

"Florica, why are you bathing here with the boys and the men?" I asked.

"Because it is where I must bathe—here both with them and removed from them. There is no other place for me."

"Why?" I asked. "I don't understand. Why aren't you with the other girls?"

"Because, my friend," she started and then bit her lip. "I am not really a girl." I lifted my eyes and looked into hers, trying not to see anything below them. Thankfully she was up to her neck in suds. "My mother makes me dress like a girl," she whispered, breaking eye contact to inspect the bubbles. "It's a lie. I am a boy, like you."

"Why would your mother make you dress like a girl?" Florica patted the side of the tub with her palm saying, "Come, bathe with me and I will tell you everything. It's okay." I hesitated, then stripped down to my undergarments and climbed the ladder into the basin, taking a seat across from her. I held my gaze to her face, still afraid to see anything below her neck. Even though she said she was a boy, I wasn't sure I believed her.

"I am gifted with the *sight,*" she began. "It runs in my family, all the way back for innumerable generations. Only with me there is a difference; I am the only boy who has ever had the gift. *Ever!*" She wagged her head in dismay. "It always falls to the daughter, no?" She raised her eyebrows as if the answer was self evident and then, for a moment, it seemed she felt ashamed. She looked away from me and made a pile of bubbles in front of herself and then scattered them.

"My father died before my mother had a girl." She laughed. "I am it!"

Silence lingered between us. I wasn't sure what to say in response to her strange confession. Finally, Florica leaned forward and held my gaze, as if sizing me up.

"I can tell, Yorgos Godevenos, that you are not one to judge. So I will tell you the rest. I am more fragile than most boys and better suited to the tasks of girls. Do you understand what I am telling you?" I considered her words.

"No, I don't think I do. You really look, well, you seem like a girl to me."

Florica smiled wide like what I said made her glad, or amused her. Her smile seemed to be tainted with regret, and then it vanished completely. With a shrug of resignation she rose from the soapy waters of the basin and stepped up on the submerged bench. Her naked body was fully revealed to be that of a young man. And the size of her tender manhood dangled in front of my eyes. I looked away.

When she splashed back into the water I looked at her but said nothing.

"I don't like to dress like a girl, Yorgos, but my mother insists that I do it. She thinks people will be kinder to me if they see me as a girl. She thinks it makes it easier for them to ignore what makes me different from other boys if I do not present myself as a boy. I hate it. I am not a girl."

"Does it work?" I asked. "Are they more kind to you?"

"Mostly it works, until it is time to bathe. No one wants me when it is time to bathe. Do you think the women want to bathe with *this?*" With both hands Florica indicated her male body. "And the men . . . ?" She left that sentence, unfinished, hanging in the air between us.

"Florica, if you hate it so much, you should tell your mother what you want. You have to trust what you know. You must know yourself."

"Djordji." She said. I thought she called my name, so I looked at her. "No–it is my true name, my *male* name, same as you, no?" She pointed at me and said "Yorgos," and then she pointed at herself and said, "Djordji. Your name means gardener, does it not?" I nodded. "My name does too. You're named after Saint George?"

"Yes." I nodded again.

"So am I." I leaned into the space between us and bridged the gap with my offered hand. "You see," she said "We are the same, yes?"

"Yes." I agreed. "It is a pleasure to meet you, Djordji." She smiled, without a hint of shame, and accepted my hand.

"I like you, Yorgos," she said, only her voice was different. It was deeper, more resonant. She dropped her pretense like a mask. Still holding my hand Djordji turned it over. He gripped my wrist with one hand and uncurled my fingers with the other, revealing my palm. He squinted in the dimming light of the darkening sky, and pushed his long wet hair out of his face.

"You have a beautiful palm," he said. It is difficult to read here, under the single lantern. You must come to my mother's tent where there is plenty of light and let me get a better look at it."

Djordji climbed out of the water. The droplets that dotted his honey-colored skin glistened like diamonds in the lantern light until he toweled them off. He looked up at me a couple times, to see if I was watching, and smiled generously when he saw that I was. He wrapped his towel around himself and left. My cheeks flushed and my chest hurt delightfully. I felt the familiar prick of guilt and made the sign of the cross.

"Come soon, Yorgos. It won't take me long to dress. Do not delay."

I nodded. "I'll come soon. I promise." I watched him walk away with rapt attention. Djordji was a handsome man with a beautiful body. It was a shame that his mother forced him to hide it from the world.

I, too, toweled off, dressed, and wandered through the camp. I listened to the music, watched the dancing, and even accepted some strong alcohol. I only took a couple of sips before I abandoned my drink on the top of a table. While I continued to press through the merry crowd, I found that my feelings were mixed. Djordji intrigued me. I could look at him all night and still be refreshed in the morning. However, I was on my way to Mount Athos to give my life to God. The way Djordji made me feel seemed to contradict that. I shook my head, wanting to clear it.

Hoping I had waited long enough, I asked someone which tent was Dika and Florica's and went to it straightaway.

"Hello," I called out. "I'm here, like I promised." I stood outside the bender that I had been directed to, kicking at the soil with my heel.

"I'm in here, Yorgos. Come," he answered. I pushed through the flaps and parted the curtains that were hung just inside. Outside it looked like nothing more than the makeshift dwelling that it was. Inside it was comfortable, even luxurious. I found Djordji sitting on a chair with Dika standing behind him. She was braiding his hair. Djordji, fully dressed as Florica with traditional jewelry, face paint, and all, looked up and flashed me a smile.

Pillows, cushions and blankets were scattered everywhere; candles and oil lamps, too. The bender was filled with light. A meter or two to their left was a small table and a vacant chair.

"Have a seat, Yorgos," Djordji said, and then he wrested from her agile fingers the lock of hair his mother had been twisting.

"Leave us, Mother. I want to read Yorgos' palm in private." Dika acquiesced, but not before glowering at me with her eyes reduced to slits.

"Mother! Take that back." The woman frowned at her son and then spit in my direction. Djordji dragged his chair through the dirt and sat on it across the table from me.

"Thank you, Mother," he said. The woman spit again and inspected the nails of her right hand before leaving.

While mumbling to himself, Djordji glanced down at his many gold chains and strings of beads, selecting a simple strap of leather from which hung a blue-glass eye. He lifted it up over his head and down over mine, in a single movement.

"To ward off the gruesome gaze," he said. "Mother does it quite easily and without thinking."

"Don't all mothers?" I asked. We both laughed. "What were those words you mumbled? I couldn't understand them."

"I spoke the words of a traditional prayer. In Greek I would say: 'This is espand, it banishes the evil eye. The blessing of King Naqshband. Eye of nothing, Eye of relatives, Eye of friends, Eye of enemies. Whoever is bad should burn in this glowing fire.' Now, the evil look she gave you cannot touch you."

"Oh," I said, my stomach fluttering. "Thank you." He answered with a smile.

I extended my arm and pulled it back. He reached for my fingertips and drew my arm to him, fully extending it.

"Relax." He looked me in the eye and turned my arm so that my palm faced up.

"Hmmm," he said simply. He drew his index finger over the longest line on my palm a couple times.

"This is most interesting–"

"Listen, Djordji," I interrupted. "I don't want Florica to read my palm. I want *you* to do it. Djordji. *Please?"*

Withdrawing his hand from mine, Djordji stood. He removed the jewelry from his ears and neck, and placed it in a dish on the table. Then, he lifted the dress up and over his head. His plain taupe pants, rolled up to the shins, were exposed. He tossed the dress carelessly to the dirt and looked at me. The tiny bells jangled while it fell.

"Better?" he asked.

"The face paint too," I answered. He laughed, reaching for a damp towel, and removed the mask of paint from his face.

"Now?"

"Come closer."

He did. Resting his bottom on his heels, he knelt beside me. He rose up on his knees and brought his head so close to mine that there wasn't any space between. Inhaling his breath, I placed my palm on his bare chest and felt his heartbeat. It pounded strong and sure beneath my hand.

I leaned closer. Our lips touched. He wet mine with his tongue and my groin leaped. I was awash with tingling heat from head to toe. Guilt pricked my heart. I didn't know exactly what we were doing, but I knew I shouldn't proceed. I pushed him off and stretched my arm across the table again.

"Shall we begin, Djordji?" I said. He nodded and rose from his kneeling position to take his seat across from me. All the while he did not stop staring into my eyes.

"Djordji," I finally said. "My palm? Shouldn't you be looking at my palm?"

"Yes," he said, blushing. Again, he traced the longest line on my palm with his finger. His expression was unreadable. Lifting my hand, he held my palm, horizontally, in front of his face, studying it closely. Rising to his feet he shook his head no.

"I cannot," he said simply. "I cannot, Yorgos."

"You cannot what? Read my palm, or tell me what it says?" Djordji pressed his lips together, shook his head again and said, "Perhaps both." An unconvincing smile touched his lips.

"Have a seat," I insisted. "I am curious, please."

Djordji sat down again.

"Alright, if you insist."

"I do. Tell me everything you see, Djordji. Don't hold anything back." He lay his palm on mine so that his fingertips touched the crease in my wrist and vice versa.

"What do you see?" I prompted. He removed his hand from mine, and looked at my palm.

"Sorrow," he said simply. "Deep sorrow." My heart ached, and I wished I hadn't coerced him so effectively. It was too late to stop. I had to know everything he could tell me.

"Go on. Please."

"Before that, you will know love . . . and purpose. You will be happy." Again he traced his finger along the longest line on my palm. "Hmmm. You are called by God, Yorgos. You are called by God to go into the heart of darkness with your light. It is your sole purpose. I see now that the sorrow can be avoided."

"How?" I asked. "How can I avoid the sorrow?"

"Like you said to me, you must know yourself. For you, it is the only way to avoid the sorrow." I exhaled. It sounded simple enough.

"I noticed that you keep touching this line." I said and I traced the long line as he had. "What does it reveal?"

"That is your life line. It is most unusual." Again he touched the tip of his finger to my palm and traced the line to the place where it stopped and then started again. "I have never seen one quite like this. If it stopped here it would seem that your life line was uncommonly short. But this is only a tiny gap in it. In truth, you have an extremely long life line."

"What does it mean?" I asked.

"Life lines, like every feature of a palm, can be interpreted in various ways."

"How would *you* interpret it?" I pressed. Djordji paused and lowered his gaze. He focused on the flame that flickered and popped on the wick of the oil lamp between us. He lifted his eyes and looked at me.

"I think you will soon experience death, but for you it will only be temporary." His words were well measured. Equal weight was given to each. I laughed at the absurdity of what he said.

"You're teasing me! There is only one person in all of recorded history whose death was temporary."

"Yes. I know the story of your Jesus. Yorgos, don't look for a literal interpretation. Ponder these things that I have

129

been privileged enough to see and tell you. Perhaps you should ask your Jesus for the interpretation."

"Perhaps," I agreed. I stood up and reached into my pockets, knowing that they were empty. Throwing my hands up in mock surprise, I twisted my brows. "I'll have to ask Father for the money."

Djordji took hold of both of my wrists and gently forced my arms down against my thighs. I didn't resist. He pressed against me. I pushed him off. He stepped back and bent to retrieve the dress he had earlier discarded saying, "The only payment I wish to receive from you, Yorgos Godevenos, is your gratitude." Before he lifted the dress over his head I grabbed him by the wrist and yanked it from him.

"Don't you have a manlier shirt you can wear?" I asked.

"No, not really." I stared at him blankly. "Let me see . . ." he amended. He riffled through his trunk for a suitable shirt. Standing beside him, I saw black suspenders and a plain white button-up shirt. I retrieved them and pushed them into his chest.

"I think these will do nicely," I said. After he put the shirt on, I tucked it in for him and secured the suspenders. Then I pulled his hair back and tied it in a tidy ponytail. He turned. He was a few centimeters taller than me, so when we stood face to face his lips were even with my forehead. He kissed me there. My heart ached with equal parts pleasure and pain and a twist of guilt. He leaned down to touch his lips to mine, but I turned my head and instantly regretted it. To both want and not want something, simultaneously, can be paralyzing. I hoped that he would try to kiss me again, so that I wouldn't have to choose. He didn't make the attempt, but he didn't move away either. Recklessly I turned and pecked him on the lips and then I turned away. But I didn't turn *him* away, I reached for him.

"Let's join the others," I said. I took a step forward to leave. He squeezed my hand while taking hold of a lantern that hung at the entrance.

"Wait," he said, pulling me back. "I've thought of a way for you to pay me."

"Yes?" I asked. My voice quivered.

"Please, for me, make every effort to avoid the sorrow. Know yourself, my friend, as you have taught me to know myself."

"Alright," I agreed. "I'll do my best. I promise."

"To know this, that you will avoid the sorrow, makes me happy." We stepped toward the curtains and flaps that separated us from the world. I gave his hand a firm squeeze and let it go while we pressed through.

I was astonished to see that, at such a late hour, the festive atmosphere, though quieter, had not completely died out. While we walked through the camp most people did double-takes when they saw the handsome young man who guided me.

Someone said, "Did you see that? That was Florica walking with that boy!"

And someone else said, "Was that Dika's girl?" There were several other variations on the same refrain.

"Ignore them," I said.

"Oh, I intend to."

We first went to the fire to find my father and brother, but they were not there. Several musicians still created their lovely music. Joyful, yet sorrowful, it wounded and consoled at once.

Djordji and I meandered our way to the perimeter and walked around it to Fonso's tent, guessing that's where we'd find Father and Theophilos. While we walked, the sound of the music receded to a whisper in the background. The crunching of leaves beneath our feet filled my ears, but

I thought I heard something else, too. Something in the low growing foliage at the edge of the clearing kept pace with us. Taking Djordji's hand, I pulled him to a stop. The sound continued for a couple of seconds, and then it stopped too.

"Did you hear that?" I asked.

"What?"

"We're being followed."

"By whom?"

"I think the proper question is, 'by what'?" I whispered.

"You, my friend, have a vivid imagination." Djordji resumed walking, drawing me along with him. I heard the sound again and tugged him to a stop.

"*You,* my friend, don't know what I have been through in recent days." There was a quiet rustling again and up ahead I saw a black form pass quickly through a gap in the shrubs.

"There!" I pointed. "Did you see that?" I shouted louder than I meant to. Adrenalin amplified my voice.

"Shhhh." Djordji touched his finger to my lips "I didn't see it, but I did hear the sound it made," he said. Frozen and mute with fear, our mouths dropped when the swift black shadow passed back the way it had come. I pointed and my heart raced.

"I see it," Djordji whispered in my ear, so close that his lips touched it, and shivers went down my neck.

The creature looked at us. Its eyes flashed when they reflected back the light of the lantern. I gasped.

"It's okay," Djordji said. "You are not alone." I turned and kissed him full on the mouth. He slipped his hand into my pants and took hold of what he found there. Unbuttoning his shirt, my fingers fumbled, when a voice called out.

"Yorgos, is that you?" It was my father. His intrusion destroyed the silence. The black cat ran off, blending into the shadows.

"Yes, Father." I turned to Djordji, kissed him on the cheek and ran to join Father and Theophilos in Fonso's tent.

I couldn't sleep. It wasn't the sound of Father's snoring that kept me up. My heart was too full. I had no idea what to make of it all. Forget, for a moment, that I was finally on my way to Mount Athos to give my heart, my love, my all, to God. That alone would be enough to keep me awake, I am sure of it. That wasn't it.

I had developed a crush on someone who did not run away from me when my attraction was revealed. In fact it was clear he felt the same way. *He.* I lay awake wondering if something was wrong with that. I had never seen a man who openly loved another man. The only couplings I had ever seen were men with women. *Are we the only two?* I wondered. If so, it seemed lucky that we should have found each other. As *my* luck would have it, however, there wasn't any room in the life of a monk for any type of coupling. Couples of any form do not exist in the world of Greek Orthodox monasticism.

I ached with fear and desire. Again, this alone would normally be enough to keep me awake from midnight to dawn, but there was more. Many of Djordji's words randomly intruded on my thoughts, echoing in my mind, 'deep sorrow,' 'unusual life line,' and 'temporary death.' None of it made much sense, but I must admit it scared me.

The scariest thing he said, however, was that God was calling me into the darkness. *What could that possibly mean?* I was going to Mount Athos, not into the heart of the pagan world. I couldn't fathom it, so I tried to hold on to the words he said about my finding love and purpose and being happy. I found his words of encouragement to be small, insignificant, and light. Too light to yield much peace.

Exasperated and tired, I rolled to my side and recited the Jesus Prayer over and over hoping that it would console me and help me go to sleep. It did neither. It only dulled the blade of fear that cut into my soul.

When the scent of breakfast wafted through the flaps of the tent, I rose. It was early. Even Fonso was still sleeping. Except for my shoes, I hadn't undressed for bed, so I was fully clothed in the previous day's attire. I considered going out like that, barefoot and all, but I thought of Djordji. I wanted to be presentable for him.

I opened my bag to riffle through it for something suitable to wear. Right on the top were my ikons. Remorse seared my heart. I hadn't prayed with them since the first day of our journey. I missed them. I missed spending time with them while contemplating the mysteries of faith. I missed the way they connected me so tangibly to God and the saints. I knew that I could, at that early and quiet hour, steal away to pray with them, and a part of me wanted to. I thought, again, of Djordji. I hoped he was already awake. I would always have the ikons. I wouldn't always have him. I lay them down next to me and selected my clothes for the day. Then I placed the ikons in my knapsack and pulled the drawstring closed over them.

When I exited the bender tent, it was dark out, but morning light was driving the night away. Most of the Gypsies were awake. Some of them were already tearing down the tents, others were serving breakfast. I headed to Dika and Djordji's tent and found that it had already been dismantled and their belongings packed on a couple of the small carts. I walked through the space between the tables looking for my friend. I couldn't find him. I worried, for a moment, that I wouldn't find him when a handsome young man who wore a cap smiled at me over his lifted cup of tea. I smiled back and looked away, still trying to locate Djordji.

"Yorgos, it's me!" I turned back to the young man who had greeted me so warmly. With a shrug he lifted the cap off his head.

"Djordji, your hair!" I exclaimed. He ran his fingers over his scalp as if in search of longer locks.

"Do you like it? he asked, wincing. "I hope you do, because my mother is furious."

"I love it." I said, taking my seat next to him. "You're very handsome."

"Then it is worth enduring her wrath." We sat together in sweetly awkward silence for a moment. "Go get your breakfast and some tea," he finally said.

When I returned, Dika was sitting with her son. She glowered at me.

"You are the one who has changed everything!" she accused, regarding me with a steel jaw. Her eyes flashed, mere slits, and went wide again. Instinctively I took hold of the eye-amulet, hanging from my neck, which Djordji gave me. He nodded with a sly smile, and Dika stared at her fingernails.

"No," I corrected. "Djordji did it. I just encouraged him to tell the truth."

"Hmm," said the woman. "Let me see your palm." Without hesitation I yielded my hand. "Hmm, yes," she said. "My son is right. Everything he told you is right." She held my hand, palm up, for several seconds, thinking. In light of my sleepless night I wasn't consoled by her words. "Yorgos," she said while laying my hand down on the table, "people do not want for a man to read their palms. They want for a woman. They *expect* a woman. Your encouragement has ruined everything until my son's hair grows back."

I screwed up my courage to speak to her plainly. "If Djordji is gifted with the *sight,* does it really matter if he dresses like a man or a woman? I think people want to go to someone who can really *see*. Why should it matter if they wear pants or a dress? Maybe if you stop hiding him behind face paint and long hair and put him out there, just as he is, even more people will come to see. Their curiosity about the man who is unusually gifted will bring them." Dika pressed her lips together for a moment, considering my words.

"Perhaps," she said simply. Her hard, cold countenance softened and then warmed. I saw that she was imagining the possibilities. She smiled, almost imperceptibly, and spit in my direction.

Fonso approached us with Father and Theophilos right behind.

"Djordji, Djordji, Djordji!" Fonso exclaimed. He ran to his great-grandson, quicker than you'd expect a man his age would be able to, and wrapped his arms around him from behind.

"I have missed you," he said loudly.

"Where is Florica?" Father asked, glaring at my new friend.

"She is gone, it seems," Dika answered.

"I have always been here Grandfather," Djordji said to Fonso while turning to embrace him.

After breakfast, Father drew me aside. "As long as we travel with the Gypsies, I want you to avoid that boy," he said, with no preamble to soften his words.

"Which boy?" I asked.

"You know the one. The one you have been with since the Gypsies arrived here last night."

"Father, he's my friend."

"Why make a friend you can not keep? Your friendship will be over when it's time to part ways." I looked my father in the eye. He looked away. "Please, just do what I ask.

There is something about that boy that doesn't sit right with me."

"I like him, Father. He's been kind to me."

"Yes, son. I know. That's what I'm afraid of."

I didn't avoid my new friend. I avoided being seen with him by Father. Though we never spoke of it again, Father made it difficult for Djordji and I to be alone, but we accepted the challenge and were creative in meeting it.

Fonso decided that when we reached Salonika, their destination, the bulk of the group would stay and a smaller party would take us by horseback the rest of the way to our destination. I was relieved when it was time to say good-bye. It was over. Father and I could relax and enjoy our last days together before we parted ways for only God knew how long.

Dika was the first to embrace me. In the brief time we spent together, she came to love me. Djordji was next in line. With Father glowering over Djordji's shoulder, we whispered our goodbyes.

"Yorgos, what can I do to compel you to stay with us?"

"There is nothing you can do that you haven't already done," I said. "God is jealous, and I love Him. I *want* to go to Mount Athos. If it wasn't for that, I would find a way to stay."

Dika and Fonso approached Father and Theophilos and, when they got their attention, walked them over to the horses. When Djordji and I saw that we were free of Father's watchful eye, we reached for each other's hands. Our fingers and thumbs, all twenty of them, tangled in a greedy mass. We wanted to exchange as much touch, affection, and love as we were able in our last few moments.

"I guess a mere Gypsy boy can't compare with the One who created the cosmos." When he put it that way I laughed.

"No. I think not," I said, smiling. "Djordji, thank you. I won't forget you."

"And how could I ever forget you? You have changed everything. My mother was right."

"No, you did it." We both shrugged. It was a silly thing to disagree about. I looked over Djordji's shoulder at Father and Theophilos. Fonso and a couple younger Gypsies were showing them how to saddle up the horses. I turned back to my friend with a sly smile touching my lips. I stepped on the tips of my toes to kiss him. He bent his neck, meeting me part way. It was a short kiss, but filled with passion. I walked to Father's horse without looking back. I climbed on behind him, and we were off.

9 Athos At Last

S etting foot on the sacred soil that I longed to walk on and one day be buried beneath proved to be far more difficult than I expected. Although Mount Athos is a peninsula and not an island, it is usually reached by water because travel by land to Mount Athos is prohibited. In an attempt to keep the masses away, an ancient law was established which forbids the building of a road 'upon which a wheel can turn' between the Athonite capitol of Karyes and the rest of the world. For that reason, the Gypsies took us to Xerxes Canal and could take us no farther. Father's resolve was firmly set by the difficulty. He gave me his solemn word, "Whether on the backs of mules, or in boats, whether by foot, sea, or land, I will get you there."

From Xerxes Canal we traveled by foot. By late afternoon, we made it to the tiny port town of Ouranopolis, on the mainland, where we found an inn to pass the night. Early the following morning, we split up. I went with Father to the administration building to secure the proper permissions and get the papers that we needed to travel to the Holy Mountain.

Theophilos set out to secure passage by boat to the port of Daphne on the Athonite peninsula, which was the official point of entry.

The representatives from Mount Athos stationed at Ouranopolis reminded us of what I recently learned, namely that in 1060 Emperor Constantine Monomahos established, in an official Chryssobul, several restrictions that pertained to the admittance of visitors to the Holy Mountain. It stipulated, among other things, that only males were permitted to enter. Overnight stays were forbidden to anyone who had not secured permission ahead of time, and boys younger than eighteen were not allowed to stay more than three nights. Clearly, I would be sent home.

Father fought for me. He argued with the officials, he begged for leniency, showing them a copy of the letter of recommendation written by Father Elias. In desperation, he even suggested that if someone would simply spend an hour talking with me they would see that I had a unique calling and must be granted special permission to stay.

When he encountered only the hard impermeable wall of rules, he told them of his fears. Evil incarnate, in an unknown stranger, invaded our home and tried to abscond with me. If only for the protection of my soul, and the preservation of my life, he argued, I must be allowed passage to the Holy Mountain. His plea was an urgent cry shouted to men who wouldn't hear.

While Father fought with the officials, I stood at his side until I couldn't take it any longer. I knew what was coming. *Why delay the inevitable? It will only make it worse.* I tried to persuade him that it was time for us to go home, I was ready. But he wouldn't have it. I feared he would stay and argue until he was escorted out, and I wanted to avoid the embarrassment of that. I turned to go to the marina and find Theophilos. I hoped that he would be able to convince Father that it was time for us to leave.

While I headed to the heavy wooden doors, a hieromonk entered through them, smiling at me. He was traditionally dressed in a plain black cassock that reached from his neck to the floor. On his head he wore a cylindrical skouphos, also black. In the crook of his arm he cradled a square-shaped bundle that was wrapped with a brown cloth.

Greeting him in the customary way, I bowed from the waist and touched the floor with the back of my right hand saying, "Father, bless." I straightened, presenting myself with my hands stacked, right over left, palms up.

"May the Lord bless you," he said, forming a Christogram with the fingers of his right hand in order to bless me in the name of Christ. He made the sign of the cross before placing his hand in mine. I kissed his hand, mindful that he touched the body of Christ every time he served the Holy Mysteries during Devine Liturgy. By kissing it I showed my respect to his priestly office and, indirectly, to Christ.

I continued on my way until prompted by a feeling to stop and turn back. Wearily I obeyed, afraid to get my hopes up. There was something about the hieromonk's warm and generous smile that caused me to halt and trust my intuition.

"Are you Master Yorgos?" he asked.

"Uh . . . Yes," I faltered. "I am."

"Your brother has been telling me all about you. I am most interested in speaking with you." I looked behind myself to where father pleaded with the officials.

"But–?"

"Come with me, my friend," he said. "Your father will be busy here for quite a while." I lingered for a moment to watch while Father tirelessly argued my case with the representatives from the Holy Mountain. I didn't know if I should laugh, cringe, or be embarrassed. The hieromonk only smiled and motioned the way with his right hand. His eyes were bright and clear. They were more lucid than any eyes I had ever seen. How could I say no? He led me down a dark hall and out a door to a small enclosed garden with a large cypress tree in the center of it. A stone bench was beneath the tree. The hieromonk sat down and patted it.

"Please have a seat," he said, and he placed his small square burden between us. "I am Hegumen Evangelos, the superior of Grigoriou monastery." For a moment his eyes were fixed elsewhere. I followed his gaze and saw only the bright blue of the sky framed by the four walls of the garden. He absently ran his fingers through his scraggly beard before reaching for my hand. It wasn't a traditionally formal shake. It was more of a warm familial clasp. He looked at me.

"You already know my name," I said unsure what else to offer.

"Yes. Tell me, son, who are you?" I squinted when I looked at him, unsure how else to answer than by giving my name. I shrugged.

"I'm named after Saint George," I offered.

The hieromonk only nodded saying, "I see . . . . Are you the elder son, or the younger son?"

I stammered, "Oh, uh, I . . . I . . . Theophilos is the eldest. I'm the middle child, really, only the twins come after me."

"I trust you know the parable of the prodigal son?"

"Yes, of course I do."

"Good. What I am asking you is this: which son from the parable are you more like? Don't tell me which one you think you should be, but which one are you really?"

"Are those my only two choices?" I asked, and he chuckled.

"Yes, son, for now. Which are you like? Take your time. Your father won't get anywhere with the administrators anytime soon."

I pondered his question. I didn't think I was either of them until I thought of how I was sometimes jealous of

Theophilos' easy relationship with Father. And sometimes I felt that Zosimos didn't take religion as seriously as I did. So I was jealous and proud. When I saw it clearly it made me feel ugly inside.

"Perhaps I'm like the older son," I said, looking at my feet.

"Are you positive?" I reflected more deeply. I thought of my shameful feelings for Djordji, the kisses we stole, and the fact that I wanted to do a lot more with him than that. I would have, too, if it weren't for Father.

"I think I might be a little of both, and also neither," I said. His eyes shined though his countenance hardened, to the point of seeming grave. His nod was nearly imperceptible.

"Yes. Most of us are both. Why do you think you are also neither?"

"I don't want to think I am better than my brothers, or be jealous of them. And I don't want to let sin get rooted in my heart either. I want to be a better person than that." He reflected on my words, lifted the cloth-wrapped bundle from the bench and placed it on his lap.

"Very well. What can you tell me about these?" When he unwrapped the bundle I saw that it was a stack of ikons. An ikon of the Crucifixion was on top. He invited me with a wave of the hand to take a closer look. I was surprised to see that it was an ikon I had painted. He lifted it from the top of the stack, gave it a good quick glance and moved it to the bottom. He repeated this until he had seen them all: the Good Shepherd, Saint George, and Theotokos with the Christ Child enthroned within her womb. They were all my work.

"Where did you get these?" I asked, gingerly reaching to touch them with the tips of my fingers.

"Your brother brought them to me saying that they were yours. When I asked him why he was giving me your private collection, he corrected me. He told me that these aren't merely the ikons that you pray with but that you wrote them. Is this true?"

"Yes," I whispered. "I painted them." I looked at my toes, afraid to make eye contact with the hegumen.

"I see." He quickly re-bundled my ikons and rose to his feet. He reached for me, saying only, "Come."

Hegumen Evangelos and I collected Father and we found Theophilos waiting for us at the marina. With him were a number of monks, all adorned in the ubiquitous black from head to foot, and four other plainly dressed men.

Theophilos decided to stay behind and wait for Father to return to Ouranopolis. I threw my arms around my oldest brother not wanting to release him to his own fate.

"I don't want to say good-bye, Theophilos," I said squeezing him. "I'm not ready. I don't know when I will see you again. I don't even know if I will ever see you again."

He squeezed me back and whispered into my ear, "Go with Father, Yorgos. Your future on Athos isn't yet secured, but there is nothing more I can do." He held me at arms length, gripping my shoulders with his hands.

"I love you, Yorgos. Go with the blessings of God."

The boat sailed all the way along the western side of the peninsula and around to its southeastern tip. The trip took several hours, during which Hegumen Evangelos explained that he went to Ouranopolis to pick up the four young men who aspired to become monks. He believed strongly that I should come with them too.

A small disagreement, which turned into a full-blown debate, broke out among him and a couple of the older monks. They reminded him that I was too young and accused him of breaking the ancient rules. Father and I sat in the center of the sailboat between Hegumen Evangelos, my advocate, and the others, listening to their debate.

Being so totally powerless unnerved me. Worse was to recognize that strangers would decide my fate.

Evangelos and the monks reached an agreement. The boat would stop at Grigoriou, but only to let off the aspirants and most of the monks. Father, Hegumen Evangelos and I, with the two monks who were sympathetic, would go on to the Great Lavra, where the head of all the monasteries on Mount Athos lived. He was called the Protos, a title meaning 'the first'. Evangelos would make his appeal to him directly.

With that decided, a hush settled and I was more able to focus on the beauty of the rough terrain while we sailed around it. Hidden within the landscape's nooks and crannies were ancient and majestic structures that seemed to grow out of the rocks themselves, just as the entire mountain peninsula rose, verdantly lush, out of the Aegean Sea. *No wonder they call this the Garden of Theotokos,* I mused.

It was late afternoon when the port of Great Lavra came into view. Ahead of us was a little structure that looked like a small, fortified castle, with a dock at the water's edge. It was the boathouse. *My journey is finally over,* I thought, while the monks docked the boat. *I'm here.*

The boat landed, the ropes were tied, and the two monks accompanying Evangelos helped him to the dock. Father insisted that I go next.

Hegumen Evangelos reached for me. When he helped me from the boat to the land, I faltered, but Father steadied me and gave my backside a push. I stumbled, but I didn't plunge into the water or strike the rocks because Father and the Hegumen were both here to guide me, one from behind me and the other in front. Together, they delivered me from one life into the next. My boyhood, my work at the inn, my responsibilities to my family and my fears about my emerging sexuality; all of it was behind me now. I was starting something new.

With my feet firmly planted on Mount Athos, I crossed myself and exhaled. I couldn't believe I was there.

The monks accompanying us relieved Father and me of our bags, and tried to relieve the Hegumen of his bundle of ikons. He wouldn't relinquish it. The way he held it close to his breast you'd think it was the infant Christ Himself. The Hegumen escorted us to a small unoccupied cell inside the boathouse where he instructed us to stay until summoned. After that he disappeared with his companions into the landscape.

Within minutes, a young monk–invariably dressed in black from head to foot–brought us the traditional tray of hospitality. It was laden with food and drink; ouzo, which I didn't like, water, with which I washed it down, fruit, bread and candies made of sesame seeds and honey called pasteli. Hungry from our journey, we consumed the food and waited.

The following morning the same young monk who brought us our food the day before came with another laden tray. Once we ate, he hurried us out of the boathouse, up and down windy and narrow trails, to a broad dirt road that was thickly lined with lush vegetation on both sides. Ahead of us was an immense structure resembling a small medieval town. Surrounded by a fortifying stone wall, complete with fifteen guard towers, the sight filled me with a dreadful sense of awe.

"The Great Lavra," he said, while we traveled to it down the road. He allowed the awe to settle before continuing.

"She was the first of twenty monasteries built on the peninsula and is considered the mother of all that came after." We continued our approach in silence.

When we passed through the entrance, it seemed our true journey had only just begun. Our guide led us down open-air corridors and through many verdant courtyards until we stood before the double doors of a cavernous room.

"This is where your fate will be decided," he said. "May Theotokos go with you and smile on you. Mount Athos is her garden. If she wishes it, you will be allowed to stay. Of that I am quite certain." While pulling the door open, he blessed us with the sign of the cross.

The room was awash with ethereal golden light, creating the illusion that we were entering a three-dimensional gilded ikon. Sconces holding lighted candles lined the four walls, illumining religious frescoes with a gentle radiance. A rectangular table ran along one wall, perhaps four feet from it. Along the center of the table, from end to end, a series of candles and clay oil lamps flickered and popped.

Thirteen monks and three hegumen, who visited Lavra from their own local monasteries, sat on the far side of the table, with their backs to the wall. All of them were dressed in the traditional black robes of an eastern monk. When Father and I stepped through the door, their quiet debate faltered. Seeing us, each monk and hegumen closed his mouth.

"Is this the young man in question?" Queried a solemn faced man who sat at the center of the table. I learned that he was the Protos.

Hegumen Evangelos ushered us in, saying, "Yes, yes, this is Yorgos and his father." The Protos waved us over, squinting at me.

I wasn't sure how to properly greet him, so I bowed quickly, sweeping my hand to the floor and asked for his blessing. He doled one out, regarding me closely. Then, reaching across the table, he cradled my face in his hands, and forced my mouth open with his fingers to peer into it. Angling my head just so, he examined my teeth and my tongue. I felt like a sheepdog. I didn't resist him, even

147

when he ran his fingers through my hair and tugged my head with it to the left and right. Satisfied, he slapped my cheek and sat back down.

"So, you are the young man from the mountains. Father Elias highly recommended you." He paused and stared at me for a moment as if he could see my future in the smoothness of my skin, or the pigment of my eyes. "Tell me, young man, why do you want so desperately to come to Mount Athos?"

"I am not desperate," I said. "I only know it is what I am meant to do. It is my Father who rushed here. It disappointed me to hear of your decision, but I am prepared to wait the four years that you require of me."

"Not just you," he corrected. "None may stay more than three days if they have not yet reached the age of eighteen."

"I understand," I answered. I expected that the audience with the Protos was over, but Father wasn't so ready to give up. He squared his shoulders.

"Please, Sir, if I may, my son is in grave danger. If you would only–" The Protos waved my father to silence.

"What is this danger that your father speaks of?" he asked, peering at me.

"A man–my father believes him to be a vrykolakas– came and stayed at our inn. He became interested in my . . . companionship." When I said the word 'vrykolakas' every monk and hegumen made the sign of the cross. A couple of them gasped, and all of them whispered private prayers.

"Your home must be cleansed," the Protos said. "Surely, if your home was clean, no such evil thing would have been able to enter it." The Protos looked directly and steadily at my father.

"Your local clergy will help you. But that changes nothing here." He directed his attention at me saying, "You are

148

to wait until you are eighteen. I will pen a letter for Father Elias. You will take it to him yourself. It will instruct him on what you must do to cleanse your heart and home, and how to prepare yourself for your future here. Seek his guidance." I nodded my acceptance of his decision.

"So that's it?" Father said, squaring his legs. "Even in such dire circumstances, you so easily turn my son away? Perhaps you should hand him over to the vrykolakas yourself."

When Father glared at the Protos I detected something more than anger in his voice. I could tell that his heart was cracking under the weight of his concern. A quiet murmuring rippled around the table.

"I do not turn your son away forever," the Protos interrupted. "Only until he reaches the proper age." Hegumen Evangelos came and stood beside me. His angular face was set like flint.

"Who is to say the proper time is not now? I see a light in this child that is most uncommon."

"Tell me, Hegumen," the Protos said, "who is this child that we should break the rules for him?"

"We break whatever rules we want, whenever it suits us," Evangelos answered. He took a deep breath, and his countenance softened. "He is, already, at such a tender age, a writer of ikons," he amended. He produced from a pocket in his robes the ikon of St. George that I painted from memory before Theophilos gave me the new one. He looked at it, kissed the image, and turned it over to the Protos.

"For your inspection," he said. The Protos held it before his eyes. A hush fell on the assembled men. Almost imperceptibly the hard lines of his countenance softened. Just as quickly he set his face again.

Without speaking the men passed ikon, from hand to hand, around the table. When he held it, each man made the sign of the cross. Most kissed it. Five recited the Our Father, or the Jesus Prayer, and three began to cry.

After a long period of silence, Hegumen Evangelos was the first to speak, "There are more of them tucked away in my cell. They are all made with the same skill and beauty. This child is gifted. He has been delivered into our hands. It is foolish to turn away such a gift because of our stringent formalities. We must receive him." All of the men entered into prayer while they sought answers to the questions raised by Evangelos.

At length the Protos crossed himself before addressing Father and me. "Please wait outside," he instructed.

We did as we were told. Prayerfully, I put my trust in God and Theotokos. If it were God's will, and if my presence in her garden pleased her, I knew Theotokos would permit me to stay. To me it was really as simple as that.

Father and I sat on the floor with our backs to the wall and I fell asleep with my head on his shoulder. When the double doors creaked open, I stirred and woke up. Hegumen Evangelos called us in. I took a deep breath and exhaled, hoping it would relax me. I set the pace, Father followed, and Evangelos accompanied us. We stopped at the center of the table, across from the Protos.

"He is too young," he said, looking at Father. "He is too young to begin the life of a monk."

"There is no other life for me," I said, and then I clapped my hand over my mouth. I had determined that I would receive news of their decision, which I was certain would not be in my favor, with dignity and respect. Turning his back on the men, Father tugged on my sleeve for me to follow him.

While we headed to the door, murmuring broke out among the men. It quickly became a muted squabble, until Hegumen Evangelos shouted over the din, "The decision was not unanimous," he said. "Many of the men along this table were in favor of your staying here. However, they are afraid to counter the Protos." Father and I stopped, but did not turn around.

"I am not afraid," Evangelos announced. "The boy will stay with me. I will share my quarters with him, if I must, until he is old enough to wear the cassock. He will be my servant and my student."

"There is no precedent for this," the Protos argued.

"Respectfully, Protos, I will set the precedent. That or I will leave Mount Athos. I will find a monastery elsewhere. One that will have the both of us." The Protos narrowed his eyes to slits and regarded the hegumen before his expression slacked.

"Very well," he answered. "The boy is your responsibility. His instruction and his life are in your hands."

"Yorgos. His name is Yorgos," corrected Evangelos. "The responsibility you have given me is a happy one."

Soon after, Father and I said our good-byes, and the Hegumen and I set sail for Grigoriou. Once there, Hegumen Evangelos showed me to the cell that would be our shared home for the next four years. It was barely large enough for even two small beds.

I couldn't sleep that first night. I was too excited by the unexpected and favorable turn of events. I had expected to be turned away. Theotokos must have indeed looked on me with favor.

Long after the hegumen went to sleep, I sat on the edge of the mattress provided by him. I was in deep contemplation, praying with the ikon Theophilos gave me, when the sound of it striking the hard floor jolted me awake. The Hegumen mumbled, while rolling over, his back now facing me. I retrieved the ikon and inspected it. It hadn't been damaged, thank God. I kissed the image, crossed myself, and placed it on the shelf along with the hegumen's ikons while extinguishing the light.

While I slid between the sheets, I became aware of an intruding presence in my mind, and a soft rhythmic vibrating filled my ears.

"The cat!" I exclaimed. Evangelos huffed and turned in his bed again, facing me. The sound didn't awaken him. I threw off the sheet and went to the window. Sure enough, there it was, outside the monastery's protective wall. Though I had never seen it before I left my home, it was fast becoming a fixture in my new life. I didn't know what to make of that.

The cat paced with its penetrating gaze fixed on me. It seemed as if intelligence greater than that of a beast directed it.

Evangelos stirred, stumbled to his feet and asked, "What is it?" rubbing his eyes.

"It's . . . it's a large black cat. It's been following me." I didn't turn away from the creature when I spoke of it; I merely pointed out the window and stared at it. It stopped pacing and stared back.

When Evangelos came up behind me the creature nodded once and dove into the dense ground cover. Evangelos peered over my shoulder to the spot where my gaze was fixed.

"Did you see it?" I asked, while wiping sweat from my forehead. I didn't realize how frightened I was until I spoke of it, or how much I hoped that Evangelos would say he had seen it too.

"It's your imagination, son," he answered. "Sleep now. The call of the symantron will wake us too soon, I'm afraid."

10 First Days

The next morning, the hegumen asked me to accompany him on a visit to an aged monk called Old Father Maximus.

I carried the man's piping hot breakfast with both my hands cupped around the bowl. The thick, nondescript porridge was so void of texture it didn't require teeth to be consumed.

"Old Father Maximus has seen many unusual things, the nature of which I cannot even begin to imagine," explained the hegumen. "I want you to tell him about the strange guest your family entertained just before you left to come here. Leave nothing out, not even the smallest detail, no matter how insignificant it may seem. He will know better than anyone what must be done to ensure your safety and prepare you for life here."

While we continued on our way, I made sure each of my steps were well placed and on even ground. I half-believed that the porridge I carried to Old Father Maximus was a sacrifice of grain meant to appease him before Evangelos asked him to perform a special ritual of protection over me. I was afraid I'd trip over a rock or even one of my own two feet, and spill the man's breakfast on the cold, hard dirt, and that my ineptitude would make him unhappy.

Evangelos stopped at Old Father Maximus' cell on the ground level of the dormitory. After a loud double knock, the hegumen pushed the door.

"Maximus?" he called out. Peeking in, I saw that the old man resembled a starved carrion bird. He sat in his chair propped up by pillows that kept him from leaning too far to one side or the other. A thick wool blanket covered him from the waist down. He was praying the rope.

I scanned the sparsely appointed room. Other than a magnificent and ornate domed-lidded trunk which seemed oddly out of place, the room had few furnishings; only a lumpy bed, a dresser, and a couple of chairs, including the one he occupied.

"Who have we here?" he asked, folding the black strand of knots into the palm of his hand. I tore my eyes away from the curious trunk and looked at my mentor.

"It's Evangelos. I've brought someone." Ushering me through the door with his palm flat on my back, Evangelos stopped before the old man to make the traditional greeting. Saying "Father Bless," he bowed low and offered the man his hands, right over left, palms up.

"May the Lord Bless you," Father Maximus said, making the sign of the cross and placing his right hand in Evangelos' palm. Evangelos kissed Maximus' hand before beginning his introductions.

"Father Maximus, meet Yorgos Godevenos."

"Hello," I said. When I offered him my hand, he didn't respond. I straightened my back. Evangelos and I waited quietly while Old Father Maximus squinted at me.

"He sounds like a young man," he said, glancing over my shoulder.

His eyes searched for me, and when they found me they were spikes nailing me to the place where I stood. "You are a little young yet to be with us, are you not?"

"Yes, Father," I answered. The man continued to scrutinize me, for a moment, before his rigid countenance softened.

"Looks may be deceiving," he added. I placed the bowl in his lap and plunged a spoon into the thick porridge. I turned taking my place beside Evangelos.

"Come here, young man," Father Maximus said. "Let me get a closer look at you." I squatted in front him so that our eyes were level with each other. He reached for my face and felt its contours with his fingertips and thumbs. When he was satisfied he cupped my head in his palms and pulled it closer to his eyes.

"Yes, one's looks never tell the whole story. Your wisdom exceeds your years, I think, but we will see about that." The hegumen took a step closer, to stand behind me.

"Yorgos, tell Maximus why you have come," he encouraged.

"I want to devote my life to God, that's why." I glanced over my shoulder and gave Evangelos a quizzical look.

"Yes, Yorgos. I am glad that is your primary reason, but I want you to tell Maximus what we discussed on our walk here. Tell him why your father defied the Protos and brought you here even though you are not old enough."

Maximus leaned forward in his chair and the bowl of porridge fell to the floor. "Yes, answer me that," he said, ignoring the mess at his feet.

"My family has an inn in the mountains. We had a guest; an artist from Romania called Mister Dumitru."

"A man from Romania? Hmmm." Old Father Maximus invited us to sit with a gesture. After bringing the only other chair I could find to the hegumen, I sat cross-legged on the floor in front of our host.

"My father fears that Mister Dumitru is a vrykolakas, and that he took a liking to me. That's why he brought me here. To keep me safe."

"What kind of vrykolakas did your father suspect this man of being?"

"I don't know, how can you tell the difference?"

"Tell me the rest of your story. Let's see if I can help you figure it out."

"He arrived just before dawn and was in a hurry to get inside and to bed. I really can't recall much else. It's a blur."

"Try and remember anything about the man that was out of the ordinary." My brow creased from the effort.

"He could lift things, things too heavy for a normal man to lift without help."

"You saw him do this?"

"Yes. He carried a box, a long narrow wooden box. It was big enough to fit a person. He asked me to bring four bags of soil from his wagon to his room. I thought that was strange." I glanced over my shoulder at the hegumen again. He appeared to be more upset by the details of my story than the older man did. Maximus merely pursed his lips and urged me to continue.

"I was curious about him, and I wanted to know what he kept in the box. When I sneaked into his room, it was unusually dark because he hung wool blankets over the windows."

"And the box?" asked Maximus. "What did he keep in the box?" I shuddered. My body remembered something that my mind did not. I wanted to leave it that way.

"I . . . I don't know." A creeping sense of fear came over me. I felt the emotion alone would animate my skin, that my skin itself would flee, if the rest of my body could not.

"Did you peek in the box?" he pressed. When I closed my eyes I could remember tiptoeing up to it. I could see my own hands reaching for the lid.

"No . . . . Yes . . . . I don't know. I don't remember." The truth was I *couldn't* remember. I couldn't have recalled it, even if I wanted to. I could recall everything up to reaching for the lid and nothing more.

"You must try." My face scrunched. My heart raced so quickly that it hurt. I covered it with my hand.

"Maximus, that's enough," Evangelos said. I was encouraged by his compassion to continue as best I could.

"That's all I can remember, except that in the middle of the night, a couple nights after Mister Dumitru arrived, I had a nightmare. In it, I saw my grandfather in his casket, and he turned into Mister Dumitru lying in that big box of his, looking very dead. He opened his eyes and I fell into them. I woke up after that, screaming in my bed. My whole family came to check on me. After I told them about my dream, we all ran to Mister Dumitru's room and discovered he had already left. That's why Father decided to bring me here; we headed out at once. He was afraid that Mister Dumitru would come back for me."

I opened my eyes and saw that Maximus had unfolded his prayer rope and was passing the knots through his fingers.

"Your father was wise to do that. The Garden of Theotokos is a holy place. You will be safe from Mister Dumitru here." Maximus pointed to his own heart and continued. "The evil that resides within is the evil that should concern you the most. The cunning of your own heart will do you more harm than that man, or any other, ever could. Here, your primary work will be to master your passions, to uproot and pull out any sin you discover lurking within yourself, no matter how gross or subtle."

"Okay," I said. "I want to do that. It sounds hard, but I am willing to do my best. I'm curious, did you figure out what kind of vrykolakas Mister Dumitru is?"

"Yes," he said without hesitation. "Undoubtedly he is one who drinks blood, but now that you are here, he will have to go somewhere else to find it."

The old man leaned so close that our foreheads touched. "You are safe," he said again. I sighed and the tension left my body.

"Okay. I'm safe," I repeated, believing it.

The old man straightened up and said, "Let us pray."

Evangelos placed both of his hands on my shoulders while Maximus made the sign of the cross on my forehead with his middle finger, fore-finger and thumb pressed together, saying, "Holy God, Holy Mighty, Holy Immortal, have mercy on this young man and preserve his soul from the evil one and all of his agents. Holy God, Holy Mighty, Holy Immortal." The three of us bowed our heads and said, "Amen."

"Thank you, Father," Evangelos said, while making his way to the door, where he waited for me.

I bent to the floor and scooped up the spilled porridge with my hands, returning it to the bowl saying, "Hegumen, may I speak alone with Father Maximus? I'll catch up with you." Evangelos nodded.

When he was gone I bent over Maximus' ear and whispered, "One more thing is bothering me, Father."

He closed his eyes. It was an attentive and prayerful expression. "Tell me, son, what is it?"

"I am being followed by a black cat." His eyes popped open, and they sparkled with unexpected mirth.

"Have you not noticed? Cats are everywhere here!" he chuckled softly. The sound was incongruous with his stark features.

"No. It's not one of these. It's huge. It followed me down the mountain from my village. I've seen it three times now.

Including once last night." The old man's eyes narrowed. He was silent for a moment.

"A dark spirit made flesh . . ." he whispered. "Have you told the hegumen about this?"

"Yes. Last night it was lurking outside his window. When he came to see it, it was gone. He thinks I am imagining it."

Father Maximus ran his prayer beads through his fingers and mouthed a prayer, his attention turned inward. Finally he nodded to himself and lifted his eyes.

"Our prayer has covered you," he said. He leaned forward and made the sign of the cross on my forehead again adding, "Peace, child. You are safe now. Go with the grace of God."

I thanked him and began to rise. He gripped my shoulders more firmly than I would have expected he could, and pulled me back down. I felt he was pressing his blessing into my body. "Peace," he repeated. He held my gaze without wavering. "If you should see the creature again let me know." He released me. "I am confident that you will be free of its menace now."

I nodded, without comment, and ran to catch up with Evangelos, cleaning the porridge off my hands with my shirt.

"Any man wishing to join a monastery must begin his vocation as a novice," Evangelos said. We had passed through the gate and traveled a short distance up the trail to an alcove made of whitewashed stone. The side walls and ceiling of the narrow structure were one continuous line that gradually curved up overhead, with built in benches opposite each other. On the back wall, exactly between the benches, hung an ikon of Theotokos framed in blue. "Though God's son, he learned obedience from the things he suffered." Evangelos quoted, asking, "Do you know what the word novice means?"

"No, not exactly," I answered.

"It means one 'under obedience.' In a sense, even the Lord himself was once a novice."

The idea that even Christ had to learn how to obey God made me smile. That I could learn from *His* example was all the encouragement I needed.

"It will be a few years until you can officially be made a novice yourself," Evangelos went on. "Until then, I will expect from you the same Christ-like obedience that I expect from any other man. Our way of life is not easy. We intentionally deprive ourselves for the sake of knowing God. Even though you are young, I will not make things easy for you. Do you understand what I am saying?"

With my elbows on my knees I made my hands into a double fist on which I rested my chin.

"Yes. I understand," I said. Lifting my chin from its resting place, I looked at him. "I can't say that I am not afraid, but I am ready."

At that he laughed and, feeling chagrined, I dropped my chin to my fist again.

"One is never truly ready, but one can always be willing." I nodded, feeling my chest expand and become hollow. It ached.

"I am willing."

"I know you are, son," he said mussing my hair. "I could see it the moment I met you. I want to make things clear from the start. You must be patient and trust my guidance. When I feel the time is right, I will invite you to officially join the monastery as a novice. There isn't an established ceremony for this. I will simply grant you permission to wear the inner cassock and the skouphos that mark you as one of us, and give you my blessing. Between now and then I don't want you to feel like an outsider. In my heart, I already feel you belong."

He lifted my chin with his finger. "Your day will come, son. You must be patient."

"I understand," I repeated. "So much has changed so quickly, I need some time to get used to it all."

"You've got all the time you need," he said with a wink. "You're still young."

"—That was the last time my village was ever troubled by the likes of him."

We were in the parlor where the men gathered after supper for conversation and fellowship. The structure was built on the cliff's edge, with the ocean raging far below. The plate of pasteli in the middle of the table was a welcome distraction. After unwrapping them, I shoved several pieces into my mouth, one after the other. With my cheeks plumped, and while the exchange of supernatural tales continued, I twisted my body around and placed my elbows on the sill of the window that ran the length of the room. Resting my chin on the bridge created by my interlocking fingers, I watched the slow approach of twilight through the glass.

"I've got a story," said a middle aged monk, named Christopheros. "When I was a boy, the sheep and goats of my entire village were devoured, one by one, by a pair of rogue vrykolakes. At first, only a couple were missing for the morning count. We thought we were dealing with a natural wolf. Over time, the creatures became more careless, leaving tracks that no mere animal could leave and killing more sheep and goats than they could possibly eat in a single night. Before too long, they killed them all. When the sheep and goats were all dead, they started to come after the people."

I turned around for a moment and listened to Christopheros thinking, *He has no idea what he's talking about.* It seemed he, like the man who spoke before him, was telling a tall tale, or something recited by rote. Their stories lacked a certain resonance that one who actually experienced such things would convey without effort. I lost interest and twisted back around so I could watch the sun follow its daily trajectory to the horizon.

"What did you do about it?" asked the monk with whom I shared the window bench. Watching their antics reflected in the glass amused me. I felt removed from the immediacy of the conversation and that suited me just fine.

"My father and uncle shot them with arrows. One each, straight through the heart, and they were done for."

"Well I've got both of you beat." Every monk and novice, except for Father Maximus and me, shifted toward the new speaker, a monk named Symion, indicating their readiness to hear the coming tale. Maximus lifted his hand.

"I've heard enough," he said with quiet authority. "Your village ran the blood-drinker off. Is that correct?" he asked the first speaker.

"Yes, Father." The man muttered. "The vermin wasn't welcome in our town." Maximus frowned.

"What was he vulnerable to? By what means did you drive him away?"

"Our numbers frightened him. The entire village–every man, woman and child–confronted the blood-thirsty bastard, and he fled."

"Your numbers. Hmmm? So the evil that menaced your community was permitted to continue to exist and harass another. Is that what you are telling me? Perhaps he even made more creatures like himself. Have you considered that? Who would take the blame?"

"I don't know exactly what happened. It was before I was born, to tell you the truth. It's a story that my grandfather told." Maximus pursed his lips while twisting his scraggly beard.

"I understand," he said. He turned to Christopheros. Though I'm sure he couldn't make out the details of his face it was clear that Maximus' vision did not depend on his eyes. He held Christopheros' attention without wavering.

"And you, brother, tell me, what were the arrows that killed the meat-eaters made of?"

"Bronze."

"Bronze?"

"Yes, Father. Bronze."

"One arrow each did the trick?"

"That's right."

"Your father and uncle must be expert marksmen." Maximus stood to address them all. I turned from his reflection in the rippled glass and looked at him.

"Stories like these should never be told for amusement's sake, but for instruction only. These creatures are damned. It is a pity that they went to their graves having turned their backs on God. Having done so, the grave has rejected them. If they had remained true to God to the end, they would be with him now in paradise. Let that be a warning to you all."

Turning full circle, Maximus directed his powers of perception at every man. His prayer rope was wound tight around the hand that clutched it. Seeing it, I reached into my pocket for my own and began to pass the knots through my forefinger and thumb while whispering the accompanying prayer.

Most of the men lowered their eyes. Maximus sat down.

"I know that your stories are not authentic," he said, turning to Christopheros.

"Bronze would scarcely have wounded a vrykolakas, be he a blood-drinker or a meat-eater. It certainly wouldn't be enough to kill one. Meat-eaters are vulnerable to weapons made of one thing, silver." He turned to the first monk.

"A crowd of ten thousand wouldn't be enough to scare away a blood-drinker unless they knew how to arm themselves. A stake right through the heart would have immobilized him, but there is only one thing to which a blood-drinker is vulnerable unto death."

The man shook in his seat. "What is it, Father?" he asked. I shook too.

"Sunlight," I whispered, with my eyes fixed on my prayer rope. Surprised by the sound of my own voice I flinched. I looked up and repeated myself with more conviction. "A blood-drinking vrykolakas is vulnerable to sunlight. They are nocturnal. Sunlight weakens them."

Maximus nodded, gravely saying, "Yes, and fire reduces them to ash."

The men began to murmur, asking questions like, "How could one so young know that?" and "Isn't he only fifteen?" Maximus interrupted them.

"Listen to this young man. He knows. They cannot sustain the light."

When I realized I made myself the center of attention I looked past the prayer rope that hung from my hand between my knees, to stare at my feet.

"Yorgos, would you share your story with us so that these men can learn the difference between fact and tall tales?"

I shook my head saying, "No, Father. Please don't ask me to do that."

"Very well," he said. "I will share my own. Many years ago . . . ." Every man in the sitting room turned to face the Father, except for me. I had heard enough. I rose to my feet and started for the door.

"When I was younger even than young Yorgos . . . ." I lingered in the threshold for a moment, listening. "My village became a hotbed of devilish activity . . . ." Caught between curiosity and dread, I was certain of one thing. I wanted to forget about my experience with the dark man, Mister Dumitru, to put it far behind me and start my new monastic life. I crossed the threshold but lingered on the other side while he continued to spin his dark tale.

"Supernatural beings of every imaginable kind were drawn there, to wreak their unholy havoc. After much deliberation, and when no one would come forward to volunteer, I was one of three chosen by lot to deal with the problem. I was the only one to survive the first year. By the grace of God, and by trial and error, I learned how to fight them and how to win. The hardest thing I've ever done was stake my own brother and burn him alive. I learned from his screams that even creatures such as he deserve one last mercy. From then on, I have ordered every vrykolakas I have captured, whether by silver or stake, to be drawn and quartered. Such a death is instant, but the magic that fixes the blood-drinker to the world of the living is especially insidious. Unless they are burned to ash, blood-drinkers will return."

I decided I had indeed heard enough. I came to Mount Athos to learn how to love and serve God, and to escape the darkness of the world. How to destroy a vrykolakas was not something I wanted to learn.

I ran down the stairs, with my prayer rope folded into my palm. I was glad that the sun had not yet plunged below the horizon. That meant the only point of passage between the outside world and Grigoriou would still be open. I needed to walk, pray, and sort my thoughts. The space between the four walls that encompassed the monastery was not expansive enough.

I sprinted out the gate, through the neighboring olive orchard, and to the footpaths that went along the cliffs. Halfway to the cliff's edge I slowed to a walk and unfolded the rope. I passed the knots through my fingers while I recited the Jesus prayer aloud, "Lord Jesus Christ, son of God, have mercy on me, a sinner." I decided I was done thinking about Mister Dumitru or being afraid of him. He was long gone now, and I was safe. In fact, I believed there could not be a safer place than where I was, and that gave me a deep feeling of relief. I felt as if God himself lifted the burden of fear from my shoulders and threw it into the sea. I raised my arms and spun in a circle three times, giddy in the lightness of being He granted.

Night was falling on the Garden of Theotokos. It was time for me to return to the protective walls of the monastery.

Enough sunlight lingered that I didn't feel the need to rush. I strolled back the way I had come, kicking stones out of my way and humming.

While I progressed along the path, something rustled behind me. I turned and saw nothing. I laughed out loud, amused by my own fear and determined that I wouldn't allow the peace I now possessed to be snatched away so soon by an imagined stalker.

A fist-sized stone lay on the ground ahead of me. I skipped up to it and sent it flying with a kiss from my toes. Again, I heard something behind me. I turned and saw a shadow pass. Another sound echoed, this time in the path ahead. Fear encroached on me again. I knew what it was. The cat had returned. Apparently, I surmised, there was more to be done before I was rid of this particular menace.

Careful not to trip, I made my way along the path while glancing over my shoulder. I tried to keep aware of anything that might approach me from any direction. Behind me, the shadow crossed the trail again. This time it was accompanied by a low throaty rumble. Ahead of me, I heard another animal pass through the bushes. I was being surrounded. *Is there more than one large black cat now?* I wondered.

I turned and looked behind myself and saw it. A barely discernible shape charged me. I screamed and protected my face with the backs of my hands. Through my laced fingers I saw it leap. I dropped to the ground and the beast jumped over me. I rolled in the dirt and scrambled up to my knees. It tackled a wild boar only a meter from where I fell. I watched while it ripped into the animal's throat with its claws and teeth. For a moment I froze, but my reason prevailed and I ran, stumbling up to the gate. The cat abandoned its kill and followed me from a distance. I watched it through the narrowing gap while the gate closed. I had the distinct feeling that it was pleased that I was safe. I decided, then and there, that I would not tell Maximus that I saw the cat again. It no longer scared me.

Nearly every night, I found the creature pacing and keeping watch outside my window or following me if I walked the trails just before dusk. For the longest time, I was the only one to ever see it. It possessed the uncanny ability to avoid being seen by anyone else, but I came to prefer it that way.

11 Word From Home

Mother had a desk in the corner of the common room where she composed letters to family and friends who lived far away. Some were in Thrace, where she was born, and others were in cities along the coast. One of her brothers moved as far away as Athens.

I used to watch her at her desk and feel jealous of those to whom she wrote. It seemed she was giving them a part of herself that she would never have reason to give to me. Well, I didn't have a reason to be jealous anymore. In August, a little more than three months after I fled the village, Evangelos came alongside me while we filed into the refectory for supper. He had a gleam in his eyes and an envelope in his hands.

"This came for you," he said, handing it to me. I recognized Mother's handwriting. 'Grigoriou' was written on it in big letters with my name, in smaller letters, underneath it.

"Who brought it?" I asked, looking around to see if I could spot the messenger.

"A friend of your village priest, Father Elias, is on retreat here. He delivered it to me. I know you've been feeling homesick. Perhaps this will help." He smiled and left me to read in peace.

I thanked him and tore the envelope open. Hearing Mother's voice in my mind, I devoured the letter like it was a piece of her spanakopita:

May 3, 1633

Yorgos, my dear son, my little monk,

Greetings from home! I have great news: Uncle Petros and Aunt Petra are engaged! Once they are married they will be moving out of the inn into their own home. I will certainly miss having their help around the house and inn, but I am equally happy for them as they start a new life together. With all of the vacant rooms, we can receive more guests! I wish you could be here on their happy day.

Everyone else is doing well. Zosimos has been sick but is holding on, as he always does. Zoe-Sophia is growing up nicely. I took her rag-doll away from her and hid it. I fear that she will never forgive me, but she is getting old enough to attract attention. No man wants to marry a woman who carries a doll around by its tiny hand. She will forgive me, won't she?

Well, I must be off. There are always chores to be done around here, as I am sure you remember quite well.

Please, my son, know that I love you. Never forget it.

Mother.

PART TWO:
OF MONKS & MEN

12 The Daily Routine

It was made clear from the start: I would not become a monk before I turned eighteen. I had three years to wait, but I would not be allowed to wait passively. Hegumen Evangelos saw to it that I was kept *very* busy.

In addition to keeping the Divine Services and a stringent rule of private prayer, I was assigned work in the kitchen. From there, my duties expanded to working in the garden and with the livestock. During this time, and throughout my first six months on Mount Athos, the closest I came to painting ikons was when I fed and cared for the chickens.

Daily, I delivered fresh eggs to the ikon studios, lingering for as long as they'd allow. My heart swelled with longing, as one's heart might who was allowed to stand in proximity to the one he loved, but never to touch, or to speak, to or to otherwise directly acknowledge him. It was excruciating.

After a number of months, Hegumen Evangelos recognized my heart sickness. He knew the remedy. I was relieved of my duties in the kitchen and reassigned to the ikon studios. However, the chickens and the garden were still my responsibility.

In the studios, I was told to observe. I wasn't permitted to touch anything. This lasted several weeks. Finally, I was allowed to clean the brushes and anything else dirtied by the ikonographers. I was surrounded by easels, paints,

brushes, and ikons in various stages of completion; all I
was permitted to do was menial labor! I was so very close
to the thing I loved the most, but not close enough. How
I longed to join my brothers and set brush to the wood. It
was like being invited into the banquet hall but not being
allowed to eat.

One morning after the services, Evangelos asked to
meet alone with him in one of the studios. When I entered,
I saw at once that he was holding one of my ikons. The rest
of them were stacked on the table by his elbow. Each one
was wrapped with a soft, protective cloth.

"It is time you learned to prepare the ikon boards," he
said. "This is an important task for a writer of our sacred
images. Without a properly prepared ikon board, one cannot properly write an ikon." I nodded, saying nothing.
Evangelos handed me an ikon of Saint George that I had
painted.

"Your attention to detail is impressive, particularly
here." He pointed to Saint George's tiny eyes. "Amazingly,
there is depth and life in the eyes. But, look at this! The
wood is too rough. All of the imperfections show through. It
nearly ruins your work." With his index finger he indicated
several rough spots and a subtle knot in the surface of the
wood. "While there *is* life in the image that the imperfections cannot touch, the fact that you have been especially
gifted can only take you so far. It is time to add skill to your
gifting. Are you ready?"

"I've been ready since the day I arrived," I said. A slight
smile curled his lips.

"Very well, then. Let us get started." His smile broad-
ened. He set Saint George on top of the stack and pushed
the stack aside to the corner of the table. He stood and
indicated that I should follow him to a workbench where
unfinished ikon boards of various sizes were set in several

stacks and pushed flush against the wall. On the surface of the workbench were various tools and pots of thick liquid I couldn't yet identify. He lifted one of the boards from the top of a stack and ran his fingers along the edges and the surface, indicating that I should follow his example. The wood was rough.

"This is a lot like the wood you found and used at home, is it not?"

"Yes. I made do with whatever I had at hand. I didn't have all the proper—"

"There is no need to make explanations or apologize, son. I know you did your best with what you had. You now have more resources at your fingertips than you know. You can finally perfect the gift that God has given you."

"I am ready for that," I enthused.

"Fine." He pointed to several items on the workbench and named them. Among them were gesso, linen, and a wood scraper. He pointed to a pot of thick bubbling liquid that boiled over a fire. "Rabbit skin glue," he said. Indicating the stacks of ikon boards he continued, "These panels have been cut for us and all the materials have been mixed. Later you will learn to do everything yourself. Now, let's start with teaching you to prepare the surface of the wood."

I learned that preparing the wood to receive the paint is an exacting task, more so than I would have guessed. Each panel takes days to prepare. Ikon painting is an act of prayer and an exercise in patience. I learned how to properly adhere the linen to the wood with the heated rabbit skin glue, making sure that the glue was applied evenly, without air bubbles.

While he demonstrated how to do this, Hegumen Evangelos taught me its deeper significance.

"Every detail of an ikon has meaning. The linen," he said, lifting a piece of it from the table, "reminds us of the shroud our blessed savior was wrapped in for burial. Meditate on his suffering and his death when you apply it to the wood." I nodded with all the solemnity the lesson required.

"And the wood reminds us of the cross our blessed savior was nailed to." When he said that, we both crossed ourselves. "I see that you understand that every seemingly mundane detail has meaning and is significant."

"I do," I answered.

"Yes. I could see that about you. That is why I fought for you to stay."

I learned my lessons quickly. For example, the linen must be allowed to dry completely. After that, the gesso is applied in layers. Each layer must cure, dry, and be sanded before the next is added. When enough layers have been applied and the surface of the blank ikon is thoroughly dry, it is sanded smooth with the wood scraper one last time.

Sometimes as few as four or five layers of gesso will be enough. In the course of my studies, and by trial and error, I learned that each piece is unique unto itself. I've prepared some panels that required ten or more layers to achieve the desired smoothness. Once the surface is prepared to our exacting standards, the panel is ready to receive the sacred image.

For several days, Hegumen Evangelos repeated the lesson and expounded upon it, until I learned the basics. Within no time, in addition to preparing the surface of the panels, I was cutting wood, preparing gesso from scratch, and making the rabbit skin glue. For the next year and a half, that was my sole purview, as far as writing ikons was concerned. Every day, after I was finished with the chickens and my work in the garden, I retired to the studio to focus on my real work: namely preparing the panels for the monks who painstakingly applied the images of Jesus, Theotokos, and the Saints. How I longed to be allowed to touch the brushes and the paint.

"All in good time," Hegumen Evangelos would say. And I had learned, on my first day, that I could trust him.

When, a year and a half later, Evangelos finally allowed me to set the brush to the wood, I feared that I would discover that my talent, or rather my gift, had left me due to neglect. With trepidation, I lifted the pigment-soaked brush to the panel for the first time since my arrival on Mount Athos. To my relief I found I could still write the images. Writing my first ikons felt like throwing light on some dim, dark, forgotten corner of my soul. I felt more like myself than perhaps I ever had. However, I wasn't let loose in the ikon studio. Further instruction was required.

Evangelos selected two seasoned ikon writers to continue my lessons: Brother Christopheros and Brother Yannis. Daily, between the sixth and ninth hours, according to the schedule of the Divine Services, I was required to report to the studio to work under the tutelage of one or both of the masters.

The focus of their instruction was first and foremost that I approach the task of rendering the sacred images prayerfully. That had been my habit from day one, as they quickly discerned. Secondly, I was expected to learn the established canons, or rules, that pertained to how to write an ikon. That included learning and mastering the proper form, proportion, and color of the sacred images. I was encouraged to learn by heart the meaning of their symbolic language and how to represent it in my own work.

Once they were satisfied that I understood what was expected of me, my instructors gave me the task of copying, without error, ikons they painted. This continued until *I* began to recognize and correct *their* mistakes. This happened in the third week of my instruction.

In the years that I taught myself, I may not have had the knowledge, skills or tools necessary to properly prepare the panels, and I may not have had a full palette of colors available to me, especially the ubiquitous gold leaf, but I did have plenty of love for the medium and an abundance of time to practice.

It turns out that I spent so many uncounted hours praying with and copying the ikons that Mother supplied me with, I unwittingly internalized them. My tutors believed that I had accidentally stumbled on some of the proper techniques. Evangelos knew that it was providential and that my understanding of the symbolism was intuitive.

"Your hands, your eyes and your heart are blessed," he said.

It reminded me of the words of encouragement that Nona had given me so many years before when I showed her the copy of Christ Emmanuel I made for Papus.

So, only months after my seventeenth birthday, at least half a year before I expected to become an official novice, Evangelos entrusted me with the task of teaching monks and novices how to write an ikon.

Wakened by the symantron, I found the floor with my toes, sat up in my cot, and rubbed my sleep-encrusted eyes. I blinked, trying to adjust to the light of the oil lamp that was already lit.

Evangelos knelt in prayer with his elbows on the mattress of his bed. I crossed myself and was about to kneel beside him when he pushed against the mattress to stand up. He smiled while taking a seat across from me.

"I think it is time for you to move to your own cell. We've shared my cell years longer than we should have, I think."

"No," I countered. "I've been happy here."

"Yes, it has been too long. Every monk needs his own space to pray and practice solitude. I am afraid as long as we continue to share this tiny space—"

"You won't have the privacy you need," I guessed. "I'm sorry."

"No, son, I am thinking of you. Like I said, every monk needs his own space." While he spoke, Evangelos went to his dresser and retrieved a garment and a skouphos from it.

"These are for you." He placed the skouphos on the top of my head, while handing me the garment saying, "The inner-cassock." I stood and shook it out, holding the shoulders of the inner-cassock up to my own. It unfurled and reached to the floor. "If I were one to follow the letter of the law, you would still have to wait another six months, but I feel you are ready. You have been under obedience from the first day. You have earned it."

I hugged the inner-cassock up to myself the way I imagined a bride-to-be would hug her wedding dress. I had anticipated this moment, but now here, it felt surreal. I wished the Hegumen would pinch me to prove that I wasn't dreaming. I nearly asked him to.

"Yorgos, I must ask, do you still wish to become a novice?" Tears collected in the corners of my eyes and I blinked them away.

"Yes. Absolutely." I answered, when I could speak.

"Very well. You are now *officially* one under obedience. Now you will be clothed in the inner-cassock and wear the skouphos on your head. I don't expect much else to change."

"No, Hegumen. I will obey you, as I always have." Evangelos smiled broadly.

"These are the first two parts of the habit you will be permitted to wear," he explained. After your novitiate, you will pass through the three progressive monastic ranks: the

Rassaphore, the Stravaphore, and the Great Schema. Each of these represents an increased level of asceticism. With each successive rank, you will receive another part of the habit until you are fully vested. The process of becoming a monk is intentionally slow, but I am keeping in mind that you have been here for nearly four years already. If you continue on the path as you have been, you will progress to the first rank within the year, assuming that is what you choose when the time comes."

"I won't change my mind, if that is what you are asking."

"No, I don't expect that you will."

February 20, 1637

Yorgos, my dear son, my little monk,

Greetings from home! I hope my letter reaches you on, or before, your Name Day. Please know that you are always in my thoughts and prayers, and will be especially so on your special day. I want you to know how proud of you I am. It pleases me immensely to hear that you have become a novice.

I have a couple bits of news. First: Uncle Petros and Aunt Petra are already expecting their second child. Can you believe it? It seems like little Titus was born yesterday. I can't believe they've been married for three years. Where does the time go? It feels like ages and ages have passed since I've seen you, even though you've only been gone a year longer than they've been married. Perception is a funny thing.

We are all excited about the baby, but I am also saddened, because it means that Yaya will be leaving the inn to help my sister with her ever-growing brood.

However, I no longer need your Yaya, as I once did. While Petra's brood is getting larger, mine is getting smaller. This brings me to my second bit of news:

It is your sister's turn to get married! She recently turned the head of a wealthy guest who was traveling from Salonika. He is a kind man. I expect that with this marriage in place, your sister will have a good life and will want for nothing. Don't worry about her.

The courtship has been fast. They only met six weeks ago and the wedding is this Saturday. Of course, by the time that you read this, the day will have passed.

After the wedding, your sister will be moving to Salonika, to start her married life. If I thought there was a chance that you could come be with us, I would have notified you much sooner, but I know it is not easy for you to get away. Besides, I have been so overwhelmed with preparations. Please forgive me for not telling you sooner.

That leaves only your brothers at home. Theophilos is working as hard as ever in the fields. We still take guests, but not as many as we did when I had more help.

And Zosimos. What can I say about Zosimos? He is still sick, though for the time being, his health has stabilized. The village healer believes he will be with us yet a while longer. Your brother is determined as ever to be well. I think it is his determination as much as any prayers that have been said on his behalf that has kept him alive. I think he might outlive us all! Please know this, dear son, before I sign my name—we are all happy. I wish for you the same. Be happy.

Love, Mother.

Your sister would like to add her own greeting:

Yorgos, I miss you.

I hate that I can hardly remember what you look like. If it weren't for the portrait of you that was made when you were a boy, I would have forgotten entirely. You were young then, and now you are a man. I hate that I don't know what your voice sounds like either. You are living the life that you wanted, and for that I am glad.

Can you believe I am getting married!?! I must confess, I am a little scared. It has all happened so quickly, and I fear I hardly know my husband-to-be. Father assures me that he is a good man, and I trust that he is. Since the day we met, he has always been kind and good. He has already given Mother and Father the dowry, so what more can I say?

I have one request, brother. Please paint for me an ikon of your patron saint. I will consider it a wedding present, though of course I don't expect it to arrive on time. It would mean the world to me, to have an ikon of Saint George, painted by your own hand. I still remember fondly the night you told the whole family the story of your Saint. You told it with such vivid detail, how could I ever forget it?

I love you, my brother, and because I know you will do as I have asked, I will thank you in advance.

Always, your sister,

Zoe-Sophia.

13 A Day Like Any Other

1637, The Feast of Saint George, Mount Athos, Greece

At four in the morning, the repetitive beating of the symantron awakened me. Though it was my Name Day, I didn't expect it to be different than any other day. A few well wishers might think to greet me accordingly, but I didn't expect anything more than that. I didn't need to single out this day, or any other, as a special day of observance. My Name Day would be like all the days that came before, and all the days that would come after: I would do my chores, say my prayers and spend hours writing ikons. The day would be a perfect blending of the sacred and mundane, just like any other day.

Raised by the symantron, I greeted the Lord by making the sign of the cross. After throwing on my cassock and skouphos, I shuffled from my cell to the Katholikon for the service, struggling to wake up.

The aroma of frankincense mixed with essential oils swirled around my head and clung to my clothes, reminding me that the space I entered was holy. The fragrant smoke represented our prayers going up to God and the pleasure they gave him.

While I made my way through the sweetly pungent haze, I closed my eyes and rubbed away the residue of sleep. Waiting in line to kiss the ikon of Saint George, I crossed myself and whispered, "In the name of the Father, and of the Son, and of the Holy Spirit."

When I opened my eyes they were still bleary from sleep, and from being rubbed, and because the light in the Katholikon was dim. But there, kneeling before me, I saw with increasing clarity, a young man I had never seen before. He venerated the ikon of Saint George with his unruly hair cascading like water to the rocks of his shoulders. Dressed in ordinary clothing, he was either a visitor or an aspiring novice. Clothed or not, he was Michelangelo's David; rendered not in stone, but flesh and blood.

His posture exuded penitence. His puffy eyes, though open, were turned inward. With a tortured expression and tear-lined cheeks, he was clearly troubled by some private torment. Making the sign of the cross, he murmured. I recognized the words of the Jesus Prayer while he formed them with his lips. After a long moment, he stood to light a candle which he placed in front of the likeness of Saint George. With his head bowed and eyes closed, he didn't move for several breaths. Returning suddenly to the present time and place, he blushed, wiped his tears and turned to greet me. His smile, at first, was false. I don't mean to say it was dishonest; he merely wanted to keep his grief and pain private.

When we looked into each other's eyes, something happened; a sort of emotional transmutation. His false smile became real and my pulse quickened. We were meant to meet, I could feel it. In that briefest of moments, our hearts were knitted together by the threads of faith, hope, and love.

When I remembered that other men were waiting to venerate the ikon, I motioned with my head that he move on. He smiled, shrugged, turned and walked away. When I knelt before the ikon I crossed myself, and implored the saint to pray for me.

"Help me slay the dragon of this desire," I prayed. "Give me strength, and courage." I held myself still before my namesake's stylized likeness. How I hoped to find that, like Saint George, I had the grace of God to do what must be done; only I wasn't sure what that was. Resolving that I would not be swayed by temptations of the flesh, I rose to my feet, crossed myself again, and went to the sanctuary.

Footsteps came to a stop behind me, to my right.

"Constantine," the young man whispered. I ignored his impertinence, and he leaned closer to my ear. "That's my name, Constantine," he whispered again. "My friends call me Tino." I gave him a curt nod, looking straight ahead. Externally, I made every effort to appear unaffected. I came to worship God, after all. Inside however, the sound of his voice chipped away at my recently set resolve. I feared that I would be defeated even before I put up a fight.

I turned my head to acknowledge him and couldn't help but smile. I stepped aside and saw, from the corner of my eye, that he smiled too.

During the service I couldn't focus on the chants and prayers. I wrestled with my own temptations. Accordingly, I eschewed the formal written prayers, and improvised my own entreaties.

The intense desire I felt for Constantine surprised me. In my first months on Mount Athos, I told Evangelos about the gypsy boy, Djordji. He called it a temptation, pure and simple, sent to distract me from my life's true purpose. Under Evangelos' guidance, I determined, in my earliest days on the Holy Mountain, not to let anything else distract me from my call or my love for God. I feared that meeting Constantine was the first real test of that determination. I didn't think I was ready.

I crossed myself and inched farther away from Constantine. Gazing at the ikonostasis, I meditated on image of Theotokos holding the infant Christ. Careful not to glance temptation's way, I prayed that Theotokos would hold me, and that the Lord would preserve in me the innocence of a child.

When the service ended, I hurried to the refectory for the day's first meal. Constantine followed close behind. I harrumphed, feeling that I had been found by a stray dog that I couldn't shake. He sat next to me at the table.

"You didn't tell me your name," he whispered, leaning in. I cocked my head to the brother at the lectern who read the story of Saint George while everyone else ate. I listened with an intensity that suggested I had never heard the story before.

"Your name?" he persisted. The sound of Constantine's voice further chipped at my resolve.

"Yorgos," I said evenly, without looking at him.

"Happy Name Day," he enthused. "Saint George is my favorite saint. I look to him for strength. I have dragons of my own I wish to slay. His example gives me hope."

Taken aback, I stared at him. "Me too."

Someone cleared his throat. Looking up and down the long table, I spotted the Hegumen leaning forward, and eyeing us, with a silencing expression. I looked down at my plate, and held my gaze there, without speaking another word, until breakfast was over.

When I finished eating, I stiffly pushed myself from the table. I went to the kitchen to collect buckets of food and water for the chickens and carried them to the coop.

I hoped to dodge Constantine and begin the day's work uninterrupted. While I passed through the doors, Hegumen Evangelos walked up along my left side and Constantine trailed behind and to the right.

"I see you two have met," Evangelos said, without inflection.

"Yes," Constantine answered, before I had a chance. He hurried along, skipping playfully, to catch up and take his place at my right. "I was telling Yorgos that I closely identify with his patron saint. I find encouragement from his story."

"I heard," Evangelos huffed. "Typically, aside from the reading from the lectern, our mealtimes are silent affairs," he explained.

"I . . . I'm sorry," Constantine said. "Forgive me."

Evangelos chuckled, saying, "Lighten up, brother, I appreciate your enthusiasm." Chagrined, Constantine laughed as well.

With temptation on my right and my confessor on my left, I wasn't sure how to proceed. I felt instinctively that I needed to avoid spending inordinate amounts of time alone with Constantine. I made that mistake with Djordji and almost gave myself over to sin. I wanted to avoid making that mistake again.

"Yorgos, you seem troubled," Evangelos said. His voice pierced through the cloud of fear and self-recrimination enshrouding me.

"Not at all. I was remembering the last time I celebrated my Name Day with my family." It was only half a lie I told my confessor. That day was always in the back of my mind, especially on its anniversary.

"I left my home to come here early in the morning the day after the feast, exactly five years ago," I added, for Constantine's benefit. "I miss them."

"Do you regret leaving them?" Constantine asked.

"No. Only . . . I miss my mother. I miss her most of all."

"Look to Theotokos," Hegumen Evangelos advised. "She will never replace the one who gave birth to you, but she can nurture your soul like no other." Constantine threw his arm around my waist, and kept a locked-step pace with me.

Water jostled from the pail, splashing us both. His attention awakened something deeper inside me.

"Yes. We are standing in the midst of her garden after all," Constantine whispered into my ear, while relieving me of the pail of water. We stumbled along, joined at the proverbial hip, until I shrugged to break free of his embrace. I rushed ahead and tried to keep my distance.

"Yorgos, speaking of the garden, I would like you to show Constantine around. Take him with you. Introduce him to all the others. Make him feel welcome. Can you do this for me?"

"Of course," I said, swallowing my complaints.

Constantine followed me to the chicken coop where I explained that hens and momma cats were the only female animals encouraged to thrive on the Holy Mountain.

"Why is that?" he asked, while I dumped the food scraps from breakfast into a bowl on the ground. He followed my lead and poured the water into the trough.

"We need the cats to kill the rats, mice and snakes," I answered. "And we need the hens for their eggs."

"That makes sense," he said. "I think it's strange that there haven't been any women here since, what was it, the ninth century?

"No. According to the story, when they were on their way to Joppa to visit Lazarus, stormy weather forced Theotokos and Saint John to drop their anchor here. Theotokos was so struck by the peninsula's rugged beauty that she asked Christ to give it to her. It is said that she heard a voice from heaven say, 'Let this place be your inheritance, and your garden, a paradise and a safe haven for those seeking to be saved.' And no other woman has been allowed here since, only the mother of Christ. So it's been well over fifteen hundred years."

"Wow," he said. "I wonder if any other place in the world can make the same claim."

"Probably not."

"Well I certainly won't be missing my sisters. They're always such nags."

I chortled. "I don't think women are kept out so we can avoid being nagged. I think it's to keep temptation and distraction away." I thought it ironic that the same rule that drove temptation from most of my brothers brought it to my doorstep.

"Evangelos tells me that you are an expert ikon painter. Is that true?"

"Hardly," I answered. "Anyone who thinks himself an expert is a fool and full of his own self-importance."

"Well that's what he said. He called you a prodigy."

"Well, I'm not."

"I've always wished I could learn to paint an ikon. If I received praise like that I wouldn't be so coy about it. Will you show me one of yours?" I opened the gate of the coop and released the chickens from their nightly captivity.

"None of them are mine," I answered. "I would like to think that the Holy Spirit writes them through me."

While we spoke, hosts of chickens fluttered out and swarmed around us, running between us and around our legs. In their haste to get outside and find food, they almost tripped Constantine. I caught him when he stumbled. While helping him right himself, I cleared my throat, trying to sound serious, "It is the image that is important, not whose hand applied it to the panel. It makes little difference whether you, I, or anyone else writes the image. The image *itself* is everything."

"Yorgos!" he said, taking me by the hand and drawing me closer. "I understand these things. You're making it hard for me to get to know you. I'm merely trying to show my interest in something you love and are good at." I swallowed my arguments, and wrested my hand from his.

189

"Well, we have to deliver the eggs to the studio. I'll show you what I am working on when we get there."

"This is where I do my work," I said, when we crossed the threshold. I put the eggs away before lighting some candles and oil lamps. Constantine pressed his palms together and with his elbows against his chest, bowed his head forward to rest the tip of his nose on the tips of his fingers. It seemed a reverent posture. He turned full circle, basking in the light. Ikons in every stage of production—from plain white panels, to completed pieces replete with sacred images and glittering gold leaf–were everywhere; on the walls, easels, and tables. The light of the candles brought out the gold, making it gleam.

"I feel we are in the sanctuary of a church," he whispered. "No, I feel we are in heaven."

"To me, this space is nearly as sacred." I crossed myself and he copied the gesture. "This is where I say most of my prayers."

Constantine reached for me and pulled me into an embrace. Before I could resist, he tried to kiss me on the mouth. I turned away from him and broke his circumferencing hold on me. I averted the danger of his affection.

Pressing my hands together, I rested the tip of my nose on my fingertips. Snagged. An impossible swell of conflicting emotions welled up. Tears came to my eyes; I blinked them away, trying to compose myself. I thought that I put this behind myself when I confessed and prayed with Evangelos. But clearly, I still wanted it. I needed it. And I wanted God. In fact it seemed, in that moment, illumined by the light of numerous oil lamps and candles, that the two complemented each other: my desire for God and my longing to be with a man. Cut from the same cloth, one the warp and one the weft, both were woven into the fabric of my soul.

190

However, this contradicted Evangelos' teaching. I trusted him. Nothing would convince me that these two desires were in anyway compatible, not even my own intuition.

I pushed Constantine off and he bumped into an easel. The easel tumbled to the floor and the ikon I had been working on with it. I bent to right the easel; he rescued the ikon from the dust. While brushing it off, he glanced at the image: the crucifixion. His complexion paled.

"I'm sorry," he whispered. With trembling hands he passed me the ikon. It had chipped and a thin crack ran through the paint right down the image, nearly halving it.

"I'm sorry," he repeated, scrambling out the door.

I held the ikon against my breast and leaned my back against the wall. Sliding down until I rested on the floor, I wept over the image of my savior.

For centuries, Mount Athos had been a refuge for those who sought to save their souls through fasting and prayer. I was no exception. For the most part, in my earliest years there, I managed to escape my strongest vice: my attraction to men and desire for a male companion. Of course I experienced temptations of this sort, but all of them were passing, until Constantine came along. If given half a chance, I believed I could love him. Somehow, that seemed worse than the physical expression of that love. Even though I was still a virgin, I knew intuitively that sex was an act that could easily be turned away from in repentance, but how does one turn away from, or repent, of love?

Most of the men attracted to the austere life of Mount Athos were blessed in that their primary external temptations were far away and removed from their daily routines. The women were in the cities and villages, as were money, and any chances at fame or establishing a name for themselves. This drove them deeper inside, to face internal entanglements.

I was not so lucky. The day I met Constantine my deepest fear and weakness came to the fore and there was no edict preventing him from entering the safe haven of Mount Athos and shaking me to the core.

14 Via Media

After Constantine attempted to kiss me, I avoided him, believing the health and well-being of my soul depended on it. However, when you and the one you wish to avoid live and work in the same small community, it's not easy to do. When our paths crossed, other than a formal and polite 'hello,' Constantine didn't speak to me, and I found reason to go elsewhere.

I knew that I should share share my burden with Hegumen Evangelos, but I was too ashamed. I dreaded seeing disappointment distort his usually pleasant features, so I kept my struggles to myself.

Even though I said nothing, I suspect that Evangelos knew that something troubled me. Early one morning, when I went to see him at the appointed time, he handed me a jug of water, and a cloth bag containing hard bread and said, "You need to go on a hike, Yorgos. There is a hermit whose wisdom you must seek."

"Who is this hermit?" I asked. "Where will I find him?" Evangelos pursed his lips, while his fingers moved slowly from one knot on his prayer rope to the next. When I didn't move, he rose to his feet, and bid me come. In silence, I followed him through the monastery, out the gate, past the stone prayer alcove, and up the little path that lead to, and from, Grigoriou. He pointed in the direction I must go. Though there were numerous trails all around, there were none in the direction in which he pointed.

"Press right on through the vegetation; you'll find your way."

"Who are you sending me to? Give me a name. How far is he?" I asked. Though Evangelos said nothing, his lips curled upward in a subtle smile.

"Can you give me a hint?"

"You will know," he said. "There are numerous hermits in the hills. Trust God to lead you to the right one." He turned and left me with my questions for company.

Confused, but trusting, I struck out in the direction he pointed. I pushed branches out of my way, and stomped my feet to scare away any snakes that might be in my path.

Some hours later, I pushed out of the dense leafage into a clearing. Three paths led in three distinct directions. I scratched my head, unsure which one to commit to. I stood at the crossroads staring down each one, wishing for guidance. Nothing. Afraid of getting lost, I sat down in the center of the clearing and sipped from my water. I gnawed on a hard crust of bread, removed my skouphos and dusted it off.

"Which way do I go?" I finally asked out loud, fidgeting with the hat. "Saint George, conqueror of dragons, in the name of Christ, lead me." Like a flame set to a wick, guidance came. *Take the middle path.* Without further procrastination, I stood and followed my intuition, with the jug of water and bag of bread in hand.

The path mostly led upward into the hills. After hiking for a few hours more, I entered another clearing. In the distance, a little hut peeked out of the surrounding verdure. Looking around, I saw several such dwellings camouflaged by the vegetation and landscape. Some were nearer than others. In all, there were six or seven of them. The first hut I saw was in the middle distance.

I sensed I had reached the end of my hike, but I didn't yet know which hut I should go to. I closed my eyes, crossed myself, and repeated the prayer I said earlier, "Saint George, slayer of dragons, in the name of Christ, lead me."

Go to the middle hut.

While I approached it, I was confounded to see Constantine emerge from it. He stood at the door, regarding me. I paused. Both joy and sadness throbbed in my chest. I lay my hand over my heart and drew in a sharp breath.

He forced a smile and began to approach me. Stepping out of his way, I pressed into the thorny bushes, to make room for him in the narrow path.

"Constantine," I said, nodding once to acknowledge him.

"Yorgos," he replied and kept walking.

Plants rustled when he passed. I turned, expecting to see his backside disappearing into the distance. He had stopped and was watching me.

I love him. I wanted to deny the thought. I tried to explain it away; *I love him like a brother.* I knew it wasn't true. *I love him.* No explanations. No qualifiers. Despite my best effort, it had happened; I had fallen in love. When it hurt too much to keep looking, I nodded and turned away from him, heading to the hut.

While I approached, the door flung open revealing a spry, elderly man. He wore the customary skouphos and black robes of a monk. His robe had been patched and mended so many times it appeared to have been made from a black crazy quilt.

He removed the black cap from his head, wiped sweat from his brow, and waved me in, all in one fluid succession of movement.

"Come, Yorgos, I've been expecting you," he said.

"Did . . . did Hegumen Evangelos tell you I was coming?"

"Who is Hegumen Evangelos?" he asked. "I do not know anyone named Hegumen Evangelos." For a moment he appeared lost in thought. "Perhaps," he amended, "I knew this 'Hegumen Evangelos' before he received his new name."

"Perhaps," I agreed. While we spoke I followed him into his simple abode.

"How did you know my name if no one told you I was coming? And how did you know to expect me? No one else knows that the hegumen sent me." Though the hermit smiled, his eyes and thoughts were focused elsewhere.

"Do Jesus and the saints know your name?" he asked.

"Of course," I whispered.

"Do Jesus and the saints know that your hegumen sent you here?" he asked.

"Of course." I repeated, whispering more quietly than before.

"Jesus told me you were coming, and Jesus told me, once I saw your face, that we shared the same Name Day." For evidence he pointed at the single ikon that hung on his wall. Saint George. I crossed myself.

"It is a good name that we share, Yorgos, and it suits you. I sense that you have it within you to slay many dragons through the power of your love, and the love of Christ that dwells in you, in here." He extended an impossibly bony and wrinkled finger and poked me above the heart with it.

"When the day comes for you to choose a new saint to emulate and be named after, refuse. Dedicate yourself to Saint George and the honoring of his name. Dedicate yourself to slaying dragons."

"But that is not our way," I protested.

"Hmmm," he answered. "It is unwise to tamper with perfection when someone has been so well named. I tell you what, when the day comes, you tell that hegumen of yours that I, the hermit he once sent you to, told you to dedicate yourself to Saint George and to honor his name. He will not argue with that."

I nodded, unsure of what to say. We lingered in silence, and I fidgeted with my prayer rope. Finally, he recalled the social graces.

"Have a seat." He pointed at an upside-down barrel and disappeared into the darkness behind a curtain. I surveyed my surroundings. The hut was small. His existence was impoverished by any worldly standard, but I sensed that he was rich by the standard that most mattered to him.

He returned with the traditional tray of hospitality: some water served in a handmade tin cup, a shot of ouzo, and several pieces of pasteli. I ate them up and downed the tiny shot of ouzo, thankful that there was so little of it. I savored the water, though, using it first to wash down the flavor of the ouzo and then to refresh me. While I consumed his offering he pulled up another barrel and perched himself on top of it.

"I don't know why Hegumen Evangelos sent me to you," I said, staring into the tin cup.

"You doubt your ability to love," he answered. "That's why."

"Yes." I glanced into his eyes and looked away. "It seems my love is so easily tainted by sin."

"You are a young man, hardly a proper novice. You have your entire life to learn to love. Continue to wrestle with your passions. Seek wise counsel. Determine to honor and follow God with your whole being, but do not be afraid to love. God will make your love pure. He will teach you to love without sin. Trust Him." He looked at me with clear and piercing eyes.

"To refuse to love someone? *That* is the sin you should fear the most. Never refuse to love." He dropped his gaze to his prayer rope and appeared to be counting the knots.

I waited a moment until it was clear he would likely say no more. I stood, thanked him and asked for his blessing.

"May you be well, and may God enlighten you always," he said, making the sign of the cross.

I slipped passed him and out the door. I was well on my way down the path when I heard him call after me.

"Yorgos, do not be afraid to love the one that you love, the one that left when you arrived. If you seek to love the way that Christ loves, your soul will always be right."

While I stared at him with my mouth gaping he shuffled into his hut and closed the door.

I caught up with Constantine about two-thirds of the way back to Grigoriou. He sat on a rock wall in a shady clearing, drinking water from a jug.

"Hello Constantine."

"Hello Yorgos. I can't help wondering what accounts for the good fortune I am having today. Twice, now, you have spoken to me without my first having to address you. I am astounded."

I laughed. "Walk with me?" He leapt to his feet and followed. Neither of us spoke until I broke open the silence with a question, "What did he say to you?"

"He told me I would learn everything I need to know, if only I'd learn how to paint an ikon." I received his words the way the iris of an eye opens to receive the light. The prospect of teaching Constantine everything I knew excited me.

"Did he now?"

"Yes. And he told me not to wait. He urged me to begin learning at once."

"Well then, we'll start your lessons tomorrow." His ample smile exposed his dimples and all of his teeth.

"I'd like that."

We walked side-by-side, when the width of the path allowed for it and single-file when it became too narrow.

Occasionally, our knuckles grazed. I tried, unsuccessfully, to find an occupation for my hand. Defeated, I gave up, and let it hang at my side where it swayed and occasionally touched him. When the path narrowed I stepped to the fore to lead the way.

"You know he's right," I said. "If you learn to paint an ikon you will learn everything you need to know. You will learn our theology, how to focus your thoughts, clear your mind, and how to be humble, teachable, and patient. Most important of all, you will learn how to pray." Constantine raised an eyebrow.

"All of that from picking up a paint brush?"

"Indeed. All of that and then some because it is so much more than simply picking up a paint brush." While we continued in companionable silence, my heart expanded to contain what the hermit said, and to make room for Constantine. I wasn't sure how to proceed, or exactly how to make sense of my feelings for him. What I did know was that I couldn't ignore him any longer.

"So what did he tell you?" Constantine asked. I shrugged, reluctant to answer.

"Well . . . ?"

"He told me that refusing to love someone is a terrible sin and should be avoided. He urged me never to withhold my love." Constantine smirked, but said nothing. I considered telling him the rest, that the hermit urged me not to be afraid of loving him, specifically, but thought better of it.

Early the following morning, Constantine came to the ikon studio several minutes sooner than I expected him to. With a child's grin, he placed a single purple wildflower on my work stand, where I could see it. Concentrating intensely, I focused on the ikon that Zoe-Sophia requested of me over a year earlier. Two or three more brushstrokes and I would be done.

When I felt him peering over my shoulder, I became irritated. One glance at him and I smiled, my irritation vanishing.

"Give me a few more minutes to finish this. Have a look around." I turned my full attention back to the ikon on the easel in front of me. While painting the eyes, I meditated on the life of my patron saint and reflected on the words of the hermit; namely that God had called me to be a slayer of dragons and that I should dedicate my life to Saint George, and follow his example. When Constantine removed an ikon from its place, I lifted the brush from the wood and lay the brush down.

"Yorgos, is this the one I damaged?" I turned to see which ikon he spoke of.

"Yes, that's how it became cracked," I answered. He inspected it.

"I thought it looked familiar. I didn't get a good look at it that morning. When I picked it up and saw Jesus staring at me . . . ."

"–You felt guilty."

"Yes, and it startled me." He ran his finger down the scarred surface of the paint. "It's beautiful, aside from the crack. It's not like your others, though. It's more crude, less . . . precise."

"So, already you're a critic?" I asked, looking him in the eye.

"No. Never," he said, and looked away.

"That one is one of my earliest efforts," I explained. "I didn't even have any gold-leaf. That's why the sky is yellow, instead of gold. There is a story about that one. Maybe I'll tell it to you someday."

I turned from him, back to my work, and meditated for a moment, before touching the brush to the image with a steady hand. I *had* learned, over the years, to be more precise. I stepped back and gazed at the image of Saint George. The eyes were correct. The halo was perfectly round. The gold leaf was smooth, and the dragon was pierced through. In short, the ikon was complete. I crossed myself, and turned to regard my waiting pupil.

"Are you ready to start?"

"Where are your other students?" he asked, looking around. Other than the two master ikon writers I shared the studio with, who worked in silence, we were by ourselves.

"Today we work alone. I sent them out."

I made it my goal to never be alone with Constantine. It seemed the easiest way to avoid temptation. As far as his lessons were concerned, I started at the beginning, showing him how to select the best wood and cut it to size. I taught him how to prepare everything, including the gesso and the rabbit skin glue. I found him to be a good student, eager to please, and quick to learn. I also found that I enjoyed teaching him.

Days later, I sneaked off after lunch to pray alone at the whitewashed stone alcove just outside the gate. With Theotokos watching from the ikon on the wall, I passed my prayer rope through my fingers in contemplative silence, practicing moving slowly from knot to knot, feeling the words form in my mouth like something with weight and substance. The prayer was nourishment for my soul.

When Evangelos first approached, I was aware of someone watching. When he slid into the seat across from me I guessed it was him, but I made sure to finish my repetition of the Jesus Prayer at the slow methodical pace I set for myself, before lifting my gaze to greet him.

He smiled, folding his hand into his lap and leaned forward. "I have a question for you. One I want you to answer with utmost honesty, and only after reflection. Do you understand?"

"Yes," I said, lowering my gaze, my stomach aflutter. I knew what he was going to ask. And I knew my answer. However I had to do my best to examine myself, in case any unrecognized doubt lurked in the secret places of my heart, places that even I couldn't see without the illumination of the Holy Spirit.

"Yorgos," he said. I lifted my gaze. "Do you wish to become a rassophore?"

My cheeks flushed. I'd waited my whole life to be asked that question. "Yes," I gushed. My body shook with excitement. I smoothed my cassock, trying to be stoic.

"I appreciate your enthusiasm," he said. "Please remember, I want you to take your time answering this. There's no need to rush. Quiet your mind and listen to your heart."

I tried to follow his instructions. Concentrating on breathing slowly and deeply I relaxed. Every corner that I looked inside myself the answer blazed like a candle flame dispelling the dark. *YES*. Every corner, that is, except for the corner where I had tucked my feelings for Constantine.

I didn't fool myself on purpose. I knew without a doubt that I wanted to become a rassophore. It's what I was born for. I knew I wanted to devote my life to the ascetic way. Only my friendship with Constantine gave me a moment's pause. I dismissed my concern out of mind. *Constantine and I are fine.* I had to believe it. I wasn't going to let something like my feelings for him get between me and my service to God. Besides, I had a lifetime to learn how to love in a way that pleased Him. *Yes.* My answer was unequivocal.

"Yes," I said, looking Evangelos in the eye. "I do wish to become a rassophore. I'm ready." I felt giddy and nervous. "I have no doubts," I said, trying to be brave.

"Very well." He placed his hand on my knee before standing up. "But don't be fooled. We all have our doubts.

The question is, are you ready to press through them and not let them limit or define you?"

"I am," I answered, though his words frightened me.

He clasped my hand warmly; "The vote will be taken after supper this evening. I will be surprised if it's not unanimous."

The vote was unanimous. After eating, the entire community supported my decision with happy enthusiasm. I looked at Evangelos, my mentor, and Old Father Maximus, who I thought of as my spiritual guardian. I wanted to make them proud.

I scanned the faces of all the other men present, feeling loved and valued. *I love these men.* Their support strengthened the bond of spiritual brotherhood I had with each of them. And with their support, I believed I was ready to be tonsured.

When I looked at Constantine, my gaze lingering on his face a little longer than it should have, my palms sweat. He seemed proud of me in a way that was sweetly possessive. My breast swelled and I looked away. Good or bad, my feelings for him were being strengthened too. He didn't feel like a spiritual brother the way the others did. He was something more. Not that our shared interest in spirituality wasn't a part of our friendship, but the romantic tension between us tempered that. I knew with growing certainty that I loved him, in a way that I believed was unspeakable.

For a moment I wavered, afraid that my love for Constantine would be my undoing; that I would lose everything because of it, even God. I knew then that I was ready. I had to be ready. Why delay? I believed that new grace would be granted me if I took this step in faith. Grace enough to rise to the challenge and love Constantine in a way that was free of sin. God would show me how.

After dinner, while the others gathered for conversation in the parlor high above the sea, Evangelos and I took a meandering walk through the trails.

The water below was a dark plane of glass, reflecting the light of the setting sun.

"As you know, it is customary for a novice to receive a new name when they are tonsured. Have you considered which saint you'd like to honor, like I asked you to?"

"I have," I answered, looking up at him sheepishly. "I'd like to honor Saint George by keeping his name."

Evangelos pursed his lips, "That is not our way, Yorgos. You must receive a *new* name to symbolize your death to your old life."

"I understand that, but doesn't the black of the cassock symbolize the same thing? I want to die to my old self by slaying the dragons of sin that lurk inside me. Saint George is the right saint for me."

He negated my words with a shake of his head. "Yorgos—"

"Do you remember when you sent me to meet the hermit in the hills?"

"Yes."

"He told me that I was perfectly named and that I should dedicate myself to honoring Saint George and slaying dragons, and he told me to tell you that he said so."

"Did he?"

"Yes. He did. And that's what I intend to do . . . to honor Saint George."

Evangelos chuckled and scrubbed his face with his hand. "Very well. Your journey until now has been peculiar. Why should I expect you to proceed any differently?"

In the Katholikon, at the close of the preceding service, the Deacon said, "Let us pray to the Lord" to mark that the tonsuring ceremony had begun.

Silently, Evangelos invited me to come forward and stand with him while, in unison, the choir raised their voices, "Lord, have mercy."

Approaching slowly, I felt the way I imagined a bride would, nervous and excited, both wanting to make the commitment and afraid. I knew that with each slow and deliberate step I was closer to crossing the threshold into a deeper commitment to God. Once I crossed it, there would be no turning back.

There are no formal vows when a novice is raised to the rank of rassophore, which means "robe-bearer." The candidate is merely asked to affirm his commitment to persevere in the monastic life. Formal vows aren't made until one takes the next step and becomes a stavrophore.

Waiting to be asked to make my affirmation, I closed my eyes, concentrating on Christ; my dependence on Him; my love for Him; and my determination to please Him.

According to the custom, once I affirmed my intention, Evangelos cut a small amount of my hair from four places—to symbolize a cross—intoning the Name of the Father, and the Son, and the Holy Spirit. He paused between the names of each person of the Holy Trinity, for the choir to intone 'amen.'

When all the cuts had been made, he clothed me with the rasson—or outer cassock—a black garment, like the inner cassock, that reached to my ankles and had wide sleeves. He also fastened a leather belt around my waist. With these few simple words and acts I had officially become a monk.

15 The Chip In My Resolve

Gathering my cassock with both hands, I ducked out of vespers before the end. My prayer rope– all but forgotten–hung loosely from my wrist. My thoughts were too scattered. I couldn't stop thinking about Constantine. I tried, but found it too difficult to focus my attention on the liturgy. I didn't have it in me to rise to the challenge.

While I sneaked out, I heard footsteps behind me. I shut my eyes, *Please be Constantine,* and berated myself for thinking it. Making the sign of the cross, I muttered a quick prayer for forgiveness and dashed under cover of shadows. Footsteps followed. While I neared the gate, I glanced over my shoulder and sighed. Constantine caught up with me.

"Wait here," he said, and he left me, a lone centurion, standing at the gate. He returned shortly with a blanket and a carafe of wine. When I parted my lips to protest he touched them with his finger.

"Come," he said, taking me by the hand. We rushed past the gate, and took the paths that wound down to cliffs overlooking the eternally turbulent sea. Though it was still light out, the sky was beginning to darken. My mounting excitement distracted me from paying any more than rudimentary attention to it.

We spread the blanket at the cliff's edge and sat down. Constantine chugged a mouthful of wine and passed the bottle to me. I held it by the neck, flicked my wrist, and watched the red liquid swirl up the sides of the glass and streak down in thin rivulets to collect at the bottom. I passed the bottle back without touching it to my lips.

"You didn't drink." He thrust the bottle back at me "Drink!" I hesitated before lifting the carafe to my mouth. I sipped from it carefully. Constantine wagged his head, grabbing the bottle from me.

"It's not hot tea, Yorgos!" He threw back a mouthful, swished it around and swallowed it. I followed suit, feeling the hot flush hit my cheeks.

"I don't drink too often, other than the wine of the Eucharist." I admitted. "It's a personal vow I've made." I shrugged.

"You've vowed not to drink?" he asked, his muscles tensing.

"I've vowed not to drink too much." He relaxed.

"Well, you've hardly had any, so you're not even close to breaking your vow." He thrust the bottle back at me, and I took it. "Not yet, at least," he added, with a quick arch to his eyebrow. I frowned. I threw my head back, anyway, and downed a mouthful. Thick on my tongue, it was acidic, tart and sweet. I liked it. Constantine reached for the bottle; I twisted away, and held it up to my lips, taking another hearty swig.

"That's better," he said.

I turned toward him saying, "Get thee behind me . . ." and smiled for good measure, surrendering the bottle to him.

"Tell me about your vow. Why did you make it?"

"I don't like to have my senses dulled and I hate to lose control. When I drink, I drink only enough to feel the heat of it in my cheeks."

"Some would say that that is already having too much, if one is trying to avoid getting drunk."

"No, for me that's the sign to stop." It was my turn to drink, but I dropped the carafe to my lap.

"Constantine, why are you here? On Mount Athos, I mean. You don't seem much like the other monks."

"What do you mean?"

"Well, from what I've observed, you certainly like your drink, you–"

His laughter interrupted me. "I am not the only one here who likes his wine–"

"No, I suppose not. However, you don't follow the fasts very closely either. You skip out on a good number of the services. You sleep in often and–"

"Whoa, Yorgos. I didn't realize I was being watched so closely. Are you judging me? I'm hurt." A quick glance at his face and I could tell that I had indeed hurt him.

"I'm sorry, Constantine, I didn't mean . . . ." He shook his head, lifted the bottle from my lap and drank deeply from it.

"I'm here for my mother," he answered with a satisfied gasp, handing the carafe to me. I sipped from it and passed it back. "Her favorite uncle is here on Mount Athos at Esphigmenou Monastery. Before he came here, they were close. I grew up hearing how much I reminded her of him and how proud she'd be if I followed in his footsteps."

"Then why aren't you with him at Esphigmenou?"

"Trying to get rid of me?"

I laughed. "Never! I'm just curious." I lifted a green twig from the ground and twisted it into a circle, fidgeting.

"I tried to go to Esphigmenou first. The hegumen there said it was best for me to start out on my own. If, in time, I do decide that this is what I am called to, he'll have me."

"Well, then you're in luck," I said. "There is never a shortage of time here."

For several minutes it was quiet except for the sound of the ocean repeatedly throwing itself against the rocky face of the cliffs below and then dragging itself back into the sea.

Constantine spoke first, "Yorgos, I do feel called to a life of prayer and solitude. I am just not as singularly focused as you."

"You make me sound like some kind of a saint."

"I'd carry your ikon in my pocket if you were. You're the only saint I'd petition."

"Constantine, stop it." I threw the twisted twig at his chest.

"I have a question for you, Yorgos," he said. "Why do you avoid being alone with me? Do you realize that since the day I tried to kiss you, this is the first time we've been alone?" I reached for the carafe and sucked a mouthful from it, drinking nearly as deeply as he had.

"That's why I avoid being alone with you Constantine. I'm too weak. I'm afraid that could happen again."

"Would it be so terrible if it did?"

"Yes! I can't just give up." He pursed his lips and stared at me.

"Doesn't it make you tired?" he asked.

"What?"

"Always having to be so perfect. I know it did me. I can't fight anymore."

"No." I answered quickly. "Well . . . yes. Isn't that what the call to the ascetic life is? A call to constant vigilance against our passions?" Constantine considered my words and shrugged.

"Maybe you're right," he said. "Maybe I'll be a terrible monk."

"I never said that." I held the bottle out for him, a peace offering. He pushed it away and climbed to his feet.

"Will you believe me if I say I've had enough?" He reached for me.

"I've upset you," I said, while he helped me up.

"No. It's getting dark. If we don't hurry, the gate will be locked, and we'll be out here all night."

On our way back to the monastery, I became acutely aware of the world around me. I had been so focused on Constantine, our conversation, and my own inner landscape, that I failed to see that it was indeed quickly getting dark. We hurried, hand in hand, to the gate and found it to be shut and locked.

"We're too late!" I said. "What will we do now?" I didn't wait for him to answer. I grabbed hold of the gate's handle, with both hands, and shook it, shouting, "Hey! We've been locked out!"

Constantine shushed me, grabbed me by the shoulders, and with firm hands turned me to face him.

"Yorgos, you know they won't unlock the gate until sun up. Besides do you want to have to explain what we're doing out here?"

"What *are* we doing, Constantine? We haven't done anything wrong." I turned to the gate, taking hold of its handle with one hand, and raised my fist to beat on it with the other.

"Maybe not," he answered, intercepting my fist and pushing my hand away from the gate. "Admit it; it does look kind of funny. We've got a blanket, a bottle of wine, and we're so late that we've been locked out." His lips twisted in a cocky smile.

"Oh, shut up!" I said, slapping him on the chest. And then, in spite of myself I laughed. "Okay," I amended.

Still holding onto the gate with one hand, I reached for Constantine's hand with the other and squeezed it. It took me a few seconds to fully embrace the moment, including the fact that I had reached for him. I was no longer the passive one waiting for him to make the first move. "What should we do?" I asked.

"I suggest we find a place where we can spread this out to sleep on." He lifted the blanket, and shook it. "And then we get up with the sun and sneak back in once the gate has been unlocked. I don't know about you, but I don't want to have to explain this, whether or not there really is anything to explain." I closed my eyes and took a steadying breath.

"Okay, I'm with you," I said, feeling a liberating sense of relief. I released my grip of the gate, and turned to him. "There's a little clearing that should do nicely," I said, and I pulled him along, pushing branches out of our way. "It's a good thing I don't share a cell with Hegumen Evangelos anymore, because there would be no way I'd get away with this if I did."

We spread the blanket out under the sprawling canopy of an olive tree. The moon, a polished and radiant silver coin in the sky above us, shone through the leaves and branches illumining us in a sterling wash. We lay side by side on our backs, our heads in our hands, our elbows overlapping.

All God's nocturnal creatures came together to perform for us, especially the crickets and the frogs. Nature's music so enchanted me, I didn't feel compelled to speak. It was Constantine who eventually broke the spell.

"Yorgos, you once told me there was a story about the ikon you painted for your mother. Will you tell it to me now?"

"I've never told anyone that story, not even Hegumen Evangelos," I said. He rolled onto his side to face me.

"Please?"

"Alright," I said, exhaling. "My mother gave me a copy of the ikon after Divine Liturgy one Sunday."

"The one of the crucifixion?"

"Yes, that one. She asked me to copy it for her. It was her way of encouraging me to learn the sacred art. She often brought me new ikons and asked me to paint them for her." The memory made me smile. I hadn't realized what lengths she'd gone to to encourage me until I spoke of it.

"I took the ikon into a ravine behind our house. There was a nice spot down there where I used to pray."

"That's so cute. I can picture it as if I'd been there. I think you've always been a monk, waiting to be tonsured to make it official." I elbowed him for his interruption and continued.

"At the bottom of the ravine was a flat rock. I used to lay my ikons on it when I prayed with them. I had a little ritual, with candles and everything."

"What happened?"

"Nothing, at first. Something had been troubling me for quite some time. The crucifixion was a perfect image to meditate on with my struggles in mind."

"What troubled you so badly?" I looked away from him, weighing my words, and fearing speaking them aloud.

"It's funny, Constantine, even though you've tried to kiss me, I'm afraid to tell you this. Up till now Evangelos is the only person I have admitted it to.

"What is it?"

"I had a crush on a boy and it terrified me. I feared it would ruin everything. No matter how hard I tried to stop, I always thought about him, the way I always think about you."

Once I said the words, I wished I could take them back. I hadn't meant to reveal quite so much. Constantine looked away from me, to the dappled light of the moon that shone through the canopy above us.

"I think about you all the time too," he whispered.

"I thought about Niko's smooth skin, and the way that he smelled. I wondered what he'd look like naked. I always wondered what his skin would feel like under my hand . . . . I wanted to feel his heartbeat . . . . Anyhow, I took the ikon of the crucifixion to the flat rock and set it down to pray with it. To this day I don't understand what happened next."

Constantine sat up. I reached for him and he pulled me up to a sitting position too.

"What happened?"

"While I prayed with it, the ikon opened up for me and came alive. I was drawn into it. The Lord hung naked on the cross. The sight moved me to tears, as well as to worship him. When I approached Him, sand crunched under my feet. I could smell people's sweat and the sun beat on me. I knelt under the cross and was shocked when blood started to drip from him onto my forehead. Like I said, the Lord was naked. I felt simultaneously aroused and terrified.

"The Lord's nakedness aroused you?" He held the back of his hand to his lips, his brow scrunched up.

"Not like that, Constantine. It's hard to explain. What I felt aroused in me was love, gratitude, and the feeling that I would do *anything* to lessen his suffering. So I removed him from the cross and ministered to him. I kissed him. Once I started kissing him, I couldn't stop. I kissed his forehead. I kissed his wounds. I kissed his cheeks. It was passionate without being sinful. When I kissed his lips however, I feared I had gone too far. In a flash, He hung above me again, and His tears dripped on my forehead. Before I could comprehend what happened, the whole scene snapped closed, and I looked down at a normal flat ikon. I've pondered this for years and I still don't understand it."

"Do you remember the day we met?"

"Yes, of course I do. I don't think I'll ever forget it."

"I struggled with the same thing. I feared that this would ruin me."

"I understand that fear."

"It hasn't, Yorgos. Above all else, I came here to escape this. The morning after I arrived, before the sun even came up, I met you. I don't think I was ever supposed to escape this temptation and I don't fear it anymore. In fact, temptation is the wrong word for it. 'Temptation' implies that it's wrong. I don't believe it is." He reached for my hand and clasped it. I liked the feeling of the warmth of his skin on my own.

"I love you, Yorgos." He brought my hand to his lips and I yanked it away.

"Don't."

"Do you know why I think Jesus cried?" he asked.

I sighed. "Go on. Tell me."

"Because you were ashamed when your passion reached its peak. I think He cried because you feel so much shame. He loves us, Yorgos. Our shame keeps us from knowing it fully."

"I wish I could agree with you Constantine, but I can't. I believe he loves *me,* but how can he love *this?* This part of me? No, I don't believe it."

Constantine snatched up my hand again and kissed it before I could pull it away. My chest expanded with both fear and passion and I brought his hand to my lips. I feared slipping beyond the point of recovering myself when the words of the hermit came back to me. He said that I was young and had a lifetime to learn to love the way God would have me love. I hoped that he was right.

Constantine and I lay down again and listened to the music of the night. With my back to him, he enfolded me in his arms and squeezed me close. After a while, he shifted behind me. "Are you awake?" he whispered. I turned in his arms to face him and, wrapping my own arms around him, drew him infinitely closer to myself. I kissed him.

"Yes, I am," I answered, with our lips touching.

"Me too. I can't sleep." The growing pressure of his groin against my thigh aroused me.

"I wonder why," I teased. Even by the pale light of the moon I could see him blush.

"I've been thinking about your story. I wish I could have seen it for myself. I've never had an experience like that. The closest thing would be if you'd paint it for me, exactly the way you saw it."

I mashed my lips up to his and spoke while kissing him, "Yes. Whatever you want." Trying to undo it with one hand I struggled with the lace of his pants. He grinned wildly and grazed his teeth over my upper lip.

"I didn't think you'd ever let me touch you," he said. "I've wanted this–" The heat of the moment burned away my guilt. From its ashes rose something brazenly unapologetic, something burnished into pure radiance by both lust and love.

"Shhhh," I admonished. "Just promise me you'll never stop touching me and then shut up." At that he grinned even wider and held me tighter. Mustering all of his strength, he rolled me onto my back.

"No, Tino!" I exclaimed, and I fought to wrestle myself to the top. He was bigger and stronger than I was. He pinned my arms to the ground and straddled me in triumph. When he released them I pounded on his chest with both my fists before surrendering. I felt, in my own way, just as triumphant as he.

Stripping off each other's clothes, we halted, half naked, when another voice joined the night symphony. It was a voice that extinguished our passion like water thrown onto a flame. A single wolf howled at the moon. He was very close and moving even closer.

I pressed my back into Constantine's chest, wishing I could meld with him. He responded by hugging me so close it hurt. I discovered deep comfort in the pain of his embrace.

"Be quiet," he whispered. Another wolf answered the first.

"I'm afraid they're going to kill us."

"No, they're not. Wolves rarely attack people." The duet of howling continued and gradually became louder while the second wolf approached the first. When it sounded like the wolves were right on top of us, it became perfectly quiet. The stillness continued, until the crickets and frogs began to fill the night with their orchestrations once again.

When the tension in my body began to ease, a small white deer burst from the foliage, shooting past us like an arrow. The wolves followed. They dashed through the clearing so swiftly that my eyes only registered a blurry grey streak. I yelped and buried my face in Constantine's chest.

The wolves dragged the deer down. I didn't see it, but its collision with the earth was unmistakable, as was its resulting cry: so bestial and and yet child-like. The cry was cut short, followed by the wet sounds of snarling, ripping, and tearing. I covered my ears with my hands. Once the sounds of the outside world were sufficiently muffled, they were replaced by a sound that originated from somewhere within me. It was the now familiar steady and rhythmic purring of a cat. Constantine pulled my hands away from the sides of my head.

"Listen," he said. "I think another wolf is moving through the bushes." Behind us, in the thick foliage that bordered the clearing, leaves rustled quietly and a twig snapped.

"No," I said. "It's a cat. A large black cat." The purring grew louder. "Do you hear the purring too?" I asked. My question seemed to startle, and then confuse him. Finally Constantine shook his head.

"No, I only hear something sneaking through the bushes." I heard both. The creature bypassed the clearing, moving slowly and deliberately toward the wolves while it stalked them. It gave me an odd sense of relief to hear the purring.

"It's the cat," I whispered, more to myself, than Constantine, and I smiled. He began to inquire what I meant when a fierce roar interrupted him, followed by a brief scuffle. The wolves scattered. I was seized by panic once again. *What if they were startled back the way they came?* Constantine drew me close. He pressed his lips into my ear and quietly chanted.

I couldn't sleep for several hours. I couldn't even close my eyes, though my eyelids were as heavy as weighted curtains. Unfortunately, it wasn't passion that kept me awake, but fear. Only Constantine's singing comforted me. Well, that and the fact that there was a large cat out there, somewhere, watching over us.

Just before the break of dawn, I was awakened by Constantine scrambling backwards, away from where we had fallen asleep, a tangled mass of arms and legs.

"What is it?" I groggily asked, rubbing my eyes.

He said nothing, but his gaze was fixed. I followed it and saw, curled at the foot of our blanket, the same impossibly large black cat that I always saw at night. It stretched its back in a perfect half circle, yawned, and regarded us each in turn. It looked into the brightening sky, where the sun pierced through the fog, and dove headlong into the concealing ground cover.

"You saw it?" He didn't respond right away, his gaze was fixed to the spot where the cat had been.

"Yes, I saw it," he said, nodding absently. "Cats are everywhere here. I've never seen one so big. You knew before we saw it. How did you know what it was?"

"I've seen it before, many times. The first time was when my brother, my father and I were coming down from the mountains on our way here."

"It followed you all the way?"

"I can't believe it let you see it. No one else here has, even Evangelos. He thinks I'm imagining it."

"No, you're not imagining it. I saw it, Yorgos." Constantine crawled across the blanket to me and lifted my hand to his chest.

"Your heart is pounding."

"That thing scared me even more than the wolves did." I rose to my knees and pressed my lips up to his, believing my kiss would have the power to stop his heart from pounding.

"It's nothing to be afraid of," I said, and I pressed my lips to his again. "That cat has been following me for five years now and it's never done me any harm. I think it watches after me."

"That's troubling." Constantine stood and helped me to my feet. "There is something about that creature that I don't trust. Aside from its size, I can't put my finger on it."

"If it meant to hurt me, it would have done so by now. It's had plenty of time."

"I hope that's true for your sake, Yorgos. How do you know for sure? What if it's an evil spirit?" Constantine's words echoed what Old Father Maximus said when I told him about the beast. He called it "a dark spirit made flesh." I paused to consider that for a moment, and Constantine wagged his head at me. With a nod he indicated the rising sun. "We should hurry back."

Constantine retrieved the half-emptied carafe of wine and downed a third of what was left of it. I gathered up the blanket. With Constantine following me, we struggled through the tangle of bushes finding our way to the trail.

When I stepped onto the path, my foot struck something that was concealed by ground cover. I nearly stumbled, but Constantine grabbed hold of my forearm and broke my fall. A humming swarm of flies took flight and buzzed around our heads. I expected to see the deer. When I looked down, I saw something quite different and much worse than a dead animal. It was the bloodied naked body of an adolescent girl. Her throat was ripped open from chin to chest, and the contents of her stomach were exposed. I dropped the blanket. Its slight weight was too great for me to carry. The carafe of wine dropped from Tino's loosened grip and shattered on the ground. He covered his mouth and turned away from me toward the bushes where he dry heaved. A wave of nausea hit me too, but courage fortified my stomach.

She had been tall for a child, but was shorter than me and unusually thin. Dried blood tangled her long wheat-colored hair. Other than that, her features were nearly too perfect. In death she seemed to have become a statue of a wood nymph or a nereid. I dropped to one knee for a closer look at her face.

"That 'evil' cat saved us," I said, glancing over my shoulder. "This could have been us." The girl's round, oversized brown eyes stared vacantly, focusing on nothing. There was something animal-like about her features. I was reminded of my pet lamb that died, also attacked by a wolf before I ever gave it a proper name. To avoid looking at her fatal wounds, I looked into the girl's eyes and wondered what name she had been given. I reached down to close them, while saying a silent prayer, and pressed the back of my hand against my mouth to stifle my own urge to vomit.

Constantine reached for me. Our fingers fused into one knotted mass.

"Come," he said, "if we want to sneak back in undetected, we should go."

"But . . . ." While he dragged me along I looked behind us. The verdure obscured the body as we left. Soon I couldn't see the body at all.

We covered ground quickly, leaving the girl behind. It felt like an evil thing to do, a sacrilege, but we needed to hurry back before anyone noticed that we were missing.

When we approached the gate, I was relived to see that it was open. I disentangled my fingers from Constantine's before we were near enough to pass through.

"Wait," he called after me, "Your cassock is filthy." He beat off of me the clinging evidence of our night together. I returned the favor. That done, I pressed through the gate, crossed the courtyard, and entered the Katholikon in seconds, not even looking to see if he was behind me.

At first I lingered in the darker corners of the sanctuary, unable to receive the solace that venerating the ikons usually afforded me. I didn't even try. Constantine stood beside me but, aside from knowing he hadn't left me, there was little comfort.

I couldn't shake the sight of the dead girl. It didn't matter if my eyes were open or closed, her lifeless eyes constantly gazed back at me. I found my heart grasping for something that could steady it. It took possession of the words of the Jesus Prayer. While I repeated that prayer, and crossed myself innumerable times, an inescapable conclusion became clear to me.

16 The Body

Iknew I shouldn't, couldn't, remain silent about the dead girl. With or without Constantine, I had to tell Evangelos about her, even if it meant the nature of our night together would be discovered. Though I could live with that secret, I couldn't live with this one–the one about our finding a dead body and leaving it to rot because we were more worried about not being caught than we were about doing the right thing.

I turned to Constantine, imploring him with my eyes. He nodded, and followed me to the candle stand where several tapers of various lengths stuck out of the sand and clumps of beeswax. We each took one and separated. With the small sphere of light cast by the taper showing the way, I searched for Evangelos, weaving through the assembly of black-clad monks. I acted with the determined impatience of a man who needed to unburden a guilty conscience.

With the prayer candle and its flickering light, I drew attention to myself, interrupting the orderly worship and prayers of my brothers.

Evangelos came up behind me from out of the shadows. He grabbed hold of my bicep and gently, yet firmly, guided me out into the light of the morning.

When we crossed the threshold into the cold outdoors, he released my arm. I turned to face him. To my great relief Constantine followed behind. To my greater distress, however, I saw that behind him, a swelling number of our brothers had gathered, made curious by our odd behavior.

"Hegumen, we've been looking for you," I explained, unable to look him in the eye.

"You've interrupted morning prayer. What is so important that it couldn't wait until after breakfast?"

"I . . . I . . . We . . . ."

"Yes, you what?" he pressed. He seemed to believe, or strongly wish, that only something of utmost importance could cause us to act as we had.

"When, when . . . when we were on our way up the trail we came across—"

"Yes? You came across what?"

"A body," Tino said.

"A body?" The tone of Evangelos' voice wavered between concern and disbelief. "Whose body?" he asked, following Tino and me to our grisly find. He brushed branches out of his way. Guessing the direction we were headed, he rushed to take the lead.

"We don't know," I answered. "Neither of us have seen her before." Evangelos stopped and released the branch he had been holding away from his face. It swooshed through the air, struck me squarely across mine, and sent me staggering backwards.

"You've come across the body of *girl?* How on earth could a girl get this far onto the peninsula without being seen?"

"I don't know," I said, climbing to my feet with Constantine's help. The Hegumen watched us. An odd expression contorted his face. Understanding dawned, but ignorance was chosen in its place.

"Wait," Evangelos raised his hands. "Perhaps you can start by answering this: What were you doing out here so early in the morning?" Constantine and I glanced at each

224

other. Our fused gazes should have been answer enough; a confession.

"We went for a walk beyond the gate last night and were locked out." I explained.

"We slept out here in a clearing," Constantine said.

"But we didn't get much sleep because of the wolves," I added.

"Wolves?" Evangelos repeated the word with an air of incredulity and a chuckle. His deep voice was laced with doubt.

"I heard wolves last night."

"So did I." The three of us looked toward the sound of the voices, and saw that a small number of our brothers had followed us. Each one, with his prayer rope in hand, pinched a black knot between his thumb and forefinger.

"Yes, wolves." I said with more confidence. "They attacked and killed a deer, at least that's what I thought I saw run past us in the night. Only this morning, we stumbled across the mutilated body of a young girl." Concern and disbelief played across the Hegumen's face, each fighting to replace the other. Disbelief was winning.

"The body is over there, down the trail. It's not far," said Constantine, pointing. Evangelos' gaze turned inward while he tugged absently on his graying beard. Compassion overcame his doubt.

"Take me to her."

This time Tino took the lead. I wanted to take him by the hand and face this together, but I fought the urge. Instinct told me that it was best if our affection and the depth of our solidarity remained a secret, so I merely followed close behind. I hoped that the Hegumen's suspicions would wither and die if we did nothing to confirm them.

When we came around the final bend in the trail a huddle of white deer surrounded the body. Snapping branches and rattling leaves announced our approach. Four deer lifted their heads. Before Evangelos and the others reached us, they were gone.

My eyes went wide. Tino gave me a look that said *I saw them too.*

"She's right up there, at the edge of the path," I said, rushing ahead. I scrambled to the spot and halted. She was gone. No trace. I looked all around, even stepping off the trail into the dense plant growth. She wasn't there. She wasn't anywhere in sight.

I looked at Constantine first, and then at the Hegumen—shaking my head.

"Not here!" I exclaimed. "I don't understand. She was here. Right here!" I stamped my foot in time with my words, to emphasize them. There wasn't a trace of her left; no imprints of her body in the soil, no marks left by her scuffle with the wolves, not even a drop of blood. Less than and hour ago, there had been plenty to cause even a butcher to lose his lunch.

For several heartbeats, Evangelos said nothing. Stepping off the trail and combing through the bushes with his hands, he scrutinized the ground on which we stood. Nothing.

He stood slowly, like a man who was so old he wasn't sure his body could make it all the way up. He looked at me, and then Tino, and wagged his head.

"Certainly you have duties to attend to," he said, looking past us, addressing the others. When the three of us were alone, he spoke with a whisper.

"I don't see any evidence of a body." The words lingered, naked and cold, in the brisk morning air. "What I do see evidence of is something that concerns me." His eyes looked first to the crumpled blanket left half hanging from the shrub I dropped it on and then to the shattered carafe. A red circle stained the ground underneath the shards of glass. "Is there something more you want to tell me? Something, perhaps, you *need* to tell me, but are afraid to?" He looked from Constantine to me.

"No."

"It appears to me that your night out here was not an accident at all, but something you two planned."

"No sir," Constantine answered, stepping forward. "I asked Yorgos to join me for a walk. I brought the wine and the blanket to sit on. It was early when we came out here. It was an accident that we were locked out." Evangelos pursed his lips.

"I don't know," he said. "Your behavior this morning has been most peculiar and very unlike you." He pinned his gaze on me. He then regarded both of us, each in his turn and his eyes lighted on Constantine. "Perhaps you merely drank too much? Imagined the whole thing, hmmm?"

"Perhaps," Tino said. I glanced at the Hegumen and then looked away. I feared he would see into my soul and recognize my secret shame. His voice softened.

"Very well." Before releasing us he narrowed his eyes. And then he simply said, "Go attend to your duties."

Walking in brittle silence, Constantine and I headed first to the kitchen, then the chicken coop. I felt fragile, raw, and a little bit dirty. Was my soiled conscience a result of the affection that we so freely shared when no one was looking, or was it due to the fact that we nearly left the body we found to decompose without the dignity of a proper Christian burial?

"I know what I saw," I said. I hoped that he would agree without a second thought, but once the words were spoken, brittle silence enfolded us once again.

In that space I recalled to mind the girl's pallid face. There was something familiar about it. Not her face, specifically, but its general contours and the structure of her bones. I met someone who looked like that once before, when I was a child. I held my tongue. I feared that Constantine was choosing to doubt what we witnessed the night before. If he could doubt the things he saw with his own eyes and heard with his own ears, why would he believe an extraordinary tale from my childhood, something he had not seen or heard himself.

"Tino?" I whispered, trying to coax a response from him. I opened the gate to the chicken coop. It creaked on its rusty hinges. The sound unnerved me. The hens came rushing out, in their usual frantic flutter, but we were both ready for it. Our feet were positioned correctly and our shoulders were squared. This time they wouldn't topple either of us.

"I don't know, Yorgos," he said at last. "Our night started out normal enough, but it got so weird." He poured the water into the trough.

"Yes, it did," I agreed while dumping the food scraps into the dish left on the ground.

"I mean, the wolves are one thing," he said. "Yes, I believe we saw the wolves. Both Christopheros and Yannis said they heard them too."

"But . . . ?" I prompted.

"But the black cat and the girl, they don't make sense. I don't know. Looking around us now, in the morning light, it all seems like a dream. It couldn't have really happened."

It seemed that for Constantine, the sun was a light that could burn away the memories of the things that haunt him in the night, making them seem less real, less substantial. I'm sure to him, in the light of day, it all seemed like so many compounded nightmares. I wished that the sun was as bright for me.

My chest swelled and my breathing became ragged.

"I thought you saw the cat. You assured me that I hadn't imagined it."

"Maybe we both imagined it," he suggested. I drew air into my lungs through my mouth, and forced it out my nose. I nodded, not in agreement, but in acceptance. That cat had been a secret, of sorts, one I really wanted to share with someone who would believe me. Though he was beside me, I felt utterly alone.

I split the eggs I carried between the studio I worked in and the one adjacent to it. I then asked Constantine to deliver the contents of his basket to the ikon writers who preferred to work in their own cells. Before he set out to do what I asked, I excused him from that morning's lesson, saying that I wanted to work alone.

When I entered the studio, I was glad to find it empty. I lit the candles and lamps, and rummaged through my things for the ikon I wanted to work on. I found it buried under one of the stacks of plain white panels I prepared ahead of time to receive fresh images. The tortured image of Christ was still halved by the crack that ran its length from top to bottom. I ran my finger up and down the blemish, hoping I could save it. I though I could. Thankfully, the crack was superficial. I would repair it and alter the image to match the vision I shared with Constantine.

First, I set the ikon aside, made the sign of the cross, and paused a moment to center myself. I invited God's spirit to come. I offered him my hands, and asked that he would use them to his glory, while I sought to capture on wood the image of his suffering. And then, as was the tradition before starting any sacred task, I asked God for the grace to pardon my enemies. Having done that, I reached for the ikon. Before lifting it I hurriedly added a postscript to my prayer, "Father please forgive me if the image I intend to write does not please you."

While I began the task of repairing it, self-understanding brightened my mind. I pursed my lips, shaking my head at myself. Tino was always in my thoughts and intentions, even when I was upset with him.

I pushed all of that out of my mind. A damaged ikon needed repairing. I prayerfully focused all of my attention on that one, single task.

17 Coming Undone

All that day, I remained in the studio pouring myself into the ikon. Thankfully, the others I shared the space with preferred to write their ikons in contemplative silence. Conversation was not expected or desired. That was perfect for me. I preferred to brood over both what I worked on and my bruised emotions.

As the day wore on, everything simply fell away; the fear from the wolves, the horror of our grisly find, the loneliness of not having someone to bear witness to the cat, and the nagging guilt about the intimacies I shared with Constantine. Yes, it all fell away until only I, and the image of Christ upon the cross, remained. It didn't open up or come alive like I always wished it would since my first animated encounter, but a subtle Presence that felt like healing balm poured over me.

While I smoothed the edges of the crack and began to repaint the image, I agonized over how I should render it. I had second thoughts. Should I be faithful to my vision of the Crucified One, or should I be faithful to the cannons of the church? I knew that representing it exactly like I had seen it, which is what Constantine requested, was absolutely not canonical. It would be frowned upon as a novelty and probably worse.

After spending the better part of the day preparing the panel and beginning the repairs, I set it aside to allow the day's work to dry and went outside. I was hungry. I passed the entire day so focused on my work that I forgot to stop and eat. Since I missed all the services and both meals, I decided to go for a walk. I retrieved my topcoat from my cell and set out.

With my attention diverted from sacred work to more mundane matters, all my troubling thoughts returned.

I meandered along the switchback trails, passing my prayer rope through my fingers knot by knot, repeating the Jesus Prayer like a mantra. I didn't stray far from the gate. I had no desire to be locked out again. I merely wanted to clear my thoughts, and, if possible, to further unburden my soul of its troubles.

When twilight laid claim to the sliver of time between day and night, it was time to return to the protective walls of the monastery. I walked along the path that threaded through the olive grove on the cliffs above the sea. I turned, and with the ocean now behind me, began the trek back. A familiar sound began to pulse between my ears: purring. I stopped in my tracks and looked around, trying to locate the cat with my eyes. In that moment, I feared perhaps it had tricked me into believing it was benign. Perhaps Constantine was right to be suspicious. It was the cat, above all else, that I feared would come between us. So great was my disappointment when Constantine doubted he had really seen it.

The sound between my ears grew louder. The beast was approaching me. I crouched low to the ground and ran my hand over the dirt. I gathered several stones, both rough and smooth, which I transferred to my passive hand, then I held myself still. Several paces ahead of me a shadow crossed the trail. I palmed one of the stones in my dominant hand. The cat crossed the trail again. It stopped midway and turned to look at me. Its yellow eyes reflected the moonlight and glowed with the same intensity.

Charging after it, I threw the stone. The cat turned to flee, but looked at me over its shoulder while it retreated. I threw another stone and struck its head.

"Go away. I don't need you," I shouted. "No one believes in you, so why should I?"

I palmed a third stone and launched it at the beast, striking its flank. It dove head first into the ground cover and disappeared from view. I ran up to the edge of the trail and released a volley of stones from my left hand. "Go," I yelled, "and don't ever come back."

I stood still for a moment gasping for breath, trying to calm myself down. I wondered why I didn't feel any better. With my hands on my knees, I forced deep breaths into my lungs, and expelled them slowly.

"Yorgos, is that you?" I tensed when I heard Constantine's shout. "They are about to lock the gate."

"Yes! It's me," I answered.

"I'm coming." I sprinted to him. When I caught up, he threw me a hunk of bread and tossed a pear into the air. I reached out and caught it before it fell into his upturned palm.

"I saw you weren't at supper," he explained, "so I brought you these." I devoured the bread and bit into the pear while we headed home together. When he reached for my hand, I smeared juice on his fingers.

While we passed out of the shadows into the light of the lanterns that were hung along the walls at the entrance of the monastery, we parted from each other like the waters of the Red Sea, and the gates thundered shut behind us before being locked for the night.

At the door of my cell, I looked up and down the hall before straining on the tips of my toes to reach his lips. He crooked his neck to meet me, but instead of kissing me he licked pear juice from my lips and chin with a mischievous smile.

"Thank you for the food, Tino," I said, nudging him with my shoulder. He backed away from me, winking before disappearing down the stairs.

Having said our good-byes for the night, I shut the door and drew the latch closed before collapsing onto my mattress.

With my middle finger, I traced the space between my parted lips. Tino brought me food and walked me to my cell to make sure I made it home safely. I wasn't as alone as I felt after all.

It was then I understood something I hadn't understood before. There are some things a person cannot believe, or his world just might become too dark for him to bear. And there are people who cannot deny the darkness, once they have seen it, no matter how badly they wished they could. In that sense, Constantine and I were different kinds of people. That didn't mean I was alone, not in all respects at least.

The wolves came out again that night, and the night after. Both nights, hoping to spy a glimpse of one, I stood without resting before the slit window of my cell. I came to believe that the moon was a source of both pleasure and torment for them. Something about their plaintive song that rose above and silenced the singing of crickets and the frogs, enchanted me and kept me on my feet into the wee hours of the morning. On the third night, sometime after midnight, an emotion like fear took hold of me. But it wasn't fear at all, it was more like awe. An instinct told me that another world, one usually unseen by humankind, yet co-existent with us, had come out of the shadows into the light of the full moon. *But why now? And why on Mount Athos?*

Though the monastery was unsettled after the second night's commotion, no one considered the wolves to be a serious threat, even after Old Father Maximus said that he had a bad feeling. We were protected by a wall and several guard towers, after all.

On the morning after the third night, however, when what was left of the bodies of three wild boar and a badger were discovered strewn along the nearby trails, panic broke out, and more than a few of us took the old Father's trepidation more seriously.

As soon as word about the dead animals reached him, Evangelos apologized to Constantine and me that he had doubted us about the wolves. To my disappointment, he made no mention of the girl.

By nightfall of the fourth evening, the monks of Grigoriou were armed and ready for the hunt. We even accepted provisions of arrows that Old Father Maximus crafted from silver when he was a young man, as it was his duty to protect his village from malignant supernatural beings. In addition to those arrows, our quivers were filled with conventional ones.

Those of us who did not know how to shoot an arrow, like Constantine and me, were hastily taught in case any wolves breached the strong enclosure. The walls were built to keep pirates out. How could a wolf scale them?

Throughout the fourth night, Grigoriou and the land surrounding it was empty and quiet. The wolves did not return. On the fifth and sixth nights, the monks of Grigoriou remained ready to defend themselves from any wild beast that might breach the defenses, but none did. So, after a few days, the threat that wolves would come so close to a human settlement was forgotten and written off as an odd occurrence. Everyone in our little brotherhood of ascetics returned to life as normal.

Everyone, that is, except for Constantine and me. As the days turned to weeks, all the sneaking around and keeping of secrets began to wear on me. I missed more of the services than I attended and my prayers suffered. Though I loved Tino dearly, I missed God, for I had to push one of them out of my mind to be able to focus my thoughts on the other. The problem was, I couldn't ever really stop thinking about Constantine. I found myself wishing I could split in two. One of me would pursue my vocation with a singular passion and love God with all of his heart. The other of me would court Tino and love him with all of his. I was beginning to fear that as a whole, singular person, I couldn't love both. A choice had to be made, and I loathed making it.

The one constant for me was my work in the studio. I focused my energies on repairing the damaged ikon. It was fitting that it was an image of the crucifixion. What better image is there to meditate on when one is being utterly undone by his passions?

18 Where Many Equals One

O n the first night of the next full moon, long after most of my fellow brothers had gone to bed, I knelt prostrate on the floor of my cell. Though the singing of crickets and other nocturnal creatures filled the air, I didn't find pleasure in it like I usually did. I felt too desolate.

Arranged on a shelf in the corner, my ikons loomed above me. Because of the passion that ravaged my heart, I feared the perfection they exemplified would always elude me. Yet I called out to every saint I could think of; even Nona and Papus, asking for their prayers.

When my affair with Constantine began, there had been a sweetness to it that was all but gone now. Now, it was mostly bitter and pained. It's not that I didn't love him, I did, and I cherished every moment that we spent together. The affair was spoiled by guilt. I feared I knew what I must do, but wasn't ready to do it. I needed strength. To find it, I looked to the example of the saints who went before me, because they had, undoubtedly, encountered similar struggles of their own.

I repeated the Jesus Prayer more times than I could remember when I noticed the sudden and peculiar absence of sound.

I finished my silent repetition and rose from my knees. While looking to the slit window, I crossed myself. Moonlight flooded my cell with a silver wash of cool light.

Then, from a distant place, howling began. It sounded sad, small, and unimposing; an echo of my own inner state. At first, only a single wolf howled. While I remained on my knees, listening to it, the sound grew louder. I felt I was being summoned, *but by what?* I rose and strode to the window. The single voice, echoing through the darkness, seemed lonely to my ears. I was drawn to answer its loneliness, to be instrumental in ending it, until two more wolves raised their voices to the moon, making a chorus of three. They were heading to the monastery!

I had an urge to go outside so I could hear them better and share in their experience of the cold and lonely night.

I dressed quickly and went out, taking the stairs three at a time. Soon, I stood in the middle of the courtyard.

When I stopped to catch my breath, I heard something sharp scraping stone. From the other side of it, a form scrabbled to the top of the wall and ran along it, until it was parallel with me. It was like nothing I had ever seen before. If I felt awe a month before when I listened to the wolves from the safety of my tiny cell, I felt a holy terror now. Something that was neither human nor animal–but inexplicably both–paced the wall with its gaze fixed on me.

In the light of the moon, I saw the beast's silhouette in profile. It had arms and legs, but it mostly walked on all fours like a dog. All ten of its digits were sharply clawed. The beast's body–starting with a slobbery, fanged snout– was long, muscular and sleek. It ended in a tapered tail that whipped about excitedly. Its white fur reflected the moonlight.

The great monster drew air into its nostrils while it turned toward me, scenting me. I backed away, wishing I hadn't ventured out. The beast took a deeper breath, its body expanding with it. With a howl, it leapt from the wall and landed, crouching on its feet before advancing toward me on all fours.

I screamed. The awe and holy terror I felt before were gone. I felt fear now, plain and simple, fear.

I threw myself onto the stairs that led to my cell and the beast was on top of me. It cornered me with my back pressed against the rough masonry. The vrykolakas–I knew that was what the creature was, one who eats living meat–closed its eyes to slits and pressed its nose against my neck, its hot breath bursting on my skin. It drew my scent into its nostrils before opening its jaws. When its fangs pricked my skin, I closed my eyes and pictured Christ upon the cross washing me clean with his blood.

"Have mercy on me," I whispered.

I believed I had prayed my last prayer. I would have crossed myself too, but the beast was too close. Its breath on my neck was so impossibly hot I believed the fires of hell burned in the depths of its stomach. To my surprise, the vrykolakas did not crush my throat; it drew back. I sensed it was confused.

Numerous doors opened and the sandled feet of many monks came slapping down the hall to the staircase.

"Wolf! Wolf!" Tino screamed while the bells of the monastery rang to rouse them all. Tino's cry was repeated by several monks at once, followed by a stampede of black-clad men down the stairs and from their cells.

The vrykolakas cocked its head and eyed me peculiarly until armed monks led by brother Christopheros descended upon it like a ragtag band of soldiers. The creature retreated on its feet before touching its paw-like hands to the ground and sprinting away.

I trembled where I stood, unable to move. Constantine came to me. He kissed me full on the mouth, without fear or shame. I leaned into it.

"I thought that wolf was going to kill you," he said, while he pressed his lips to mine again. I closed my eyes, allowing his touch and his affection to comfort me. When I opened my eyes, I saw Evangelos watching us keenly. With pandemonium all around, our kiss concerned him the most.

Two other vrykolakes scaled the wall and bounded to the white one. They ignored the monks that descended upon them until brother Christopheros stood in their way. The first, with mottled gray and black fur, captured him in its jaw and tossed him aside. He slammed into three more brothers, knocking them to the ground.

The monks rushed in and scattered. The grey and black beast placed itself between the white vrykolakas and the monks. The second, a multicolored animal with steel-blue eyes, cornered the white one. Grabbing hold of one of its legs with its paw-like hands, it snapped the bone in two and the white vrykolakas wailed. While the white one struggled to break free of its captor, a host of silver arrows hissed through the air, striking them all.

Brother Christopheros, scratched and bloodied, charged the beast with bow and arrow in hand. The gray and black vrykolakas lunged at him. It crushed his neck with its jaws, before throwing him over its shoulder and escaping over the wall with him.

The multicolored beast, having lost its ivory prey, began to limp to safety. It resembled a pin cushion with so many silver arrows quivering in its hide.

The white one fled, favoring its broken leg. While it ran, its body shifted back and forth, between two different forms. One moment it was a white vrykolakas, the next it was a white deer. In between, it was an impossible cross of the two. When it disappeared into the distance, I swear it became the smaller form of an adolescent child. However, the shadows obscured it, and I couldn't be certain of what I had actually seen.

In the courtyard, mayhem continued. My brother monks descended on the multicolored vrykolakas. I rushed forward to see what was happening, and was astonished to see that they surrounded not a fierce and deadly beast, but a badly injured human female with numerous silver and bronze arrows protruding from her skin. I looked from her to the place where the adolescent limped away. A strong suspicion came over me. In spite of my fear, and the fact that I barely escaped death from the adolescent's monstrous jaws, I felt an overwhelming compulsion to follow her into the shadows.

I looked up to see Hegumen Evangelos bearing down on me with Constantine close behind him.

The Hegumen, with his gaze turned down to the woman on the ground, opened his mouth to speak, and Constantine called my name. I ignored them both and ran after the girl.

Constantine continued to call after me, but only followed me to the edge of the light. I ventured alone into the ever deepening shadows.

The farther I went, the less light there was to see by because the buildings of the monastery and the surrounding wall with its guard towers blocked out the moon. I cursed under my breath, wishing I had thought to bring an oil lamp. It was too late for that.

Still in shock from my encounter with the vrykolakas, I trembled while traveling deeper into the moonless darkness. Vrykolakas. The word alone staggered my heart. Though I hadn't heard it spoken aloud since my earliest days on Mount Athos, I remembered it well; because it was the only word I ever knew to cause my stoic father to fear. He spoke of vrykolakes the night before we made our hasty departure for the Holy Mountain, warning me of their terrible, godless existence. He uttered 'vrykolakas' to the monks of Mount Athos when he begged them to let me stay, even though I was four years too young. And now, I had seen one up close. It could have killed me. No wonder my father feared them.

Since my eyes were rendered useless by the dark, I followed whatever senses I could, especially my sense of sound. It led me back to the chicken coop. Something was upsetting the hens.

I went to the shed next to the coop, and fumbled through it for the lantern and two pieces of flint I used whenever I collected eggs before sunrise. Gathering lint from my pockets, I patted the earth in search of dry twigs, sticks and leaves. I made a pile with what I found and banged the pieces of flint over it until a spark ignited the kindling. With a burning stick from the tiny fire, I set flame to the lantern's wick. Once it ignited, I stomped the fire out.

All the while, commotion inside the coop continued. Over a guttural, yet human growl, I heard the chickens clucking and beating their wings. Making my approach slowly, I held the lantern in front of myself as far as I could reach. When I opened the squeaky gate, several of the hens came rushing out, but there were fewer of them than usual.

What I discovered inside the coop astonished me. A naked girl–I guessed she was the same one who the wolves attacked a month earlier–was squatting in the corner. Several arrows, both silver and conventional, protruded from her body. She held a squawking chicken up to her mouth and bit into it, tearing off a mouthful of warm feathered flesh. Piled knee-deep around her were the carcasses of chickens that had met the same fate. Some of them still twitched their wings and legs. The rest were more thoroughly dead than that, though all of them had been torn into and bitten from when they were yet alive.

Broken eggs were everywhere. It grieved me to see them wasted like that. While I approached her, shells crunched under my feet. I winced with every step.

"I need sustenance so I can heal," she mumbled, while trying to pull a silver arrow out of her thigh. The shaft snapped off, leaving the arrowhead lodged under the surface of her skin. She let the shaft drop to the floor, tossed aside the hen she gnawed on, and looked up at me while shielding light from her eyes with her blood-smeared hand. Scenting me, in much the same way she had when she was still in her wolf-form, she pressed her back into the corner of the coop, edging away from me. Disgust flashed across her face and her lip curled to reveal her merely human teeth.

"You're the one mother sent me for," she said, while successfully dislodging one of the arrows. She dropped it to the floor. "She didn't warn me that you'd smell like that."

"Like what? What do I smell like?" I asked, feeling surprised that with all the questions I had, that was the first one I chose to give voice to.

"I smell the blood on you," she answered.

"What blood? Whose blood?" She ignored my questions.

"I know you are only a mortal," she continued. "My nose tells me that too, but you sure smell like a blood-drinker." My breath left me. "The only way I can think of to prevent it, is to make you like me," she continued.

"You mean to make me a vrykolakas, one who eats meat?"

"Yes."

Most of my questions fell out of my mind, replaced, simply, by fear. One question did remain, "The only way to prevent what?"

"The blood-drinker from turning you into a creature like himself. You've been marked. He will come." I backed away, wishing I hadn't let my curiosity compel me to follow her.

"Those are my choices?" I asked, crossing myself. "I don't want to be either kind of vrykolakas." When I backed into the gate I reached behind myself for the rake that I knew was leaning against the jamb. Exactly what I planned to do with it, I wasn't sure. I had no intention of hurting her unless she attacked me first.

"Put your weapon away. I am too weak and wounded to harm you," she said, and she laughed adding, "Or to help you, rather."

"I don't need your help. Not if it means making me like you." I approached her again slowly, watching while she pulled two more arrows out of her flesh, and lay them atop the others. "Besides, from the looks of it, I would say you need my help. You said your mother sent you? How do you know I am the one she sent you to find?"

"Is your name Yorgos Godevenos?"

Mouthing the word 'Yes,' I nodded.

"She sent me for you. She said you'd know where the Man of God lived. She said only you could take me to him."

"Man of God?" I stammered. "I don't know who you are talking about. I'm sure you've got the wrong person."

"No," she countered. "You *are* the right person. Tell me, how is your brother Zosimos doing?" My pulse thrummed painfully under the surface of my skin. It emboldened me. I was certain that if I were to run, or fight, I would be successful either way. However, I steadied myself.

"He is alive, but still sick," I answered. "At least he was, last I heard."

"He won't die. You can count on that. The water you gave him is potent."

"How do you know about that?"

She chuckled lightly saying, "Even still you do not understand. It was my aunt who helped you." I covered my mouth with my hand and nodded my head again.

"And now . . . ?" I said, speaking through the space between my fingers.

"My mother requires your help. She says you owe my family this debt." Yes, I was beginning to understand.

A silver arrow was lodged in her shoulder. I knelt in front of her and reached for it. She recoiled from my touch, but relented and let me pull it out. The shaft snapped off, leaving the arrowhead inside her open flesh.

"I'm sorry." Without aggression she brushed my hand away, along with my apology.

"You will come, won't you? Mother said you would come." Hegumen Evangelos calling my name distracted me from answering.

"Yorgos? Where are you?" I gathered a wool blanket from a shelf and gave it to her saying, "Cover yourself and wait here."

I ducked out of the coop to face my mentor. The sky was lightening. Morning would soon break. When he saw me, the Hegumen sighed deeply, seeming relieved.

"I feared the worst," he said.

Off in the distance, from within the monastery's encompassing wall, a pillar of smoke snaked into the sky.

"What's happening?" I asked. "Did something catch fire?"

"We *started* the fire. Where is the white vrykolakas?"

"It's gone. What is the fire for?" Something banged inside the coop and several more hens came rushing out into the safety of the morning light.

"It is a pyre for the monsters," he said, approaching the open gate. I covered my face with my hands and pressed the tips of my fingers into my eyes. "Yorgos, where is the girl?"

I knew what the girl was. I knew that in the light of the full moon she became a flesh eating beast. But what Evangelos suggested was just as unconscionable as any evil she might be capable of. Surely there had to be another way. I shrugged, unwilling to answer.

Evangelos crossed the threshold into the coop saying, "Never mind, I found her."

I paced the open air hall muttering prayers and crossing myself. Three floors below, Evangelos and others stoked the flames, making them burn hotter and reach higher.

I had gotten myself into an impossible predicament. I saw no way out of it that was easy or guiltless. I could disobey the Hegumen by abandoning my post, or I could follow through with what he required and be party to the young girl's death and destruction. I didn't particularly like either choice.

"Yorgos, is that you . . . ? Yorgos . . . ?" I placed my hand on the door and pressed my ear into the wood. "I know it's you. I could recognize your scent anywhere."

"Yes, I am here," I answered.

"What's happening?"

"They're building a fire."

She beat on the door, "You must take me to my mother. She will explain everything! Please! Don't let them burn me up!" I turned away from the door and paced again, trying to shut out her pleas.

"Say something. Are you still there?" The fear in her voice made her sound small, weak, and vulnerable. How could she be a threat? It became easy, for the moment, to forget that a terrible beast lived within her, one that would be released each and every full moon unless, or until, she suffered the flames. I stopped and went back to the door.

Reaching into my pocket for the key, I fumbled with it at the lock when I heard footsteps coming up the stairs. My cheeks blanched and I shoved the key back into my pocket.

It was Tino.

"What's happening?" I asked.

"They've drawn and quartered the woman," he answered. I could tell by his grimace that the present turn of events disturbed him as much as they did me. My stomach churned.

"And then?" I prompted.

He turned his gaze to the pyre burning below. I went to the bannister and placed my palms on it, taking in the inferno. I wished to God that this would end without any more casualties, beast or man.

Through the wooden door that separated us, I heard the girl shout in desperation, "Yorgos! Please help me! You must repay your debt!" I looked from the door to the fire. Tino turned my head, with his fingers on my chin, forcing me to look at him.

"What did she mean by that?" he demanded.

"There's no time to explain. I've got to help her escape." He blocked the way.

"I'm afraid for you. I want to understand. Take time and explain it to me."

Sighing deeply, I relented. "I once spoke with a nereid in the hills above the village where I grew up. I was young." Once I started, the story came rushing out of me. I told it quickly, leaving out all but the most pertinent details.

He listened, without interrupting, while I described Papus and his penchant for telling stories. I explained about the illness that nearly ended my brother's life, and told of his deathbed request that I retrieve the water from the nereid cave that he believed would save him. I ended by telling of my encounter with the nereid princess and

247

how she blessed the water, promising that my brother's life would be spared, and it had been. My brother was still alive.

"Now the nereids expect me to repay my debt by helping the girl."

"How? What can you do that a nereid can't?" And then he laughed. "Listen to what I am saying! I don't even believe in nereids. They're just stories old people tell."

"You're wrong, Tino. I've seen things . . . ." I glanced down. Evangelos and Maximus were approaching the ground-level stairs. "I can't say I understand it, but this world is much more than it seems." I looked him in the eyes and placed my hands on his shoulders to move him out of the way. He yielded and stepped aside.

"I'll be back, Tino. Please, go talk to them. Stall them for me. I have to do this." He nodded reluctantly, with tears filming his eyes. He wiped them away and sprinted down the stairs without speaking or looking back.

I fumbled with the key to open the door and found her balanced on her one good foot with the blanket wrapped around herself. Her other foot was black and blue, twisted out of shape and broken at the ankle.

"If I am going to help you get home, I want to know what to call you," I said.

"I'm Galatea."

Footsteps ascended the stairs and Tino rushed to the two elders, trying to engage them in conversation. We both looked toward the stairwell and understood that the time for talking could wait.

"Come on." I waved her over. She hobbled into the hall and stumbled into me. "Climb onto my back," I said, squatting.

While we escaped down the back stairs, my thoughts kept turning to the one who had been drawn and quartered.

I didn't speak until we made it past the gate and were well on our way.

"The woman . . . the one . . . ."

"They're burning her pieces now." Galatea said dispassionately.

"I'm sorry I wasn't able to help her."

"Don't be."

"I thought she was with you. I thought they were both with you."

"No. A month ago, on the last full moon, the two vryko-lakes who followed me over the wall last night attacked me. They left me for dead like vrykolakes always do."

"I remember. I was there," I said. She ignored my interruption.

"Their cursed magic worked and I quickly recovered from my wounds. They've come back for me, and I don't know why. I fear they want to take me from my family."

"How can I help you? I'm only a man, a mortal man."

"You are much more than that, Yorgos. You exist in a crossroads between the supernatural and natural worlds. You always have."

"No, that's ridiculous," I scoffed. "I'm a writer of ikons. I have faith and I pray. That's supernatural enough for me."

"No it's not. It never will be. Think back over your life, Yorgos. You just happened to be there when this happened to me. You've received the aid of nereids and have met–"

"Mister Dumitru."

"Yes, the blood-drinker. I only hope you'll be spared."

"Stop it, Galatea, please. You're making me uncomfortable."

I traveled with her on my back for as long as I could stand it until the heat of the day beat on us and sweat dripped into my eyes. I needed a break. Feeling we had put Grigoriou far enough behind us, I set her down on a large boulder and leaned against it for support. We were in a clearing surrounded by various kinds of trees. I winced in sympathy when in the clear light of day I saw her many wounds. From some of them, I saw the glint of metal where the shafts snapped off leaving the silver arrowheads lodged under her skin.

"You might be small, but you're heavy," I said, panting and thrusting my bent elbows behind myself to crack my back. "I don't think I can carry you any longer." She tried to stand up, but her foot couldn't sustain the weight of her body. She collapsed back onto the rock.

I had an idea and took a look around.

"You said earlier that the wounds you sustained from the vrykolakes healed quickly. I wonder, why aren't you healing quickly now?"

"I think that the silver in my body prevents spontaneous healing." While we spoke, I saw what I hoped to find; a broken off branch of a laurel tree that was shaped perfectly for what I had in mind.

"Will it help you if I dig the silver out?" She grimaced.

"No. I'd rather have my mother do it. Besides, it would take too long."

I snapped off the excess wood and fashioned a crutch she could support herself with.

We traveled all day, hiking up the steep face of Mount Athos, stopping frequently to rest and drink from the springs and creeks we passed along the way. I am sure her foot slowed us down. However, Mount Athos is so steep; it would have taken skilled hikers the better part of a day to scale it.

While the humid day burned on, we kept conversation to a minimum, and a companionable silence embraced us until the sun began to set. At last, it began to cool and a refreshing breeze soothed my skin.

"I need to rest," Galatea said. She stopped hobbling and leaned against an old gnarled oak. Her body trembled, like the canopy of leaves spread out above us. She closed her eyes and scrunched her face.

"Are you alright?" I asked.

"Yes. I think I'm feeling the call of the moon, I don't know for sure. Last night was the first time." She winced again, moaning. Though human, it echoed the cry of a wolf.

Fear stole my breath and I backed away from her. Looking at me, she lifted her chin, her eyes fluttering.

"The blood smells stronger on you tonight," she said, sniffing the air. Her hoarse voice sounded bestial and her breath was labored. She struggled to stand. With the support of the crutch she took several faltering steps.

"You must become like me, it's the only way. Let me do it . . ." Her skin, and the bones beneath it, quivered. It appeared that the wolf inside would tear through the shape that contained it, if it could.

"Galatea!" I snapped. "Galatea! Do you really want me to suffer as you have?"

I backed into a pine tree. She grabbed my wrist and pulled it to her mouth.

"Galatea!" I wrested my arm free before she could bite it. She shook her head, and opened her eyes.

"I'm sorry, Yorgos. The wolf wants to come out and play."

"The wolf wants you to attack me," I said, my voice trembling.

"Yes, I know, but you are safe. Though my body wants to change, something is preventing it. Gingerly she touched one of the wounds. "My mother will know what to do."

"I hope so," I said, without confidence.

We traveled on. Soon we came across a creek where we stopped to refresh ourselves.

"If we follow this ribbon of water, we'll find my village," she said. I worried that the wolf might indeed have its way with her, and then with me, because the brighter the moon became, the more Galatea seemed to be caught in a fight between her two natures. Under my breath, I called out to Saint George, asking for his guidance and protection.

Galatea struggled to cross the steep terrain and remain as much in possession of herself as she could. She winced and groaned with every step. I regretted that there was nothing more that I could do for her than help her get home.

"My village is straight ahead," she said at length. She stopped, and leaned against the crutch with both hands. I looked where she pointed and saw only a deep ravine over-grown with many kinds of ancient trees and low-growing vegetation. The ravine cut into the side of the mountain which rose sharply to tower over it.

"I can only see trees," I said, turning to make sure she was steady.

"Look again." While the glamour that concealed the vil-lage from mortal eyes lifted, a series of overlapping concen-tric rings rippled vertically through the air in front of me.

It was then that I saw the village. Everything within the ravine burned with a subtle luminosity. The trees held homes within their branches. From their wide-open doors and windows, a thick honey-colored light came pouring out. Farther in the distance, caves with ornately carved entrances were hewn into the side of the mountain.

We followed the creek into the ravine where it widened into a small lake. Many nereids danced in circles on its shore and sang with their arms held high. Some of them randomly turned into little twisting clouds and disappeared into the darkening sky. Others assumed the shape of deer and ran through the trees down into the water where they drank before taking flight on four legs again.

Along the lakeshore, four nereids washed white clothes and hung them on the branches of surrounding laurel and oak trees. Galatea rushed to them calling their names. In her excitement, she tripped over her crutch and landed palms-first on the ground.

One of the nereids looked up.

"Galatea's come home!" she sang out loud. "Call her mother. Tell her Galatea's come home!" She rose from the rocky ground and came rushing upon us with silent swiftness of the wind. The other three nereids followed, and together they all carried Galatea to the water where they bathed her and cleaned her seeping wounds. While they ministered to her, they sang rhymes and lullabies in harmony. It reminded me of the chants and hymns that my brothers and I sang together in the Katholikon, and was nearly as moving.

"Thank you, Monk, for honoring your debt and being brave," they said together. Each one emphasized a phrase or two in turn, before deferring to the voice of another. "Thank you," they continued in like manner "for bringing our daughter home to us." Their voices were sweet, with a musical quality to everything that they said. I bowed, not sure how else to address them, and smiled.

Other nereids rushed upon Galatea and helped her into a white dress. Wood-folk came pouring out of the caves and homes in the trees to greet her. They pressed in on us from all sides until I was a lone mortal lost in a multitude of gods. I didn't belong there. I wanted to go home and be with my own kind. I wanted to return to my normal life and put this whole strange experience behind me.

"Is my debt paid? May I leave now?" I asked. The surrounding nereids only laughed. They lifted their eyes. I followed with my own and saw a white funnel twisting through the air, heading in our direction. It upset branches and leaves in its wake. Upon its final approach, the crowd of nereids that pressed in on me from all sides backed away, creating a large circle, leaving me in the center of it.

The funnel cloud touched down in front of me and continued to turn. Though the wind tugged on my hair and clothes, I stood my ground. The form of a human female coalesced inside the cloud. I could see through it, at first, but it quickly became more substantial until the wind subsided, collapsing into the woman.

Leaves and twigs dropped to the ground in the shape of a circle around her. She was taller than most Greek women I had ever known, and skinnier. Her features were nearly human; too perfect to be mortal and reminiscent of a deer.

Only one blemish marred her perfect features; a shiny scar that ran the length of her forehead and ended at the corner of her right eyebrow.

"No, dear one," she said, meeting my gaze. "You may not yet leave us. You have not yet repaid your debt."

"But!" I began to argue. And then I looked away, feeling ashamed, and not a little bit afraid. An instinct warned me not to pick a quarrel with a nereid.

"What more do you require of me?" I asked instead, my voice trembling. She lifted my chin with her fingertips so she could peer into my eyes.

"I see why you so impressed my sister," she whispered.

"Your sister?" I asked. "You mean, you and the nereid I met in the hills above my village are really related?"

She laughed saying, "All nereids are sisters, brothers, aunts, uncles, fathers, and mothers. Come."

The wind bore me up and lifted me through the air into the largest of the houses in the trees. All around, like whispers, I heard countless nereids singing "We are all one, one and many, many and one.

19 Family Secrets

The house in the trees was comfortably appointed with a simple crafted beauty and elegance to its wood, bone and hide furnishings.

Ambient light gave the room the golden glow of late afternoon. We were in what could only be described as an infirmary, however, it seemed that the tools of healing kept there were seldom put to use. They were so clean, sharp, and shiny, that I guessed the nereids didn't often suffer from injury or illness.

"Your guess is correct." The woman said, apparently reading my mind. I didn't like that she could do that. I felt altogether exposed. "Many of us bear the children of mortal men, who are more susceptible to injury and disease, like my dear daughter. It is true that the half-breeds heal quicker than mere mortals, but not always, and not from everything."

Thalia, that's what she called herself, had her back to me. One by one, she dug the arrowheads out and dropped them into a metal bowl filled with water. I sat on a tall wooden stool that had a place to rest my feet. After the hours spent hiking up the sheer face of Mount Athos, I needed more than a foot rest if I was going to regain my strength.

"All in good time," Thalia said. "Tonight you will rest well, I promise you that. We have things to discuss first."

I jumped from my perch and went to stand beside Galatea where she lay.

With some kind of magic or medicine that was unknown to me, her mother had caused her to fall into a deep sleep. I envied her that.

The first thing Thalia did was set the broken bone and immobilize it with a splint. Next, she turned her attention to dressing Galatea's wounds. Thalia only extracted the bronze arrowheads and left the three silver ones untouched.

"I offered to dig the silver out." I said. "It seems to have weakened her, but she wanted you to do it."

"You are so thoughtful," Thalia said, while extracting the last of the bronze arrowheads. She dropped it into the bowl. With a crimson splash, metal clinked against metal.

"Is there ever a time when showing kindness isn't your first thought?"

"You make me sound like a saint," I said.

"Aren't you a saint?" Turning my eyes away from hers I glanced down at the array of medical equipment spread out on the counter.

"Hardly," I scoffed.

"I can see into your thoughts, Master Godevenos the things you fear aren't nearly as bad as they seem."

"Tell that to God," I said.

"God!" she responded with a gasp. "Such a vast mind. Who can know it?"

Thalia passed her hands back and forth over her daughter's wounds. Her vibrating fingers and palms emitted a barely discernible light. She gently kneaded Galatea's flesh and the gashes without silver knit themselves closed beneath her touch.

"As long as the silver remains in her body, she will not become the wolf. So far, that temporary fix is the only solution I have been able to find. I hoped to avoid implementing it. I hoped we would be able to free her of this curse before piercing her with silver became necessary, but your brothers have done it for me."

She turned to wash her hands in another basin, one filled with fresh water. "Lucky for you," she continued, turning to face me, "the monks you live with are well armed. She might have attacked you if she were able." Once again, I noticed her scar. I winced, imagining the pain that must have accompanied the wound when it was fresh. Thalia saw me staring at it and gingerly patted it with her fingertips.

"Is the scratch still so visible? It should be completely healed by now."

"What happened?"

Galatea groaned and stretched, beginning to wake up.

"She scratched me last night when I tried to restrain her," Thalia said, turning to her daughter to continue her ministrations.

"It can't be that recent. It's almost completely healed."

"For a nereid, this one is healing slowly." She corrected.

Galatea stretched again and sat up. She looked around, as if trying to locate something, and said, "Mother, I've already apologized for that. I wasn't myself when I scratched you." While she spoke she covered her nose and grimaced. "What is that awful stench?" she asked. Her mother sniffed the air.

"I only smell the earth and her trees."

Searching for the source with her eyes, Galatea located me. "Oh, it's you, of course," she said. "I might have known. You smell even worse. I wish you could wash it off."

"What is my daughter talking about?" Thalia asked.

I looked away from her saying, "I have no idea."

"He smells like a blood-drinker. He's been marked. Take the silver out and let me make him a creature like myself."

Thalia's eyes narrowed. "Would you really do that, pass your curse on to another? And one who has shown you kindness, no less?"

"Anything is better than becoming a blood-drinker."

Thalia raised an eyebrow. I shrugged and Thalia looked into my eyes.

Memories came rushing back from the time when Mister Dumitru visited my family's inn. Some of the images were things I couldn't properly call memories because they were so deeply buried I could never have recalled them without Thalia's help, and they were things I didn't understand.

Thalia wiped her hands dry. She nodded to herself, with a look of regret, and spoke to her daughter, "It is not for us to decide whether being one kind of vrykolakas is worse than being the other."

Galatea pushed herself up from her bed with both hands. "I know which is worse. I must prevent it. I feel it in my bones."

"That is the meat-hungry wolf within you speaking. You are a higher order of being than that. You must try to remember it." Galatea fell back into the pillows. Thalia wept into the palms of her hands, a mortal gesture, and then looked at me with plaintive eyes.

"You must help her."

"I don't understand what you believe I can do. I am only a man, a mortal man."

"Yes, I agree," Thalia said. "However, you are also a monk of the religion that replaced Greece's ancient gods. And you owe a debt to my people. That makes you the only mortal on this peninsula who can help Galatea get to her father. There must be magic that he knows of which I am unaware. He can break the curse, I am sure of it."

Galatea pushed herself up to a sitting position, with her feet dangling over the side of the bed. Her broken foot already showed signs of healing. It wasn't as swollen or bruised as it had been mere hours before. "Can you take me to the Man of God?" she asked.

I was completely at a loss and Thalia knew it.

"Her father is the one you call Protos," she explained. "I watched him from the time he was a young man, but I could never approach him. Never. It wasn't allowed. Long ago, we promised the Holy Synod that we would not interfere with their ways. We also promised that we would not enter their fortresses or come anywhere near them. We have kept our promises. In exchange, they vowed to leave us be. We have been here for eons. That we should leave because your people, your men, decided to build fortresses devoted to your God here, was unthinkable, so we arrived at a truce.

"If you weren't allowed to approach him, how did you and her father meet?"

She sighed. "Many years ago, by your standards, he stumbled into the ravine where I was alone and washing my garments. He approached me, saying my beauty bewitched him. In time, I gave birth to Galatea. Since her attack, I have done all that I can, tried every cure known to nereid kind, and nothing has worked. Her transformation last night is proof of that."

"How do I explain all of this to him?" I asked. "Does he know what happened to her?"

"He was there the night the wolf-women—the vrykolakes—came for her. I bathed in the ocean while he taught Galatea one of his prayers. It was sweet." She smiled at the memory—a bitter expression, with little sweetness to it.

"I sensed her distress. When I came rushing from the depths of the water, they were both gone. That is the last time I saw him."

"How do you know he wasn't attacked too, if you couldn't find him?"

"The vrykolakes came after me. They didn't touch him," Galatea said. "Please take me to the Man of God."

"I am not sure if he can help you. Besides, Galatea, you saw what they did to the other woman they captured."

Thalia stepped forward.

"He would never hurt his own daughter. He would find a way to save her, I know it."

It didn't take me long to consider my options. As I saw it, I didn't have more than one.

"I know where the Protos lives," I said. "And yes, I will take you to him."

Thalia was true to her word. My sleep that night, in addition to being without interruption, was deep and restful. The full light of day streaming through the window woke me. I stretched and moaned, feeling reluctant to leave the comfort of the bed. In comparison to it, the furnishings in my cell at Grigoriou left much to be desired.

Soon, however, I felt the pangs of hunger made all the more intense by the aroma of breakfast being prepared. The knowledge that I could trade the comfort of soft pillows and blankets for the comfort of warm and tasty food drew me out from under the covers. The austerity of a monk's daily diet was something else that left much to be desired. I knew that on this occasion I wouldn't deny myself. I needed my strength, after all.

I found fresh clothes laid out for me. They were a perfect fit, even the shoes. I dressed and followed my sense of smell into the large kitchen which was filled with many aromas I didn't know, and some that I did. The table in the center of the kitchen was piled with Greek specialties. Seeing spanakopita, my favorite, delighted me. The smell always reminded me of Mother. The bittersweet pang of nostalgia pricked my heart. I hadn't seen her in nearly eight years. I wondered, for a moment, how I could stand the separation. I pushed the thought from my mind.

"Eat up," Thalia said. I grabbed a plate and utensils.

"Your mother finds the separation to be intolerable too. With a saint for a son, how could she not?"

I nodded my thanks while chewing on an oversized bite.

"Where is Galatea?" I asked with plumped cheeks. The task of leading her to the Great Lavra gave me the jitters. If I was going to take her to her father, why delay it? It was best to get it over and done with, so I could sooner face the consequences of what I had done. *Evangelos must be worried and angry with me. And Tino.* My thoughts went to Tino for the first time since I asked him to distract Evangelos and Maximus so I could help Galatea escape. I knew that he would be the most worried of them all. I regretted putting him through this: disappearing for days without any way to let him know that I was alive. Yes, I wanted to get this done so I could go home.

"Her aunts are helping her dress," Thalia answered, drawing me out of my thoughts.

"Her foot?" I asked.

"Nearly healed. She responded well to my treatment. She's already able to wear shoes!"

When Galatea and her aunts entered the kitchen, I dropped my fork onto my plate. I almost didn't recognize her.

"What do you think?" she asked, turning a slow circle, with her arms spread like wings, so I could see her from all sides.

"First, if you want to pass as a boy you've got to move like one. Most adolescent boys wouldn't do that if they knew someone was watching." She dropped her hands flat to her sides and looked at me straight on.

"Now?" She asked.

"Better," I said. I put my plate down–after shoveling another bite into my mouth–and went to her. I ran my fingers over her head. Her hair was cropped close to her scalp. I winced. Even I could feel the pain of that loss.

"My hair will grow back," she said. "I don't mind." The clothes she wore were not unlike my own: plain and boyish–purely utilitarian.

"Do you think she will pass?" one of her aunts asked.

"We hoped this would help if he takes her into the fortress."

"I am sure it will," I said, forcing a smile.

"You seem unconvinced?" Thalia said.

"Yes," I answered. "I am unconvinced. Not that this disguise will work, I believe that it will. I am unconvinced that there is anything the Protos can do for her."

"Do you not have faith in your own God?" The five women asked in unison, each one emphasizing a word or two the same way they had done the night before.

"I do have faith," I said, unwilling to confess outloud that it wasn't my God that I doubted, but Galatea's father. The lack of compassion he showed me on the day I arrived left a lasting impression on me.

We decided in committee that the nereids would take us as close to the Great Lavra as they were able, without breaking any of their promises to the Holy Synod. I would take her the rest of the way on foot, and make sure she arrived safely and found her father.

The five nereids came together and began to dance circles around Galatea and me. While the seconds passed they danced faster, and faster, until they blended together, and became one great white funnel-cloud which lifted us up into the air.

We passed out of the ravine in which they lived, around the holy mountain, and down the side opposite the one

Galatea and I had climbed. Within minutes, the nereids deposited us on the road merely a twenty minute walk from the Great Lavra. While hugging Galatea good-bye, they looked hopeful. I still had my doubts. When they said their good-byes to me, I avoided making eye contact with any of them, lest they might detect my unbelief.

Once alone, I noted that the sun had just begun to rise. The air was cool and crisp. It seemed to be hours earlier here than it had been back at the nereid village. I wondered at that.

Galatea chuckled.

"Look at you," she said, pulling twigs and leaves from my hair. I returned the favor, and brushed debris from her shoulders and back as well.

"You look presentable," I told her.

"So do you."

"Shall we go, then?"

She nodded, with a hopeful smile saying, "Which way?"

I pointed down the hill toward the Aegean Sea. "Straight ahead."

I muttered a hasty silent prayer that things would go well, and that I was wrong about the Protos. I prayed that we would find him quickly.

"I'm ready," she said. Without further delay, we began our descent.

Our hike was short. Within minutes, the imposing wall that encompassed The Great Lavra and the fifteen guard towers atop it was within view. From our vantage, it appeared that the monks of Lavra had not yet risen, however I knew that couldn't be true. At the very least, some offered prayers and chants in the Katholikon, and others busily prepared breakfast in the kitchen.

"Is that my father's fortress?" she asked, her voice tinged with wonder.

"Yes. That's where he lives."

While I dutifully trudged on down the hill, she ran ahead with a new aura of lightness about her. When I caught up to her, she was hiding behind the leafage of a low-growing tree near the sloping hills of an olive grove that reached all the way down to the sea. Through branches and leaves, she watched while a monk harvested olives and placed them in a basket that he cradled in one arm.

"Father?"

The black-clad hieromonk looked toward the sound of her voice, squinting.

"Father!" she repeated. She stepped from behind the tree and said, "It's me!"

When he saw her, he threw his bounty down and sprinted up the gently sloping hill. In his haste, the skouphos tumbled off of his head. He looked naked without it. Any monk would.

Though I hadn't seen him since I arrived on the Holy Mountain almost eight years before, I recognized the man. It *was* the Man of God, as the nereids called him, her father, the Protos.

Galatea dashed down the hill to him. When they reached each other, he greeted her with a hug and lifted her off her feet. Swinging her in a circle, he set her back on the ground.

"I can't believe it," he said. "I hardly recognized you. What a clever disguise you've got on." He mussed her hair and smiled broadly. "I am so glad to see that you are alright, that you haven't been harmed."

I stood behind the tree where she had been, watching them.

"Well," she stammered, "I have been harmed. The vrykolakes attacked me. And two nights ago, at one of your other fortresses, men with silver arrows shot me." She looked away from him. "I wasn't myself at the time."

He dropped to his knees and pushed up her sleeves, one at a time, finding in her shoulder one of the wounds that still had a silver arrow head lodged in it. She lifted her shirt to show him the one in her side.

"I have a third wound here." She pointed to her thigh. "There were many others. Mother extracted all of the arrowheads, except the ones made of silver."

"I understand," he said. "Your mother always knows the right thing to do. I have so many questions. What were you doing at one of the other monasteries?"

"Mother sent me to find a man."

He stood to his feet, his eyes narrowing, and his forehead furrowed like a freshly plowed field.

"What man?" he asked, his voice colder, and his countenance darker, less open.

"She sent her to find me," I answered, stepping away from the tree. "I owed the nereids a debt. They decided it was time for me to pay."

"Evangelos' ward," he said. "Nearly all grown up. To which nereids are you referring, exactly? I am uncertain." He scratched his scalp. The ear he brushed his hand against was freshly pierced by a tiny silver spike. Blood crusted the wound, glittering in the morning sun like polished rubies.

"Mother said he was the only one who could help me get to you."

The Protos stepped away from his daughter.

"I don't know who you are talking about." He brushed dirt from his hands and retrieved his skouphos, placing it on his head. Then he shoved his hands into the pockets of his cassock.

"Father?" When Galatea reached for him, I pulled her back and guided her away.

"I think we've come to the wrong person," I said, leading her up the hill to the road. She resisted me, looking

265

over her shoulder. "No, no, that's my father, the Man of God." Her voice broke into sobs. "That's him!"

"No, Galatea, we've made a mistake."

Trailing behind, he followed us up to the road. I looked at him over my shoulder again and he regarded me coldly. His unspoken message was clear: *Don't tell anyone.* Looking away, he retreated back down the hill.

When we put enough distance between us and the Great Lavra, I pulled her by the wrist to a stop.

"Your father loves you, Galatea. I could see it when he thought he was alone with you."

"Why did he act the way that he did when he saw you? His behavior confuses me."

"He acted that way because he has broken one of our rules. More than one, I think. If he acknowledged you in my presence, it would be the same as admitting that."

"I don't understand."

"I can't say that I do either, but listen to me. I am so certain that he loves you, and that he cares about your well being, that I am going to pretend to leave you alone on the side of the road. See the thicket up there?" I pointed to a tangled mass of bushes, shrubs, and trees no more than fifty meters away. She nodded. "I am going to hide in it for as long as it takes. I know that he is going to come find you." I hugged her and headed to the thicket.

"Don't leave me," she pleaded.

"I won't be far. Just watch. He'll come." I dashed off into the concealing foliage and waited.

Approximately an hour and a half later, the Protos came wending up the road with an air of secrecy. From where I hid, I couldn't hear their conversation but from their actions it could easily be surmised.

He dropped to his knees in front of her and wrapped his arms around her waist. She bent forward with her hands on his head. She appeared to be imparting a blessing to a penitent. They held onto each before he rose to his feet, took her by the hand, and led her to the monastery. When they neared it, he dropped her hand and they entered the gate side by side; an elder monk with an aspirant.

20 A Confession To Make

I arrived at Grigoriou at dusk the following evening; tired, famished, and well beyond dirty. Supper had been served and was in fact, nearly over. It had been so many hours since I'd eaten more than what I could glean from the land that I would have been happy to eat the scraps from the table.

When I entered the refectory, even the monk reading from the lectern stopped what he was doing to look at me. Every man dropped or set down his spoon. Both Evangelos and Tino rose, followed by several others, who came pushing forward to greet me, to touch me, to make sure I wasn't an apparition. I hugged Tino and walked away from him with the Hegumen, who shepherded me outside with a guiding hand and a lantern. It hurt me to leave Tino standing there without apology or explanation, but I felt an urgent need to speak with my mentor. Tino would have to wait.

Evangelos shooed the men away, except for Old Father Maximus. The knots of his ever-present prayer rope moved through his fingers while he waited for the others to get a good look at me.

The three of us passed through the gate and walked several meters more before Maximus was satisfied that we were beyond earshot of any of the others. He began his inspection. Under the light of his own lantern, which he held above his head, I lifted my shirt to show him that there weren't any bites or scratch marks on my shoulders, back or stomach. He scrutinized my skin the best he could with his failing eyes and then passed the tips of his fingers over the surface of my flesh, searching, I assume, for any scabs or open wounds his eyes may have missed. I showed that my arms and legs had not been bitten either, and he followed the same procedure.

Satisfied that I bore no wounds, he held my face steady and stared into my eyes before lifting the silver crucifix that hung from his neck and pressing it to my forehead. It was cold and hard. I didn't have any noticeable reaction to it.

Throughout the examination, Evangelos kept his head bowed and passed the knots of his prayer rope through his fingers while muttering prayers under his breath.

"The beast did not attack him," Maximus said. "If he had been bitten, it would be too soon for his body to have healed so thoroughly," Evangelos sighed and looked up. He thanked the elder, who departed.

Without speaking, the Hegumen guided me up the trail to the stone alcove made for contemplation and prayer. We sat opposite each other, with Theotokos presiding over our conversation from the ikon on the wall.

"Brother Christopheros has not been found," he said, his focus on his prayer rope, which he held between his knees with his hands resting on his thighs. "I feared we lost you too. I feared the young girl bewitched you and lured you into a death trap, or worse."

"Worse?" I asked. He looked up from the rope.

"That she had made you into a meat-eater like herself."

"She was too weak. There was too much silver in her body." He nodded his understanding.

"Thank God for that," he said. "Some think that gold is the most sacred of metals, but they're wrong; silver is."

"Yes," I agreed.

"Yorgos, what happened to her, the beast-child? Where is she?" I averted my eyes, turning them down to my own prayer rope, also held between my knees. I felt I had swallowed a rock.

"She's been taken care of."

"Hmmm. It's never easy ordering one of God's creatures to her death. It's even harder to carry out the sentence. I will always weep when I think of the woman we burned. I can't get the sight of it out of my mind, or forget the stench." With searching eyes he inspected me.

"You've changed, Yorgos. You seem grown up now."

"She said something that I can't shake. It still bothers me," I said, dismissing his appraisal. He signaled with his hand that I should continue. "She said she could smell blood on me. She meant Mister Dumitru. Do you remember?" He nodded.

"He is the reason your father begged us to be lenient regarding your age."

"She said he had marked me." Evangelos rubbed the corners of his eyes with his forefinger and thumb.

"Lies, Yorgos, lies! When you first came to the Holy Mountain, we dealt with that."

"That's what I thought, but she was so certain that it frightened me. I don't want to be marked."

"You are not marked. If you were to become a vrykolakas, it would be a consequence of your own sin. The servants of the evil one will always tell you lies to disorient you, to seduce you into lowering your defenses. That is why we say the prayer of the heart without ceasing. It is our protection, our seal."

"It is my habit."

"It's a good habit to have."

"Hegumen, in light of all of this, I feel I have something to confess. Do you remember the night Constantine and I were locked out of the gate?" He nodded.

"I lied when I said I had nothing more I needed to tell you." I paused to gather my courage.

"Go on."

"That was the first time I kissed Constantine. We would have done more, but the wolves interrupted us. We were too scared after that to do anything else. Ever since that night, we've been more intimate than we should. We've never . . . you know . . . but the way things are going, it's only a matter of time."

Evangelos looked up at me from his prayer rope, a smile on his lips.

"I am glad you had the courage to tell me this yourself, and that you didn't wait for me to bring it up. I had a feeling this was going on." With pained and tear-glazed eyes he continued, "This is what I meant when I warned you of consequences. There are some who believe that the sin you speak of, the sin of two men loving each other as only a man and a woman should, will lead to someone becoming a vrykolakas after they die. I don't have to warn you, do I, what a serious consequence that is?"

"No," I answered. "Do you really believe that's true?"

"I believe as long as someone is alive he can make amends for his sin, but why tempt fate? The vrykolakes we speak of steal the blood, the very life, from the living so that they can have something that merely resembles life. What quality of life can the living dead and hopelessly damned really have?"

"I understand," I said, lowering my gaze. "If I am in danger of it because of my own sin, how do I make the required amends?"

He smiled again. "It pleases me that you have asked that, Yorgos. Dedicate yourself to our way of life without distraction. Purify the passions of your heart, that's how. It will take you a lifetime. It does everyone.

"I see great potential in you. Your calling to the monastic way is without question. Don't let the evil one steal it from you." He rubbed his chin with his fingertips and thumb, twisting his beard into a wiry point, inwardly reflective.

"I want to share something with you that I have not yet shared with anyone. Not far from the isthmus that connects the Holy Mountain with the mainland, a small party of monks have established a new kind of monastic settlement called a skete. I have been asked to join them as their Gerantas, their Spiritual Elder. I haven't known if I would accept or not until now. I will accept, and I'd like you to come with me. We don't yet have a master ikon painter among us. We can use one." I knew what he was asking of me. The moment to make the choice I had been avoiding had come. It was time to choose between Constantine and God. In light of my recent experiences, I knew there was no other choice for me to make.

"I will come," I said. My cheeks glistened with tears.

"If your love for Constantine is true, you will do this. You will free him from temptation and avoid taking the risk of either of you becoming a monster."

I nodded but didn't speak, tears clogging my throat. I pressed my fingertip and thumb into the corners my eyes. Evangelos leaned forward and placed his hand on my shoulder, attempting to give me what comfort he was able. At first it wasn't enough.

"I will send you ahead of me with Father Maximus," he said. "You will leave by the end of the week."

I nodded, still trying to quell my tears. We both stood up and I threw my arms around his neck, anchoring myself to him. I hung from him like my sister's boneless doll, taking the support I needed from him, until my weeping passed.

Hours later, Constantine and I sat at the edge of the cliff. In my sorrow, the waves crashing against the rocks below sounded like an invitation. I pushed the idea out of my head.

"How soon will you be leaving?" Constantine asked, staring at the sea.

"By the end of the week."

"I see," he inhaled deeply. His voice broke, and his hands shook. "What about what the hermit said? He told you not to be afraid to love me."

"He did," I agreed. "Perhaps, if he knew the nature of my feelings for you, he would have said differently."

"Perhaps," Constantine said.

"I have something for you. I intended to wait until your Name Day, but that's several months from now."

"And you won't be here anymore."

"That's true." I reached into my jacket pocket and drew out the gift, handing it to him. With enthusiasm, he liberated it from its wrapping.

"It's beautiful," he said. My gift made him smile, in spite of his sadness. "You wrote the ikon the way I asked you to?"

"Yes, I did."

I'm sure it was the most unconventional representation of the crucifixion ever written by an ikonographer who was trained in the canons of the church. It was certainly not a blessable ikon. There wasn't an Orthodox priest alive who would hang it in his own home, let alone the sanctuary of a church.

Jesus hung stark naked on the cross. His blood poured in a profusion of red upon the head of a child who knelt in the sand beneath him. The usual people depicted in the traditional ikon were arranged around the child on his knees, astonished at what they beheld.

"This is what you saw?"

"Yes, exactly the way I remember it."

"And this is you?" he asked, pointing to the blood-soaked child.

"Yes." He turned it over. I grabbed his wrist.

"Please, don't read the inscription yet. Wait until I am gone."

"For my beloved," he read out loud, ignoring me. I looked away from him. From the corner of my eye I saw his shoulders rising and falling while his body shook with his tears.

"I am sorry, Constantine."

"I love you, Yorgos. You've never been able to say it, though I've always wished you would. You don't have to say it now. I know you do." He clutched the ikon close and continued to cry.

PART THREE:
SAINT GEORGE'S SKETE

21 Saint George's Skete

Located on the northeastern corner of the peninsula, Saint George's skete was a mere fifteen minute walk from the coast and a forty five minute walk from Xerxes Canal. The skete was comprised of four newly constructed stone and wood dwellings. Each one had two stories and, in addition to four cells, its own kitchen, a common room, and chapel. The Katholikon, where we collectively celebrated the Divine Liturgy on Sundays, stood in the physical and spiritual center of the community. Every other day, community members celebrated in their own homes with their housemates.

My life at Saint George's skete was much like my life before Constantine, except for two things. It wasn't possible to go back to before and I found I could no longer write the sacred images. I tried.

Gerantas Evangelos honored me when he invited me to write the ikon of Saint George that would be set in a place of prominence in the Katholikon. I set up the easel, paints, and other supplies I needed to complete the task and attempted to begin the sacred work at once.

For weeks, my cell was more a workshop than a place to sleep, and for weeks I sat in front of the plain white panel with an array of paints, brushes, gold leaf, and egg yolk arranged around me. Everything I could possibly need was within my reach, except for inspiration.

Typically, when I began an ikon, I sat in front of the blank panel and prayed the rope until the image I meant to capture presented itself to me in the eye of my heart. Once it had, the task before me was easy enough. I simply had to represent, in the physical world, on wood, with tempura paint and the egg medium, the image I imagined.

After sitting with the white rectangular piece of wood and passing the rope through my fingers day after day, week after week for more than a month, I knew that my heart had gone blind.

From a purely technical perspective, I suppose, it would have been possible for me to produce a finished piece, but something vital in me broke when I left Constantine.

Perhaps it was my soul that broke. It didn't really matter. The passion that I once knew for the sacred art was gone. I grieved the loss of my passion nearly as badly as I grieved the loss of Constantine. A cold ache replaced it, one that got worse any time I tried to do something that once brought me joy.

However listless I may have been, my daily routine remained much the same as it had been at Grigoriou. When I wasn't prostrated, blind, mute, and dumb before the blank ikon, I dutifully performed the actions that were expected of me, because there was always something that needed to be done. I cared for the chickens, worked in the garden, and followed my usual rule of prayer, thanking God for it, because if my life depended on spontaneous prayer, I would have been dead already.

Before Gerantas Evangelos sent me to the skete of Saint George, he cautioned me to carefully and thoroughly examine my heart and turn away from the sin that had taken hold of it. Under his guidance, I placed the Jesus Prayer even more squarely at the center of my spiritual practice than I had before.

While time passed and I waited for Evangelos to join me, it became unmistakably clear that I was in this for life. No manner, or amount of prayer, with or without his guidance, would change me. I would always be attracted to men. And I would always, no doubt, love Constantine, even if I should never see him again.

The best I could hope for was to lay that aside and devote myself to a celibate life. In that, I was no different than any other man on the Holy Mountain. The only difference between me and them, as I have noted before, was that they—assuming that the majority of them were not like me—had left the objects of their sexual and romantic desire on the other side of the isthmus. I was surrounded by mine and had left the singular object of my love not far behind at the village where I grew up, but at the monastery where I passed from adolescence to manhood. Constantine was close, yet infinitely far. I found living with that paradox to be excruciating.

During our services, I forced myself to practice stillness; but when I wasn't worshiping or focusing on a required or needful task, my anxiety drove me out, away from the community of men I lived with, into nature. I spent my time hiking through the surrounding canyons and ravines and along the nearby coast until I exhausted myself, at which time I would return from my wanderings and collapse onto my mattress waking, not with the symantron, but with the light of the sun.

Late one evening, after an unusually exhausting hike, I fell asleep before my head reached the pillow. Soon after, a rap on my door roused me.

"Yorgos? It's Evangelos. I heard you come in," he said, speaking in a false whisper, meant more to be courteous than quiet. I blinked, wanting to focus my vision, before inviting him in. He opened the door a crack. The light from the oil lamp he carried stung my sleep-blinded eyes.

"I've hardly seen you more than a few minutes a day since I got here. You're gone sunrise to sunset. The others tell me you've been keeping to yourself like this since you arrived." He towered above my bed regarding me. "And the ikon I asked you to write . . . I think that's what troubles me the most. You're not yourself, Yorgos."

"Come in." I sat up and curled my legs to make room for him and patted the mattress.

The door closed with a snick behind him. "Where have you been going?" he asked. His wrinkles were made deeper than usual by his concern. The strange play of light and dark across his features exaggerated the expression.

"Just outside. Anywhere, really, as long as it's outside. I feel closer to God out there." I turned my attention to the slit window and parted the curtain to peek out. The moon, three-quarters full, was bright, illumining my cell, rivaling the light from the lamp that Evangelos held. "He seems more present to me in nature, now, than anywhere else," I continued. "I can't stand to be inside, or standing still, for that matter. I feel that if I am still, something will catch up with me."

Evangelos placed his hand on my knee.

"What are you running from? Do you need to speak to Maximus?"

"No," I answered. "It's nothing like that. It's Constantine. I understand that our relationship put us in danger, but I still have feelings for him. I don't know how to put that behind me."

I turned from the window toward my mentor and found that I couldn't bear to look at him too closely. I feared that disappointment had twisted his features beyond recognition. I didn't want to see that. Instead, I focused on the flickering flame of his lamp until the intensity of the light made my eyes water.

"I had hoped to keep progressing up the monastic ranks, but I'm not so sure right now. I might be a Rassaphore for a long time at the rate I'm going. I hope that doesn't disappoint you."

He clutched his prayer rope, but didn't pass the knots through his fingers; instead he gently rolled the same knot between his forefinger and thumb, as if carefully pinching the juice from a grape.

"No, Yorgos," he answered, progressing to the next knot. "You haven't disappointed me, but I have been concerned. Now that we've spoken, I feel you are working out your struggles the best you can. You have my blessing to continue to sort this out as you've been doing, but please don't shut me out."

I nodded and he continued.

"The ranks are not something one rushes through. The point is not to have arrived at some highly esteemed place, but to put God's will above all else and to keep one's heart pure. I see that you are struggling with that very thing. The struggle *itself* is good, Yorgos. Please remember that."

When he left me, Evangelos patted my hand and said, "Sleep now."

My anxious wanderings did not stop after our conversation. They continued with a new fervor. Over the next weeks, there was little ground surrounding the skete that I hadn't covered.

One day however, perhaps nine weeks after my arrival at Saint George's, I scrambled into a ravine that cut through the rolling hills down to the ocean. From a distance, I spied something I hadn't seen before; the slanted roof of an abandoned guard tower and the jagged remnants of a stone wall. My curiosity stole my breath, making me forget the angst that had been spurring me on. I sprinted to the tower.

I guessed that it was all that remained of a monastery that had been destroyed by fire. When I pushed through the vegetation, I saw that the old tower was built only meters from the shore and that trees of various heights grew up around it.

I paused, panting at the door of the dilapidated structure. With a slight push from my toes, I sent it creaking open. The door was solid. The hinges, though badly rusted, were strong. I pushed it all the way open, allowing the light to enter before I did.

Inside, telltale marks of fire marred the stone walls and blackened the wood, but the structure seemed to be sound enough. The main chamber, echoing like the steeple of a Roman cathedral, was sparsely furnished with a crude, uneven table and two chairs, all covered with dust.

I walked to the center of the room and turned a full circle, looking above and around myself. Cobwebs fluttered overhead. The wood roof had broken in a number of places. Sunlight streamed in through the holes, creating a dappled pattern of light and dark on the floor and walls.

Inside and to the left, another door led to a smaller room with a lower ceiling. Just as dusty as the larger room, its only furnishings were a straw mattress with a low table beside it. I backed out into the main room and followed a spiral staircase to the loft above. I sprinted, taking the stairs two by two, until I came upon the first one that was missing. I counted the remaining stairs that spiraled above my head. Every second or third step was broken or completely gone. I continued with more caution until I reached the top. The loft had a tiny window and a door that opened to a covered porch overlooking the sea. I strode out the door and up to the half-wall of the porch.

The ocean raged against the rock barrier that had been built to protect the tower from the waves. Paradoxically, the angry sound comforted me, as if Poseidon himself gave expression to the grief I had not been able to. I listened until the sky darkened. It was time to return to the skete.

The following morning, I rose with the beat of the symantron. The dull ache that had come to characterize my waking hours greeted me as soon as I opened my eyes. Ignoring it, I followed my morning rule of prayer, and dressed in my cassock, pocketing my mother's bottle of perfume that I kept hidden under my mattress.

Skipping matins, I raided the pantry for provisions and began my trek to the tower while wrapped in a blanket and carrying a lantern.

After a cursory dusting, I deposited the food on the wobbly table and climbed the stairs. From the covered porch, I watched the sky grow steadily lighter. Returning to the ground level, I sat–legs crossed–with my back against the cold rough wall, and I prayed the rope.

While the knots passed through my fingers, I took stock of the weeds that sprouted through the cracks in the stone floor. I tucked the rope into the pocket of my cassock and pulled out the weeds that were within my reach. When they were cleared, I crawled the length and breadth of the room on my hands and knees, extracting them all.

Once started, I continued to clean, making the tower less rustic, more habitable. With a leafy branch I broke from one of the nearby trees I cleared the cobwebs, and I thoroughly dusted everything with my undergarment, before discarding it in the corner of the little room.

Once I cleaned the tower, I spritzed it with my mother's perfume, enjoying the bittersweet pangs of homesickness that the scent of jasmine stirred in me.

And so it went, day after day, week after week, for more than a month. I spent so much time at the old tower that it started to feel more like home to me than the skete did.

285

I decided, after braving the treacherous stairs for so long, that it was time for me to repair them. I stuffed a bag full of things I thought I might need. In addition to a hammer, nails and wood scraps I gathered from one of the ikon writers, I brought a loaf of bread, a knife, and some fruit from our garden.

I spent my day alternately making repairs and watching Poseidon throw his angry waves against the shore. I was tempted to discard the blanket I wrapped myself in, jump over the banister and plunge into the sea, extending my arms as if stretching for something beyond my reach. I wondered what it would feel like to pierce the surface of the water, fingertips first, and then to be swallowed whole. More than that, I wondered what it would feel like to be thrown against the rocks–again, and again–to be caught in the ocean's ebb and flow. *How long would it take before I lost consciousness?*

The tumbling waves enchanted me, and so did my own dark thoughts, until my own morbidity frightened me. I shook my head clear and followed the stairs back down. After dropping the blanket at the foot of the stairs, I was off and running a race against the dark.

A thin beam of sunlight pierced the slit window waking me with a start. I had wanted to wake with the symantron and begin my day early, but the morning was half over now. I found the floor with my feet, threw on my cassock and bolted out the door like a mad man. I had to get out. I had to get to the refuge of my tower.

When I arrived the front was ajar. I pushed it open and entered with caution. The scent of my mother's perfume hung heavy in the air, heightening my sense of apprehension. Though I spritzed it the day before, the scent had dissipated by the time I left. In a world populated by vrykolakes, large menacing black cats, and who knows what else, I was learning to be more cautious.

Standing in the threshold, I surveyed the main chamber. Things were not as I had left them. The heavily perfumed air was the first giveaway, but I couldn't put my finger on what else was out of place.

I scanned the chamber again. The blanket wasn't at the foot of the stairs. Much of the food I left on the table was gone and so was one of the lanterns. A cold fist clenched my stomach.

Something thumped in the adjacent room. My muscles tensed. Holding the pull-string that released the latch between my forefinger and thumb, I steeled myself before opening the door. While it swung, a hot burst of adrenalin hit my bloodstream. Though my body was ready to fight or flee, I planted my feet, imagining roots anchoring me to the ground.

Pieces of bread and other scraps of food were scattered across the floor. The knife was stabbed into the table, with the remnants of the loaf beside it. And Mother's perfume bottle lay on its side in a heavily scented puddle, with the nozzle popped off.

A monk in his cassock lay on the mattress. He reached for the knife, knocking the perfume bottle to the floor. The knife sliced through the air and struck the doorjamb centimeters from where I stood. I uprooted my feet and ran; fear now doing my thinking for me.

"Yorgos, wait." Recognizing Galatea's voice, I stopped and willed my body to stay. Three deep breaths later, I turned to face her. She settled back onto the mattress and gathered the blanket around herself. She hadn't changed much since I left her with the Protos, except that her hair had grown, though not enough to destroy the illusion that she was a young man.

"I should have trusted my nose. Your scent is all over this place," she said with a grimace. "In fact, it was your scent that led me here, but you startled me."

"All I smell is my mother's perfume. You used too much." Still trembling, I glanced at the knife sticking out of the jamb.

"I'm sorry I scared you," she said.

I retrieved the perfume bottle, glad that I was able to pop the nozzle back on and that it hadn't all been spilled.

"What are you doing here?" I asked, while fixing it.

Rubbing her stomach, Galatea looked away from me and then down at her hand. I followed her gaze, and saw that her wrist was badly scarred. Yanking her sleeve down, she met my gaze. She sniffled and rubbed her nose with the back of her hand.

"I need help," she said. "I didn't know who else to turn to."

"Will my debt to the nereids never be paid?"

"You don't owe us anything. I was hoping you would think of this more as helping a friend."

"A friend who wants to maul me?" I said, raising an eyebrow. "No thank you." Her nose scrunched.

"The smell is getting worse, but I won't bite. I promise. Mother said what happens to you in the future is none of my business, no matter how bad the smell gets."

"Your father wasn't able to find a cure?"

"I don't think there is a cure. Not one that leaves the afflicted alive. Father came to fear that the only way to free my soul from the wolf was to destroy my body."

"Yes, with fire," I said, without inflection. "I've heard that before."

"With fire," she agreed. "Just like they did to the woman the day you helped me escape. There's more, Yorgos. You should know this before you make your decision. Father had been stalling. He said he hoped he was wrong, that he'd find a better way, but last month the other vrykolakes came back. There were three of them again. My father's men drove them away, but he's afraid they'll be back and that they'll keep coming back, until they get what they want."

"You," I said.

"Yes. Me. He changed after that. He said that there was no way he'd give me up to those 'damned godless creatures.' The flames were better, he said, than joining ranks with them, it wasn't just talk. After they came, he started to build a pyre."

"I see why you fled. I agree that there's got to be a better way, but what can I do?"

"I don't know, but I'm desperate." She tried to stifle her tears without success and pushed the blanket off. Smoothing the cassock, pulling it tight around her belly, she revealed the cause of her desperation.

"And pregnant," I said. "When did that–? *How* did that happen?"

"I think it happened the night Mother sent me to find you. I don't know for sure, that entire night's a blur."

"That was only four months ago, Galatea. You look like you've been pregnant a lot longer than that."

"That's not possible. Please, tell me you'll help me. I don't know where else to go or exactly what to do, but no one will lead me into the flames, not when I'm expecting, especially not my own father."

"Why don't you just go back to your mother if your father won't help you?"

"Do you remember the scratch on my mother's face?" I nodded. "As long as I'm a threat to my people, I won't go back to them." I snorted, finding it darkly humorous that she didn't have a problem being a threat to me, but I accepted it. If I were in her position I wouldn't want to be alone either and I certainly wouldn't want to be a threat to my family.

"Alright," I agreed. "You can stay here until we think of something better." I exhaled from my guts. "What happens if the others find you here? Or your father? I'm not even sure which possibility I am more afraid of."

"Neither am I." She flashed me a weak smile and patted the mattress beside herself. "Tonight is the first night of the full moon. We should prepare for the worst."

"Tonight? Right. The worst!" I said taking a seat beside her.

She reached into the pocket of her cassock for something. "Help me put these in," she said, palming the items. She pulled both sleeves past her wrists before dropping a tapered pair of thick gauge silver hoop earrings onto my hand.

Both hoops had a sharpened point at one end, and a sphere where the metal had been held to a flame and melted to a ball at the other. "The wound has to be fresh," she explained. I glanced at her earlobes. Indeed, scarring indicated that they had both been pierced and healed multiple times already. "Father removed the silver arrowheads and made these from them. He made a pair for himself too. He said he wanted to share in the pain of my affliction so he pierces his ears every time I have to."

"Would he also walk into the flames with you?" She answered with silence.

Later that afternoon, while trembling at the door of Maximus' cell, I fought to steady my nerves. With one hand I held a lighted candle, and with the other, an empty shoulder bag with a drawstring. Even at that moment, when it was far too late to turn back, I lied to myself thinking, *Relax. I'm just here to borrow some things.* If my intentions were that straightforward why did I hope to find him napping? And why did I count on his poor hearing? Taking a deep breath, I released it slowly, giving myself a chance to change my mind. I didn't.

I pushed the door open as quietly as I could and took another deep breath.

He sat upright in his chair, propped up with pillows and covered with a blanket. He was snoring. I sighed, and walked over to the magnificent trunk beside his chair. Taking each step with care, I tested them before placing my full weight. The floor creaked but he didn't stir.

I placed the candle on the floor and squatted in front of the trunk. Taking another deliberate and controlled breath, I pulled the trunk away from the wall and swung the rounded lid open. It creaked more loudly than the floor had, but still he didn't stir. I thanked God and felt guilty. Did I really expect God to bless my intention to steal? I crossed myself and and continued.

Like I expected, Maximus' weapons made of silver filled the trunk. I opened the bag and began to stuff it with loot. I grabbed chains of various gauges and lengths by the handful. They jangled and clanged while I shoved them into the bag. Next into the bag were two full quivers followed by a couple small bows.

I paused when I uncovered two manacles linked by a chain, remembering Galatea's wrists, and her effort to conceal the scars. It was a brilliant discovery. Silver manacles were sure to hold her, especially if the rings remained in her ears, but I didn't want to be the one to put them on her. I came close to returning them to the trunk, but changed my mind, adding them to the contents of the bag with a wave of guilt splashing over me.

I began to close the lid when something caught my eye. I reopened it, and lifted a cylindrical bottle of what I guessed to be particles and flakes of silver suspended in liquid. On a hunch I stuffed that into the bag along with everything else. I closed the lid, pulled the drawstring tight, lifted the candle from the floor and began to stand up. Maximus shifted in his chair. I froze. For what seemed like an eternity, but was probably only seconds, I stood in place like someone turned to stone by Medusa's glance. A deep melodious snore came from the sleeping man, and I relaxed. I tiptoed to the door, carefully pushed it open, and began to pull it closed behind myself when I heard his wheezy cough. I froze in place again.

"I am too old," he said. I opened the door. He coughed again and said, "I am too old for the hunt. Unburden me of my weapons, please."

"No . . . no." I stammered. "I don't want them. I only wanted to borrow the–"

"Borrow? Did you say borrow? It seems like stealing to me. One cannot steal what is freely given. They're yours." I rushed in and fell prostrate at his feet, like a trembling slave before a king.

"Please, Father Maximus, forgive me. I only wanted to help a friend. I'll bring them back, I promise."

"No. You may take all the silver that is mine; I'm ready to part with it. If you do, do not return it to me. I have no use for it anymore."

Maximus held up his shaky hand and made the sign of the cross before dropping it into his lap.

"The weapons are yours, Brother Yorgos. It falls on you, now, to rid the world of supernaturally evil beings. Be uncompromising. Learn to use your weapons well." I scrambled up to my feet and hoisted the bag over my shoulder. My knees buckled under its weight. "A man never chooses the hunt," he said, while I swung the door closed behind myself. "The hunt chooses him."

22 Preparing For the Hunt

I ran with haste to the refuge of my tower. The bag of silver jangled and clanged while I went, nearly weighing me to the ground. Halfway there, I stopped to rest and unceremoniously dropped my burden. Maximus' words were not as easy to surrender. In fact, they were unshakable. The hunt. My dealings with dark beings were beginning to feel inescapable. I was either in danger of becoming one or chosen to hunt them. Could both be true?

It was twilight when I returned to Galatea and already dark inside the tower. I lit both lanterns and hung them from the rafters in her room. I found her asleep on the mattress and covered her with a blanket, careful not to wake her.

I returned to the main chamber where I left my bag of loot and dumped the contents onto the stone floor. I selected a long, thick gauge chain and the pair of manacles. I rummaged through the pile for the key and pocketed it. With it all gathered in my arms I moved carefully trying, with minimal success, not to rattle the chains. It was best for me if Galatea didn't wake. Though I knew that she wouldn't consent to what I had in mind, I was as determined to protect myself from her as I was to protect the both of us from any unwelcomed guests that might show up.

Using the bedside table as a stool, I swung the silver chain over one of the rafters and wound it around several times. When I was through, equal lengths of the chain dangled limply on either side of the beam, glinting in the lantern light.

I went to Galatea next and lifted one of her arms. Her wrist was so badly scarred that I almost couldn't do it. I closed my eyes before closing the manacle around it. I set it down and went to lift her other arm, when she rolled over on top of it. I paused before making another attempt. She rolled right back and blindly swatted my hand away. I tried again, only then realizing what an obstacle her swollen stomach would prove to be. Once I'd freed her arm, I lifted it and held the manacle up to her wrist.

"What are you doing?" She mumbled, half asleep. She flailed her arm, swatting at me with more aggression. The second manacle fell to the floor, clanking on the stones, and I backed away from her. With effort, Galatea stood to her feet. The chain that linked the two cuffs hung from the one closed around her wrist, jangling against her leg.

"I don't feel safe with you, not with the full moon coming. If you were to leave here tonight and harm any of my brothers, I would be responsible."

"That won't happen," she said, struggling against the manacle. "I'm wearing these." She pointed at the silver hoops I helped her force through her ears. The fresh wounds were crusted, and glistening with blood. "Remember?"

"What if they get pulled out?" She negated my words with an adamant shake of her head.

"They won't. I don't want anyone to get hurt either." I backed into the door.

"Still, I would feel safer if you wore the manacles. You said it yourself that we should prepare for the worst."

"I did," she agreed. "I meant we should prepare to face the vrykolakes that did this to me."

"What could be worse than the earrings getting torn out and you hurting me or someone else?"

Galatea straightened her back and narrowed her eyes at me. "Please don't. Father did this to me too. It hurts and it's humiliating."

"Did it work? Did it keep you from hurting anyone?" The look of defeat she flashed was the only answer I needed.

"You're right," she said, slumping her shoulders. She lifted her uncuffed hand and offered it to me. "I surrender with reluctance."

The chains hanging from the rafter were short enough that once both cuffs were attached to them she couldn't sit on the mattress, let alone lay down on it. I went to the main chamber for a chair and also brought her one of the blankets. Once seated, she reminded me of a begging dog, her useless hands hanging limply over the silver cuffs at the wrists.

"I'm sorry that this can't be more comfortable. It's the best I can do with so little warning."

She shrugged saying, "I'm used to it. Apparently this is my life now."

"It's getting dark," I said, avoiding making eye contact. "Will you be alright?"

"You're leaving?" I glanced at her and wished I hadn't. The look of fear darkening her features cast a shadow over my own. "I'd feel better if you didn't leave me alone here. I'm afraid all chained up like this you've made it extremely easy for them to come and get me." I opened my mouth ready to respond but found that any argument I may have posed simply lacked conviction.

"Good point," I said instead. "I hadn't thought this all the way through." I dropped down to the mattress and hugged my knees up to my chest. "If they should come, that means I'm going to be the only thing that stands between you and them." She raised an eyebrow.

"Are you trying to make me feel better?"

I ignored her and ruminated over our predicament, while a cold sensation hardened my gut, making me shake.

"We don't stand a chance," I said, lifting my head from my knees to look at her.

"Don't say that. Can't you go for help? Some of the monks have fought vrykolakes before."

"You don't want their help. *You* are a vrykolakas. If any of them come here they are going to shoot you with arrows made of silver, draw and quarter you, and burn the pieces. That is all they believe can be done. To be honest, I am not sure they're wrong, but I pray to God that they are."

"So do I," she said, dropping her gaze. "So, you're not going to leave me?"

"No. I'm not going to leave you." I went to her and squeezed her hand. "I'll stay here, no matter what happens."

Her lips formed an inaudible "Thank you."

"What else did the old man give you?" she asked.

"His name is Father Maximus. I'll show you."

I retrieved all the items and laid them out on the floor in front of her.

"That's quite a collection of weapons and chains," she said. "Two bows and too many arrows to count."

"Just two quivers of silver arrows, that's only 24 in all, and a handful of conventional ones. I'm afraid we'll run out if we find we need to use them."

"What's that?" she asked, pointing to the bottle containing the mixture of liquid and silver.

"I'm not sure. I think it's silver particles suspended in water." I lifted it off the floor, shook it, and held it up to the light. It twisted and turned inside the bottle. "I do have an idea though . . . ." I lifted my mother's perfume from the bedside table. I hesitated. What I had in mind felt like a sacrilege, but nostalgia wouldn't save me. If my hunch proved true, I would have one more weapon in my arsenal.

Decidedly, I found the undergarment I tossed in a corner after cleaning, shook it out, and emptied the bottle onto it. I held it to my nose and inhaled, allowing memories of my mother to flood my mind. I saw her smile, felt her touch, and smelled and tasted the spanakopita she served almost every morning and on special occasions because she knew it was my favorite. I remembered the way she supported my budding interest in writing ikons. The scent of her perfume beautifully conjured and summed up my memories of her. I drew it into my lungs, my chest expanded with it until it ached, and then I shook the memories away. While exhaling, I replaced the perfume with the mixture of silver and water.

"I don't know what this will do. I'll bet eyes will make a good target though."

"And the nose," she insisted. "I can only imagine what breathing a silver mist would do to me and I don't want to find out." I pocketed it.

"If I have to use it on the others, I'll make sure you're upwind."

"Thanks, that makes me feel much better."

"I need to prepare myself," I said, ignoring her tone. "I won't be long."

I spiraled up the stairs to the porch, remembering the many times in recent months that the ocean had called to me and the many times I resisted the call by not hurling myself in.

I found that at this moment, with another life to consider; two lives, to be exact, the temptation to jump had lost its allure.

Reaching into my cassock pocket, I lifted my prayer rope by the knotted cross at the end. I squeezed it between my forefinger and thumb.

"Lord Jesus Christ . . . ." I whispered, letting the words linger and the rest of the prayer remain unsaid. The moon continued to climb the sky, illumining the world like a lantern.

A wolf howled in the distance. *And so it begins.* Another wolf answered, one that sounded much closer. From the room below, as if she too were answering, Galatea struggled with the change. If I hadn't known any better I would have believed that she'd been caught in a hunter's trap and gnawed on her own flesh to get free. Her cries were so sharp that I would have sworn she was with me on the porch and not downstairs. The cold sensation returned to my gut.

Fear, and the responsibility I felt for Galatea and her child battled in my breast while I flew down the stairs. When I reached the door to her room, only seconds later, something on the other side of it slammed against the floor. The chains rattled so loudly I thought she would pull the roof down with the rafters. I expected to find her free of the earrings and transformed. And if she was, she would likely target me.

I hesitated before pulling the latchstring and pushing the door open, fingering my prayer rope. Instinctively, my fingers passed over it and went to the bottle of liquid silver instead. Though I knew using it was a betrayal her trust, my fight or flight instinct was strong. If I had to fight for survival I would use any weapon within my reach. I clutched the bottle, believing it would ward off the devil himself, should I find him on the other side.

I opened the door. Galatea, still in human form, was on her knees and slumped over her fallen chair. She convulsed. Only the chains kept her from seizing on the floor. I sighed with relief and returned the bottle to my pocket.

Outside, the wolves continued to serenade the moon, moving closer to the tower. It sounded like their approach was slower, less directed by reason or want than it had been at Grigoriou. Strangely, it seemed less driven.

"Galatea? Are you okay?" She looked up at me baring her teeth.

"Help me," she whispered.

"I don't know what to do," I said, sitting on the floor across the room from her.

A low growl issued from her throat. "I'll tell you what to do, Yorgos. Come here."

"What is it?" I asked, crawling to her. She lunged at me, snapping her jaws. The chains rattled.

I scrambled away, climbed up to my feet, and brushed myself off. "You are not yourself tonight, despite appearances," I said.

I stood over her for a moment. It looked like worms writhed just beneath the surface of her skin. And her bones looked like they were trying to unhinge and rearrange themselves. The change didn't come.

"You reek, friend," she said. "I can't bear the smell."

"Then I will leave." I bent to the floor for the bow and quiver, shouldering the latter. Passing through the door I hesitated and looked over my shoulder at her. Still breathing heavily, she had slumped and stopped writhing. The vrykolakes outside became quiet.

"Don't leave. I'm sorry."

"I know. I gave you my word. I'm not going far."

The duet of howling started up again, and her body twitched and writhed in time with it. I nocked a silver arrow and went outside.

The howling continued. It sounded like the vrykolakes were moving closer. I waited for the duet to become a trio, but as far as I could tell the third vrykolakas didn't show.

Even through the thick door, I could hear Galatea's struggles. I couldn't listen anymore, not as long as I was powerless to help her in any meaningful way. I stepped away from the safety of the tower and, with bow and arrow held ready, tracked the vrykolakes with my ears, wondering why they tarried. Certainly, with their heightened senses, they already knew where she'd been hiding.

I sneaked through the vegetation. Following the sound of their howling, I traveled through ravines and up a small hill. The moon shadowed their silhouettes on the next hill over.

When I reached the top, sheltered by the canopy of trees and the thick ground cover, I got a better look, but it was hard to make out any details. Bile bubbled into my mouth. I spit it out. I had hoped to see some identifying marks so I could tell if any of them was the vrykolakas that escaped over the wall the night Galatea came to find me, but it was too dark. All I could tell for sure was that they were large, though not as large as the creatures that came for Galatea on that fateful night.

I found them, two dark shapes, tumbling over each other, and across the ground, in the mooncast shadows of a laurel tree. One of them unleashed a ferocious growl, the other whimpered. The first dark form towered over the other, growling at it, before backing away.

I pushed through the foliage hoping to get a better look. Two more vrykolakes came up the far side of the hill from the right, and two more from the left. Their numbers were growing! I kissed the tip of the silver arrowhead, praying that if I had to let it fly, it would swiftly find its mark.

A seventh vrykolakas and the largest so far, came up between the two pairs, and challenged the victor. I retreated back into the shadows as the two beasts tussled. The others formed a circle around them, barking and growling like drunken thugs cheering a fight.

Backing farther into the shadows and leaves, I stumbled over a fallen branch and dropped my weapons. Scrambling up from the ground, I crouched and readied my bow and arrow again. The vrykolakes stopped fighting and turned their heads toward me. I screamed and accidentally released the arrow, sending it into the flank of the vrykolakas nearest me. It ran away, whimpering, scattering the others. When some of them passed into the full light of the moon, I saw that they were wolves, merely wolves, and nothing more.

I collapsed, feeling an odd mixture of fear and relief. My body shook and I spit out another mouthful of bile before I could stand up.

When I returned to Galatea, she was seated again. Though less dramatically than before, her body still showed signs of the change that the silver would prevent as long as it remained inside an open wound.

"What happened?" she asked. "Did you scare them away?"

"Yes, I think I did. But they weren't vrykolakes. They were wolves, real wolves. They're gone now."

Galatea sighed. "Thank you. I'm sorry about the things I said."

"I know. You're not yourself when the moon is full, even with the silver."

"It's worse when the moon first appears."

"Is it painful?"

"It is," she laughed. "It feels like the wolf wants to scratch its way out. It makes me afraid to give birth."

"How is the baby? I was afraid it would be hurt the way you were thrashing around."

"That worries me too. But it's better for the baby than if I changed. Mother says that babies don't survive the change. That's why nereids don't change shape when they're pregnant, but this is something else. I don't control it as much as it controls me. Though hurts me, I am glad to wound my flesh with silver. It's what's keeping my baby alive."

I clasped Galatea's hand. "You are a brave young woman, Galatea. I'm glad to know you."

"What do we do now?" she asked.

"Those wolves weren't the vrykolakes we're waiting for. It's still early." I brandished the bow. "We're ready for them. Let's stay ready."

"Ready for the worst?"

"Exactly." I seated myself cross-legged on the mattress with the bow in my lap and the quiver over my shoulder.

Sometime around dawn the cry of a rooster woke me. I looked at Galatea. She had fallen asleep too.

"Wake up," I said, patting the back of her hand. I waited while she stretched and moaned. She peered at me and presented me with her wrists.

"Unlock me, please." I retrieved the key from my pocket and released her. The scars she had initially tried so hard to hide from me were fresh again. When she saw me staring she yanked the sleeves of her cassock down and said, "I guess I should get used to it."

"Look," I said, "I've never stayed out all night before; I've got to go home. Evangelos and the others will be worrying. I'll be back before sundown, I promise. Make yourself at home and eat whatever food is here. I'll bring more."

When I made it to Saint George's skete, I discovered a mule tied to a tree. That wasn't something you saw there every day. A strong suspicion warned me to enter with caution, not so much because I feared I was in danger, but because I sensed some kind of trouble afoot. I tip-toed into the building. Indeed, Evangelos was deep in conversation with someone.

"I am sorry that you and your uncle have lost your home. Under normal circumstances, I would welcome you both with open arms, but I am worried that this isn't in Yorgos' best interest. He's been uncommonly sad since he left Grigoriou. He's gotten in the habit of leaving in the morning, before the sun rises, and returning long after it sets. I have no idea where he is going. Last night he never came home. Honestly, I am afraid I am losing him. Lent is his favorite time of year, yet he hasn't participated in any of the Lenten services. Have you asked any of the other monasteries?"

"No, you are the first I've spoken to. I thought it best we go where I knew some people." Hearing Constantine's voice opened an oddly pleasurable void in my heart. "It's been drafty since the fire. I am afraid my uncle will die if we stay much longer."

"Are repairs underway yet?"

"They've just begun. I've been excused from helping so I could stay with my uncle and look after him."

"Space here is limited. I have a bed for your uncle. The brothers and I will look after him until the two of you can be reunited. In the meantime, I am sure they will take you back at Grigoriou."

I composed myself and stepped through the short hallway that opened into the common room of the building. Their conversation halted.

"Yorgos, where have you been?" Evangelos said.

"Nowhere." I glanced at the Gerantas and then Constantine. It appeared that a candle hidden beneath his skin had been lit before my eyes.

"Yorgos!" he stammered. He shoved his hands into his cassock pocket. I followed suit. The magnetism between us drew our bodies closer, in spite of our determined efforts to abstain from the sin of loving each other.

"You've been tonsured?" I asked.

"Yes. Four weeks ago, at Esphigmenou. It was only days before the fire. I decided I was ready to take the first step and join their community."

"That's good," I said. "I overheard what you two were discussing," I addressed Evangelos. "If they need a place to stay, they should stay here. I'll be okay." I averted my eyes and looked at my sandaled feet. "It's not like I am really ever here anyway. Put them in another building, away from me, and everyone will be cared for as they should be."

Evangelos cleared his throat. When I looked up at him he held my gaze without wavering. "Are you sure?"

"Yes. Separating them can't possibly be the right thing to do. They should both stay." I walked past Evangelos toward the stairs and smiled at Constantine.

"Wait, Yorgos," he said. "I have something for you. It arrived at Grigoriou a couple days before I left to join my uncle. I promised the new hegumen that I would deliver it to you." From his pocket Constantine produced an envelope addressed to me in my mother's handwriting.

"I'm sorry it took me so long to get it to you."

Reaching for it, I felt a mixture of anticipation and fear. I hesitated, drawing my finger along the edge of the home-made envelope. I hadn't heard from Mother in months. Panic fluttered in my chest. Because I knew I might never see Mother again, I was always glad to receive a letter from her. Her letters, written with her own hand, might be the only contact I would ever have with her. Though bitter-sweet, it was the best joy I knew. But I also feared, with every letter, to learn that Zosimos had died. So, each time word from Mother arrived, I both couldn't wait to tear it open, and dreaded doing so.

"Thank you, Constantine," I said. When I received the letter, I touched the back of his hand with my finger, making it look like an accident. My body rejoiced with goose bumps. The brief moment of physical contact threatened to reawaken in me something I had worked hard, with little true success, to put to sleep. I withdrew my hand like someone burned while lighting a candle. "Thank you," I repeated, flashing a self-conscious smile before taking the stairs, two by two, up to my cell.

Evangelos and Constantine resumed their conversation. I stopped at my door, holding the latchstring without pulling it, and eavesdropped.

"We can stay here?" Constantine asked.

"Yes. You can stay until repairs are completed. But I want you to avoid spending time alone with Yorgos."

"I understand." Constantine agreed. "I will return with my uncle in three days."

"Preparations will be made for you by then."

I listened while they said their goodbyes and ran into my room after I heard the front door close. From the slit window, I watched Tino untie the mule and ride away. He had long disappeared into the distance before I collapsed onto my cot. Lying on my back I held the letter above my head and stared at it. I tried to guess at what news it might contain. Finally, my excitement overcame my fear. I tore it open.

Yorgos, my dear son, my little monk.

I pray this letter finds you. I know you've moved, but I am not sure where to, so I will send it to Grigoriou with hopes that someone there will know how to get it to you.

The family needs prayers, yours, and those of your entire community. Out of all of my children, I find you are the one I pray for the least. That sounds awful, doesn't it? It's because you are also the child I worry for the least. I know that as long as you live on Mount Athos you will be healthy, safe, and well cared for. God has certainly blessed that place and blessed you to live there.

We, too, have been blessed to live so far up in the Mountains. It's hard for the Turks to maintain an effective presence here, and so our way of life has been unchanged. Those not living in the Pindus have not had it as easy. Word has been reaching us, as it always has, from those living lower down in the foothills, the plains, and along the coast. There, land seizures, exorbitant taxes and forced conversions are not uncommon.

Theophilos has decided he has heard too much and done too little. He's gone all the way to Salonika to join the fight against the Turks. I am afraid he's going to get himself killed. The only thing at all that comforts me in this is that he and Zoe-Sophia can look after each other as long as he is there. I pray he comes to his senses and returns to us and to the safety of the mountains, before he is hurt or killed.

This leaves only the three of us at home until he returns. I've closed the inn because I spend so much time looking after Zosimos. Without help, I can't do that and run the business too.

Speaking of Zosimos, there is nothing new to report about him, as far as his health is concerned. As always, he's got one foot in Charon's boat and one foot on the ground. Either your brother has an extremely willful soul, or God has a purpose for him that is yet to be revealed. Either way, even though he is physically weak, and it seems he is close to death once again, it is his soul I fear for the most.

He's become so obsessed with recovering his health that he's been reading mystical writings officially condemned by the Church. He is certain there is a secret to living forever and that he will find it if he searches hard enough.

He's become delusional if you ask me. But then, if I had lived with the threat of dying for as long as he has, perhaps I wouldn't be any better off.

I have less to say about your sister. On the surface, she seems happy, and in her letters she always says that she is. A mother has to trust her instincts. Mine tell me that something is off between her and Paulos. Call it a hunch, but I'd feel better knowing that you were praying for her.

As far as your father and I are concerned, we are both well. Do not worry about us.

I love you, my son. I always will, of course. In closing I want you to know how proud of you I am. You are, and always will be, my little monk.

Mother.

I read the letter three times before dropping it to my chest. Crying, I refolded it, stuffed it into the envelope, and slipped it under my pillow. Having done that, I fell asleep in no time at all.

I slept all day, waking with a start, at the onset of dusk. The moon would soon edge its way into the sky. If I didn't want to break my word to Galatea, I had to set out at once.

Evangelos waited for me in the common room. When I approached he looked up from his prayer rope. "Sleeping during the day now, are you?"

"Gerantas, forgive me, I have to go." I went to the pantry and began to stuff my bag with bread, fruit, vegetables, and a couple jugs of water. He followed me and watched.

"Explain to me what you are doing, please. I want to understand."

"I don't have time for this. I'm sorry." In my haste I dumped some of the contents of my bag. I bent to the floor to retrieve them.

"Maximus told me he gave you his weapons. He said you sneaked into his room and tried to take them without asking. Yorgos! What's gotten into you? Is there anything going on that you haven't told me about?"

I couldn't look at him, or even answer right away, because any answer given would have been full of subterfuge or straight out lies. I hated feeling that I couldn't be honest with him, but telling the truth was equal to putting Galatea and her baby at risk.

"Last night I heard wolves. They were only wolves, nothing more, but it reminded me of what happened before we left Grigoriou. After everything I've seen and heard, I feel safer having Maximus' weapons close at hand. Really, there is nothing more to tell you than that." I stood to my feet, having returned the contents to the bag, and pulled the drawstring closed. I looked at him while throwing the bag over my shoulder. "I have to go now."

"Then why don't you come home? I mean *really* come home to us. You are safer here than you ever could be alone, out there–wherever it is you've been going to."

"I really don't have the time for this." I repeated. "I am sorry, Gerantas. I mean no disrespect."

I headed to the front door and Evangelos called after me, "Maximus tells me that he believes you are called to fight the dark ones, Yorgos. That is not a calling one undertakes lightly. One must be trained and spiritually fit." I paused at the threshold to answer over my shoulder.

"As he tells it, Maximus was never trained. Besides, it's not as if I am going to war. I promise." Without saying goodbye, I stepped through the threshold into the dark world outside.

23 A Wolf In Chains

I ran, racing against time and the moon's ascension through the sky. Halfway to the tower, my body demanded that I slow down. I paused, hands on my knees, panting to catch my breath. Something behind me rustled. I walked at a brisk pace and my pursuer matched it. When I started to run again, my pursuer did too.

This time I didn't pace myself, I ran full speed, glancing over my shoulder. I couldn't make out what followed me and I nearly stumbled over a boulder.

When the tower loomed ahead, I pushed myself again, achieving greater speed than I knew I could, and yelled for Galatea, "Quick, open the door! I'm being followed."

I threw myself into the tower. A glance around and I saw that she had nocked an arrow and leveled it at the open door. I slammed it closed and struggled with the bolt. A resounding thud shook the door. I leaned against it with all my weight and it rattled on its rusty hinges. I wasn't strong enough to hold it closed against the intruder and slide the bar into place at the same time. The intruder prevailed, the door flew open, and I landed, ingloriously on my butt.

I recognized Constantine the same moment Galatea released an arrow from her bow.

"No!" I shouted. Too late. In the time it took me to look from him to her and back, the arrow made itself at home inside his flesh.

I ignored his screaming and secured the door before tending to him.

"It's just me!" he shouted. "What the hell's going on here?" He grabbed the shaft and struggled to pull the arrow out of his chest, the side opposite his heart. I sensed he lacked the courage necessary to cause self-inflicted pain.

"Let me," I said. I knelt before him and couldn't keep myself from smiling, in spite of his obvious pain. I placed my hand on his left shoulder and mussed his hair.

"What's so funny, Yorgos? It hurts."

"Nothing. I'm glad to see you, even like this." He braced.

"I'm glad to see you too, but would it be alright with you if we got this over with first, before we begin to celebrate?"

"Okay. Sure. Are you ready?" he nodded.

"I think so. On three," he suggested. "Alright?"

"Alright, on three. One, two . . . ." For leverage I pushed his left shoulder with my right hand and pulled the arrow out with my left. He screamed and unleashed a flurry of swear words.

"Damn it! What happened to the three?"

"I lost count."

Galatea chortled. "I am so sorry," she said. "We thought you might be . . . well, I'm sorry."

She knelt before him with strips of cloth she tore from an old linen sheet, and a carafe of wine, most of which she poured over the wound. Tino wrested the carafe from her and downed what was left with a satisfied gasp.

"You thought I might be what?" he demanded.

"It's nothing, Tino."

"I don't have my mother's healing gifts, but after watching her dress a number of arrow wounds that I sustained, I think I know what to do."

Constantine eyed Galatea, while she bound the wound, and then eyed me, a quizzical expression contorting his face.

"Yorgos, who is this?"

"You've seen her before, Tino. This is Galatea."

He regarded her coldly. "When have I seen her?" he asked, though I knew by his tone of voice and his expression of incredulity that he had already worked it out.

"She's the one attacked by wolves on the night we were locked out; the same one you distracted Evangelos and Maximus for. I helped her escape before they sent her into the fire. Do you remember?"

He drew a long breath, "Yes," he said, raising an eyebrow. "I do remember. What is she doing here?"

A low moan rose from Galatea's depths, and her arms went rigid before she collapsed to the floor. She writhed while Tino looked on dumbstruck. I glanced out the window. Sure enough, we had tarried too long, the moon was rising.

"I'll explain later, Tino. First, I need you to help me lock her up."

"Help you what?" In different circumstances I would have found his being completely confounded to be endearing, but we didn't have time for that. While restraining her, and trying to prevent her from harming herself, or the child she carried, I pointed to the manacles on the bed-stand.

"Bring me those." He stared at me dumbly. "Tino! Bring me the cuffs!" He scrambled to the table for them.

"Now what?"

"Get off of me, you bloody, reeking bastard," Galatea barked, clenching her teeth, "or I'll bite you." She struggled. Tino stared with open mouth while backing away.

"Constantine, you've got to put the cuffs on her. I'm holding her for you." She lay, face to the ground. I held her by the wrists, spread-eagle on top of her, trying to be mind-ful of the child she carried. With the rush of fear pumping through my veins, that was no easy task. "Tino!" I shouted. He scrambled over.

"I'll bite you! If I have my way with you, you'll never become a blood-drinker." She twisted her neck and snapped her teeth at my arm.

"No, you'll make me into a meat-eater, like yourself, instead. What's the difference? Both are monsters." I held my tongue, after that, knowing better than letting her wolf-self bait me into a pointless argument.

The first manacle clinked closed and Tino crawled around to her other arm. After the second manacle clinked closed we hoisted her up and into the chair. He held her while I secured the chains to the manacles.

Confident that she was secure, I held Tino's hand say-ing, "Come with me." On our way out I scooped up the bows and quivers, handing Tino one of each. While we passed through the door, he gripped the jamb and peered in.

"Her wrists are so raw and bloody."

"I trust you remember how to use these." I said, pulling him away from the door and closing it.

"Yes, of course. Where are you taking me?"

"You'll see. I want to show you something, but be ready with those just in case."

"Just in case what?"

"Nothing. Just . . . in case. Don't worry."

Holding the railing with one hand, and his hand with the other, I guided him up the stairs.

"This is what I wanted to show you," I said, opening the door with dramatic flair, as if revealing a masterpiece. The moon had reached its zenith. Its reflection danced on the obsidian colored water like fireflies. Tino squeezed my hand, turning to kiss me. I resisted, holding him at arms length, with both hands on his shoulders.

"Let's not start that again, Tino. I *am* glad to see you, but things have changed. Loving you that way isn't worth the risk."

"What risk? How can loving someone be a risk?" he asked.

"Loving someone is always a risk," I said. "For me, the risk of loving you is too great. I don't want to lose my soul."

I resisted the temptation, incongruous with my words, to pull him close and press my lips against his. I wanted to explore his mouth with my tongue and sample the flavor of his skin. I pushed him off and turned from him to the view of the ocean.

"I just don't believe that our love is so dangerous," he said, standing beside me.

"It is, Constantine, I assure you." Beneath us, Galatea thrashed about and howled with an all too human voice. "I don't want to end up like her, Tino. Our love puts us in danger of some nasty, unnatural consequences."

"If you are so afraid of becoming a monster, why are you even helping her?"

"Because she has no one else. Her mother doesn't know how to help her. Those who did this to her want to take her away against her will, and her father has threatened her with flames. If it weren't for me, she'd be all alone and probably dead."

"Perhaps she should go into the flames," he said. "I mean, if she's really become a monster."

"No. Not that. There's got to be a better way to free her of the wolf."

"What did she mean when she said 'If I have my way with you you'll never become a blood-drinker'?"

"She claims she can smell blood on me."

"What does that even mean?"

"It means that she thinks I've been marked by a blood-drinker who will come for me and turn me into a creature like himself, unless she attacks me first." Tino pressed his body against mine and drew a long, deep breath through his nostrils, while running his nose up my neck to my ear lobe.

"You smell good to me, nothing like blood." His lips lingered near my carotid artery. Little peaks of pleasure appeared up and down my arms and neck and across my shoulders.

"I don't know. I might enjoy it if you bit me," he whispered. "Go ahead, drink my blood."

"Stop it, Tino," I said, pushing him off me again. "You're not making this easy."

"I don't want to make it easy, Yorgos. Why are you making it so hard?"

"Please respect my wishes. Ever since I left you at Grigoriou, I've struggled to get my thoughts, my feelings, even myself, under control. Evangelos was right. We shouldn't be left alone. It's too dangerous."

"You eavesdropped on us?" he said, chuckling.

"Yes. I wanted to know why you came back. Why did you come back, tonight I mean? I thought you planned to return with your uncle in three days."

"I never made it all the way to Esphigmenou. I was too worried about you. After everything Evangelos said, I turned the mule around, tied it to a tree near Saint George's, and waited. I wanted to see where you've been going and what you've been doing."

"You waited for me all day?" Tino stepped alongside me and held my hand. I allowed it.

"Like I said. I've been worried."

"I'm okay, Tino. It pleases me that you're here, but it's not easy for me. Once you've left with your uncle, I will have to start all over again."

"Start what all over again?"

"Grieving." The word dropped from my lips with the weight of a stone, and I extracted my hand from his.

"Perhaps I should—"

He didn't finish his sentence. Until now, we managed to ignore Galatea's cries. We couldn't ignore her any longer. She fought the chains with such force, it felt like a stampede charged through the tower.

"I want you to stay," I said. "Let's check on Galatea."

Tino followed me down the stairs. When we reached her she was in the throes of the transformation that the silver would not allow. Tino looked on in apparent disbelief.

"What's wrong with her skin and bones?" he asked.

"Her body is trying to change," I explained. "Don't worry. As long as the silver earrings stay in her ears she won't be able to. She'll settle down in a bit." While he watched, his expression of disbelief turned into one of shock, and then horror.

"I can't watch anymore," he said, going into the main chamber. I followed.

"I don't like this, Yorgos. Not one bit. Don't assume I believe your understanding of things, but it's not like you to lie to Evangelos and Maximus, or to hide important details from them. Evangelos thinks you slept outside last night. If he knew the truth—"

"You can't tell him, Tino, promise me you won't. I don't want anyone else to know about this place, or about Galatea." I implored him with my eyes. He looked away from me. "Tino?"

"Okay. I'll keep your secret."

"Thank you." I rewarded him with a kiss on the back of his hand. I thought it would be innocent enough. But, when I felt his skin against my lips, my groin began to rise. It took a concerted effort to redirect my thoughts and several repetitions of the Jesus Prayer before it went back down again.

I explained that Galatea feared the vrykolakes responsible for her condition could return for her at any time; most likely during a full moon. We remained vigilant most of the night, sitting cross-legged on the floor across from the front door with our backs against the wall and our bows and arrows ready.

I woke when the rooster crowed. Tino had fallen asleep with his head in my lap. I untangled his curls with my fingers, glad that the rooster hadn't wakened him too. I meditated on his beauty for as long as I could stand it. Finally, I shook him awake, feeling ready to head home to the skete.

Before leaving, I released Galatea from her bonds and the three of us began our goodbyes.

"I'll come back tonight," Tino said, while we walked out together. "I don't want the two of you facing an army of hungry meat-eaters alone."

"Do you think one more person will really make a difference?" I asked.

"Sure, why not?"

"You don't even believe in vrykolakes."

"I'd hate myself if I was proven wrong and you died for it."

I walked him to where he tied his mule.

"We'll be okay," I insisted. "Besides, I don't think they're going to come tonight. Why would they wait until the third night of the full moon, when the moon is beginning to wane? Go care for your uncle. I'll see you at the skete in three days. We'll be okay."

"You're sure?" I placed my palm flat over his heart and pushed him gently.

"Go." He backed away from me, holding my gaze. He waved, turned to mount the mule and galloped away.

24 The Calm Before

After the third and most uneventful night of the full moon, I gathered up all of the silver and stowed it. It wouldn't be needed for a month and I wanted to spare Galatea the daily reminder of the pain she chose to bear to keep her baby alive and the wolf inside her at bay.

Released from manacles for the interim, Galatea was free to come and go so long as she steered clear of the skete and the neighboring monasteries. However, she didn't take advantage of her new freedom. Instead, she spent much of her time asleep. When awake, she ate jaw-dropping amounts of food. She ate in a single day what Tino and I ate in three. When I questioned her, she said she was famished, weak, and hadn't the energy to do much else.

It was no wonder. The child inside her grew at an exponential rate, something which confounded and concerned me. I learned not to bring that up. It seemed, after the first and only time I mentioned it, that her own concern for her child was enough to rouse the fury of the wolf, and the wolf was not something I was eager to entertain.

Three days after he departed, just as promised, Tino returned to Saint George's Skete, transporting his uncle and their few belongings on two mules. His cargo included a long rectangular object wrapped in a blanket.

The next day, Tino used the same mules to help me transport Maximus' trunk with the remaining articles of silver inside to the tower. We waited until well after midnight to set out, so we could move about in secrecy. In addition to the trunk, Tino packed the blanket-wrapped bulk, which had piqued my curiosity. When I went to take a peek, he slapped my hand away saying, "Leave that alone. It's a surprise for Galatea."

The surprise, however, was his. "Dear Theotokos," he said, when she greeted us at the door. "Look how big you've gotten. In just three days!" She threw the crust of bread she'd been gnawing on, hitting him squarely in the forehead.

"Never say that to a woman who's expecting if you value your life."

"Especially if she's a vrykolakas," I added.

Chuckling, he apologized saying, "I have just the thing to make it up to you. Yorgos, help me with this."

We hoisted the blanket-wrapped burden into the tower, carrying it between us on our shoulders.

"You won't need to be chained up again, once these are in place."

"What is it?" she asked, lifting the corner of the blanket. She uncovered three thick wooden planks that were twined together, along with several metal brackets and other pieces of hardware.

"These are for the door to your room. I salvaged them from the wreckage at the monastery."

"This won't work," I complained. "She's vulnerable to silver, not this." I tossed one of the brackets to the floor after inspecting it.

"Well, I should think that piercing her ears with silver is enough to keep her from changing. This will keep her confined to her room."

I eyed him, doubting that the wooden planks would be strong enough, and shrugged. "I guess it's worth a try, but I'd feel better if it the metal parts were made of silver."

"Well, I'm thrilled," Galatea said, dismissing my pessimism, and running the tips of her fingers down the length of one of the planks. "Thank you, Constantine. Now my wrists can heal." She beamed and her eyes glistened with tears. She wiped them away with the back of her hand. Turning to me she said, "You can hang all the silver chains you want on the door and from the planks, but leave them off me."

In the morning, after Tino left to care for his uncle, Galatea and I shared a simple meal of porridge, fruit and bread.

"Do you ever eat meat?" she asked, with her elbows on the table between us. She eyed the food I placed before her with palpable disinterest. "I need meat, not this mush."

"I thought nereids didn't eat meat," I answered.

"Well, I'm more than a simple nereid now, aren't I? Apparently my dietary needs have changed."

"I don't have access to any meat. We eat simply, I'm sorry."

She picked over the breakfast, consuming little of it, but devoured the piece of bread, tearing a second helping off the loaf.

"Tell me about Constantine," she asked, while gnawing on the bread. I looked up from my bowl.

"What?" I reached for the carafe of wine and downed a mouthful before offering it to her. She swatted the carafe away.

"I've been watching you two. You have something."

I downed another gulp of wine. "I don't know what you're talking about. He's just one of the monks I used to live with before I came to Saint George's. He'll be staying for a while. There was a fire in his monastery." With both hands, I tugged my cassock at the waist to straighten it.

Galatea dragged her chair closer to the table and reached for my hand. "He's more than that to you." I stared at my bowl and found I had lost interest in the porridge. I pushed it around with a crusty heel of bread.

"Yorgos, you can be honest with me."

I pulled my hand free of hers, pushed my chair back, and stood to my feet.

"He's just another monk." I smoothed my cassock with my palms. "What do you want me to say?"

"The truth. You love him. I can smell it. There's no point in denying it."

"If your nose knows," I said, avoiding looking her in the eye, "Why do you need to ask?"

"I want to help you, that's why. It's clear you love him, but something is holding you back."

"I didn't ask for your help and there's nothing going on." I walked to the corner of the room, where the planks were leaned against the wall, and ran my fingers over the ends of them.

"I don't believe you." I met her gaze, but held my tongue. "Your fear gave you away when I mentioned him. I could smell it."

"That nose of yours doesn't miss much, does it?"

"No. Not anymore."

I pursed my lips considering what she said. "You're right. I am afraid. People like me who act on their feelings, come back after death as something monstrous. Something like . . . like . . . ."

"Like me?" she asked.

I looked at her squarely while taking my seat across from her. "Yes. It's a consequence of sin."

"Who told you that nonsense?"

"Everybody I respect and love. My feelings don't matter. Tino and I can never be together."

"How serious a sin does it have to be? Do you even know? I didn't commit any grave sin and still this was done to me."

"I don't know exactly what causes it. According to the teachings of the Church, committing murder, being declared anathema, or speaking blasphemy can make someone a vrykolakas, as can living a sinful life, dying with unrepented sin on one's conscience, dying before one is baptized, or being buried in unconsecrated ground."

"That's quite a list, Yorgos!"

"It is, but there's more. The worst thing is being a man who loves another man. If Tino and I ever act on our feelings, we're done for." She laughed out loud and covered her mouth with her hand.

"It's not funny," I said, lowering my eyes.

"I know it's not. I'm sorry, but you make it sound like the two of you falling in love will usher in the end of the world as we know it. You know, with a list like that, it's a wonder everyone doesn't come back from the grave as some kind of monster. I don't believe it. I don't think sin has anything to do with it, especially in your case. Love doesn't turn people into monsters, other monsters do. I should know."

"I hope you're right. I don't know how it happens, but however it works, whatever the cause, I don't want to risk it. It's not worth it."

She fixed her gaze on me. "I think I get it. You're afraid of that man, aren't you? The one who was a guest at your family's inn when you were a boy. You believe if you can manage to live without sinning, he won't be able to get to you."

I fidgeted with my cassock again, looking down to straighten the belt. "I'm not comfortable talking about Mister Dumitru. Besides, I'm safe from him as long as I never leave here."

"You do realize, don't you, that I was turned into what I am here, on Mount Athos? You're no safer here than you would be anywhere else."

I sighed, relenting, and looked up at her, "I know that. That's why I have to be vigilant."

"Maybe being religious causes it. Have you considered that?"

The fingers of her right hand gingerly traveled over the raw skin of her left wrist. She winced and withdrew them from the wound as if she had touched fire. Ignoring the pain, she continued, "If officials of your church know that being declared anathema or being buried in unconsecrated ground can turn people into vrykolakes, why do they keep doing it? I think they're responsible for creating the very same monsters they condemn to the flames."

How ironic and how true. Now it was my turn to laugh.

"I hadn't thought of that before. But face it, Galatea, we come from different worlds. The Protos may be your father, but you are not Orthodox. I don't expect you to understand what we believe or the way we order our lives."

"You're right about that. Nereids are a different kind of people."

"Are nereids even people at all?"

"Raising her chin at me she said, "We are, after a fashion."

While the days passed and Galatea's belly continued to swell, so did my concern. I had observed that the decline of her stamina was exactly opposite to the growth of her baby.

By mid-month, her face was gaunt, her limbs were frail, and her skin was pale as ash. The baby, however, so thrived that her stomach rippled with ceaseless activity. That worried me. She was far too weak to look after herself, let alone the acrobat child she carried.

If I am to defend them, I decided, *I need to hone my skills, and fast.* Thankfully Maximus' trunk was filled with a number of conventional arrows, as well as several dozen silver ones. I could practice with the bronze arrows without reservation and still have the others when I most needed them.

I practiced daily, using targets I made myself that more closely resembled scarecrows, than traditional bulls-eyes. Aiming for the 'heart,' I incrementally lengthened the distance from which I could strike, until I was satisfied that my arrows would go where I wanted them to.

Tino felt torn between his responsibility to his uncle and wanting to practice his skills with the bow and arrow. His uncle took precedence, which was as it should be. He insisted on joining me as often as he was able, saying that on the occasion of the next full moon he had no intention of leaving me to fend for myself.

At first we managed–by God's grace and by keeping ourselves busy–to avoid spending an inordinate amount of time together. We were never alone; accept for when we practiced shooting. I can only speak for myself; the seriousness of the coming threat helped me to keep my mind focused on the task at hand.

Besides, our energies were required separately and we didn't have the luxury of spending them on each other. While the month passed, however, and the next full moon drew nearer, he began to join me for practice more often– almost daily.

25 Trial By Fire

"That was great!"

Tino, who had aimed his next shot, lowered his bow-arm and lifted his eyes. "I'm catching up with you," he said, grinning. He nudged me with his shoulder, knocking me off balance and then lifted his arm, fiddling with the weapon.

Regaining my footing, I shrugged. "Well, that shouldn't be too hard, since I'm just a beginner myself."

"You're a natural then," he said. The target, an effigy hanging from a tree by a rope around its neck, swayed in the breeze perhaps twelve meters away. Exacting his aim, Tino locked his bow arm into position. He cocked his head and winked before following through. Drawing the bowstring until his hand brushed his cheek, he sent the bronze arrow whizzing through the air. He moved fluidly; drawing, aiming and releasing with one continual motion, ending with his elbow behind and slightly above his shoulder.

"Show-off," I said, hefting my own bow and arrow. "I've been doing this a lot. If anything, you're the natural. You've practiced less than I have and your skills are on par with mine."

"Practice is paying off?" he asked. "For the both of us?" I nodded, absently.

I focused my attention on my target, a couple meters farther away than the one he struck. I squared my feet, keeping them a shoulder's width apart. Balancing my body weight over the balls of my feet, I straightened my back to absorb the recoil. At the last second before releasing the arrow, I shifted, aiming for the same target he struck. I sent the arrow flying. It sunk into the center of the red circle on the effigy's chest, right next to Tino's arrow, with not so much as a quarter of a centimeter between them.

"Who's the show off now?" he asked.

"It's me," I shrugged. "We don't have a lot of day light left. Let's collect all the arrows and go. Meet here again tomorrow?"

He nodded, adding, "If my uncle's still doing well."

With Tino at my heels, I strode over to the target. Both our arrows protruded from the middle of the effigy's straw heart. Tino's face turned red.

"What?" I insisted, with my hand around both shafts. "Why are you looking at me like that?" One swift tug and the arrows came out.

"I like the way you grabbed those, is all," he said, becoming aroused, "with a firm hand."

"Stop it!" I said, throwing an arrow at him. It glanced off his chest, thudding softly on the ground. I tried, for all it was worth, not to blush, or become too visibly aroused myself. Tino didn't need the encouragement.

He bent for the arrow and slapped it in my hand. "I can't help myself. When I am around you, it has a mind of its own."

Reaching around him, I dropped both arrows into the quiver on his back. "Then you should ignore what its thinking; try to use the head that's bigger and hopefully smarter."

Taking advantage of my proximity, he lowered his head and kissed me. It was chaste: a peck on the forehead. I liked it.

"Do you wanna know what my head is telling me to do?" he asked. Tapping his skull he added, "This one, I mean." I raised an eyebrow. "It's telling me that I should tell you how much I love you and that I should convince you to run off with me, far away from here."

"And where would we go?"

He shrugged, an oafish grin smeared across his lips. "We could see the Parthenon. I've always wanted to see the temples and ruins in Athens."

I was struck at that moment, by how natural and good it felt to accept his affection, how easy it was to love him and how much I wanted to run away with him. *What am I afraid of?* "And from there to Italy?" I asked, flashing a sheepish smile.

"Yes, Venice."

"Venice," I agreed with a nod. "It's a nice fantasy, Tino, and tempting, but I belong here." I offered him my hand. "Take a walk with me. I'll get the arrows later, after you've gone."

"By then it'll be dark."

I started off down the trail and pulled him along. "Then I'll do it tomorrow. Come on."

I had been thankful, on a number of occasions that the monks I lived with neither ventured far from the skete, nor the established trails. I had no reason to fear that it would be discovered that I made my lodging in the abandoned tower or that I harbored a girl in it. Tino and I were safe. No one would spy us traipsing, hand in hand, down the overgrown trails heading away from St. George's to the tower. No one would notice if we stopped for another kiss, chaste or not.

"I wish I brought my coat," I said, dropping his hand. Twilight was falling, and the temperature with it. I crossed my arms and rubbed my shoulders and elbows with vigor, hoping the friction would warm me. Tino pulled me to a stop, with his hand on my shoulder, and wrapped his arms around me from behind. I felt the crush of my quiver into my shoulder blade, while he squeezed me close.

"Let me warm you," he suggested, rubbing my arms and nibbling my earlobe. Turning me to face him, he pushed my back up against a rough tree and pressed his body and lips against mine. I pressed back, coaxing his tongue from his mouth with my own before a wave of guilt hit me. Licking my lips, the way someone does when they can eat no more, I eased him off me, pressing firmly with the palms of my hands.

"It's getting late, Constantine. You should go to your uncle before it gets any darker."

"Damn it, Yorgos! You go from hot to cold so quickly, my head is spinning."

"I'm sorry. I'm trying to be your friend. What more do you want from me?"

"My *friend?*"

"Yes, your friend. Is friendship so terrible?"

"Under normal circumstances, no, it's not, but with you it's excruciating and confusing."

With a shrug I threw up my hands, "I have nothing more to offer you. I'm sorry."

"Yes, so am I." Turning away from me he shoved his hands into his cassock pockets and shouted over his shoulder, "You're right, I need to get back to the skete. You had better hurry, I'm sure your girlfriend is expecting you."

"She's not my girlfriend," I shouted to his back. "She's like a sister–" I was cut off by the sound of someone yelling.

"Show yourself, goddamn it! I know you're here."

Squaring his shoulders first, Tino stopped, and turned around. "Who's yelling?" I didn't have the time to answer.

Instead I tore a path to the sound. It was coming from the tower. Swiftly Constantine closed the gap between us.

"Yorgos, who was that?" he insisted, catching up with me.

We bounded from the foliage and shrubbery, into the clearing in which the tower stood, only the tower wasn't there, and the Protos, in full regalia, with his ear freshly pierced, was cutting a semi-circle in the dirt–like a rabid dog–pacing in front of where the tower should be.

"Get out here!" The Protos demanded. He was accompanied by a monk I had never seen before, who stood by motionless and impassive, watching. From behind I could see that both of the monk's ears were badly scared and pierced with a single, blood encrusted, hoop earring, made of silver.

"Shhh." I said, touching my finger to my lips. I pushed Tino back into the overgrowth, hiding with him behind a thick-trunked laurel tree. "If it's not one group of vrykolakes, it's another," I whispered.

"What do you mean?" he asked, his voice hoarse under the strain of trying to whisper with adrenaline pumping into his blood. He peaked out from behind the tree with his mouth gaping. I pulled him back.

"Nothing, it's just a hunch."

"Where has the tower gone and what is the Protos doing here?"

"Enough questions," I said, adding, "He is Galatea's father." Tino's eyes became as big as apples. "It's a long story that I'm sure I don't even know the half of."

"Her father?" He mouthed the words with apparent incredulity.

"Yes. And the tower?" I shrugged. "I have no idea."

"Buildings don't just disappear, Yorgos."

I nodded my agreement saying, "No, usually not, but this one has."

We both peeked from behind the tree. The Protos stormed up to where the tower's entrance should be, shaking his fist.

"Show yourself. I know you're in there." He rushed up, slammed against an invisible barrier, and stumbled backwards, landing in the dirt on his rear, losing his skouphos. He retrieved his hat, and—with his palms flat against its surface—found the invisible door. He stood up, using it for support. "I know this is some kind of nereid trick," he yelled. "A glamour! Your mother told me all about those."

With his palms flat, he found the door's edges with the tips of his fingers, establishing its length and breadth, before positioning himself in front of it.

Taking a moment to compose himself, he swat dirt from his backside, pulled his cassock down at the waist, and squared his shoulders. Then he raised his fist and, for all appearances, began to beat the air, each knock resounding loudly.

Galatea opened the door. He stumbled into her but managed to regain his footing before hitting the ground. Though a glamour still concealed the tower's exterior, the candle-lit interior was visible.

He grabbed Galatea by the forearm and pulled her out.

"Could you please help me now?" he asked, waving the monk over to assist him.

Galatea protested, pushing against the earth with her feet, but they both had her by an arm, and dragged her away from the rectangle of light that spilled from the open door.

"Let me go," she yelled, resisting them. While they dragged her farther into the open the glamour lifted. The air rippled with vertical concentric rings, and the tower materialized behind them.

"Ever since we met, I've seen the strangest things." Tino whispered.

"Welcome to my world."

While they dragged Galatea through the dirt, our eyes connected. The weak smile she flashed me was almost imperceptible, but she did smile, and then she went limp, pulling them down with her.

Tino and I followed, placing each footstep with care. Avoiding the crunch of twigs, branches and dried leaves was impossible. I counted on them making too much noise themselves to hear our approach. At length, they entered another clearing ringed with burning torches that stuck out of the ground. Another monk, his back to us, added the finishing touches to a pyre. I dropped to the ground before we were noticed, pulling Tino down with me. We hid behind a thicket of tall grass and bushes.

"This is the girl?" the monk asked, turning to face them. His voice sounded familiar. I parted the grass with my hands to get a better look, and could still only barely make out his features, distorted, as they were, by the dark of twilight and the interplay of shadows and light cast by the flickering torch-flames. When I got a decent look at him, I gasped. It was Brother Christopheros.

"We should do something," Tino whispered. I nodded, finding I couldn't speak, and my limbs felt as if they had turned to water.

"Do what?" I managed to choke out.

The Protos relinquished Galatea to the monk who assisted him. He, in turn, shoved her to Christopheros.

"Please be gentle with her," the Protos said. "No need to be so rough. Now that all the afflicted are here, we can end this curse and stop it from spreading."

"I don't care about any curse," Galatea protested. "I won't go into the flames. I'll wear silver every month. I won't ever let the wolf out, I promise."

The Protos wagged his head, a mournful look contorting his harsh features.

"It's not advisable. Tell her, Christopheros. Tell her about the silver."

"Yorgos, we have to do something," Tino whispered. Trembling, I shrugged, ashamed that when danger finally called, I put my own life above that of another.

Christopheros took one of the torches and lit the pyre, touching the flame to several places before tossing it into the growing conflagration. He turned back to Galatea and spoke to her like they were the only two people present, with a touch of tenderness coloring his voice. "Prolonged exposure, even intermittent exposure, causes weakness, loss of vitality, and even, I fear, serious illness. Surely you've noticed symptoms by now, but don't you worry. Everything will be okay." He reached for her, smiling pleasantly. "We will meet God on the other side, if we pass through the flames willingly, and with faith. Come with me." He grasped her by the fingertips, while backing into the flames.

"No, I won't." She struggled to wrest her hand from his. "Doesn't anyone care about my baby?" Christopheros squeezed tighter. Galatea dropped to the ground, causing him to fall.

The Protos rushed to her. "This is for your salvation," he said, standing above her, *"And* your baby's. The flesh is sacred. Normally cremation is forbidden, flesh should be allowed to return to dust, but there is nothing normal about these circumstances. There is no other known cure. Only destruction by fire will set you free. You must take heart. If you meet the flames here on earth, perhaps you'll be spared the flames of hell. That is all that matters now."

He reached for her with a helping hand. She swatted it and pushed herself up from the ground. While backing away she glanced over her shoulder, realizing that she was edging toward the same destruction he spoke of. The fire crackled and popped, sending sparks into the darkening sky. Serenely, the monks waited, with enough space for her to pass between them and into the flames. Christopheros, prayer rope in hand, mouthed the words to a prayer. The Protos approached Galatea. Grimacing, she inched back.

"Don't waste your time pleading with me, Father. I don't believe in your hell or your God," she said between her broken sobs, "Please, let me be."

He turned his head and indicated the tiny silver spike that he had driven through his ear. "I admit it, I've not been piercing my flesh only to share in your pain, but because I, too, bear the curse. I'll be right behind you, darling. We'll do this together." He approached her slowly, as one might approach a cornered, frightened dog.

"Darling? If you ever loved me, you wouldn't be hell-bent on destroying me."

Perplexity darkening his face, the Protos acted like she had slapped him across the mouth. "Destroy you? No! I am trying to save you!"

She shook her head, taking one more careful step back. "Mother will come for me. I doubt you've ever seen a nereid's full fury."

I looked at Tino, and through the tears filming my eyes, saw the bouquet of feathered arrows blooming from the quiver strung over his shoulder. *ARROWS!* In my fear I forgot about the arrows. I reached over my shoulder and drew one out of my quiver. Tino followed suit and we gave each other a single nod, and then directed our attention on the task at hand.

Stepping closer to her, the Protos laughed. "Your mother is a woman of honor. She would never break her agreement with the Holy Synod. We are too close to Saint George's. Now, stop this foolishness and come."

He took another step, reaching for her. She ran, with the determination of a ram, shoving him aside with her shoulder. He turned swiftly and leapt, taking hold of both of her wrists from behind.

"You can help me now," he called over his shoulder to the waiting brothers.

"Now," I whispered. "I'll take Christopheros."

Tino and I sprung to our feet and sent a volley of arrows into the advancing monks. They both staggered back, toward the fire. They tried to regain their footing, and approach the Protos, but we kept the arrows flying. With each one, they staggered back until the flames engulfed them.

The Protos, with a firm grip on Galatea's wrist, looked around to see who shot at them. Shock widened his features when recognition dawned. Galatea struggled to take advantage of his confusion and break free. His grip tightened.

"Evangelos' ward. Again!" he said. "And your lover, I presume? I thought the air was thick with the scent of lust. This doesn't concern you, boys. Mind your own business and go back to your fornicating."

He turned away, dismissing us with a grunt, pushing Galatea toward the inferno. Inside it, Brother Christopheros, and the monk I had never seen before, thrashed about in the flames. I said a prayer for them, crossing myself and wondered if I would ever be able to sleep again, or if I would ever again feel clean, after taking part in the killing of two holy men.

The fire continued to consume them, making the air thick with oily smoke and the scent of burning human flesh. Inside the pyre, with arms flailing and feet hopping, they appeared to be dancing. Christopheros chanted and prayed with agonized tones. The other monk tried to pray along but surrendered to the pain and began to wail.

"Protos," I called, sending an arrow his way, it whizzed past, grazing his ear. He turned, arms crossed and glared at me. "It's not wise to turn your back on the man who's pointing an arrow at you."

"Two men," Tino corrected, "two arrows." He pulled his bow string to its limit, and stepped forward.

"Let her go." I said, with a level voice. "Burn yourself to a crisp if that's what you want to do, but let Galatea go."

He sneered at me, and laughed. "Boys and their toys. I wondered who was responsible for all those targets hanging from the trees. Shoo! Yorgos, you and your boyfriend are bothering me." He turned from us. I released an arrow, striking his left shoulder.

"Let her go! My quiver is full."

"Lucky shot," he said, pulling the arrow out and dropping it. Ignoring Tino and me, he pushed Galatea closer to the flames. Tino sent an arrow into his right shoulder.

"We're both getting lucky tonight, Yorgos."

"I rue the day I allowed Evangelos to keep you," the Protos sighed.

I fired another arrow, striking the back of his thigh.

"Some of these arrows are silver. How many more can you take? Let her go."

Holding tightly to her wrists, the Protos turned, facing me, trying to stare me down. Tino and I both, with steady hands, aimed arrows at his heart, and we were unflinching.

"Very well," he said, releasing her. Opening his arms for her, Tino lowered his bow and she ran to him. I stared at the Protos down a silver shaft. He regarded me coldly.

"I'll be back."

"No, you won't."

"How can you be so sure?"

"I know your secret. Secrets, I mean. Unless you want Evangelos and the Holy Synod to know that you've had relations with a nereid, fathered a child with her, and have become a vrykolakas, I would advise you to go away from here, and never come back. I'll show them Galatea and the baby, and I'm sure Thalia, under the circumstances, would agree to meet with Evangelos and members of the Holy Synod in the nereid village. I will expose you."

His eyes became cold slivers. "I could kill you. Both of you. You'll never know. I'll wait until you think I've forgotten."

I shook my head. "You won't do that, not unless you are more given to evil than I realize."

"Me, evil? I'm not the pervert."

"No. I think that you actually believe that you are saving Galatea by forcing her into the fire. You believe it's what God wants you to do. Do you really believe God wants you to murder me and Tino? It would be murder. We're not vrykolakes."

"You'll hold your tongue?"

"Yes. Haven't I so far?" He nodded curtly. "And you'll stay away?"

Staring at me, he stood without moving, glanced at his daughter, and then looked back at me, and nodded again. "It seems we've reached a truce," he said. He turned from us and disappeared into the night.

26 Waiting

My legs wobbled, and I trembled, but not because I was cold. With Tino behind me, I leaned against him for support.

By now, our brothers the monks, were gone. Dead. Their physical remains were well on their way to becoming ash and brittle bone.

Galatea, a crumpled mass, lay on the ground. Taking a deep breath, I composed myself, dropping to one knee beside her.

"Galatea," I said, shaking her gently. "Come, let's go home." When she didn't respond, I feared that she too had died, perhaps killed by fear. I shook her again; a little rougher than before and sighed when she stirred.

Tino and I hoisted her up. She glanced around, her eyes wide and glassy. Standing on her own, she dusted herself off, rubbing her hands around the globe of her stomach. Satisfied that her baby had not been harmed she smiled and released her breath. Her smile became a grimace. She reached lower saying, "My water broke." I held my breath, anticipating the next words to come out of her mouth.

Still cradling her stomach with her palms, she groaned, "The baby is coming."

I glanced at Tino, knowing we were thinking the same thing: *Could this night get any worse?*

"The baby can't come now. My father will know." Her cracking voice rose two octaves. "He'll come take it from me. He'll burn it."

"No," Tino said. "He won't. We need to get you to the tower. Don't you worry. You'll be okay."

"I'm not worried about myself. My baby–"

"Will be okay," I said. "I don't think your father will come back. Not tonight, at least. And you won't be alone, we'll both be here." I looked up at Tino, imploring him with my eyes.

He nodded, saying, "Yes. We won't leave you."

With Galatea between us, Tino and I shouldered her weight about a third of the way until he urged me to go ahead to make preparations.

Prepare what? I wondered. "Theotokos, please help Galatea, I have no idea what to do." I mumbled my prayers while I ran. *And please pray for me.*

My stomach clenched when I neared the tower. I bent over the bushes by the front door, vomiting. *Two dead, and one about to be born, all in the same night! And I'm in the middle of it all!* Wiping my mouth on my sleeve, I tried to stand and my knees buckled. Composing myself I entered, leaving the door open.

One of my cousins was born in the inn when I was seven years old, just after Aunt Petra lost her husband and moved in. I remembered the occasion, but not the details. And I remembered when Zosimos and Zoe-Sophia were born, although I was much younger. All I recalled from the births was a lot of loud commotion, and Yaya and Nona needing plenty of towels and hot water.

Inspecting the linens and blankets we had on hand, I was aghast. They weren't filthy, but we didn't have any that were freshly cleaned, either. I picked through them for the freshest ones and spread them over her mattress. I fluffed the pillows and smoothed the linen, wanting it to be perfect.

Tino staggered through the door, supporting Galatea's weight.

"The bed is ready," I said, turning back to my work.

After putting a pot of water on the fire to boil, I chose an old linen sheet and tore it into hand-sized squares. I crumpled them like paper, and tossed them into the pot. Standing over it, I watched the pieces of linen slosh around, and the tiny bubbles slowly get bigger. When the water began to bubble over, I removed the pot, carrying it into Galatea's bedroom.

I found her groaning in her bed, biting the back of her hand. Her legs, bent at the knees, were spread. I stole a peek and relaxed. The baby hadn't crowned yet.

Tino covered her legs with a blanket and sat beside her. Holding her hand he brushed sweat-drenched hair out of her eyes. I sat the pot down on the floor at his feet and handed him a soggy square of linen.

"Let it cool." He nodded, a myriad of conflicting emotions passing over his eyes like dark clouds. I took a seat at the far end of the bed and fished my prayer rope from my pocket. It seemed as good a time as any to pray.

Holding it by the knotted black cross at the end, I began to center myself, or at least make the effort, when I heard a rushing wind. I lifted my gaze from the tiny knotted cross, and looked at Tino.

"Now what?" I said.

"What?"

"Don't you hear that?"

He shrugged.

"Mother," Galatea moaned, repeating the word, "Mother, Mother!" She pushed herself up with her elbows.

Tino shushed her saying, "Stay in bed."

"You're mother can't hear you," I said. "You're with me and Constantine at the tower, remember?"

The sound was frightfully loud now. Before rising to his feet, Tino wiped her head with the towel I gave him. "What is that?" he asked, cocking his head.

The structure shook. Together, we darted for the front door, collecting our bows and arrows, nocking them, while we went out.

"Mother!" Galatea called out. "Mother!"

Looking up into the moonlit sky I saw a faintly luminescent, white funnel twisting above our heads.

"What the hell!?" Tino said, shouting above the sound of the wind, and pointing his bow-and-arrow at it. The wind storm lifted twigs, dirt, and even stones from the ground, and flung them in all directions. I shielded my eyes with the back of my hand.

"Oh!" I shouted. "It's okay." I set my weapons on the ground and gently pressed his arm down with my hand on his wrist. "We're not in danger. It's Thalia, Galatea's mother. She tried to tell us."

The funnel cloud touched down a few yards away. Tino eyed it dubiously.

"Her mother is a white tornado?"

I laughed. "Stick with me and who knows what oddities you'll see."

An indistinct and human shape, which you could see through, formed in the center of the funnel, and the cloud collapsed into it. The body was solid and opaque now.

"Oddities without number," Tino said, under his breath.

"I don't know what you know," I started, while she strode toward us, "or if you've even seen her since–"

"I'm her mother. I know everything," Thalia said, passing us on her way into the tower. We swiveled on our feet, following right behind.

"This is Constantine–"

"The one you love. I know!" She dismissed my introduction with a flick of her hand.

I followed her into the room, with Tino at my heels. I waved him back, into the main chamber. Thalia, sitting on the edge of the bed, squeezed her daughter's fingers.

"I'm here, sweetheart," she whispered. She looked up at me. "Is there anywhere else you two can go? I'll call to you when it's over." She had never struck me as so human or so vulnerable.

I nodded without a word, turning. Thalia stood before the door blocking my way, yet I saw nothing of her passage through space.

"You will always have my gratitude, Yorgos," she said. "Always. Mine, and that of all nereid kind. It was a good thing you did, staying with her when your own life was in danger. I knew you'd save her." She shook her head. "Now it is we who are indebted to you. I put so much faith in that man and his God. Love must have blinded me."

"His God is my God too," I protested, not wanting God to get a bad name because of what the Protos had done, or tried to do.

She nodded. "Yes. Your example gives me hope that there is goodness in your religion. You've saved my daughter twice now." She reflected for a moment adding, "We will have plenty of time to talk when this is over."

I lit an oil lamp, grabbed my shoulder bag, a couple of blankets, and an ikon of the crucifixion. Taking Tino by the hand I said, "Come with me."

Walking at a brisk pace, we went to a ravine I knew of that wasn't far from the skete. The upper level of two buildings was visible above the tree tops, including the building my quarters were in.

I retrieved the ikon from my pocket and kissed it, crossing myself, and saying a quick prayer, before leaning it against a tree. Then I dangled the lamp from a low hanging branch.

Together Tino and I spread one of the blankets on the ground beneath the lamp and I collapsed onto it.

Tino cuddled up to me from behind, wrapped his arms over and around me and pulled me close.

"So, I'm the one you love?" he whispered.

"Do you really need to ask that?"

"Yes. My heart may know it, but that doesn't mean I don't need to hear it from time to time."

I squirmed, turning around to face him.

I ran my fingers through the tangle of curly brown waves that obscured his darker brown eyes. Brushing the hair back I said, "There you are," straining to kiss his eyelids each in turn. "Yes. You are the one I love." Sighing, I rolled onto my back, pulling him on top of me. A brand new discovery, I repeated it, "I love you." I liked the sound of those particular words when spoken to him in particular, and I pressed my mouth against his. His lips parted. I teased his tongue with mine and then drew back.

"Tino, do you think I'm good?" I asked, holding his gaze.

"Good? You? Of course! I don't know anyone who's better."

"But, those were good men we killed. A truly good man wouldn't have done that." I twisted my neck to glance at the ikon of Christ and his passion. I would have crossed myself too, but Tino's arms were in my way. "Have mercy on me, a sinner," I whispered.

"Well, I helped. Maybe you should pray for me, too. Only, I don't feel like a murderer. They were going to hurt Galatea and they were going to go into the fire anyway. Hell, they built it. Turn this around, Yorgos. We saved two lives tonight! Lives that would have otherwise been destroyed. Innocent lives. That's good, isn't it?"

He held himself above me, with his arms straight, elbows locked, palms pressed flat into the ground.

"If this is good, why do I feel so bad?" He pressed his ear against my breast, lay there, quiet for a minute, before rhythmically patting my chest with his palm in time with my heartbeat.

"This is one of life's puzzles. Only the terribly good seem to worry that they're not."

The weight of all the warnings I'd ever received came crashing down on me. Murder, lust, thieving–any sin, if not repented of–can make someone a vrykolakas. I seemed to have committed each and every sin on the list. And the worst of them all, to be a man who loves another man, wasn't I one of those all along?

To hell with it. "Take me, Tino. Tonight. Please. Do it!" *I fear it's too late for me, anyway.* Twisting around till my belly pressed into the damp earth, I reached for the ikon and turned it around so the back of the panel faced us. As if that would keep Jesus from seeing. *Forgive me.*

I waited, expecting him to push up my cassock, and to feel the pressure of his member against my muscle. "Tino, why aren't you doing it? Give it to me already!"

He chuckled softly.

"My, isn't this a change! I can't do anything when you've got that thing on." He tugged my garment.

I thrust myself up with such force that he slid off me. Trying to cast it off, I got all tangled up in it and required his help. Once free of the encumbrance, I tossed my cassock

345

aside like so much unnecessary weight and pulled him down on top of me. The weight of his body and the pleasurable crush of his naked flesh against mine was the only weight I wanted to feel.

"Tino, why are you still wearing your cassock?" He straddled me, his cassock bunched uncomfortably. He lay on top of me, without removing the clerical garb, and placed his ear over my heart again.

"I don't know, Yorgos. I know I've pressured you about this, about us, but this isn't how I imagined it. You're under duress."

"You're not forcing me."

"That's not what I mean. This has been a confusing, long and painful night. I want you to want this, to want me."

"You're right, then. I am under duress, but I do want this. I want you. You make me feel safe. I need to feel safe. Please?" I tried to keep from crying, but my chest heaved. "I don't think you could ever be close enough, even if you're inside of me." I started to sob. When the blood warmed my cheeks I looked away from him. "Please Tino. You're what's keeping me from believing that I am rotten with sin."

"Aren't you still afraid that–"

"Damn my fears! It's too much to fight. And I'm tired." I flung my arms out, making the shape of the cross on the ground with my body. "It's too late anyway. I love you. Isn't that all it takes?"

Tightening his hold on me he rested his chin on my breast, saying, "I love you, too."

"Don't use words. Show me."

Even before he touched my skin, my heart pounded in my ears and I became short of breath. I helped him off with his cassock, discarding it without ceremony and throwing it as far away from us as possible. He yanked down my undergarments and spit on his fingers. I opened my legs for him and lifted my knees. He applied the cold, slick liquid and teased my opening.

I was ready. Gripping his shoulders I pulled him down on top of me. A wickedly mischievous grin spread his lips and he reached between my legs with more saliva on his fingers. Pressing my thighs together, I denied him access. I threw my arms behind my head and arched my back.

"You tease!" he laughed.

"No, sorry, I'm not teasing." I opened my legs and lifted my knees again, applying my own spit. Once ready, I guided him into me. He didn't last inside me for long. It hurt too much. Though I needed it, I wanted him so close that I couldn't tell where he ended and I began, my body had a mind of its own and tightened up. In my frenzied state, I was determined. I wouldn't have my body making decisions for me.

"You're too tight, Yorgos. I don't want to hurt you."

"Kiss me then." Our lips pressed together. Our fluids mingled. I reached around for his member and tried to slip it in. "Try again," I demanded. He did. It hurt like hell. I loved it. I didn't think I could ever get enough.

When he entered me, I gasped, and forced my fist into my mouth, to suppress a scream. I bit down on it, my teeth leaving deep impressions.

I don't know if I merely ignored the pain until it was transformed into the most intense pleasure I had ever known, or if I accepted it as punishment deserved. But somehow it was transformed, and once it had been, I accepted every thrust until he gained access into my deepest soul.

The sky above was gray with the first light of morning when I heard Thalia calling to me in my mind. Tino had fallen asleep half on top of me. I ran my fingers through his hair and kissed him. He stirred, kissing me back. A smile, more innocent and pure than I would have imagined, graced his beautiful face and I kissed him again.

"Mine," I said. "Your lips are mine, now."

"What are you talking about, Yorgos? All of me is yours and has been since I met you in front of the ikon of Saint George."

"I know. I knew it then, but I was too scared."

"How are you, now? How do you feel, I mean?"

"If you are asking me if I feel guilty, the answer is no. I feel great!" I reached up and tickled his armpits. We tumbled and rolled in the dirt, laughing.

"I could stay here with you all day and we could do it again and again, but they're ready for us to come back. Let's go meet the baby."

"I need a moment Tino," I said when we neared the tower. "I'll be right back." He acknowledged my words and proceeded to the door. "Wait!" I emptied the contents of my bag, placing everything on top of the folded blankets, and handed it to him. "I'll be right there." Without a word he kissed my forehead and pushed the door open, going in.

I went to the spot where the pyre had been, finding the area in shambles. It appeared that the flames had been quenched by a localized deluge. The soggy, charred remnants of the pyre were scattered throughout the area, and some of the bushes and trees that ringed the clearing had been uprooted and thrown several meters. By the looks of it, they caught fire too. *What did this?* Even still, I found some charred bones and the gritty ash–mixed with mud– that now constituted Christopheros and the other monk. I collected their remains and put them in the bag.

This was what I felt guilty about, my participation in their deaths. Somehow my conscience accepted the intimacy I shared with Tino without torturing me, but *this?* I believed that I could bathe in holy water to the top of my head and still never feel clean again.

Kneeling in the mud, I twisted my prayer rope around my muddy fingers–making a fist–and held it up to my lips.

"Lord Jesus Christ, Son of God, have mercy on me, a sinner." I knew I should pray for the dead monks as well, but for the life of me I couldn't recall the appropriate words. I merely crossed myself, asking God to grant them peace, and allow them entrance into the great cloud of witnesses.

Before heading back, I slapped my hands together to brush off the muddy soot and wiped the rest off with my cassock.

When I entered the tower, the door to Galatea's room was open. Quiet laughter and conversation spilled out into the main chamber, echoing in the tower's heights.

While I passed through the door, Tino, Galatea, and Thalia all turned to greet me. Galatea, reclining in her bed, looked down at the sleeping infant she cradled in her arms.

"Isn't she beautiful?" she asked.

"You had a girl?"

"And two boys," a voice behind me said.

I turned to see a third nereid striding in, with a swaddled, and sleeping infant in the crook of each arm. Her face was familiar, but I couldn't place it. I knew she wasn't one of the four aunts I met in their village.

"My sister, Erato," Thalia said, rushing up to receive one of the babies from her.

"I finally got them to sleep," Erato said.

She strode across the room to me, brushing my cheek with the backs of her fingers. The feeling of familiarity intensified with her touch.

"You have grown up to be a fine young man," she said with a warm smile.

I squinted. "We've met, but I don't remember when."

"I see I made quite an impression," she chimed. "You were just a boy."

My mouth dropped. "You can't be the nereid from the caves above my village. You don't look any older."

"And you look all grown up! My sister tells me that you have not lost the faith and courage I detected in you, but that it has only increased. She is right. We are now in your debt."

I threw up my hands. "I don't care about any debt. Let me hold one of the babies and I'll consider us even."

When Galatea fell asleep with her daughter nestled against her breast, the rest of us moved into the main chamber. Thalia held one of the boys and I the other. I cooed at him, and Tino, standing beside me, tickled his chin. Thalia began to pace.

"Is something troubling you?" Tino asked.

Thalia pressed her lips together, locking gazes with Erato before answering.

"Yes. I haven't spoken of it to Galatea, but certainly she has detected it by now."

"Detected what?" I asked.

"The babies. They have the curse too. I suspect that is what the vrykolakes, as you call them, wanted all along."

"Will they change tonight?" I asked. My face scrunched up with horror when I imagined a tiny litter of infant meat-eaters ransacking the tower and surrounding area.

"No. I suspect the first change won't occur until they reach puberty." She sighed, dropping her gaze to the infant boy in her arms. "We are not equipped . . . ." she said under her breath.

"Tell them the rest, Thalia," Erato urged.

"What?" Tino and I both asked.

When the typically composed and stately Thalia paused, and cleared her throat, tingles of fear crackled across my scalp like a bolt of lightning.

"The father has nereid blood," she said. "Perhaps only a quarter, but he is one of us."

"How can you be sure?" I asked.

"We know these things." Nudging the baby's nose with her own, she sighed. "His blood sings to mine through theirs."

"I'm afraid to ask, because I mean no offense, but is it a bad thing that their father is nereid?"

She pursed her quivering lips.

"For starters, the father is both nereid and wolf," Erato answered. "And he attacked Galatea, one of his own kind, meaning his allegiance is with them, not us. That doesn't bode well."

Thalia nodded her agreement saying, "The little ones are doubly cursed, with were-blood from both sides.

"Were?" I asked, the term unfamiliar to me.

"Vrykolakas," Erato explained.

"It is troubling," Thalia whispered. "In recent years a small number of nereids have gone missing. All of them were children or young adolescents. Most of them were half breeds like Galatea. It has been a mystery, one we may soon get to the bottom of, but if vrykolakes are responsible . . . ."

Thalia's voice trailed off. Erato continued in her stead, "Why are the cursed meat-eaters abducting our children and afflicting them?"

I looked at the innocent in my arms, and then back up to Thalia, then Erato.

"Troubling, indeed."

Tino stayed with us until after breakfast, which was, in typical nereid fashion, a veritable and celebratory feast.

"I am glad you're not alone anymore, but I promise I'll return tonight anyway," he said. "Another full moon! Can you believe it? If the beasts that did this to Galatea should come, I don't want you having all the fun without me."

"It wouldn't be fun unless you were here," I said, giving him a chaste peck on the cheek while he departed, bow in hand, full quiver flung over his shoulder. I wanted to give him more than that, but not with an audience.

I put off helping Galatea prepare for the full moon to the last second. The idea of taking the babies from her and confining her to her room was unthinkable, but necessary. It was agreed, until the full moon passed, that the babies were safer in the care of Thalia and Erato.

Thalia took over ear-piercing duty, something I happily relinquished. When it was done, I hugged Galatea before baring her door. Then the waiting began.

When the moon edged its way into the sky, Galatea's wolf tried to emerge.

Thalia cried. "I feel so helpless," she said passing the child she held to me and wiping her tears.

The hours passed. Tino had not yet shown up and I began to worry. At about half past nine a thunderous knock shook the door, startling the three of us.

"Hide them," I said, pointing to the stairs. In an instant, Thalia and Erato went with the babies to the loft.

Do not fear Yorgos. If we sense you are in any danger, we will protect you.

The door rattled again, shaking the tower.

"Who's there?" I asked.

"It's Constantine." I released a breath I hadn't consciously held.

"Why are you knocking?" I asked, opening the door for him. The answer was readily apparent. Two unkempt adolescent boys without any traditional Greek features stood behind him. He towered above them.

They both wore armor made of boiled leather, including breastplates; shoulder, thigh, knee and shin guards; and gloves. As soon as I saw them, the smile that I had for Tino vanished.

Earrings made of silver pierced both their ears, much like the ones Galatea's father had made. Fresh blood crusted the silver spikes. One of the boys pinned Tino's arms behind his back. By Tino's pained expression, it was clear the boy was stronger than he and not showing restraint.

"What's that smell?" the boy asked, speaking with an accent I later learned was common to the Irish. The other pointed to me, "It's him." His nose twitched with disgust. His French accent was also new to my ears.

"I'm sorry, Yorgos," Tino said, looking at his feet. "I was patrolling the area to make sure no one was lurking around and, well, these boys were."

"We're not boys," Irish said. Freckles covered his fair skin and his oily red hair reached to his shoulders. He shoved Tino at me and threw down his bow, which had been snapped in two. The pieces scuttled across the floor and stopped against my foot. Tino stumbled into me.

"We're men," French said. His hair was shorter, dirtier, and black. From clenched fists, he released a volley of arrows that were twisted out of shape. They thudded dully. "They don't send boys out to do a man's work."

"You two may possess the proper weapons, but you certainly don't pose a threat to us," Irish said.

"No, not to us," French agreed. "Your friend is brave," he said, indicating Tino with his chin, "but not very smart or strong."

"I'm sorry, Yorgos, they've come for Galatea."

"For Galatea?" I laughed. "Well they can't have her. She's gone. She left today. Sorry to disappoint you, boys." I started to close the door. French blocked it with his foot. "It's true," I continued, "you just missed her. Now, if you don't mind . . . ." I lowered my gaze to the offending appendage.

"She didn't leave today," French said, sniffing the air, and forcing the door open. Irish continued, "We've been sent to find her. A wolf's nose searches for and finds what is hidden from the eye. We know she's here, now get out of our way."

They pushed past, knocking us to the floor. With my eyes and a subtle thrust of my chin, I urged Tino to stand first. Once he had, I used his body to shield mine from view. "I may surprise you," I said. Palming the bottle of liquid silver first, I accepted Tino's hand. He pulled me up.

"I promised her mother I'd keep her safe. I always keep my promises." With the bottle of silver tucked in my palm, I believed myself to be invincible. "If you want Galatea, you'll have to get through me first."

"I think we just did," they said in unison.

I assumed a fighting stance, with my knees and arms bent, and my hands balled into fists. It felt unnatural.

They said nothing, only laughed. I turned my palm up, revealing the bottle, which coaxed them into even more uproarious peals.

"Perfume is your defense?" said French, his words broken up by his chuckles. "They're gonna love this when they hear about it back home." Irish agreed, slapping his knee.

"Yeah, that's right, perfume," I said, aiming the bottle from one to the other with my fingers on the bulb. A hand squeezed my shoulder. I looked, to see whose it was–it couldn't be Tino's; he stood on my other side. There was no visible hand, only the weight and warmth equal to one, but I heard the nereids singing in my thoughts.

Put the weapon away. These boys are smug, but harmless.

I pocketed the bottle, mimicking their laughter, and said, "That's silly, isn't it?" Lifting and dropping my shoulders with mock embarrassment.

"We're done being entertained by you." They both sniffed the air. French lifted his gaze to the loft, Irish indicated the bedroom. They smiled at each other with a nod, backing out the door.

"We were merely sent to find out what we're up against. Two monks and a couple of nereids don't pose much of a threat. We'll be back, and next time there won't be so few of us."

As soon as they were gone, Thalia and Erato stood in the center of the main chamber, with Thalia holding the boys and Erato the girl.

"We have to go," I said. "I have no idea where, but we can't stay here." I rubbed my chin, thinking.

"Tino, is any one living at Esphigmenou?"

"Yes. They're making repairs."

"Okay. Think!"

The two nereids regarded each other, conversing, it seemed, in their minds.

"We're not leaving," Thalia said aloud. Her sister agreed with a nod.

"This conflict has been a long time coming." They spoke together, each one placing emphasis on different words, in that nereid fashion, reminiscent of singing.

"What?" My eyebrows knit with confusion.

"No more running for Galatea. We stay put, dig our heels into the ground if we must, and run them off. For good!"

"What are we supposed to do in the meantime?" Tino asked.

The nereid's answer was simple, "We wait."

355

27 Storm Clouds

We inhabited the silence that followed uneasily. In the next room, and under the influence of the moon, Galatea wailed, howled, gnashed her teeth, and thrashed about. Tino was right. The planks he installed were strong enough to hold her, even when she beat on the door. For good measure, however, I took her suggestion, and draped it with silver chains.

Tino and I stayed close to each other, but said our prayers separately. I, pacing near him, with my prayer rope in hand, passing the knots through my fingers. He, on the floor, with his knees crossed, hands clasped, and head bowed.

Hours later, I collapsed with my back against the wall. All I wanted to do was sleep, but fear prevented it, as did the echoing sound of Tino's pacing.

"Tino, come. Relax." I said, reaching for him. He accepted my hand and sat next to me.

"I don't understand anything anymore," he said, laying his head on his knees. "I wish I could forget the last couple days and pretend none of this has happened, but how could I?"

"And what good would it do?" I asked. "Besides, it's not over yet."

"You're right," he shrugged.

We soon heard barking in the distance. I braced myself and squeezed Tino's hand, my eyes big and unblinking. Into the night sky, a single howl rose from the throat of a wolf. Rapidly, a pack joined in, becoming a terrifying cacophony.

I looked to Thalia and Erato for direction, finding them huddled together, hands on each other's shoulders, foreheads touching, in some kind of shared trance.

Meanwhile, the wolves were growing in number and closing in. I stood, pulling Tino up with me. Retrieving my bow and arrows from the table top, I fished a new bow out of the trunk for him, and we went to the door.

Together, we stood before it, stalling. However, time was too precious to waste. Taking a deep breath, I pushed the door open and stepped out into the night, with Tino beside me.

Under the moon's argent light, French and Irish were fast approaching, with the ends of silver chains wrapped around each gloved hand. At the opposite ends of the chains, wolves and vrykolakes strained against harnesses also made of silver. They both held two with one hand and one with the other, numbering six beasts in all. I was surprised that there were so few of them.

"Here they come," I gulped.

While they bore down on us, the six animals raised their muzzles, unleashing plaintive ululations. Countless others stepped out of the shadows into the cloud-dappled moonlight, as if the cries of their mates had rent the shadows in half. Suddenly, the clouds scattered and everything beneath the moon came into sharper focus, illumined by its cool, crisp light.

The moonlight revealed that French and Irish were the vanguard of a militia at least twenty deep and twenty wide that doggedly pushed through the bushes and shrubs. Every warrior walked two wolves or two vrykolakes. They headed our way with a slow but steady pace.

The soldiers parted down the middle, like the Red Sea for Moses. I wondered why until I saw a dirty-white tornado twisting and turning in its swift approach. Fear ignited my skin with tiny bumps tingling all over my body. Never before had the sight of a nereid cloud frightened me, but instinct told me that this was something different.

The funnel touched down meters from where Tino and I were standing, hand in hand. The sudden inclination to reach out and touch it seized me. It spiraled, lifting dust, and I felt the summons in my blood. The urge to obey was unshakable. I handed Tino my bow with an arrow nocked, and I took several faltering steps. Tino pulled me back, urging me to stay in the tower's threshold. I shook free of him and approached the twister.

"No!" he yelled. I paid him no heed but walked up to it while it collapsed into itself, becoming the body of a man.

Both the man's ears and his septum were freshly pierced, with a crust of dried blood circling the wounds. His oily red hair was pulled back, twisted into a single knot which reached past his shoulders.

Like every other nereid, his features were subtly like a deer, or a buck in his case. Yet in him, the resemblance was even more subtle. Foreign blood had gifted him with other features not common to nereids.

He wore a rough jacket made of wolf hide with mottled grey fur around the collar, pockets and cuffs. Because everything else he wore looked like it was fashioned from boiled leather, it seemed he was ready to charge into battle at less than a moments notice.

"Battle is not inevitable, friend," he said, as if reading my thoughts. French and Irish approached him. One of them passed the man a chain with a vrykolakas at its end, and the other one, a chain with a wolf.

"I am Liam," the man said, while the boys fell back into formation. His accent was similar to Irish's, but inflected differently, diluted by long exposure to other tongues. "I'd offer you my hand but . . ." he dropped his gaze to the creatures in his care. "And you are Yorgos, I presume?" he asked, looking at me.

"Should it impress me that you know my name?"

"Not in the least," he said, a thick smile forming on his generous lips.

The beasts leapt at me. He fought to keep them under control. The vrykolakas was strong; sleek and muscular. Though it challenged his authority, he kept his balance, yanking the chain, forcing it into submission. The creature growled, curling lips and exposing fangs. The wolf snapped its jaws at it, urging its companion to behave. While the animals fought, Liam staggered to the right and left, struggling to maintain balance. He twisted his hands in circles winding the chains around his wrists to further rein them in.

"Surrender what I came for and we'll leave," he said, staring down his nose at me.

I squared my legs, shook my head and said, "No."

The cries of the vrykolakes and the wolves behind him were so loud, Liam and I shouted above them to be heard. Snapping their jaws and straining at me, the animals tested the strength of their chains.

"Quiet!" he snapped, and the din subsided.

"We have the beasts under control for the moment. No telling how much damage they could do if we released them."

I held his gaze without flinching. "I said, no."

"Shall I give the order then?" he asked. He began to unwind the chains from his hands.

"Let us take him and you go get the girl," Irish said. "He'd make a nice addition to our family."

Liam shook his head saying, "No."

French took up the argument, "He reeks of blood. Certainly you can smell it." His nose twitched. "They all smell it and they're straining to get him."

While they argued about weather or not to make me into one of them, I shoved my hand into my cassock pocket and clutched the perfume bottle, feeling the edges of the facets press into my skin.

"His destiny is none of my business," Liam argued.

Irish countered, "He's been marked. We can take the girl and save him too." He lunged at me and Liam threw him a cautionary glance. Irish advanced another step, French followed his lead.

Liam turned and barked "Obey!" The boys fell back.

"The Matriarch gave me strict orders, which we will follow." He composed himself and continued. "Get the girl and my baby, and bring them back to her. That's it. She said nothing of saving anyone from being made a blood-drinker."

Liam turned his attention back to me. "I'm sorry about that, they're young. Now, the girl. She gave birth to the hope of my people. I won't abandon that so easily."

"They belong to no one but themselves," I said, "And they deserve to make their own hope."

"I see. How will you stop me?"

"With this," I said, lifting Mother's perfume bottle from my pocket. I held it in my right palm, with the bulb between my left forefinger and thumb. I aimed it at his face. He took a theatrical step backward, mock fear contorted his features that gave way to a broad smile.

"Perfume?" he said, laughing deeply. "The boys warned me about that." Behind him, laughter rippled through the militia under his command.

"Look closer." I countered, holding the bottle up into the moonlight. The silver flecks sparkled in the intricately cut crystal. "Do I need to tell you what this is? I wonder what breathing it would do to you." I stepped forward, the bottle aimed at his face. "And what would it do to your skin? Would you like to find out?" I stepped closer, giving the bulb a careful, little squeeze—just enough to threaten, not enough to wound. A faint silver mist, smelling of jasmine—a residue from Mother's perfume—blossomed in the air. He, and every vrykolakas present, whether in the form of a person, a wolf, or something in-between, took three steps back. He, and those closest, coughed.

"That's what I thought."

"You're brave for such a little man," he said. "I admire that, but don't be a fool. Do you really think that will subdue my soldiers or keep us at bay forever?"

"I'd like to find out," I challenged.

Before I had a chance to try and see Irish and French released their animals from their muzzles. They fell on me and we scuffled in the dirt like a tangle of tumble weeds in the wind. Tino hollered at them, sending random arrows into the blurry fray. One of them struck my thigh. The shaft snapped off in the tussle. When he exhausted his supply of arrows, Tino rushed up and beat them off me with his bow.

1641, The City of Salonika, Greece, Mister Dumitru

My third attempt of the evening at working the moist, round, lump of clay, was more successful than the previous two by far. Finally, I was getting somewhere and would have something to show for my time. I had been trying to produce the commissioned set of matching vases for the last few nights and found the job to be uninspiring, at best. Visions of Yorgos kept interrupting me.

Anticipating the night he might need rescuing, I set up shop in nearby Salonika in an abandoned inn I bought for a pittance. Learning to safely travel the peninsula's rough terrain would be hard for him. Adapting to the rigors of monastic life would be even harder. Hardest of all, however, would be learning to coexist with so many religious men without any women to temper them.

Did I believe the monks he lived with posed a threat to him? Absolutely. I knew it without a doubt.

I had my ways of watching him, made easy by the *little exchange,* done years before. I knew that his life, and the lives of his two friends, was recently jeopardized by two monks and their leader. The 'holy men' were filthy mongrel meat-eaters, each and every one of them. I nearly went to his rescue, but, to my surprise and delight, he drove two of them back, all the way into the flames and saved his friends from destruction. Only the Protos, their leader, got away. This was a shame, but two out of three isn't bad.

My concern was assuaged by what I saw. I decided to wait. *Perhaps he won't need rescuing after all.* Instinct told me the Protos was a wily one and that I needed to keep an eye on Yorgos because of him. Though Yorgos ran him off, I strongly suspected that the Protos would soon return; I'd bet my preternatural life on it.

Work beckoned. I tried to clear my thoughts of my young darkling. Having thrown a fresh lump of clay onto the spinning wheel, I began my vase. While I shaped the clay, I saw an image, superimposed over my work, of something peculiar. Tiny tornados, scarcely larger than men, swiftly bore down on me. There were too many to number. The wind tugged my clothes and my hair rose from my head. I raked my fingers through my hair to tame it, finding it still neatly parted and combed. I squeezed my eyes closed to clear my thoughts, wanting to stay focused.

While I pulled the clay into the desired shape, I stared into the vessel's depths feeling pleased. The vision started again. A tornado spun in my vase, rising out of it. At one end, it held a tree, which it swung at me. Startled, I screamed and stumbled back. The vision vanished, replaced by a picture of Yorgos fighting four vrykolakes. I smelled his fear. I tasted it. *This can't end well.* I feared losing my darkling to the meat-eaters. They love nothing more than preventing us from fulfilling the demands of imprinting. The image of him fighting evaporated too.

I almost flew to him without a second thought, but calmed myself. Apparently, he had gotten caught in a melee between hosts of nereids and vrykolakes. Against such a large number of formidable adversaries, I didn't stand a chance.

I had to wait. I drew a deep breath, unnecessary for my survival, but nearly effective in calming me. My potter's wheel still spun. I looked at it. The vase was misshapen and had collapsed in on itself. I watched while the wheel wound down and the clay became an unrecognizable lump. Briefly, superimposed over that was an image of a white vrykolakas rescuing Yorgos and protecting him. I released my breath, muttered a Christian prayer of thanks, and began my fourth attempt at forming the vase.

Though I knew I must wait until it was safe for me, I also knew that the time for his transformation was drawing near.

1641, Mount Athos, Greece, Yorgos

The sky went dark, like God had snuffed out the moon and all the stars. From the tower's entrance came a large cracking sound.

In the form of a white vrykolakas, Galatea broke out, splintering two doors in her wake. She charged, grabbing my attackers one at a time by the skin of their necks, and tossed them into the crowd, driving it back.

Tino helped me to my feet. I watched Galatea while holding my breath, feeling a mixture of gratitude and horror at the violence she displayed.

Tino pointed to the sky with a cry, noticing that hundreds of whirling white forms blocked out the light. They crowded the sky, heading in organized rows toward the place where the tower stood nestled between land and sea.

Galatea cleared the space around us, positioning herself between us and those who came for her. She stopped growling and bared her teeth to lick my hand.

Hundreds of twisters hovered above our heads. Everyone's hair stuck up and waved erratically. A number of the twisters broke off, some heading to the ocean, others to the ravines. The rest lighted briefly on the heads of the all the vrykolakes: the wolves, the hybrids, and the people locked in human form by silver. The twisters sucked up the bodies and spun them out with great force, sending them flying several meters.

The other twisters returned, dumping ocean water on the crowd, and swinging whole trees by their trunks, like clubs, drenching and knocking Liam's militia over. Most scattered, taking cover wherever they found it. Those who remained fell back and were contained by the funnel clouds, unable to step out of them.

Only Liam remained close with Galatea between us.

The twisters not imprisoning a member of his militia assumed human form, and held their ground.

Liam approached with caution, his arm extended, palm turned down. Galatea growled, exposing her canines.

I reached down and scratched the scruff of her neck and under her chin.

"What is it you people want with her?" I asked.

Liam stepped closer and Galatea nipped his hand. He withdrew and surrendered, backing up, lifting his hands, palms facing out.

"Let's all calm down," he said. "Let me explain."

Thalia and Erato emerged from the tower with the babies, making their way to where we stood. When they reached us, Erato handed one off to Tino. Her right hand was clenched into a tight fist, and her fingers were smeared with a small amount of blood.

When Tino received the baby I watched Liam's reaction with interest. His eyes welled with tears and his chest puffed. He straightened his spine.

"He's beautiful," he said reaching for his son.

Galatea lunged at him, barking her warning. I wrapped my arms around her neck from behind and wrestled her back, feeling something cold and wet on my cheek. I brushed it off, finding blood on my fingertips. The silver rings had been torn out of her ears. I should have known. She sat beside me–seemingly oblivious to the wounds–eyeing Liam keenly, every muscle taught.

"They're beautiful," Liam whispered.

"I believe you were about to explain yourself," Thalia said.

"Yes. I see that an explanation is in order. My ancestors, my *mortal* ancestors, that is, are of Irish descent. The family has long carried this curse, becoming uncontrollably violent during each and every full moon. They were good people before the curse; God-fearing, gentle and kind. In their effort to tame their inner beasts, they've tried everything. Even their religion failed them. To this day, the curse continues to pass from one generation to the next without cessation, though we are not quite as ferocious now as we used to be."

While Liam spoke, Galatea's muscles relaxed, she walked a tight circle, and then she lay down.

Liam continued, "My great-grandmother four times past was inspired with the notion that the aggression could be bred out of us and self-control could be bred in, including control over the change. In time, the curse will no longer control us, we will control the curse." He lifted his gaze to Thalia. "Your daughter is part of her plan now, as am I and our children."

Galatea stood up, on all four paws, and nudged Thalia's side with her snout.

"She wants the earrings," she explained, turning to Constantine. "She says she dropped them on the floor. Could you—"

Erato uncurled the fingers of her right hand, revealing the tiny silver hoops. "I have them." Thalia lifted one from her sister's palm with her forefinger and thumb, like it was fragile and precious.

"Tino, would you get her a blanket?" She bent to her Daughter, whispered, "I'm sorry, I hate doing this," and forced the sharp end of the hoop through Galatea's ear. A yelp tore out of Galatea's throat, turning into wail, when her body changed. The transformation wasn't quick or smooth. It was violent, the silver forcing her body to resume its human form prematurely, while the full moon still reigned.

"I'm listening," she said when she was fully human, regarding Liam with cold eyes. Tino wrapped the blanket around her from behind and stood beside me.

"We can help you with the change. We can help you control—"

"Liar!" Thalia shouted. "You said you couldn't control it."

Liam surrendered again, lifting his hands, palms out. "In the past, yes, that was true, and we are certainly generations away from achieving the control we desire. But we have increased our ability to control the beast, at least a small amount. That counts for something, doesn't it?"

Thalia's eyes were filmed with tears, "Why us, Liam? We are your people."

"No, you're not. I've never even seen a nereid village. Until now, the only nereids I've known have been others like me. And why? You have control over your powers, do you not?"

I looked from Liam, to Thalia, to Galatea and back. Understanding dawned in the nereid's minds, just as it had in my own.

"I think I understand what your people are trying to achieve. But you've done it all wrong. You violated me. If you think I will go willingly–"

"I think you should go," I said, my words surprising even myself. All eyes turned on me. Thalia simmered with fury, and Erato seemed disappointed.

"How could you say that?" Thalia asked.

"You said it yourself. You aren't equipped to raise these babies or to help Galatea for that matter. She's already wounded you once. Add to that the fact that the Protos will not give up until he's burned the curse out of her, and I don't see any other way to keep them safe." Thalia's fury cooled.

"I don't want to leave my family," Galatea said.

"I know you don't, but all this time we've been thinking they were the bad guys. I agree that their methods aren't good. They should learn to seek consent." I gave Liam a long look, to punctuate my words. "However, I don't think anyone else can help you. The only solution you've found–the silver earring–will hurt you in the long run. I think it already has."

"It's true," Liam said. "Wearing it monthly is too often. Silver is a toxin to our bodies that builds with frequent use. Now that the children are born, it serves you no good purpose."

One at a time I looked Thalia, Erato, and Galatea in the eye. "It pains me to suggest this. To think I risk angering you–"

Erato came forward. "Your wisdom has always been evident," she said. "Even now, though I hate to admit it."

"Am I the only one who hasn't lost their mind?" Thalia asked.

Galatea reached for the child in Thalia's arms. "Mother . . . he's right. Her gaze went to each infant and back to her mother. She began to cry. "We have to go," she said, approaching Liam.

"I can't bear the thought of never seeing you again, or my grandchildren."

Galatea stopped once she reached Liam's side.

"You can see them," he said. "Our families will reach a truce. We *will* learn to seek consent."

Quicker than my eyes could see, Thalia went to her daughter and kissed her forehead and both cheeks. "With my blessings," she said, embracing her. Looking over Galatea's shoulder she said to Liam, "I will hold you to your word."

In short order, Liam dismissed his soldiers, staying until the last had gone. Then he, Galatea, and their children departed, with Liam taking the form of a twister and carrying them away.

One word from Thalia and the nereids took to the sky, returning to their respective villages. I whispered, "May milk and honey be in your path" while they took flight. Thalia smiled.

"Look at you," she said, eyeing me from head to foot. "You brave, brave man, you even stood up to me," she laughed, leading me to the tower. "Let's clean up those scratches and get that arrowhead out."

28 A Desperate Decision

Once Tino and I were alone, I couldn't bear staying in the tower. I wanted to put Galatea out of my mind. I was too exhausted to worry about her anymore. Reminders of her were everywhere and I wanted to go somewhere else.

We gathered the blankets and I retrieved the bag that held the remains of Christopheros and the other monk. When Tino asked what it was, I changed the subject, telling him how glad I was to have him with me.

Well past dawn, we reached the ravine where we passed the previous night–or was it two nights ago now? Keeping days straight gets confusing when you stay up all night.

By the time we set up camp we couldn't sleep. The sun blazed. We both needed consoling and I wanted a diversion.

What better distraction than what our bodies were capable of achieving together?

After less than an hour's rest, I was awakened with Evangelos staring down at us, disgust and disapproval vying for dominance of his face. I nudged Tino awake. The smile he had for me vanished when he saw the Gerantas.

"You disappoint me," Evangelos said. He should have thrust a dagger into my heart. It would have hurt less.

The three of us went to the skete without speaking. Evangelos escorted me to my cell, Tino returning to his uncle in another building.

While I stripped to my undergarments and collapsed onto my bed, Evangelos blocked the door, eyeing me. Under his glare I felt exposed and dirty. Shame crept up from my toes, crawling into my heart where I feared it would make its home forever if I didn't do something fast.

"I've given you more freedom than I should and allowed Constantine to live here because you promised you could handle it. I trusted you. Obviously I shouldn't have." He wrung his hands. "I don't know what to do, Yorgos. I don't know how to help you."

"I'm sorry," I said, though I could barely lift my voice, and my eyes were heavy with remorse. "I'm sorry," I said again, turning away from him.

He remained, muttering prayers, until I began to doze. I hovered between wakefulness and sleep when I finally heard him say "Amen" and close the door.

My sleep was fitful and intermittent. I began to dream. St. George was coming to rescue me from the mess I had made of things, fast approaching on the back of a white stallion. It gave me a thrill. In their darkest moments, who hasn't wished to be rescued? But then, when he drew near the skete, the horse turned black and I saw my rescuer's face. It was Mister Dumitru!

I woke with a start, a scream still issuing from my throat. I slapped a hand over my mouth. While I lay in bed, praying that no one would come check on me, an inescapable conclusion came over me. I knew what I had to do.

I waited until dark to execute my plans, sleeping as much as I could, so I wouldn't have to think or feel until I was ready to do it.

It was nearly dawn when I woke. If I didn't act fast, someone would see me. I prayed to Christ and all the saints that no one would, and heaved a sigh when I made it all the way to the front door with out being bothered.

On the way out of Saint George's I stopped by the area of land set aside for the cemetery. No one had been buried there yet, the skete was too new. I dug a small hole, placed the bag of remains inside it, and closed it. I didn't know what to pray. I didn't think my prayers would be heard. Instead, I gathered stones and marked the spot with a cross before heading back out on my short journey.

1641, The City of Salonika, Greece, Mister Dumitru

Searing pain sliced through my left wrist, and then the right, awakening me. Metal clanked against stone. I collapsed. My eyes fluttered open, confused. I was in a dank place, surrounded by darkness. Hot streams of blood flowed from both wounds. I was losing precious liquid fast!

Disoriented, I tried to sit up, banging my head ingloriously before realizing, with more than a little relief, that I was still in my coffin, having just begun the day's internment no more than ninety minutes earlier.

I checked my wrists, patting them. Both were whole and dry. A sigh of relief escaped my parted lips. I closed my eyes, clutching at the dirt from my homeland; feeling grounded by it, and lay back down, my hands crossing my chest. I wanted nothing more than to rest in peace. No sooner had I gotten comfortable than the dream began again.

I lay dying on the cold stone floor of a towering edifice, a bloodied knife just beyond my reach. Rays of early morning light spilled in through windows and were reflected in an expanding pool of blood. My life ebbed away.

I struggled to push myself up, to fight the greedy fingers of death that clawed at me. An unblinking red reflection stared back at me, but it wasn't my reflection and it wasn't my blood. Both belonged to Yorgos. His hands slipped and his face slammed into the floor causing a brilliant crimson splash.

I opened my eyes, becoming fully awake and in charge of my powers. I reached out to my young darkling, feeling the topography of his cooling mind.

His despair led him to this. I could have stopped it if I had only acted sooner. I had felt his simmering turmoil and I knew that the thread of his life had been between the blades of Atropos' shears more than once in recent days. With each trial he faced and conquered, my confidence in him only grew. I never guessed he would present the thread of his life to the fates himself and beg them to cut it.

Throwing the lid off my coffin, I lifted myself up and out of it, stumbling to floor. The energy spiraled out of me like water down a drain. I couldn't brave the sun. I would have to wait.

I found my thoughts turning to a God I didn't believe in. "Please, Christ, if you exist, if Yorgos ever pleased you, preserve his life until I can reach him."

1641, Mount Athos, Greece, Yorgos

Waking from a thick sleep felt like swimming up from the depths of the sea and trying to break through waves. Tino's voice reached me like wind carried across the water. I tried to come up for air and couldn't.

"Here! Here's the tower," Tino shouted. I heard the rushing of feet and Tino shouting, "He's inside!" while someone else dropped to the floor beside me.

"Oh my God!" It was Tino. "No!"

He started to cry. I tried to open my eyes. I wanted to tell him I was okay, that it hadn't worked, but my eyelids were too heavy. "God, no! God, no! God, no!" he kept wailing.

Someone slapped my face. Was it Tino? *Why are you slapping me?* I tried to speak, to ask, but I was dislocated from my body and my voice.

"Yorgos!" Evangelos called to me. "Yorgos!" He slapped me again and I opened my eyes a sliver. Evangelos shook my shoulders, and began weeping. "He's alive!"

Evangelos said I was lucky. If they hadn't found me when they did, I probably would have bled to death.

He took me to the infirmary but dismissed the brother who would ordinarily have dressed my wounds and did it himself.

"I'm sorry. I was too harsh," he said. "It was a moment of unguarded weakness."

"You meant what you said." He pierced one side of the gash in my right wrist, pulled the black thread all the way through and pierced the other side, drawing it closed. I stuffed my left fist in my mouth but didn't even try not to scream.

"Yes. I am disappointed in what you have done," he continued, while he drew the thread through again, in the opposite direction. "But that doesn't change my love for you." I screamed. "And it doesn't mean I've given up hope." My left arm hurt too much, the throbbing was too intense to ignore, so I dropped it and let the screams come. "What were you thinking, Yorgos?"

"It's too late," I said, wincing. I couldn't look at him. I watched him sew up my arm instead. Disassociated, slightly separate from my body, I felt like I watched Mother repair a little tear in Zoe-Sophia's rag-doll. "I've done things you

375

don't even know," I continued, while he finished with my right arm and proceeded to the left. "Too much to say right now. And I don't just mean with Constantine. It's too late."

"You keep saying that. It's too late for what?"

"For me. I'm in love with him. Before I did it, I asked God to forgive me. I thought if I died with a clean conscience I wouldn't come back—"

"A vrykolakas."

"Yes. My worst fear. I'd rather die than become one of those."

"The surest way to become one, Yorgos, is to kill yourself. Suicide is a serious sin. The living can be forgiven, but there is no repentance for the dead. Do you understand what I am saying?"

I watched while he pulled the wound on my left wrist closed and tied the knot. I nodded that, yes, I understood.

"God has shown you mercy," he said, while pouring wine over both wrists, and binding them with clean rags. "Now is your time to turn to Him with your whole heart." He sat with me for a moment before fishing his prayer rope from his pocket and laying it over my right hand. "I will leave you alone to rest and pray. I won't be far if you should need me."

I didn't want to rest. I was afraid to close my eyes. I was afraid I'd see more visions of Mister Dumitru. Too tired to pray anything more than "have mercy on me, a sinner," over, and over again, the words lost all meaning. While I prayed, clarity came to me. I failed. On the day I met Tino and probably before, I lost my vision and all sense of direction. It's hard to know where you're going if you can't see.

So, I decided to leave and go home to the village. Mother needed my help, anyway. Perhaps if I was there, she could open the inn to guests again.

It had been made clear why I couldn't separate myself from temptation by ending my life. This was the only other way I could think of doing it.

I fingered his prayer rope, moving my hand as little as possible, until it was wound around my fingers, continuing to repeat the prayer. I sought courage now, to tell Evangelos of my decision.

I didn't have to call out to him. I hovered, between being awake and asleep. When he pushed my door open the creaking brought me fully awake.

"I'm sorry I woke you," he said, pushing the door closed.

"Please, come in. I have something to say."

He sat at the foot of the bed, waiting expectantly while I summoned my courage. I was afraid to disappoint him even more.

"Perhaps you should sleep," he suggested, rising.

"No. Stay. I want to tell you. I've come to a decision." I squeezed his rope with my fingers, drawing strength from it. "Do you remember when you asked me which son I thought I was?"

He nodded, a solemn and attentive expression gracing his face.

"I've figured it out. I am the prodigal. Without a doubt, I'm him. I'm ready to go home. As soon as I'm healed, it's what I want. Home, to my village, I mean."

He nodded his understanding, tears collecting in his eyes, and he sat down again, this time closer. He reached to clasp my hand, and then–as if remembering–rested his hand on my bicep instead.

"That is a big decision."

"Please don't tell me I risk becoming–"

"No, no risk of that, but it is a big decision, nonetheless. I suggest you wait. It's good you have time to heal. That will slow you down, give you time to pray and seek God.

Remember, Pascha is this Sunday. Wait until after Pascha, will you, before you decide?"

29 Dead In A Manner Of Speaking

"When the fullness of time had come, God sent forth His Son . . ."

Galatians 4:4 New King James Version

Pascha eve, 1641, is not a night I will soon forget. In every monastery on Mount Athos–and at the Skete of Saint George–indeed, in all the churches in every land with an Orthodox Church, the celebration of Christ's resurrection would soon commence. Typically this was my favorite time of year on the Orthodox calendar. Meditating on my sinfulness and Christ's being without sin drew me deeper into the mystery of His love, which was really what it was all about. He bore sin for us! Usually, I was able to keep that in perspective. Yes, I was a sinner, in need of a cure, and Christ's love, poured out in the form of His most sacred blood, was it. The year 1641 was different, however, because I had gone astray in so many ways. I felt my sin eclipsed the love of God. For the first time in my twenty-two years of life, I felt utterly wretched.

Alone in my cell, I prostrated myself in the eastern corner, venerating my ikons, begging God to cleanse me and restore me to Himself. The sound of a hard rain coming through the open window didn't soothe me like it normally would have. Nothing in nature–or beyond it–could soothe my ragged soul.

Giving up, I rose to my knees and slowly stood, rubbing my temples with my fingers. It was almost time to head to the Katholikon anyhow, something I was not in a hurry to do, because I knew the Protos was due to officiate Saint George's first Paschal celebration.

I crossed myself and lifted the ikon of the crucifixion that Mother gave to me so many years before and kissed the image.

"It's only a matter of time," I muttered. *I will feel right again . . . I will.* My sanity depended on believing this. I returned the ikon to its place on the corner shelf and rubbed my still bandaged left wrist where the flesh itched. Lost. I felt lost.

Please, Christ, find me, I silently prayed. I wanted to skip the service but resisted the temptation. Evangelos expected me.

I blew out the oil lamps, except for one. The rain started to soften. I peered through the tiny slit window at the moon's reflection in puddles of rain water on the ground. A dark form scuttled by and soft rhythmic vibrating filled my ears, intruding on my thoughts. I hadn't heard that sound since I last saw . . . the cat! I searched for it with my eyes, pressing my head into the narrow slit, feeling the coarse rock scrape my face. There it was! Right in front of the shrubbery and trees that blocked the view of the ravine where Tino and I were caught.

Startled into action, I grabbed the burning lamp. Cupping my hand around the flame, I retrieved an ikon from the shelf and darted out of my bedroom. Urgency and a new faith rose up within me.

Whatever this creature was, whatever it meant to do with me, I meant to find out and put an end to its menacing presence in my life. I was in just the right kind of mood to be so reckless. I would vanquish the cat, once for all, and by extension, vanquish the darkness that lurked in my soul.

I flew down the stairs to the front room. Peering out the window beside the door, I stared back at the black creature that stared at me. Light steps approached me from behind. Determined to accomplish what I set out to do, I reached for the door and pushed it. A warm, firm hand came down on my shoulder and I surrendered.

"Yorgos, where are you going?" I touched my finger to Tino's lips, and pointed out the window.

"It's back," I whispered. He squinted, peering out into the night and nodded when he saw the creature.

"I have to go and confront it," I said.

"Yorgos, are you crazy?" Tino twisted me around to face him. "What could possibly compel you to confront that infernal beast?"

"That creature has stalked me long enough. I have to know what it is and why it disturbs my peace."

"I wish you wouldn't."

I flashed him a wan smile and gave the door a little push. It opened several centimeters. Before I stepped through, he pulled me to a stop.

"What if it's a demon?"

"I believe that it is. Tonight I have enough faith to repel it. Besides, I have Saint George with me," I said, a cocky glint in my eye. Setting the oil lamp on the table by the door I drew the ikon from the pocket of my cassock and showed it to him. Constantine smiled wanly back at me. I returned the ikon to my pocket.

"So reckless, sweet Yorgos. I fear your recklessness will be your undoing."

"Perhaps it will be, but not tonight. It's nearly Pascha. My faith is strong."

For too long I lingered with my beloved. Looking into his eyes, I knew that no amount or manner of penance would change the fact that I loved him. I loved him as I loved my own soul. I loved him even as I loved the Lord Himself. For some reason, at that place and time, it didn't feel wrong. I was willing, if Christ requested it, to give up the physical expression of that love, but I would not repent of the love itself.

I wanted to kiss him, but knew that I mustn't. I smiled again and withdrew my hand from his. I gave the door a final push. It opened fully. He grabbed my wrist, sending a shock of pain up my arm. I cried out. Tino drew me into his arms and kissed my lips more fiercely than he ever had before. Pushing my buttocks, he tenderly closed the gap between us until our groins touched. Another fire blazed in my body—this time in my loins. It was so intense and pleasurable that I forgot the pain in my wrist, where blood started to ooze through the bandage from the wound he reopened. I kissed him back, pressing into him. Our tongues, touching and twisting together, fused. I wanted to yield, to surrender to the physical expression of our love again, but I knew I couldn't. Not tonight, not ever, though it pained me to know that.

I ended the kiss, withdrawing my tongue from his lips, and stepped back. It took me a moment before I could speak.

"It's over," I whispered, taking deep breaths to slow my racing pulse.

Tears filmed his downcast eyes. "I know," he said, choking on the words, "But I never want you to forget that I love you." He looked into my eyes with a steady gaze.

My pulse raced once again. Laying my palm upon his breast, I took a step—closing the gap between us.

"I will always love you, too. But Christ must be my first love, and I must do what I feel would please him most, what I feel is right, and I must do it tonight. First, I will rid myself of the menace that has stalked me all these years. I am not afraid."

I turned from him. With boldness and trepidation, I stepped into the darkness of the night. I didn't look back.

The rain, a faint drizzle now, refreshed me. I welcomed it as a sign of cleansing and stepped deeper into the shadows, away from the light that poured out of the windows of the skete.

What does one say when one looks for a large and menacing black cat?

Turning in circles, I squinted trying to locate the beast. I searched left, then right. I searched straight ahead, peering into the shrubbery and trees where I first saw it pacing. It was no where to be found.

"Here, kitty, kitty, kitty," I called out in a hushed voice. I laughed at myself for being so absurd and sprinted straight into the dense foliage, where I was certain it lurked. The darkness engulfed me. I remembered that I left the oil lamp burning by the door. Never mind, it was too late to go back for it.

The farther I went, the denser the brush became, until branches, twigs and leaves scratched and poked me from on all sides. I pushed through, moving downward into the ravine, ignoring the scratches and stinging nettles until I came into the clearing where Gerantas Evangelos found Constantine and me.

A presence flooded my awareness. All around and inside me, it chilled me to the core. A presence I knew intimately and yet hadn't been more than faintly aware of for many years.

"I have waited for this moment for a very long time." I whirled around. Mister Dumitru appeared to float in the air and bore down on me from above.

"Hello, Mister Dumitru," I said. He touched down, less than a meter away. "What brings you here to the garden of Theotokos?" I asked.

"My friend, it is you," he demurred, clutching his heart. "You don't know how much grief you caused me when you attempted to end your life. Unthinkable! I felt your pain. I felt the life flow out of your wrists like it was my own. Wasted! Your precious blood poured onto the dry earth that sucked it up like so much water. I knew I must come to you straightaway. If your life were to end, my existence would lose all meaning."

Red streaks lined his cheeks. I gasped, "You're eyes, Mister Dumitru, they're bleeding!" He chuckled while pulling a handkerchief from the breast pocket of his burgundy colored vest. His alabaster skin was indistinguishable from his crisp white shirt. The rolled-up sleeves exposed his chiseled wrists and forearms.

"Only in a manner of speaking, my dear Yorgos. This is what it looks like when I cry." I must have grimaced in disgust because he cleaned his face with the handkerchief saying, "I suppose it would be a wretched sight to mortal eyes. Will you please call me Lucian? Mister Dumitru is too formal. We are way beyond such formalities." An animal approached, paws crunching on leaves. I spun around, facing the direction the sound came from.

"Shhhh," I whispered. "There is a large black cat out here. We're not safe."

"That is a figment of your imagination. What you describe is a panther. I assure you there are no panthers any where near this place."

The sound moved closer and a spotted mountain cat dashed out of the shrubs. I yelped.

"See, no panthers here." Mister Dumitru hissed and the cat bolted off, back into the shrubbery, and beyond.

Mister Dumitru grabbed me from behind, holding my biceps. He forced me closer until our chests touched. His unnaturally cold breath chilled my neck. He kissed it. His frigid lips were as hard as polished stones. He pressed them against my forehead, and my cheek, before grinding them against my own. I struggled to get away but couldn't break his hold on me. This only made him laugh and hold me tighter.

"Dear Yorgos, why do you always fight what you cannot overcome? Aren't you tired yet? You knew this moment would come." Intellectually his words made no sense. But they registered somewhere deeper in the core of my being.

"I did not. I have no idea what you're talking about." I lied.

"I have loved you from the moment we met. This is fate. Don't you feel it too?"

"No! You are the only living soul I have ever hated. But I do. I hate you."

"That is only partially correct, young Master Godevenos. First, however, let me ease your conscience. I am not alive. If what you say is true, you still have never hated a living soul.

"I remember the morning we met clearly. You both loved and hated me. You wanted to flee to the safety of your parents *and* you wanted to climb up inside of me, to be one with me." He paused until recognition altered my countenance. "Do you remember now?" he asked.

In my mind's eye I saw the moment he described with heightened clarity, like someone else pulled the memory up from the murky depths of my soul.

"And then you laughed," I said lightly. Yes, I remembered.

"And so did you, my mortal friend. Though you didn't understand why, you did. You had no idea what was so funny." Again he laughed while he spoke of it like we were life-long friends remembering one of our treasured moments.

"I still don't understand."

Mister Dumitru took a long deliberate breath and said, "I assure you, before the sun rises, you will."

My pulse throbbed in my wrist where Constantine grabbed ahold of me, reopening the wound. The cool night air chilled the blood-soaked bandage.

In my mind, I stepped back in time to the early morning hours when Mister Dumitru and I met. The memory came to me sharp and clear. Again, an outside mind helped me to remember with unnatural clarity, what I thought and felt that dark morning so many years before.

With a shock, I realized that yes, he was right. I had always known that this day would come, though my years on Athos allowed me to forget. There was no sense in denying it anymore, the moment I heard his lilting foreign accent and saw his Eastern European features reflected in the mirror, this moment became inevitable.

"Yes," he said, reading my mind. "You remember. Your life, nay, your immortality was established the moment we met like it was etched on the palm of God's hand. Of course, if you had come to apprentice with me, I never would have touched you. And certainly, I would not have turned you into a child of the night until you reached your full stature. And here you are! Full grown! Splendidly mature." He released my arms and took a step back, examining me from head to toe to head.

"What a stunning specimen of a man."

When I turned to flee he grabbed hold of me with the vice-grip of his hand. He drew me close and pressed his cold, smooth lips against mine. I cringed; feeling soiled by his touch and recalled the illicit kisses that Constantine and I

had shared. I was thankful in that moment of forced intimacy, to have so many pleasant memories to draw from,
no matter how saturated in shame they might have been.
Constantine and I had enjoyed a brief but rich affair. I imagined myself to be in his embrace. It wasn't Mister Dumitru's
frigid lips pressed uncomfortably against mine, but the lips
of my lover. The chill night air had made them cold and
hard, but I would make them warm and supple once again.

The throbbing in my wrist worsened, hurting me. I
knew the wound would have to be cleaned and redressed
soon before infection set in. Reflecting on this, I stopped
struggling. *Let him have his way with me.* The sooner it
was over the better.

He pressed his lips into various places of my anatomy:
my forehead, chin, collar bone and chest. He breathed
deeply of my essence. In the unnatural silence that enveloped us, I heard the faint splatter of liquid upon the ground.
Mister Dumitru inhaled and released my biceps. His eyes
rolled up and closed to slits. It appeared as if an intoxicat-
ing vice had seized him.

Drip, drip, drip. The staccato splatter of liquid hit the
dirt. Something hot ran down my palm and middle finger.
A burning red rivulet of blood.

"Your blood smells of copper, incense, and passion," he
intoned. "It smells of wild roses and wine. I must have it. I
can no longer ignore the scent."

I wanted to run. This was my chance, but I'd been
transfixed. Mister Dumitru closed his eyes while he meditated on the sweet mysteries of my blood. I twisted my
torso without making a sound, and then I adjusted my foot.
I hesitated before making my escape.

"Stop!" He didn't restrain me physically. The command
of his voice was enough. Yes, he had transfixed me. He held

me lightly in thrall. In the silence that followed, the splat-tering sound of my blood striking the hard earth deafened my ears. I turned to face him again, held within the grip of his command. Silent and unmoving, he appeared to be a statue of a Roman saint in meditative prayer. I stood per-haps a meter away from him now. I felt that I was too far from him, yet also too close.

"And when the fullness of time had come . . ." he whispered.

A sly grin played across his face and disappeared just as quickly. Vaguely I knew it was a scriptural reference, but I couldn't recall chapter and verse. It seemed a perverse sac-rilege for sacred Scripture to pass through his lips. In that moment, I came to my senses. A person capable of easy sacrilegious speech was not a person to be trusted. I drew the ikon of Saint George from the pocket of my coat and brandished it.

"Release me from what ever spell you hold me with," I demanded. He laughed at me again. "Lord Jesus Christ, Son of God–"

"Come, young Yorgos, my little Saint," he sang. "Come. You are so delightful! Your petty charms and incantations have no power over me."

"–Have mercy on me, a sinner," I continued my prayer, ignoring him.

"The time for patience has passed. Time itself is a swol-len belly and now, at last, the birth pains have begun. Come." Against my will, and better judgment, my body obeyed his command as if my own will had no power over it.

"Release me, devil," I growled. "May the Spirit of the Lord bind you!" He pressed his face against my neck and licked the length of my carotid artery up to my ear. His tongue flitted in, and around it. And then he nibbled my lobe, chuckling lightly.

"You mock my faith!"

"No, my dear one. Your faith is what makes you who you are. It is beautiful. However, on this occasion, you are mistaken. I am a free agent. I do not report to any hierarchies of devils or demons. Neither am I at the top of any dark and sinister chain of command. I am, 'Lucian Dumitru, Nosferatu Extraordinaire'," he boasted, taking a bow. I bristled at that word. That, and vrykolakas, were the only words that ever struck fear into my father's heart.

"Liar! You are a liar and the father of lies!"

"Yes, there is truth enough in your accusation, but make no mistake, I am not *the* 'Father of Lies.'"

He released his mental hold on me and I fell to the ground. "Very well, young one. Fight me. Give it all you've got," he said.

Stumbling up to my feet I raised the ikon of Saint George high into the sky. "Saint George, deliver me from evil," I prayed, crossing myself.

Mister Dumitru lunged at me. I brandished the shield of the ikon at him shouting, "Back, back," until all his mirth vanished.

"I've grown tired of this, and I am thirsty. I saved my appetite for you." He lunged at me again and I struck him on the shoulder with the ikon. He grabbed both of my wrists and pinned my arms to my sides. The ikon fell to the ground with a soft thud and I screamed. His firm grip reopened my left wrist. Now both wounds bled.

Unable to use my hands, I thrust my chin up and chest forward in an effort to expose the eye-amulet Djordji gave me and that I had worn ever since. Mister Dumitru glanced at the amulet and smirked.

"You think your trinket has power to ward me off? Think again." He paused, taking such a deep breath that his chest expanded, and his shoulders squared. He appeared to become taller, more statuesque. He released one of my wrists and held his hand up to the moonlight. Blood smeared his palm. In the soft luminescence of the moon the blood appeared to be a rich violet-black. He wiggled his fingers. My blood dripped down his wrist and forearm. The cuff of his sleeve, rolled to the elbow, soaked it up.

Lifting his arm he brought it to his lips and licked from the elbow to the tip of his middle finger. I struggled and he tightened his grip on my wrist. Pain shot up my arm. My knees buckled. I couldn't fight. Holding me still, he licked his fingers and arm clean.

"It is time," he said simply. With his arm around my waist and his hand on the top of my skull he forced my head to the left, exposing my neck. He pressed his nose against it and breathed in my aroma.

"Wait!" I shouted, sobbing. "I have a question." He relented. Without releasing my wrist, he held me at an arm's length away and peered at me.

"Ask it."

"Why won't you leave me? Why have my prayers not worked? Has my sin destroyed my faith?" I knew that the events unfolding were a sure sign that my faith had suffered more than I knew. Perhaps it was irreparable. Without my faith where would I find meaning? What purpose would fill my life? He cupped my face tenderly in his hands. Silently we regarded each other–I on the threshold of death, he about to deliver me through it.

"No, no, dear Yorgos, Your heart is pure. Your faith most certainly is intact. That is why I love you; because you are a man of uncompromising faith, and goodness. I believe that is why you have been chosen to imprint on one such as me. We *need* your goodness. Your prayers do not drive me away because I am not a demon. I am a human being, just like you, only I am an immortal. And tonight, you will join me in immortality." With gracefully quick and fluid movement, his arm went around my waist again and he drew me close. His hand, on top my head, positioned my neck just so.

"No!" I shrieked. "Please, don't!" I balled my fists and struck him ineffectually. I kicked, but my kicks availed nothing. A low guttural growl rose up from his insides and, like a cat devouring his prey, he plunged his fangs into the soft skin of my neck. I fought him, kicking again. The more I struggled against Mister Dumitru, the stronger he held me. He was resolute. He would not let me go.

To the casual observer, a passerby, it would appear that we were lovers holding each other in a passionate embrace. Not so. Death incarnate emptied me of, and consumed, my very life.

My heart, beating painfully against my ribs, resisted death. I tried to speak, to demand that he release me, but he drained my strength along with my blood. Too weak to raise my voice, I merely whimpered.

In one last fit of desperation, I assaulted him again; my balled fists struck his back. He released my shoulder and I fell toward the ground. His other arm, around my waist, kept me from striking it. Every muscle in my body went slack. I hung there like my sister's rag-doll, and was nearly as lifeless. Mister Dumitru glanced down at me smiling; a mischievous glint lit his eyes. Lifting his wrist to his lips, he tore through his flesh with piercing teeth. This opened a deep and ragged wound that severed the veins and tendons, exposing tender meat. I blinked. Everything became indistinct and hazy. I blacked out.

Hot liquid dripped onto my closed lips, waking me. I parted them, taking the liquid into my mouth, and blinked. My blurry vision sharpened. Mister Dumitru held his opened wrist several centimeters above my mouth, letting the blood drip down. I tasted the brackish iron taste of his blood. It struck my lips like liquid fire and burned down my throat, awakening in me a new hunger. I reached for his forearm, pulling it to my lips. He taunted me, moving it higher above my dangling head. I stretched out my arms, grabbing for it. I needed more. He laughed at me and lowered his arm. I pulled it to my mouth. Though my dull teeth could not find purchase, I clamped my jaws down. He let out a little cry of pain, yet it seemed he took pleasure in it.

His eyes fluttered and a sensual look came over his features. Until now, I had only seen this expression on Constantine's face when we were nearly spent from our lovemaking.

Simultaneously maddened and inflamed, I consumed his blood with ferocity, taking back that which he had stolen; my own blood. Mingled with his and turned into something new, the blood was some kind of alchemist's potion, an elixir, a dark-watered fountain of youth. It worked its magic on me. A euphoric sense of wellness came from my core, washing over me, clearing away the fear.

While I feasted on him, my eyes darted from one earthly vision to the next; the trees, the rocks on the ground, and the roof of the skete, visible in distance through holes in the dense shrubbery. Everything looked different, yet the same. Everything pulsed with energy and emanated light from a secret hidden source. I cataloged the world while my perception of it changed. The radiant branches of the trees swaying overhead in the gentle breeze, snapped into sharper focus. The breeze animating the trees felt like the caressing breath of heavenly beings. The stars and the moon! Their celestial light invigorated me, contributing to my euphoric sense of well being.

Mister Dumitru tugged his arm away and I resisted. My strength had increased. Forcibly, I held his torn wrist to my mouth. "Yes, you want the blood now, don't you?" he said laughing. I looked up to see him smiling down on me like a proud father. His expression angered me. Remembering myself, I pushed his arm away from my mouth and spit out the blood.

"Release me," I demanded.

I remembered my determination too. I was desperate to not be turned into a damnable creature like him. If he was successful in turning me, I would be damned, utterly damned, I was certain of it. I couldn't imagine living a mortal lifetime without God, let alone existing forever without Him, in some kind of eternally earth-bound embodied hell. It was horrifically unthinkable. I would rather die painfully than let him damn me.

I would be a martyr for my faith. I hoped the Lord would see the sincerity of my fight, my determination to overcome this evil creature that held me in a dark embrace—which I detested—and forgive all the other embraces I had sought out and enjoyed with my beloved Tino. "Stop! Let me go! I don't want this!" I knew that Mister Dumitru would not relent, so I directed my entreaty to heaven.

"Lord, please! Deliver me from evil!" Nothing. My faith had failed. I began to weep and brushed the tears from my cheeks. My tears were tinged red.

"Please, Mister Dumitru, don't damn me like this. I don't want to be like you!" I pleaded, in one last attempt to win back my soul.

"Oh, but you do!" he bellowed. "Why else would you have held the font of my blood so fiercely to your lips and drank so deeply?"

Constantine called my name and leaves rustled in the distance. His footsteps thudded on the ground, coming closer.

"Stay away, Tino! Don't come near me." My warning was too late. He burst through the bushes brandishing a broken branch. He struck Mister Dumitru in the back of the head with it. I fell, landing on leafy shrubs.

Mister Dumitru stumbled. The force of the blow split his scalp, revealing white bone which glistened in the moonlight. His skull cracked too, exposing the gray-matter of his brain. He reached up, holding it in, and to staunch the flow.

Constantine rushed to where I lay crumpled on the ground and covered me, surrounding me with his arms. His hot tears fell on my cheeks.

"Yorgos, stay with me," he whispered, while brushing my hair away from my eyes. He gathered me into his arms and hoisted me up. My limbs were limp. He supported my weight because I couldn't. With my legs dangling, he held me so that our chests touched. "Stay with me, Yorgos," he repeated, gently bouncing me in his arms, trying to jostle a response from me. Clear tears lined his cheeks and the rhythmic beat of his heart got faster as panic set in. The feel of his heart thumping against my chest awakened me, and I realized how terribly in need of nourishment I was. I lifted my head to look at him. He smiled, glad to see a response from me, and he leaned forward to kiss me on the lips. I smiled at him in kind, but my smile sent a shock of horror through him.

He let out a little gasp. "Your teeth!" And I buried my new fangs into his carotid artery, feeling the first ever hot spill of mortal blood flow past my lips, down my throat, and into my stomach. Constantine, my first love, was also my first cold-blooded kill.

His life came to me in flashes while I ended it. I saw him as a child, learning his prayers, wanting to make his mother proud. He recited them for her without error.

I saw him as a teenager, both elated and afraid from his first crush. Like me, his fear compelled him to seek refuge from temptation on Mount Athos.

I saw him on the day we met, drying his tears. He knew that we belonged together. With that knowledge came a new certainty; there was nothing wrong with who he was.

And I saw him running from the skete, to my rescue, because he loved me. He couldn't let me face danger alone. He loved me.

He didn't fight me. While I drained him, he remained still, holding on to me as long as he was able. His blood increased my strength. I could support my own body now. While I fed, I saw motion from the corner of my eye. I turned to see that Mister Dumitru had risen and watched with approval. His head, which only moments before had sustained a mortal blow, was now whole. The bones and skin had been stitched together by some kind of infernal magic.

I drew my fangs from Constantine's neck to speak to Mister Dumitru, but the words didn't come to me. Language was leaving me. I could only groan with groans that came from somewhere deeper than my intestines. In the silence Constantine struggled to speak. His voice, weak and barely audible, rattled in his throat.

"Yorgos," he said. I pressed my ear up to his lips and groaned. With a weak voice he repeated my name, "Yorgos." I couldn't speak so I pressed my ear even closer. The only answer I could give was a deeper groan. "This isn't your fault. Please don't blame yourself. I love you. I will always love you . . . ." Stung by his words, I dropped Constantine and clutched my heart. Tears lined my cheeks and dripped from my chin. I wiped them with the back of my hand, and closed my eyes to the truth of what I saw. My tears were an impenetrable inky red. My eyes were bleeding.

I stood over Constantine's dying body. He lay in the spot where Evangelos caught us only days before. A low wail rose from deep inside me, growing louder. I lost my balance and stumbled to my knees with my arms around my stomach. It felt like my guts were being yanked out of me. I struggled to speak again, to find words that seemed inaccessible to me. Language was becoming exponentially more difficult.

"No, no!" I cried, slapping my hands to my face. "No, no, no, no, no!" For the longest time 'no' was the only word I could form with my mouth. I fought to speak. Mister Dumitru would not make me into a dumb beast.

"This evil is not me." I spit out. "I hate you, Mister Dumitru. You are Satan!" He paced a wide circle around me, scrutinizing my transformation.

"Why have you done this to me? You've made me something evil."

He came to me so swiftly that I scarcely saw him move. One moment he passed the tree beneath which Constantine and I had made love; the next moment he cradled my face with his hands.

"No, my Lover, my Son. I have made you something *different* than what you were, but not something evil." He leaned in as if to kiss me. I pushed him away.

"I would not have killed my beloved if you made me something merely different." I turned to go to my love, but Mister Dumitru intervened, holding my wrist.

"He is not dead. There is still life in him."

"Is that how you console me? Is that supposed to make me feel better? For as long as I exist, I will hate you for what you have done." I wrested my wrist from his grip, scarcely noticing that the pain had gone away, and approached Constantine.

"Stop!" Mister Dumitru ordered. "We are not finished." He spoke in that fashion of his that can not be ignored or disobeyed. I stopped. "Turn toward me." My body followed his orders. "Where were we before we were so rudely interrupted? Ahh, yes, the blood. You need more of it. You haven't consumed enough." He lifted his forearm and turned it, palm up. "Look at that, will you? Healed already."

Without so much as a grimace he tore into his own flesh again. The scent of his blood blossomed into the cool night air like a freshly poured glass of wine. My senses had undergone a change. They were more sensitive. His blood was still brackish. It smelled like iron and salt, but there was something more subtle that I hadn't noticed before. It smelled like smoke, and I detected hints of orchid, night jasmine and honey. The aroma drew me, working its evil magic. Sniffing the air, I reached for his arm and took it to my mouth.

Once again I clamped my jaws around Mister Dumitru's self-inflicted wound. This time I had fangs that could grab, hold and tear. I did. He moaned as if in the throes of passion. His blood burned like fire through my veins. The intense heat went into my stomach and radiated into my entire body, working an alchemical change.

I pushed his wrist away from my mouth and held his face, cradling it between my palms. Like I had so many years before, I felt that I both loved and hated him. I felt I must have him. A fevered passion came blazing from my groin and up my torso. I pulled Mister Dumitru's face to mine and kissed his cold hard lips. He darted his tongue into and out of my mouth and along the ridges of my teeth. He licked one of my new fangs and then the other. I bit down, taking off the tip of his tongue. He let out a cry and continued to explore my mouth, letting the blood flow. I consumed every drop until the wound healed.

An icy-hot tingling shot down my arms and legs to the tips of my fingers and toes. I withdrew from the kiss and turned my palms up. The veins in my wrists emitted silver light, like molten mercury flowed through them. My skin, too, glowed the faintest shade of blue and my self-inflicted knife wounds had closed completely. They didn't even leave a hint of a scar.

I tore my sleeves open up to the elbows. Like I suspected, the mercurial light pulsed through all of my blood vessels, and my forearms glowed. I touched my carotid artery. It burned and throbbed beneath my fingertips.

I grabbed Mister Dumitru with a new ferocity and he cackled. We tumbled to the earth. He pinned my back to the ground and climbed on top of me. He supported himself with his palms flat on the soil. He bent his elbows and pressed his cold lips against mine. Straightening his arms, he flashed me a devilish grin. Taking my cassock in both hands he tore it open, all the way to the waist. He bent his elbows again and licked my ear lobe. I moaned, pressing into him, coaxing him to more passionate acts.

I mussed his hair, and twisted my fingers around it, pulling it out by the fistful. He growled, but the pain urged him on. He licked circles around my left nipple and then the right, teasing it until it was hard. He nibbled them, gently–at first, and then more savagely. I groaned, and bucked up, sending him flying. He landed several meters away. I gasped. I hadn't yet realized how much strength I had gained.

Baring his fangs, he crawled to me on all fours and straddled me again, his knees and palms supporting his weight. Hovering over me he cocked his head–this way and that–over my chest, and came down close enough to lick my erect nipple. He teased it, gently biting it with his front teeth. A low growl came from his throat, like that of a predator.

Lost to the frenzy of blood lust, he tore into the flesh over my heart. Blood spurted out of the wound. He drank like a dying man at a desert oasis, with his lips pressed to the skin around the wound. He sat up, straddling my waist, and took my smooth scar-less wrists, one at a time and bit into them, consuming the flow, losing none of it. I writhed with mounting pleasure.

"No more," I panted. "I can't take any more." I closed my eyes, trying to shut out all of the external stimuli. Taking deep breaths, I tried to calm myself. Never before in my life had I experienced a physical pleasure that was so intense that I wanted it to stop. He relented.

Within minutes, most of the wounds were clotted over. Only the large and gaping hole over my heart still issued a flow of blood. He leaned over it, biting his tongue open again. His blood trickled over the wound and mingled with mine. Like a miracle salve, it healed the wound in an instant. He rolled off of me onto the ground. I rolled to my side with my back to him.

When I opened my eyes I was face to face with Constantine. His breath came in laborious bursts, and his eyes were opened impossibly wide. The size of his pupils didn't match, and he seemed to not see me. His lips moved, but no sound came out. I recognized the words he recited: The Jesus Prayer. Nauseous, I turned away from him and wept. I curled up into a little ball, with my left hand covering my right fist which I pressed into the center of my chest. I didn't feel a heartbeat and I was becoming cold. I hated myself for ever taking pleasure in being with Mister Dumitru.

I climbed up to my feet and went to the tree. Leaning against it, I found that I was still at a loss for words. My body now possessed two minds. I had two wills, but only one rapidly diminishing vocabulary.

I hated Mister Dumitru for what he had done to me against my will, but it was finished. New instincts were rising within me; namely a singular thirst for blood. One victim was too many, but would never be enough.

My body temperature was still dropping. I lifted my arms. The white hot glow that flowed through my veins had dimmed, and the light coming from inside my skin was fading fast. My skin, in fact, had turned a subtle shade of blue.

Mister Dumitru climbed to his feet, grinning. It seemed that to him this was all fun and games. I shook my head at him, wanting to speak, but words were fleeting. I rubbed my chin with my fingers and thumb, trying to recall what I wanted to say, when the greatest, most gut-wrenching cramp I had ever known clenched my bowels like a fist tightening around them. I doubled over and stumbled to the ground holding my stomach. The pain worsened, and I fell to my side, assuming a fetal position. I wanted to ask what was happening. But I could only moan. I thrashed my head back. My body jerked. My extremities were getting even colder. Mister Dumitru circled me, looking down, like a god from on high, observing his creation.

"You are dying, my son." I lost control of my bowels and soiled myself.

"Dying?" I cried, scarcely able to articulate the word. *But, vrykolakes are supposed to live forever.* He circled like a vulture, a black-winged angel of death. A sly smile came over his lips, causing them to curl, revealing his fang-teeth.

"No matter what order of immortal beings one joins, corporeal or not, physical death is always the passage to eternity. So, yes, you are dying, in a manner of speaking, but your death is only the beginning of a greater, immortal existence." He came to me and rested one knee on the ground. His forearm rested on the other. He regarded me silently for a moment. "It is nearly finished, my son. The change is quite unstoppable now."

An impenetrable darkness descended on me, and I simultaneously ascended up and away from it, toward a radiant swirling point of light that opened in the sky. Relief! God would receive me. Mister Dumitru's plans had been superseded by a higher plan. My life was over, but I had not been damned as I feared I would be, thank God. I reached out with the hands of my spirit to take possession of the light and to let it also take possession of me. It was tangible, a living, breathing and pulsating entity in its own right. The tips of my fingers penetrated the light, and my whole being expanded and contracted with joy.

To my astonishment, I recognized Tino's presence while it rushed upon me. Our spirits touched and blended before separating. When we made contact, I was overcome with an exchange of love. He soared past me and I strained to catch up to him. My beloved continued to ascend beyond my reach.

Just when I expected to be swallowed up by the living light, I reached the end of a tether that I never knew I had been attached to. A jarring lurch yanked me back, and the radiant swirling point of light into which Constantine had gone, snapped closed. God denied me entrance to paradise after all.

I plummeted to the hard earth, descending back into the impenetrable darkness from which I had only temporarily risen. I fell all the way back into my cold, hard, dead body.

Mister Dumitru, still resting his arm on bended knee, peered down at me. How long he waited for my return from death, I will never know. When he saw the signs of 'life' reanimate my dead face, he stood and helped me to my feet. I righted myself and looked around. My vision had changed. My eyes were able to gather together even the slightest ambient light and magnify it. The world was crisper somehow, more substantial and real. Everything pulsed with its own autonomous energy and was also enveloped by a universal field of it. When I turned my new sharper vision upon Constantine, I saw what I already knew, he was dead. His body no longer pulsed with the energy of life. I rushed to him and bent to pick him up.

30 Anathema

Being declared anathema is said to be chief among the causes of Vampirization. At least in my case that is not so. My becoming a vampire is what caused my expulsion. A case of the proverbial chicken and egg? Which came first? From all the warnings I received, well before I had ever been turned, I wonder–is the Church at least partially responsible for my descent into darkness and living hell? Had the Church created a self fulfilling prophecy?

-From the Journal of Georgeo Godevenos

I heard feet thumping and saw the flames of numerous torches. I turned from Constantine's body to see what the ruckus was about. In their haste to investigate, several monks ignited the dense foliage. In an attempt to extinguish the flames, several of them beat the shrubs and tree branches with their coats. They only fanned the flames, making them leap higher and burn hotter.

"The cries came from over here!" someone shouted. At once, five monks burst through the bushes, followed by the Protos. He gasped, stepping toward me. Crouching, I bounced lightly on the balls of my feet, with my arms hanging loosely between my knees. I sniffed their scent on the air like a dumb beast. The Protos wagged his head with mock sadness, while the others brandished their flaming torches.

"Stand back," he said to them. He took two paces forward declaring, "You are an anathema! There is no repentance for one such as you." He searched out my gaze and held it. "It pains me to find you like this, lost to evil. You were such a gifted monk." Fear squeezed his heart; I smelled it in his blood. But it wasn't me he was afraid of. His thoughts were as clear to me as my own. He was afraid his secrets would be found out.

Taking a step closer, he made the sign of the cross saying, "One such as you can never be restored to the Church. Unless God is merciful, and allows your body to be utterly destroyed, you will be doomed to exist in your decaying flesh until the end of all time."

He turned away, and with a wave of the hand, released the others to descend on me. They charged with make-shift stakes. I watched the Protos walk away while they fell on me. He turned and spoke one last time.

"Anathema!"

The entire area–the trees, under which Constantine and I made love, and the shrubs that surrounded them–caught fire and blazed. When the men approached to destroy me they rhythmically chanted a single word,

"Anathema. Anathema. Anathema. Anathema. . . .

Glossary Of Words and Terms

A

Ancients, the.

The original Vampires. Secretive and reclusive, the Ancients prefer to exist in the shadows of society, anonymously feeding off of the populace. The Ancients are so old that they have lost touch with their humanity and do not waste time grieving its loss or trying to recapture it. Little is known of the Ancients; some younger vampires believe the Ancients no longer exist.

Anathema.

An official ecclesiastical curse resulting in excommunication. A proclamation of damnation. See also excommunication.

Ascetic.

A religious person (typically a monk or a nun) who forsakes material possessions, creature comforts and wealth in order to live simply and keep his or her focus on God. The ascetic life is one of extreme self-discipline and self-denial with a focus on spiritual practices like fasting and prayer.

Asceticism.

The dedicated lifestyle of an ascetic, based on the principles and practices of extreme austerity, self-denial and self-discipline. The goal of asceticism is to free oneself of anything that might hinder achieving union with God.

Athonite.

Of or pertaining to Mount Athos.

Atropos.

In Greek mythology, Atropos is the oldest of the Three Fates. Atropos is appointed with the task of choosing the time and manner of each person's death. She ends a mortal's life by cutting with her shears, the thread that tethers them to this world. She works in concert with her two sisters, Clotho, who spins the thread, and Lachesis, who measures its length. See also the Fates.

B

Bender tent.

Bender tents were used by nomadic Gypsies before their elaborately painted wagons became commonplace. Bender tents were constructed from long, thin branches of hazel trees called withies. Bender tents could be constructed and taken apart both quickly and easily. See also withy.

Blessable (ikon).

For an Eastern Orthodox ikon to be blessable, it must be painted according to the established canons–or laws–that govern the spiritual practice of ikonography. An ikon is not considered blessable, or a true ikon, if it deviates in any way from the canons.

Blood-drinker.

A vampire. See also nosferatu and vrykolakas.

C

Cassock.

The cassock is an ankle-length robe worn by clerics of the Greek Orthodox Church. The inner cassock is worn by all major and minor clergy and monastics, including novices.

Worn over the inner cassock, the outer cassock (also known as the riassa) is a looser flowing garment than the inner cassock. Riassa are worn by bishops, priests, deacons, and tonsured monastics as their regular outer wear.

Cense.

Censing in a liturgical church is the practice of swinging a censer attached to a chain toward a person or an object (like an ikon or a casket), so that smoke from the burning incense surrounds it. The fragrant smoke from burning incense symbolizes the prayers of the faithful rising up to heaven.

Censer.

A censer is any vessel made or used for burning incense. Censers are used frequently in Eastern Orthodox Churches in any number of services, including vespers, matins, and Divine Liturgy. They are also used during parastas (memorial services), and other occasional offices.

Charon.

In Greek mythology, Charon is charged with the task of transporting the souls of the recently dead from our world into Hades–the world of the dead. Charon ferries them across the River Styx by boat.

The Greek phrase "**fight with Charon**" refers to a terminally ill person's struggle to survive their illness and "cheat" death.

The Greek phrase "**He's got one foot in Charon's boat**" Is similar to two English phrases: "He's at death's door" and "He's got one foot in the grave."

Christ Pantokrator.

In Greek Orthodox ikonography, Christ Pantocrator refers to a particular depiction of Jesus Christ. Pantocrator means "Ruler Of All." A less literal translation of the word, but one that more accurately conveys the meaning associated with the ikon, would be "Sustainer of the world."

Christogram.

A Christogram is a monogram–or combination of letters–that forms an abbreviation for the name of Jesus Christ. The term Christogram comes from the Latin phrase "Christus Monogramma" and means "monogram of Christ."

In the traditional ikon of Christ Pantokrator, Christ's right hand is shown in a pose that represents the letters IC, X, and C. The same pose of the right hand is used by monks and priests to give their blessings to a supplicant.

D

Divine Liturgy.

In Eastern Orthodox Churches, the Divine Liturgy is seen as transcending both the world and time. Believers the world over–both living and dead–are said to be united in worship with departed Saints and the Heavenly Angels. For this reason, everything in Divine Liturgy is seen as both symbolic and real, inexplicably making the unseen reality manifest.

Divine Services.

Is the term used in Eastern Orthodox Churches to describe the daily cycle of public services celebrated in the church sanctuary.

E

Egg paints.

Also known as tempera paints, or egg tempera, egg paints are a permanent and fast-drying paint medium which consists of colored pigment mixed with a water-soluble binder, such as egg yolk.

Evil eye.

Many cultures around the world believe in the "evil eye," an ill-wishing expression or curse that is motivated by jealousy, envy or dislike. It is believed that the evil eye is able to cause bad luck, injury or harm.

To ward off the evil eye, such cultures have developed measures to protect against it including charms, pendants and decorations that feature a stylized depiction of an eye, typically made of glass.

To reverse the curse, someone who has purposely or inadvertently cast the evil eye spits toward the person at whom the expression was directed before inspecting their fingernails.

Excommunication.

A severe form of religious censure. In some religious traditions to be excommunicated is equivalent to being spiritually condemned by the church or her representatives.

F

Fates, the.

In Greek mythology, the Fates are goddesses who are charged with the task of measuring the length of every mortal's life, and cutting the cord when someone's time to die has come. See also Atropos.

First parastas.

See parastas.

G

Gerantas.

The title given to the spiritual Elder of a Greek Orthodox skete on Mount Athos.

Glamour.

To enchant someone (or something) by casting a magic spell over them, typically in order to hide them or conceal their true appearance.

Great Schema.

The third monastic rank. When a monk's hegumen, or superior, deems he has reached a high level of spiritual maturity, he promotes to the "Great Schema." The tonsuring ceremony of the Great Schema is the same as that of the Stavrophore, and the monk to be promoted repeats the same vows, and is tonsured in same way as he was when he took his original vows. In addition to the inner cassock given to the Stavrophore, he is also permitted to wear the outer-cassock–called the "Great Schema."

H

Habit.

Ecclesiastical garb worn by monastics, also called a cassock. Throughout the Eastern Orthodox Church, the monastic habit is roughly the same, allowing for slight regional differences. Both male and female monastics wear the same garments. Each successive monastic rank is permitted to wear an additional portion of the habit. The full habit is worn only by the highest monastic rank. For that reason it is called the "Great Schema."

Hermit.

A devout religious person who lives his or her life alone, secluded from society. The lifestyle of a hermit is very simple, eschewing–as much as possible–the most basic forms of technology and creature comforts.

Hieromonk.

Also called a Priestmonk, in the Eastern Orthodox Churches, a hieromonk is an ordained priest who has received monastic tonsure and taken a vow of celibacy. In other words, a hieromonk is a monk who is also a priest.

Holy Mysteries.

What the Western Church calls the Sacraments, the Eastern Church calls the Holy Mysteries. In the early centuries of Christianity, to keep them from becoming the objects of ridicule, the holy mysteries–or sacraments–were kept hidden from the pagans. When the Age of Persecution came to an end, the secrecy was gradually lessened, however the term remained.

Holy Synod.

In Eastern Orthodoxy, the Holy Synod is the ecclesiastical governing body of a church. On Mount Athos, the local Holy Synod is presided over by the Protos and its members are the hegumen of the 20 monasteries located on the peninsula.

Hybrid.

A meat-eating vrykolakas that was made, not born. The term "hybrid" refers to the fact that the change induced by a full moon renders a person bitten by another meat-eating vrykolakas "half wolf/half human," whereas a born vrykolakas fully assumes the form of a wolf when the moon is full. See also vrykolakas.

I

Ikon.

An ikon (from Greek, meaning "image") is a religious work of art, most commonly a painting made with egg tempera.

In the Eastern Orthodox tradition, an ikonographer has very little freedom to take artistic license. Everything within the image is seen as symbolic, such as halos, wings and even color. In ikons, letters are symbolic as well. See also ikonographer.

Ikonographer.

One who writes ikons according to the cannons of the Church. See also ikon and writing an ikon.

Imprinting.

If their souls become inextricably entwined when a mortal and vampire meet, it is said that the mortal has imprinted on the vampire. Should this happen, the vampire will have to turn the mortal into a creature like himself. It doesn't matter if the new vampire is made immediately after meeting, or years later; until the demands of the imprinting are fulfilled, the desire to do so will increase until it becomes an unshakeable compulsion. When a mortal imprints on a vampire, the vampire doesn't have a choice. The only way for the mortal to escape his dark fate is to die a natural death before the vampire changes him. Imprinting is extremely rare. It is believed to be a function of vampire evolution. Only mortals who have something extraordinary to bring to vampirekind imprint. Typically, such mortals possess skills or traits that are beneficial to vampires, or that vampires lack.

Ikonostasis.

In Eastern Christianity, an ikonostasis is a wall (or movable screen) of ikons and other religious paintings that separates the nave from the sanctuary in a church building. See also ikon.

J

Jesus Prayer.

The Jesus Prayer (also known as The Prayer of the Heart) is a short, prayer, which is committed to memory. The Jesus Prayer is held in high regard within the Eastern Orthodox Church: "Lord Jesus Christ, Son of God, have mercy on me, a sinner."

Throughout the history of the Eastern Church, the practice of reciting the Jesus Prayer has been widely and enthusiastically encouraged. Incorporating the use of the prayer rope, and reciting the prayer slowly, one progresses knot by knot along the rope with each repetition. In this manner, the Jesus Prayer is often repeated without ceasing as part of an ascetic's personal rule of prayer. The Jesus Prayer is encouraged as a method of opening the heart to

God and bringing about the "Prayer of the Heart," which is believed to be the Unceasing Prayer that the apostle Paul promotes in the New Testament epistles. See also prayer of the heart and prayer rope.

K

Katholikon.

In the Eastern Orthodox Church, the katholikon is a monastery's major church building. It gets its name from the fact that it is usually the largest church building where an entire monastic community gathers to celebrate Divine Liturgy and the major feast days of the liturgical year. At other times, the smaller temples or chapels would be used by the members of the community.

Koliva.

A ritual food made from a mixture of boiled wheat, nuts, cinnamon and sugar. During the memorial service, the koliva is placed on the memorial table or in front of an ikon of Christ. After the service, In order to bless the koliva, the priest sprinkles it with holy water. The koliva is served graveside to all in attendance at the funeral. Before the casket is covered with dirt, each mourner tosses a handful of koliva on top of it.

L

Lent.

Also known as the Great Fast, lent is a period of 40 days leading up to Holy Week and Pascha. The purpose of lent is to prepare oneself for Pascha, or Easter, by fasting, praying, repentance and other forms of self-denial.

Lenten.

of, in, or appropriate to lent (lenten fast).

Little exchange.

The little exchange is used when a vampire wants to forge an enduring bond or connection with a mortal without making them a vampire. First, the vampire consumes a small amount of the chosen mortal's blood and then the vampire gives it back, commingled with, and changed by, the vampire's own blood.

Liturgy.

An elaborate religious ritual performed publicly, usually in a church building, and according to a particular groups traditions, such as those of the Eastern Orthodox Church.

M

Matins.

The nighttime liturgy observed by monastic communities which lasts until dawn.

Meat-eater.

A werewolf, see also vrykolakas.

Monastic ranks.

There are three successive monastic ranks called the Rassaphore, the Stavrophore, and the Schema-Monk or Great Schema. Progressing from one level to the next represents an increased level of asceticism.

Monk.

The Greek word for monk is derived from monachos, which means single or solitary. A monk practices religious asceticism. He lives either alone or with other monks in a monastic community. Other than necessary daily tasks, like cooking, cleaning, gardening, and mending clothes, a monk typically spends his day in prayerful contemplation, serving the poor and sick, or in religious study.

Mount Athos.

Also called the Garden of Theotokos or the Holy Mountain, Mount Athos is a both a peninsula and a mountain in Macedonia, northern Greece. Over the centuries 20 monasteries have been established on Mount Athos. Only monks are allowed to permanently make their homes there.

The peninsula is the easternmost "leg" of the larger Halkidiki peninsula, which protrudes into the Aegean Sea, like three fingers, for roughly 60 km at a width between 7 to 12 kms. The actual mountain, and its steep densely forested slopes, reaches as high as 2,033 m. See also Athonite.

N

Name Day.

In the tradition of the Greek Orthodox Church, almost every day on the calendar is dedicated to the memory of a Christian martyr or saint. From antiquity, the tradition in Greece has been for firstborns to be named after one of their grandparents. When Greece embraced Christianity it became tradition for Greeks to be named after revered martyrs and saints, therefore in a family there may be a long line of Georges or Petras reaching generations back.

When someone is named after a saint, the day dedicated to that saint becomes their name day and is celebrated much like a birthday. Throughout childhood, most Greeks celebrate both their name day and their birthday with equal abandon. In adulthood, one's name day takes precedence and is celebrated with much joy.

Nave.

In Eastern Orthodox Churches, the nave is the main part of the church building where the congregants stand during the services. Most Orthodox Churches do not have pews. Instead of sitting, most people stand. Instead of western-style chairs, stacidia (high-armed seats with arm-rests high enough to use while standing) are provided for the sick and elderly. Stacidia are found along the walls.

Nona.

Paternal grandmother.

Nosferatu.

Romanian word for vampire. The exact origins of the word are lost to time. Its similarity to the Greek word nosophorus, meaning disease bearing, should not be ignored. It was once believed, erroneously, that nosferatu–by their very nature–bore any number of diseases that could be passed to the masses.

There is some controversy about the relationship between nosferatu and vrykolakas. In truth they are similar, but not exactly the same thing. It is believed by younger nosferatu that nosferatu and vrykolakes share a common origin, but the exact details have been lost for millennia.

Novice.

The word novice literally means "one under obedience." Anyone wanting to become a monk must begin their ascetic vocation as a novice. After spending no less than three days as a guest at the monastery of their choice, the monastery's hegumen may bless the candidate's wish to become a novice. There isn't a formal ceremony for this. The novice simply receives permission to wear the inner cassock and the monastic hat, called a Skoufos. If a novice decides to abandon the monastic life, no penalty is incurred and he may be asked to leave at any time if the hegumen discerns that he isn't called to a life of monasticism.

O

Orthodox Church.

As an apostolic church, bishops of the Eastern Orthodox Church can trace their lineage all the way back to the apostles, through what is called the Apostolic Succession. The second largest Christian Church in the world, the Eastern Orthodox Church is comprised of several self-governing bodies. Usually, but not always, the boundaries defining them are consistent with national boundaries. Though the self-governing bodies are geographically and nationally distinct, they are theologically unified.

P

Papus.

Grandfather.

Parastas.

An Eastern Orthodox memorial service, liturgical in nature, held in honor of the departed. See also first parastas.

Pascha.

The Greek Orthodox Church term for Easter. Pascha is a Christian festival that celebrates the death and resurrection of Jesus Christ as described in the New Testament gospels. Lent is a forty-day period of fasting and penance intended to help the faithful prepare for Pascha.

Pascha Eve.

Also known as Holy Saturday, Easter Eve or Black Saturday, is the day following Good Friday and preceding Easter.

Paschal.

Of or relating to Pascha.

Passions, the.

To modern ears "passion" sounds like something we should all desire to experience. If we are passionate about something we give our all, mind, body and soul to it, and focus on it with singular vision. It may surprise some to learn that the original meaning of the word, in early Christian thought, was to suffer. Consider, for example, how the term "the passion of Christ" refers to his suffering and the events leading up to his crucifixion and death. The term "The passions" in early Christian thought referred to any sin or vice that could entangle people, drawing their attention off pleasing God. Sins such as envy, lust, pride, gluttony and greed could be referred to as passions.

Perpetually burning lamp.

In Eastern Orthodox tradition, oil lamps (which traditionally burn olive oil) are used on the altar, and to illuminate ikons on display around the church and on the ikonostasis. Orthodox Christians also use oil lamps to illuminate their ikon corners in their own homes. Once lit the oil lamps burning on the altar, or placed before ikons, should be allowed to burn "perpetually." The wick and oil should be replaced before they burn out.

Pindus Mountains.

The Pindus Mountain range of northern Greece and southern Albania reaches from the Greek-Albanian border down to north of the Peloponnese. During the time of the Ottoman occupation of Greece, the villages of the Pindus Mountains were largely left to themselves and not accounted for during the census because they were too remote.

Prayer Of The Heart.

See the Jesus Prayer.

Prayer rope.

Similar to a Roman Catholic rosary, a prayer rope is used by Monastics (and others) in the Eastern Churches to help them count how many repetitions they've made of the Jesus Prayer. Prayer ropes are made of knotted black wool with a cross, also made of knots, at the place where the ends join together, to form a loop. See also the Jesus Prayer and Prayer of the Heart.

Praying the rope.

A phrase which describes using a prayer rope to aid one in their prayers, usually numerous repetitions of the Jesus Prayer. See also the Jesus Prayer, Prayer of the Heart and prayer rope.

Preternatural.

The word "preternatural" is often mistaken as a synonym for "supernatural." There is a difference, however subtle. Just as the words "evening" and "night" are similar (they both indicate hours after dark) preternatural and super-natural are similar but not the same. Both indicate something beyond the natural order of things. However, unlike supernatural, it is assumed that preternatural phenomena have rational and scientific explanations that are currently undiscovered or unknown.

R

Rassaphore.

Once a novice (who wears "street clothes" until this point) takes his first step toward being a monk, he is clothed in the outer cassock also called the "riassa." Riassa means "robe-bearer." A rassaphore monk derives his title from the riassa.

Rule of prayer.

A rule of prayer is a formal prayer routine that is followed daily. An effective rule of prayer specifies the time(s) and place where the novice or monk will practice his prayers. In addition to deciding ahead of time when and where his prayers will be said, a rule of prayer also outlines the specific prayers to be said and the order in which they will be recited. The goal of following a rule of prayer is develop discipline and draw closer to God. See also Jesus Prayer, Prayer of the Heart, prayer rope and praying the rope.

Riassa.

The outer cassock of a Greek Orthodox monk.

S

Shape-shifter.

A shape-shifter is a being (usually a human or closely related species) who can change his physical form. Polymorphs and weres are the only two known varieties. Within these two categories there are numerous variations. A polymorph is a being that can change form at will. The number of forms a polymorph can assume is virtually unlimited. They are only limited by their their own skill and imagination. Nymphs and nereids are two closely related varieties of polymorph.

The prefix "were" is typically used to indicate a shape-shifter whose transformation is dependent on the cycles of the moon or other outside forces. Weres typically only change into one other shape, besides that of their human form. Some weres, usually those who have unusually long lives—more than long enough to learn the skill—are able to learn to control the change. But this is extremely rare. Were-wolves (aka meat-eaters and vrykolakes) and were-bears are two examples.

Sign of the cross.

A symbolic gesture used by members of The Orthodox Church the sign of the cross is made by the holding thumb, index and middle fingers of the right hand together and touching them to the forehead, sternum, right and then left shoulders. The sign is made "in the name of the Father, the Son and the Holy Spirit." The purpose of making the sign of the cross is to show reverence to a saint or holy relic, to end a prayer or to practice humility.

Skete.

A monastic style of community that is a cross between the communal life of a monk who lives in a monastery, and the more austere and solitary life of a hermit. Skete communities are made up of a small number of buildings which house the monks and a central church building (called a katholikon) in which the community celebrates together on Sundays.

Skouphos.

A soft, brimless, black hat worn by monastics in the Orthodox Christian tradition. At the discretion of their hegumen, monastics receive their skoufos either when they become novices or when they are tonsured into the first monastic rank.

Stravaphore.

Meaning "Cross-bearer," Stravaphore is the second rank of monk in Eastern Orthodox monasticism. Usually this level of monasticism isn't reached until years after the initial tonsure, and only when the hegumen feels the monk has achieved an acceptable level of excellence in discipline, commitment, obedience and humility.

At this stage in a monk's religious vocation he makes his first formal vows of chastity, obedience and poverty.

Symantron.

A percussive instrument used in Eastern Orthodox Churches, especially those in Greece and on Mount Athos, the symantron is used to summon monks to prayer at the start of of a service. The symantron is made of a long planed wood, typically maple or beech.

Before the start of each service a monk assigned to the task takes a symantron and, positioning himself before the west end of the katholikon, strikes it emphatically three times with a mallet. He continues to walk around the outside of the katholikon, turning to north, south, east and west and continues to strike the instrument as a call to worship.

T

Theotokos.

The Greek title for Mary, the mother of God, Theotokos means, "God-bearer."

Thrall/enthrall.

To be held in someone's thrall is to be spellbound by them until they release you.

To enthrall someone is to control their mind, or to enslave them.

Tonsure.

A novice becomes a monk by being tonsured. Tonsuring is a rite that can only be performed by a priest or a priest-monk (called a hieromonk in Greek). If a monastery's hegumen is a hieromonk the tonsure will be done by him. The tonsure is done by cutting a small amount of hair from four spots on the head, forming a cross.

Trisagion.

A traditional prayer dating back to the earliest Christian times, the trisagion is said at the beginning of each service of the Daily Cycle. The trisagion is also traditionally used to begin one's private prayers.

In English: Holy God, Holy Mighty, Holy Immortal, have mercy on us.

V

Venerate.

To venerate is to hold someone or something in high regard, and show respect. The Eastern Orthodox Churches teach that the honor or respect given to an ikon or a relic passes to the archetype. In other words, to venerate an ikon of Christ by kissing it is to show love toward Christ Himself, not the wood the image of Christ was written on.

Vested.

"Vesture" refers to liturgical robes, insignia and head-coverings (like the Orthodox skouphos) worn by clergy and monastics.

When a monk is said to be "fully vested" it means he has reached the highest monastic rank, the Great Schema, and is fully clothed in every article of monastic clothing.

Vespers.

Eastern Orthodox liturgies of the canonical hours. The word comes from Latin and means "evening."

Vrykolakas.

When the moon is full, a born Vrykolakas takes the shape of a wolf, larger than most specimens found in nature. When a meat-eating vrykolakas dies, he or she returns from the grave as a blood-drinking vrykolakas. See also hybrid, meat-eater, nosferatu, shape-shifter and vrykolakes.

Vrykolakes.

Plural of vrykolakas.

W

Withy.

A strong flexible hazel stem that is typically used in the construction of bender tents.

Writing (an ikon).

"Image writing" is a literal translation of the Greek word eikonographia. Some hold that ikons should be regarded in a manner similar to Holy Scripture. They suggest that ikons are not merely paintings but expressions of Christian Truth similar to the way the written word is. In this way of thinking, an ikon has more in common with hand written copies of the bible than it does a portrait. Creating an ikon, then, is seen to have more in common with writing than painting.

X

Xerxes Canal.

To facilitate his intended invasion of Greece in 480 BC, Xerxes the Great ordered the construction of what is now known as Xerxes Canal. The canal was cut across the narrow isthmus that connected Mount Athos with the mainland. The canal allowed his invading fleet safe access into the Aegean.

Y

Yaya.

Maternal Grandmother.

Z

Zagoria.

A well-known mountainous region in northwest Greece, Zagoria is home to 46 villages which are constructed of stone and have a unique architecture.

ABOUT THE AUTHOR

J Michael Braiden has been threatening to write a book since he was ten years old. At 43 he has finally followed through! It only took him 33 years.

J Michael was fortunate enough to grow-up in Santa Barbara, CA but not rich enough to stay there. He spent his 20's in Portland OR, where his mother, brothers and sisters still reside. After eleven years of chronic seasonal affected disorder, caused by the ubiquitous Northwest rain, he fled back to sunny CA, determined to find a way to pay what he calls the "suntax." He hopes this book, and the volumes sure to follow, is the way.

www.ingramcontent.com/pod-product-compliance
Lightning Source LLC
Chambersburg PA
CBHW070859260626

47162CB00007B/2510